Praise for

THE PUDDING PROBLEM

"A silly, slice-of-life tale with plenty of action and lots of
(mildly gross) humor. . . . Fans of Lincoln Peirce's Big Nate and
Stephan Pastis's Timmy Failure will adore this title."
—*SCHOOL LIBRARY JOURNAL*

"The truth behind Sam's complex lies is as much fun as the
philosophical calisthenics he does to justify his falsehoods. . . .
Further reading for fans of Timmy Failure and Big Nate."
—*KIRKUS REVIEWS*

"Despite his tendency to stretch the truth, amiable, secretly
sweet-natured Sam is easy to root for. Straddling the line between
illustrated novel and graphic novel, this series starter will easily
appeal to fans of Wimpy Kid or Star Wars: Jedi Academy."
—*BOOKLIST*

To Mum, Dad, and Sis—

with memories of the Kingsdown Street Fair and loads of love

—J.B. x x x

MARGARET K. McELDERRY BOOKS

An imprint of Simon & Schuster Children's Publishing Division

1230 Avenue of the Americas, New York, New York 10020

This book is a work of fiction. Any references to historical events, real people,
or real places are used fictitiously. Other names, characters, places, and events are
products of the author's imagination, and any resemblance to actual events
or places or persons, living or dead, is entirely coincidental.

Copyright © 2018 by Joe Berger

First published in Great Britain as *Lyttle Lies: The Stinky Truth*

All rights reserved, including the right of reproduction in whole or in part in any form.

MARGARET K. McELDERRY BOOKS is a trademark of Simon & Schuster, Inc.

For information about special discounts for bulk purchases, please contact Simon &
Schuster Special Sales at 1-866-506-1949 or business@simonandschuster.com.

The Simon & Schuster Speakers Bureau can bring authors to your live event.

For more information or to book an event, contact the Simon & Schuster Speakers
Bureau at 1-866-248-3049 or visit our website at www.simonspeakers.com.

Also available in a Margaret K. McElderry Books hardcover edition

Book design by Jack Noel

The text for this book was set in ITC Usherwood.

The illustrations for this book were rendered in pen and ink, and digitally.

1119 OFF

First Margaret K. McElderry Books paperback edition December 2019

10 9 8 7 6 5 4 3 2 1

Library of Congress Cataloging-in-Publication Data

Names: Berger, Joe, 1970- author, illustrator.

Title: The stinky truth / Joe Berger.

Description: New York : Margaret K. McElderry Books, [2018] | Series: Lyttle lies ; [2] |
Summary: Sam Lyttle's mother will allow him to see the first Wolfe Stone movie at
the end of the summer only if he can avoid telling a single lie until then.

Identifiers: LCCN 2018026945 (print) | LCCN 2018034761 (eBook)

ISBN 9781481470865 (hardback) | ISBN 9781481470889 (eBook)

Subjects: | CYAC: Honesty—Fiction. | Humorous stories. |

BISAC: JUVENILE FICTION / Comics & Graphic Novels / General. |

JUVENILE FICTION / Humorous Stories. | JUVENILE FICTION / Short Stories.

Classification: LCC PZ7.B4518 (eBook) |

LCC PZ7.B4518 Sti 2018 (print) | DDC [Fic]—dc23

LC record available at https://lccn.loc.gov/2018026945

LYTTLE LIES

THE STINKY TRUTH

JOE BERGER

MARGARET K. McELDERRY BOOKS

NEW YORK   LONDON   TORONTO   SYDNEY   NEW DELHI

SAM'S BEDROOM. NIGHT.

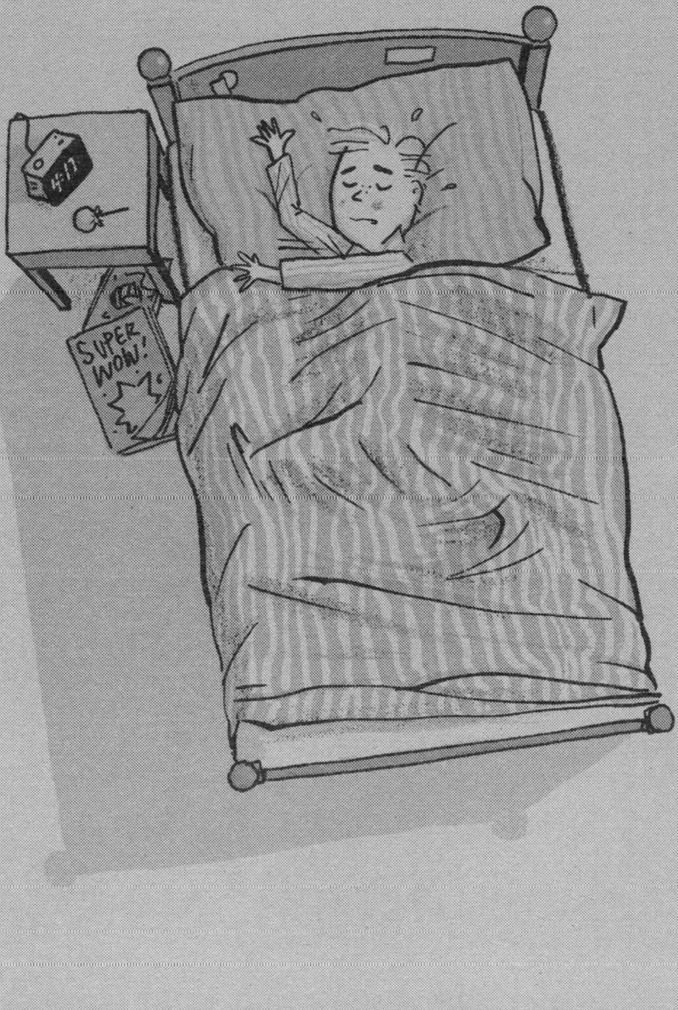
4:17
SUPER WOW!

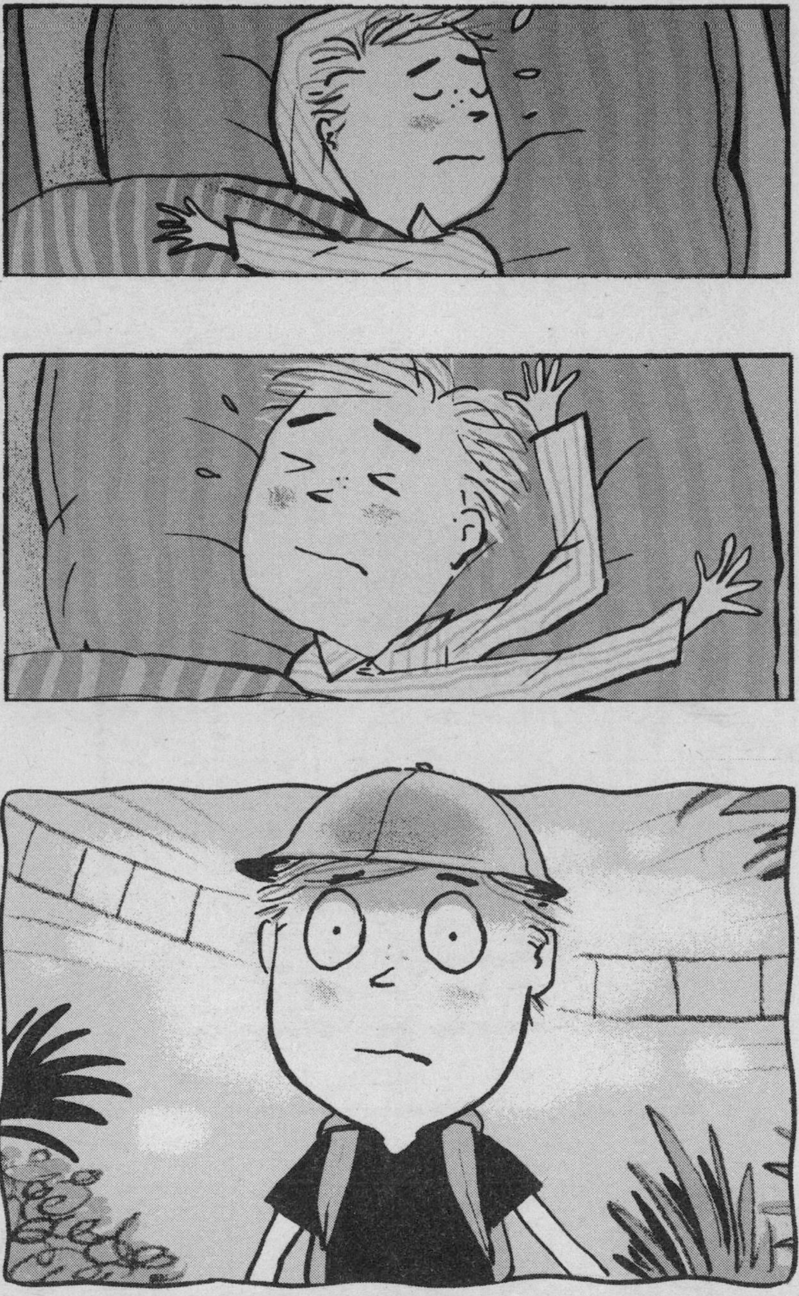

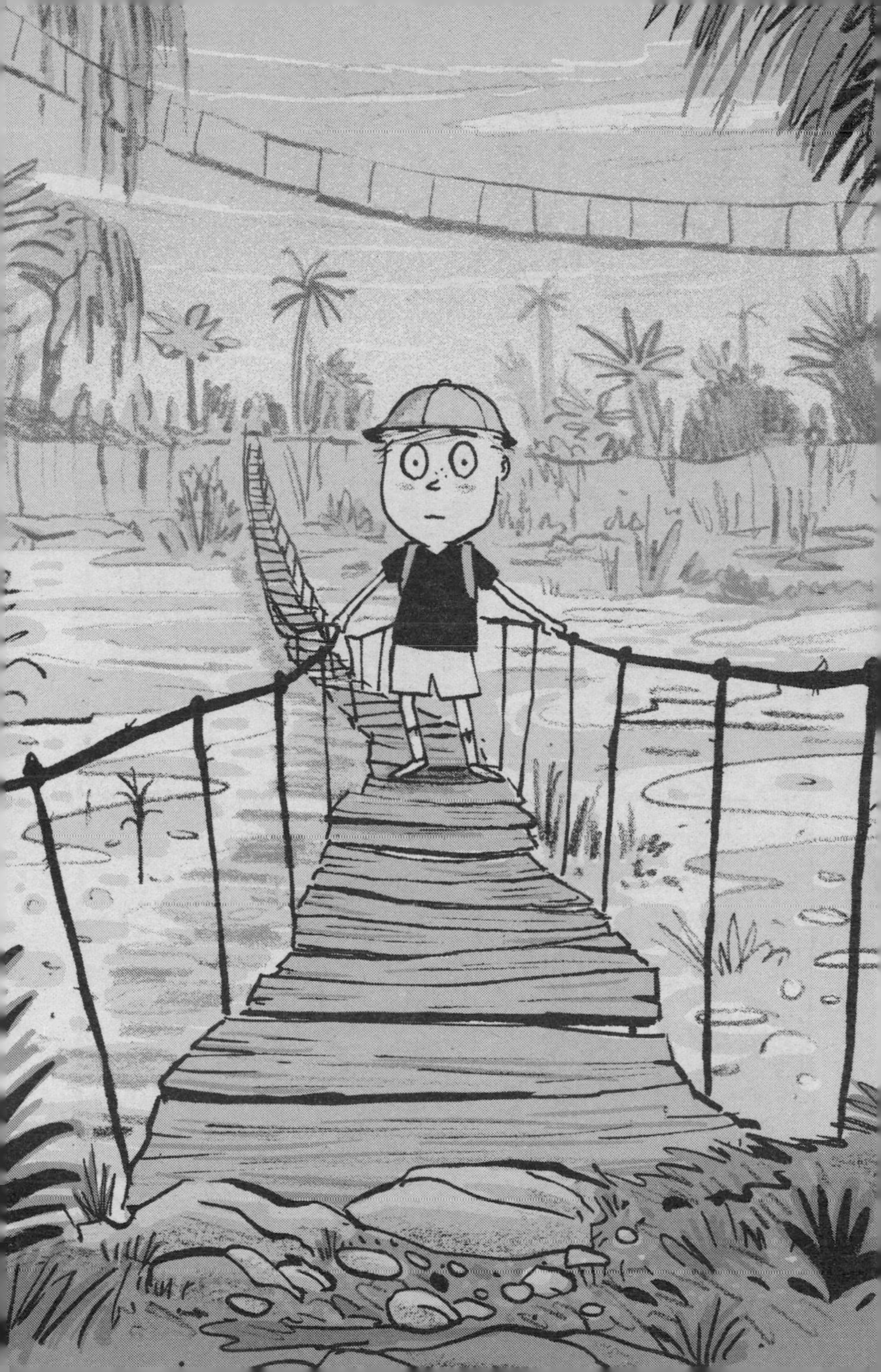

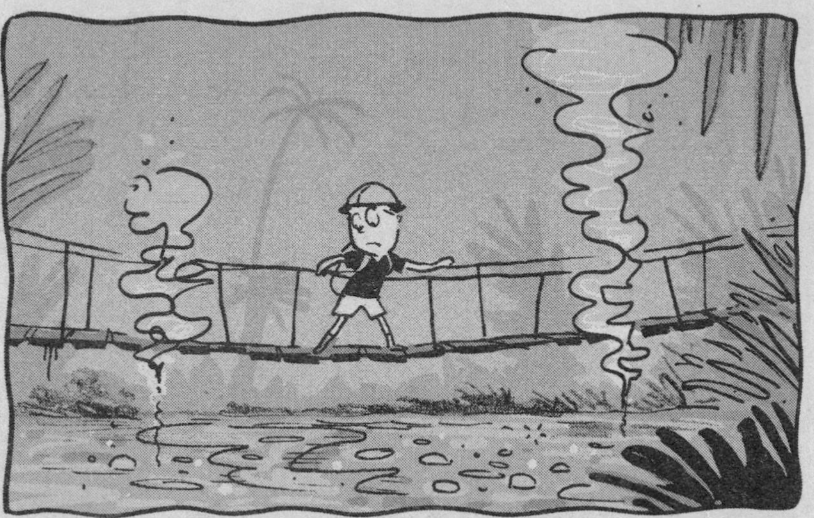

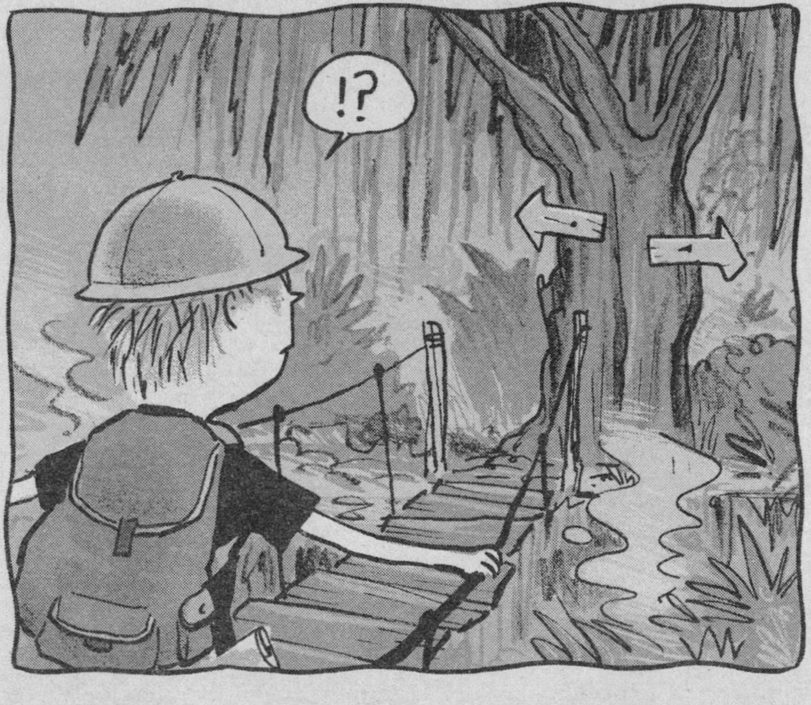
!?

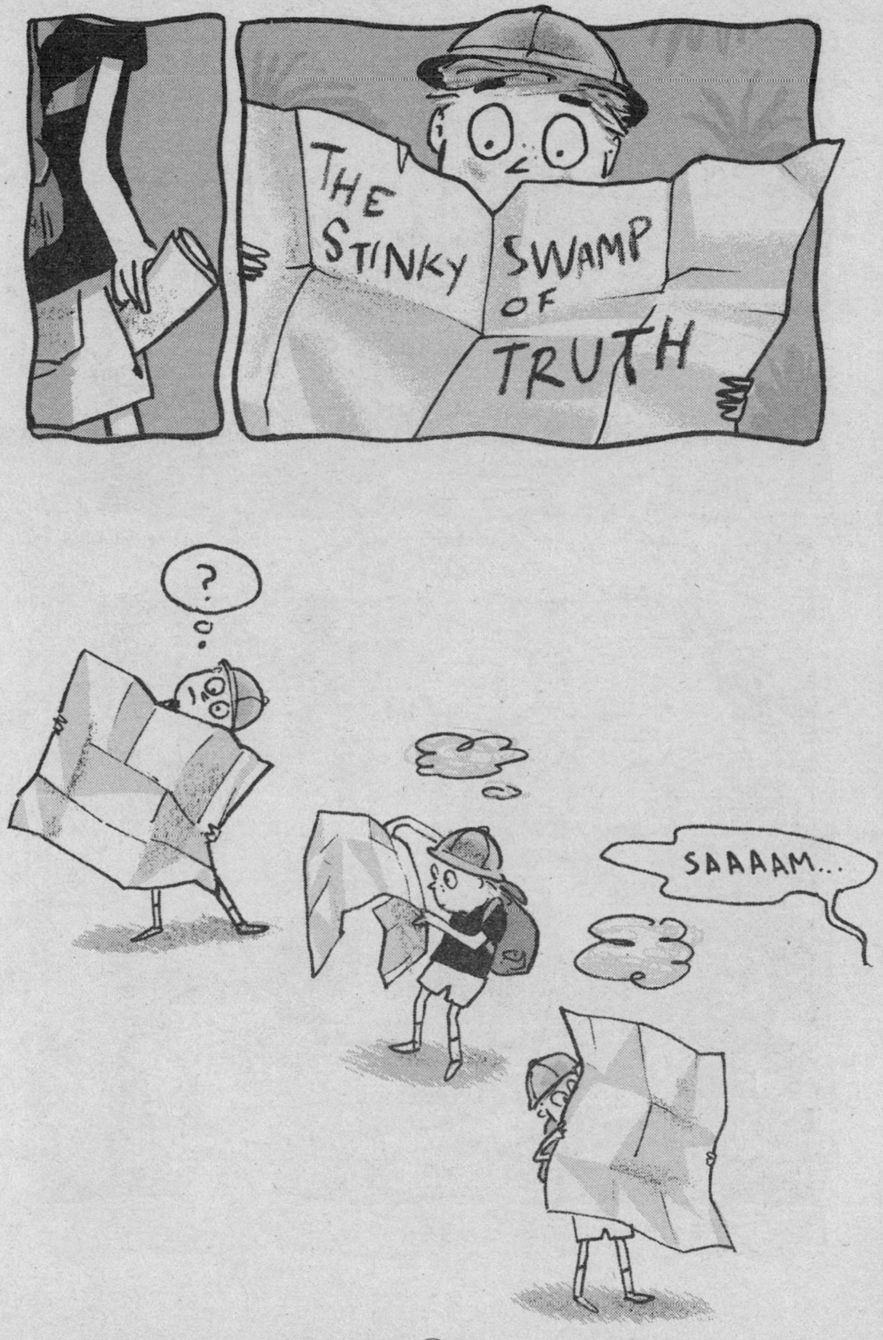
THE STINKY SWAMP OF TRUTH
?
SAAAAM...

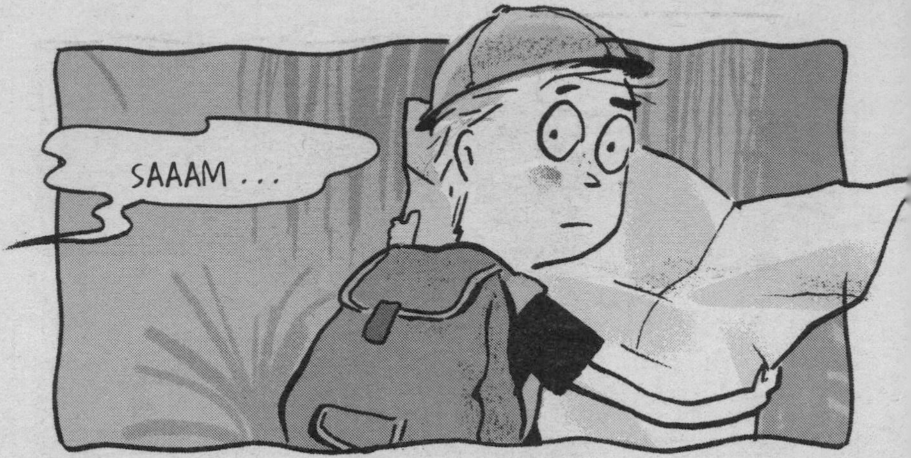
SAAAM . . .

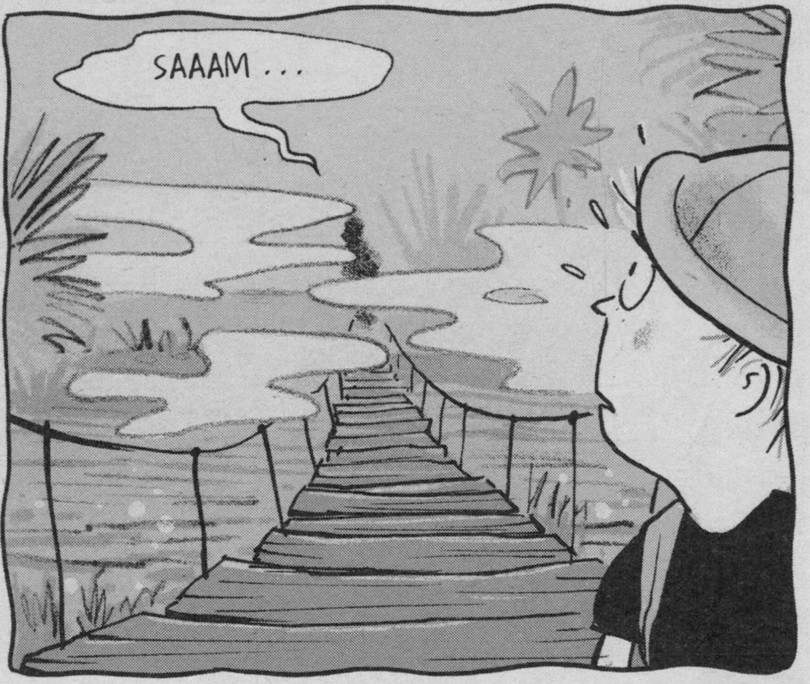
SAAAM . . .

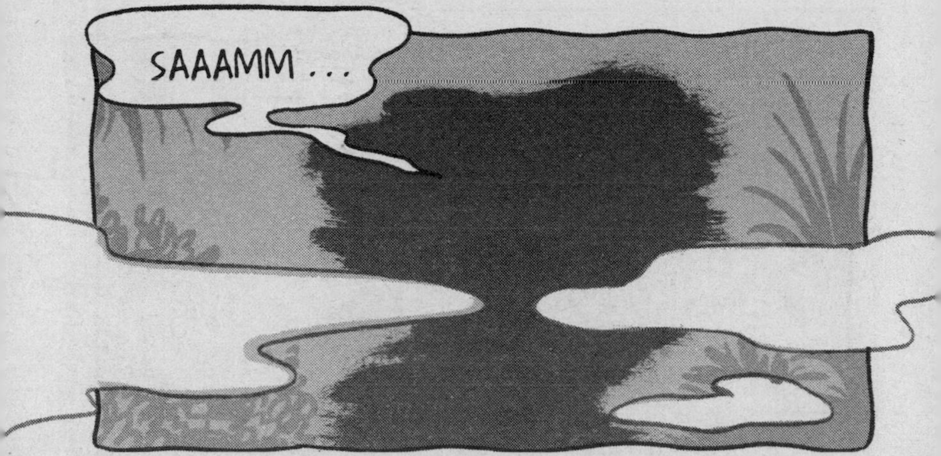
SAAAMM . . .

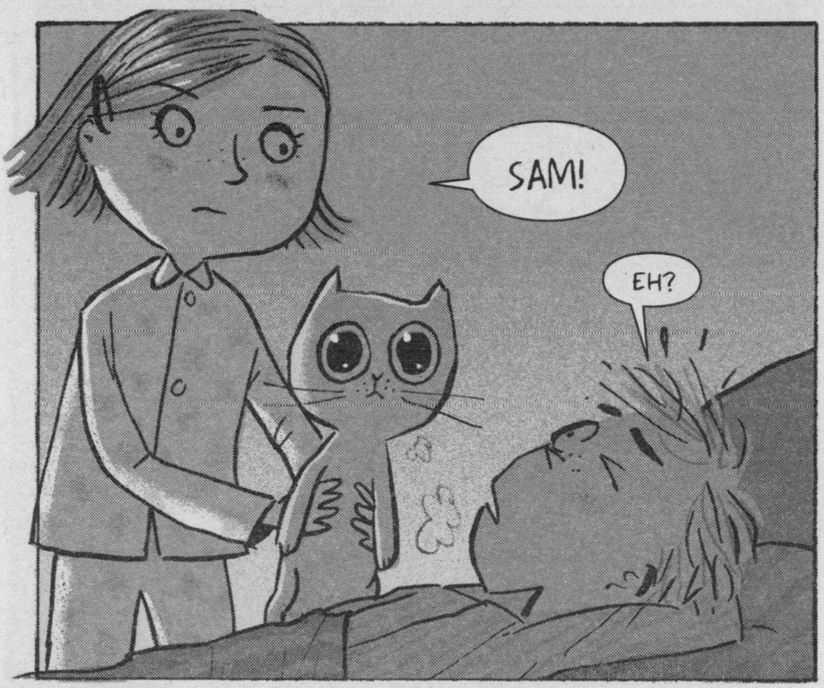
SAM!
EH?

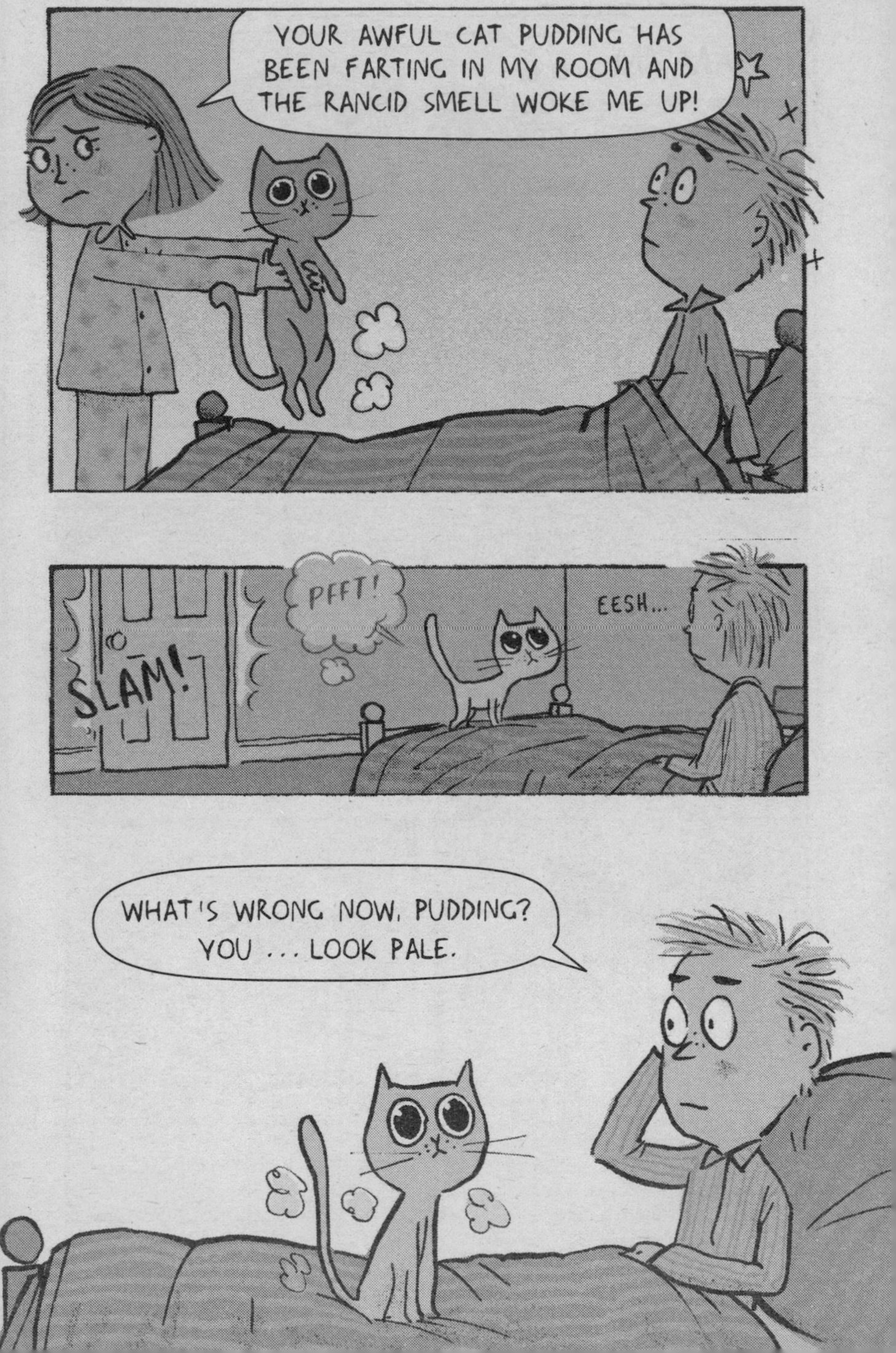
YOUR AWFUL CAT PUDDING HAS BEEN FARTING IN MY ROOM AND THE RANCID SMELL WOKE ME UP!
SLAM!
PFFT!
EESH...
WHAT'S WRONG NOW, PUDDING? YOU . . . LOOK PALE.

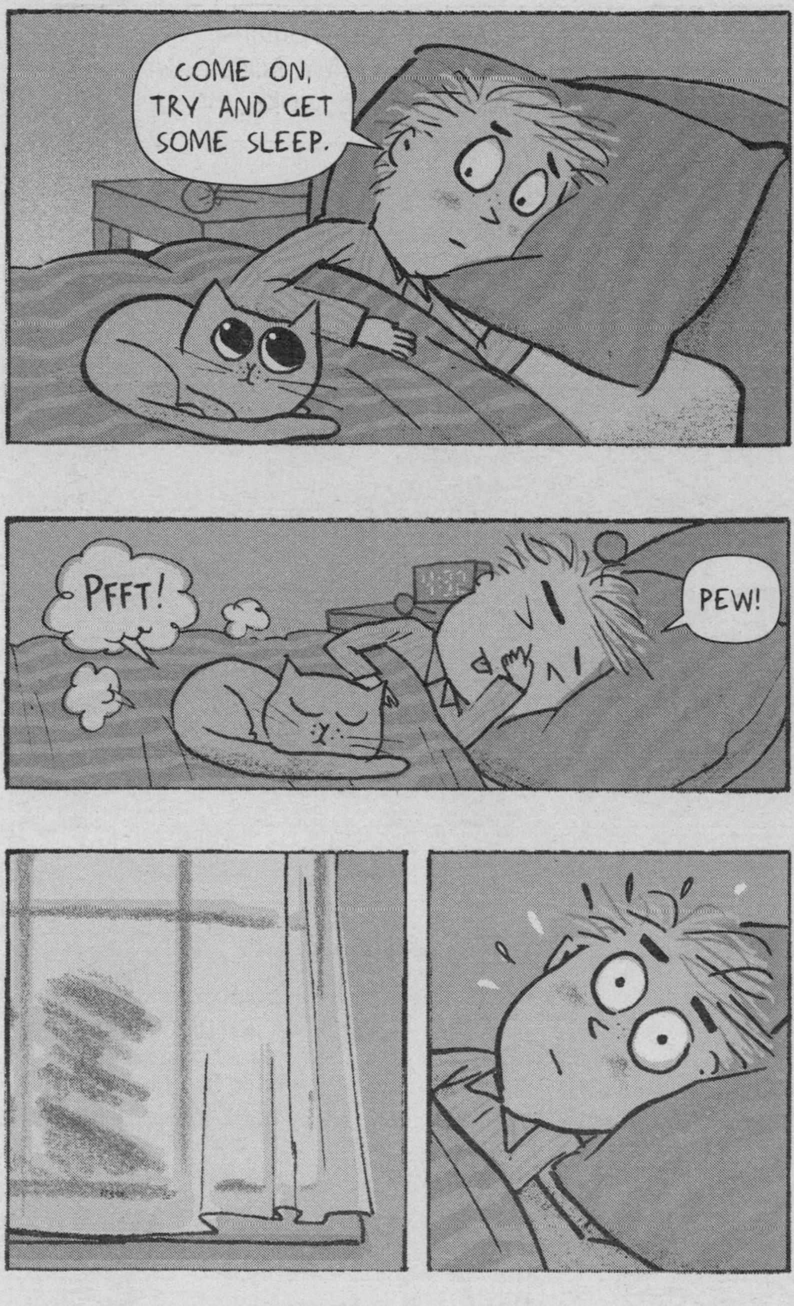
COME ON, TRY AND GET SOME SLEEP.
PFFT!
PEW!

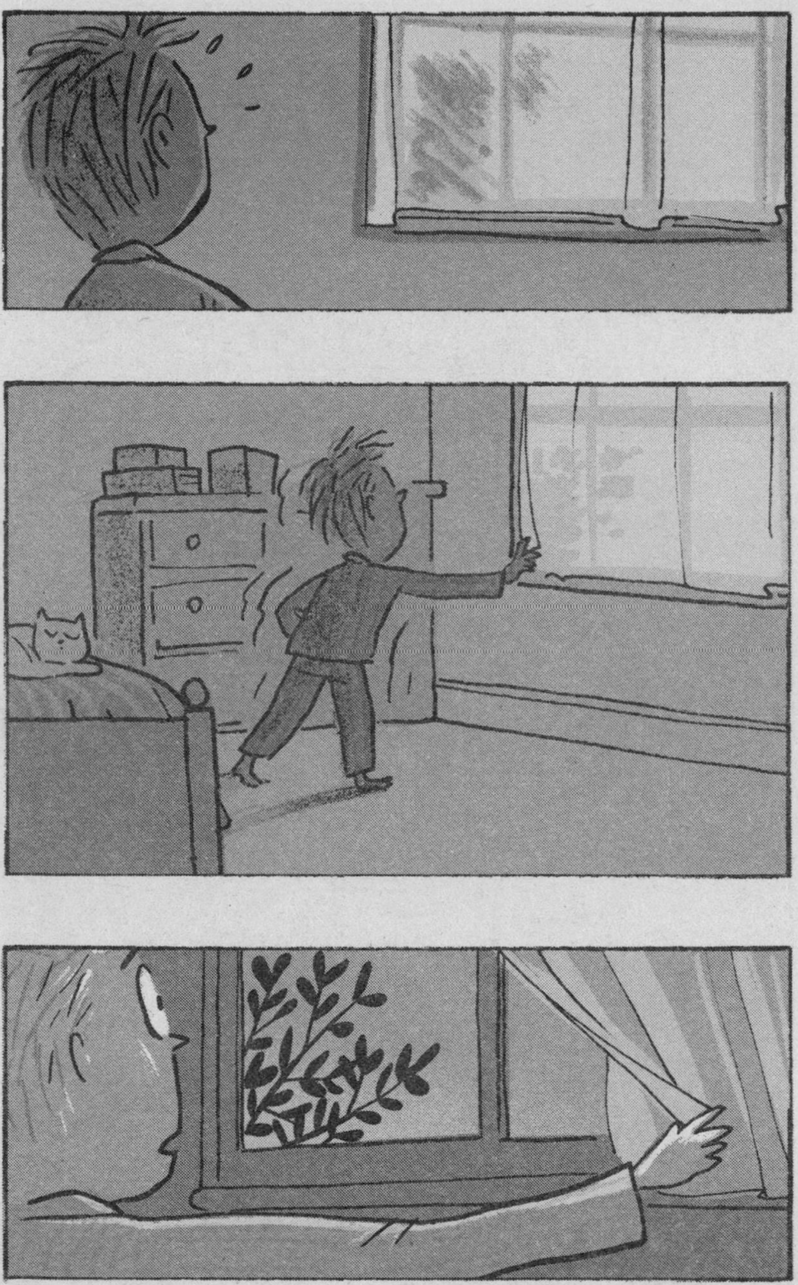

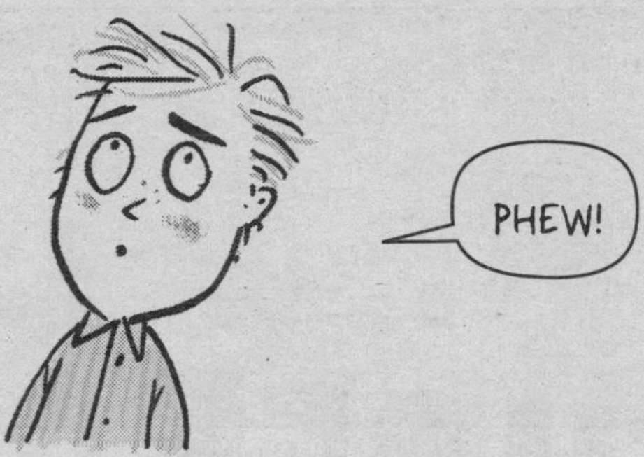
PHEW!

Have you ever felt the weight of the world on your shoulders?

Have you ever wanted, desperately, to be able to turn back the clock, and do something differently—or not do something at all?

If you haven't, you're lucky.

It's the loveliest feeling to have nothing preying on your mind, no dark clouds looming. . . . I felt like that once—for just a few fleeting moments. Three weeks ago, at the beginning of the summer break . . .

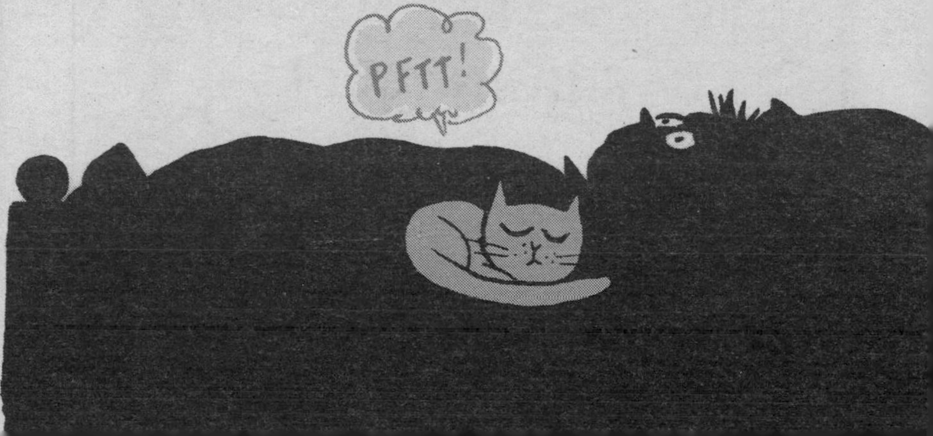
PFTT!

THREE WEEKS EARLIER

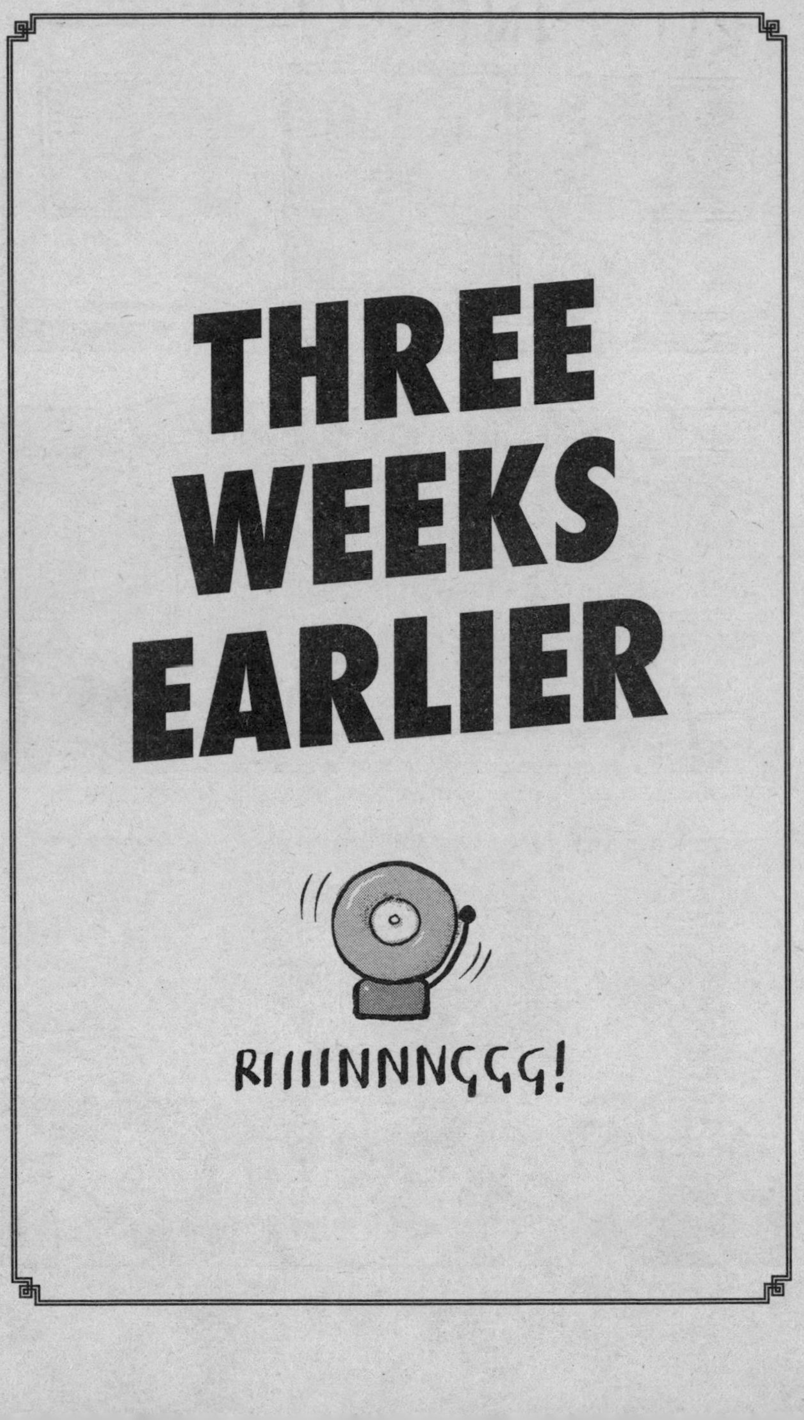

RIIIINNNGGG!

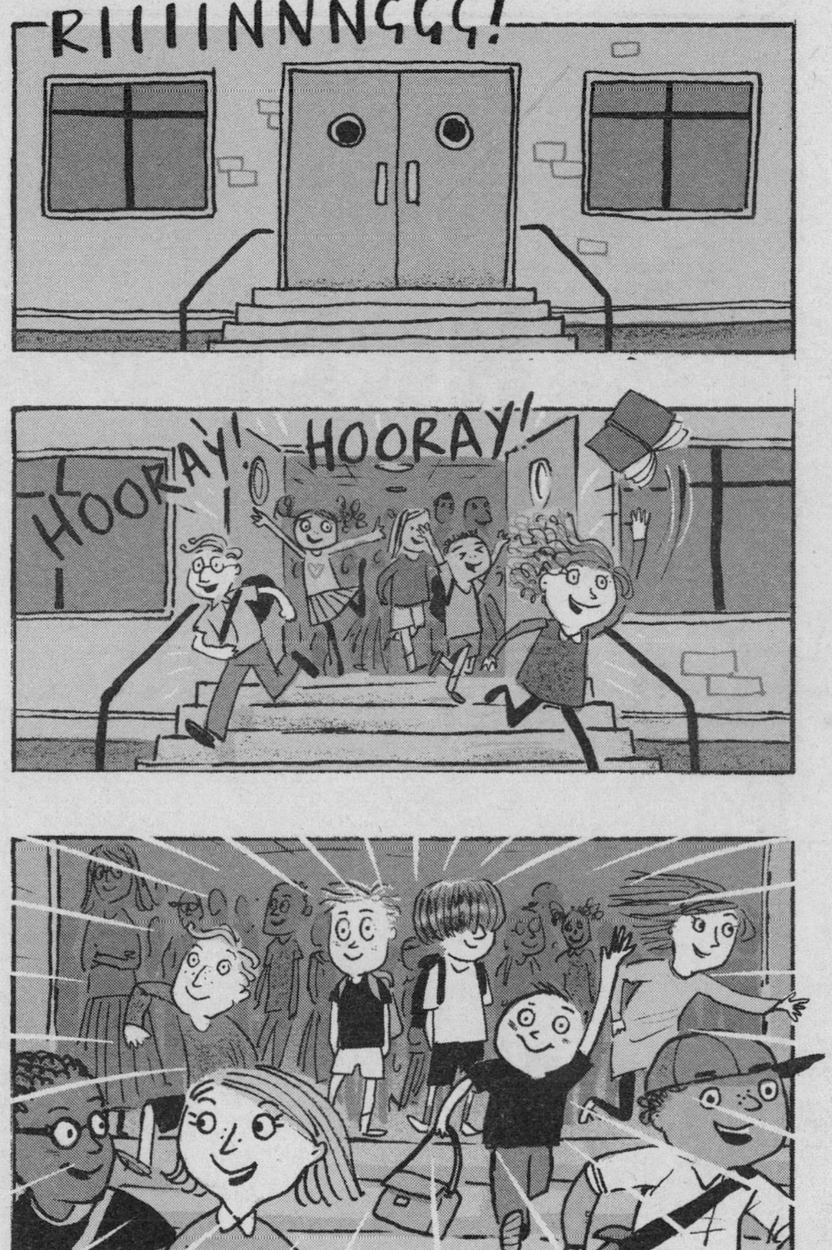
RIIIINNNGGG!
HOORAY!
HOORAY!

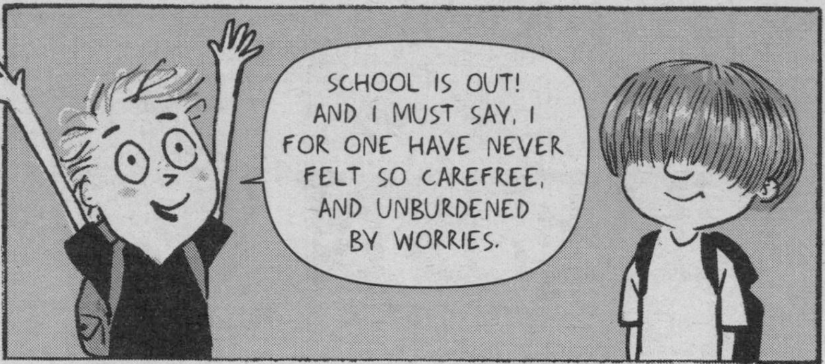
SCHOOL IS OUT! AND I MUST SAY, I FOR ONE HAVE NEVER FELT SO CAREFREE, AND UNBURDENED BY WORRIES.

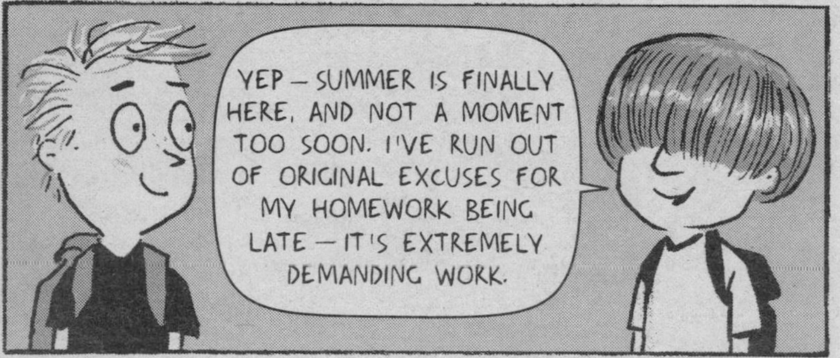
YEP — SUMMER IS FINALLY HERE, AND NOT A MOMENT TOO SOON. I'VE RUN OUT OF ORIGINAL EXCUSES FOR MY HOMEWORK BEING LATE — IT'S EXTREMELY DEMANDING WORK.

It's been a stressful year, but my worries have evaporated with the coming of summer.

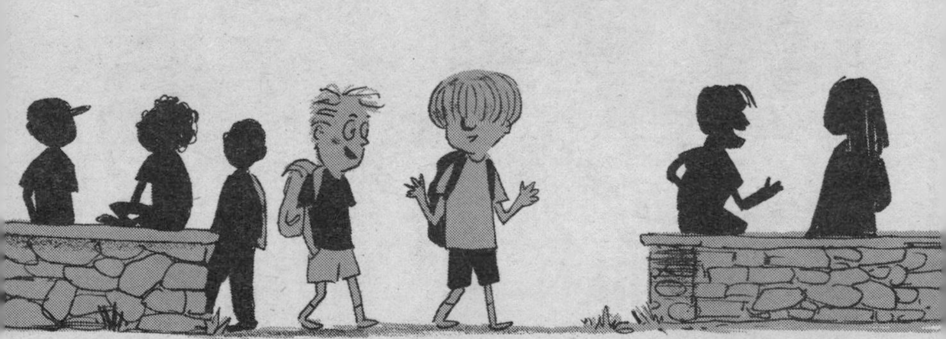

For a long time, the bane of my life was the school bully,

FEENY.

But since he got made to join the principal's Garden Gang, everything's changed. I have to hand it to the principal—it seems like his bizarre discipline technique actually has its merits, at least where Feeny's concerned. Feeny's gone from being a cheeseburger-munching school menace to a mild-mannered, salad-loving vegetarian.

FEENY THEN ➡ FEENY NOW

He's also had his hellhound Butcher rehomed, since he no longer believes dogs should be kept in the city. The only downside to all this is Feeny's show-and-tells, which are now loooong boooooring lectures on sustainability (whatever that is) and vegan recipes.

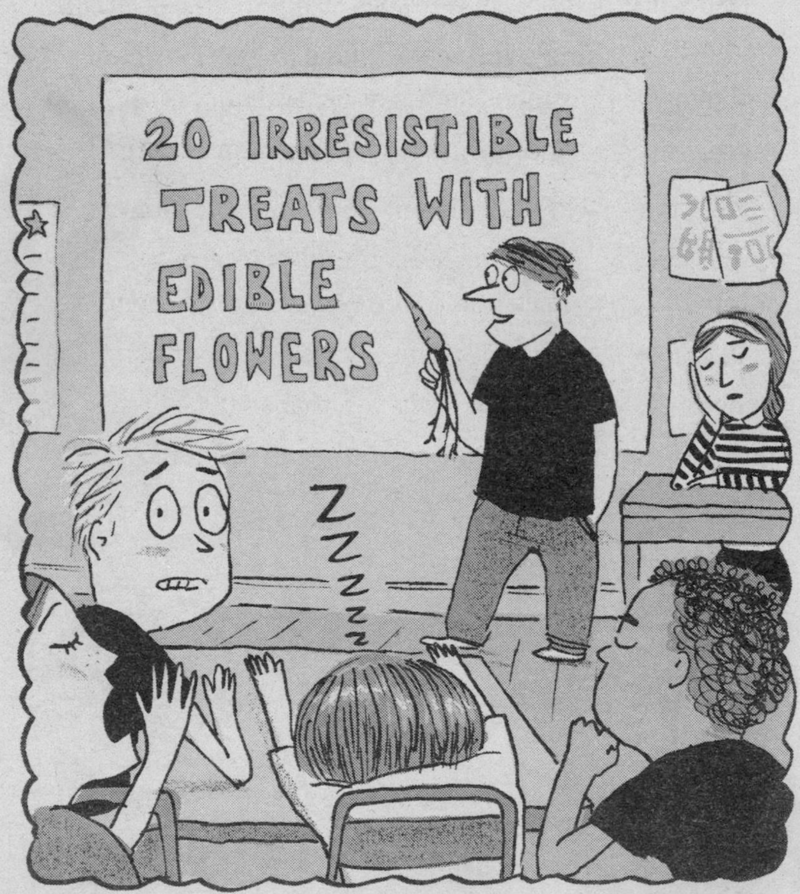
20 IRRESISTIBLE TREATS WITH EDIBLE FLOWERS
ZZZZZZ

So school is over for another year. And another, even MORE marvelous thing has happened. Drumroll, please . . .

We're **not** going on a summer vacation!!

Okay, so you're probably thinking that sounds like a bad thing, and I suppose it might be, under normal circumstances, but . . . double drumroll, please—Charlie's not going away either!!! Which means we get to spend the whole summer, every single hot, dusty, never-ending second of it, doing "that thing," what's it called? That important thing children need to do? Oh, yes, that's right— NOTHING! Hanging around to our hearts' content.

It gets even better. . . . In three weeks' time it's the neighborhood carnival.

NEIGHBORHOOD
CARNIVAL!
FLOATS! ♪
♪ MUSIC! ★
★ ♪ STALLS!
COSTUME PARADE!
OPEN-AIR
CINEMA
SCREENING!

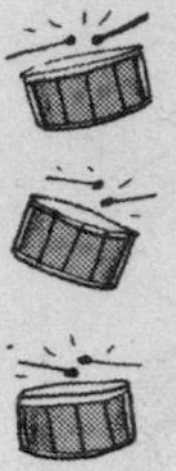

Everyone is going to be involved, even my mom (though she doesn't know it yet (ahem)). It's going to be super-fun—and the absolute best thing about it is . . .TRIPLE drumroll—an open-air screening of *Cry Wolfe*. Charlie and I are officially the world's biggest fans of the greatest crime-fighter ever:

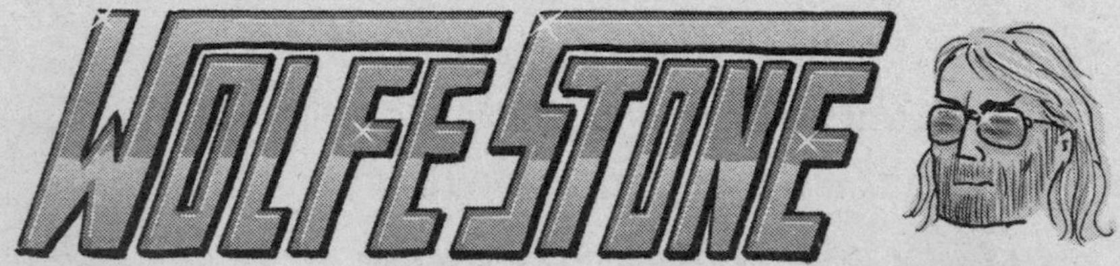
WOLFE STONE

We follow the reruns on TV, but we've never had a chance to see the original made-for-TV, feature-length Wolfe Stone movie. It's super rare, and the chance to see it on the big screen is a once-in-a-lifetime opportunity.

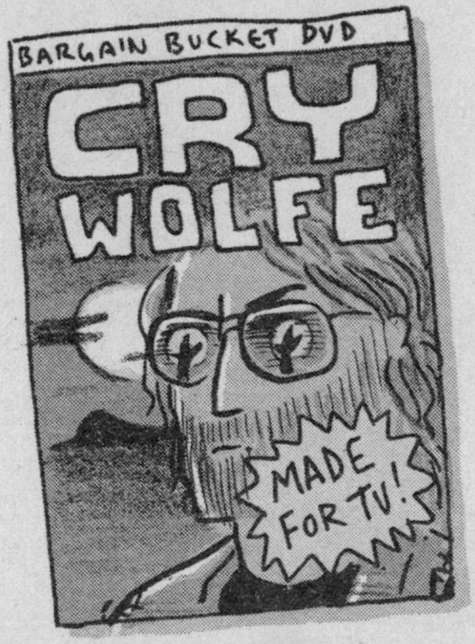
BARGAIN BUCKET DVD
CRY WOLFE
MADE FOR TV!

Who knew we weren't the only Wolfe Stone fans in the neighborhood?

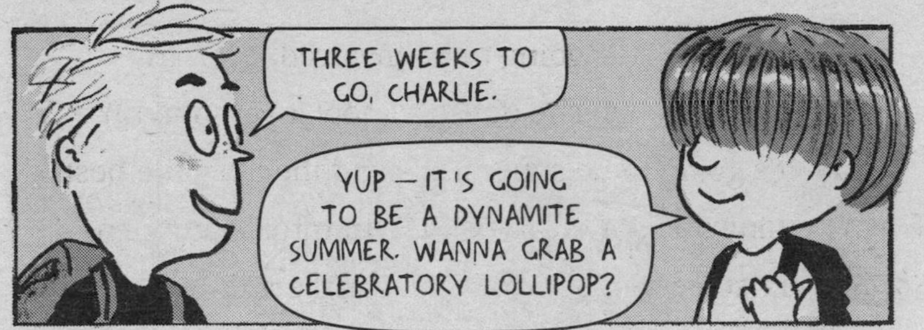
THREE WEEKS TO GO, CHARLIE.
YUP — IT'S GOING TO BE A DYNAMITE SUMMER. WANNA GRAB A CELEBRATORY LOLLIPOP?

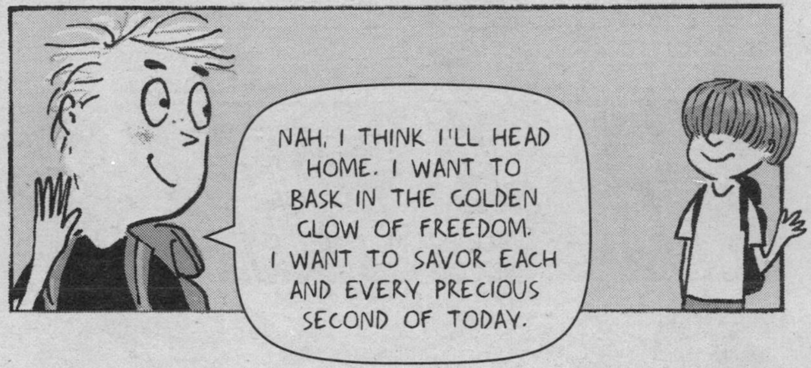
NAH, I THINK I'LL HEAD HOME. I WANT TO BASK IN THE GOLDEN GLOW OF FREEDOM. I WANT TO SAVOR EACH AND EVERY PRECIOUS SECOND OF TODAY.

Technically, the summer break starts tomorrow. And the moment it starts; well, it's begun to end, hasn't it? That's why the last day of school is so special. It's limbo time, and I love every second of it. Of which there are approximately two hundred, before I walk through the front door, back to a reality splashdown. . . .

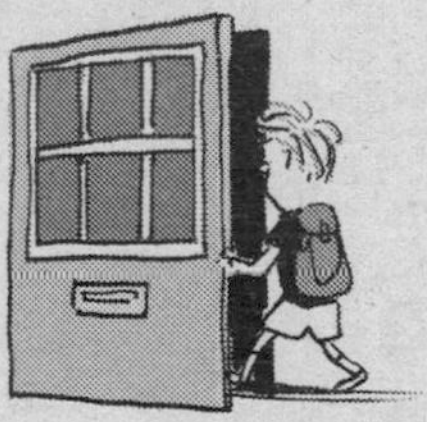

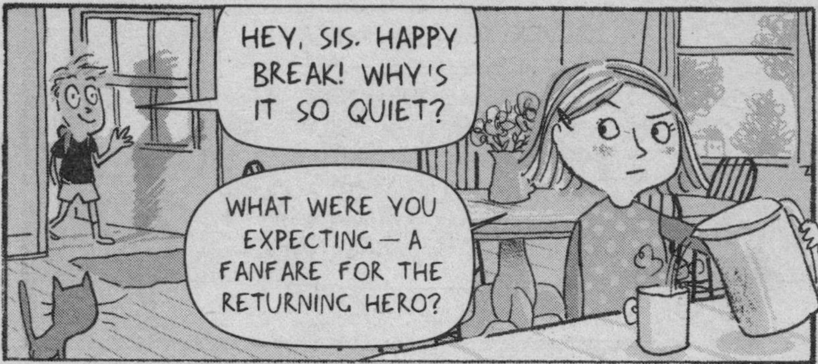
HEY, SIS. HAPPY BREAK! WHY'S IT SO QUIET?
WHAT WERE YOU EXPECTING — A FANFARE FOR THE RETURNING HERO?

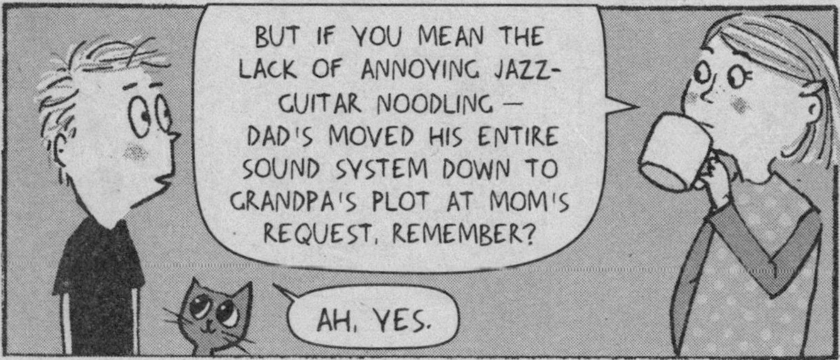
BUT IF YOU MEAN THE LACK OF ANNOYING JAZZ-GUITAR NOODLING — DAD'S MOVED HIS ENTIRE SOUND SYSTEM DOWN TO GRANDPA'S PLOT AT MOM'S REQUEST, REMEMBER?
AH, YES.

My dad spends 99% of his free time practicing his jazz-guitar noodling. Mom doesn't love jazz-guitar noodling roughly 110% of the time. So he's been banished to the plot. I think his feelings are a bit hurt, but he's putting a brave face on it. And Grandpa doesn't seem to share Mom's jazz allergy.

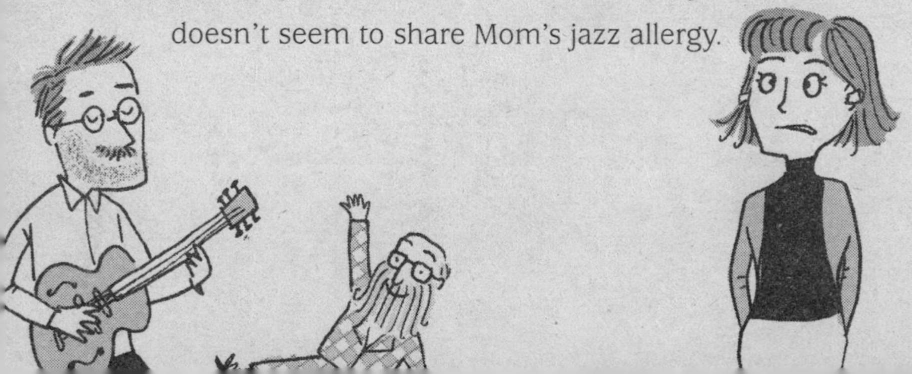

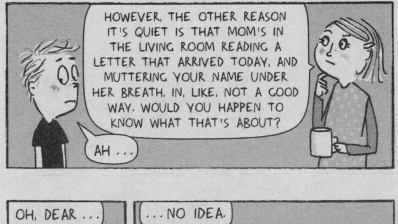

HOWEVER, THE OTHER REASON IT'S QUIET IS THAT MOM'S IN THE LIVING ROOM READING A LETTER THAT ARRIVED TODAY, AND MUTTERING YOUR NAME UNDER HER BREATH, IN, LIKE, NOT A GOOD WAY. WOULD YOU HAPPEN TO KNOW WHAT THAT'S ABOUT?

AH ...

OH, DEAR ...

...NO IDEA.

WHICH WOULD BE, I'M GUESSING, NOT ENTIRELY THE TRUTH.

PICTURE OF INNOCENCE
↓

EXPLAIN, PLEASE.

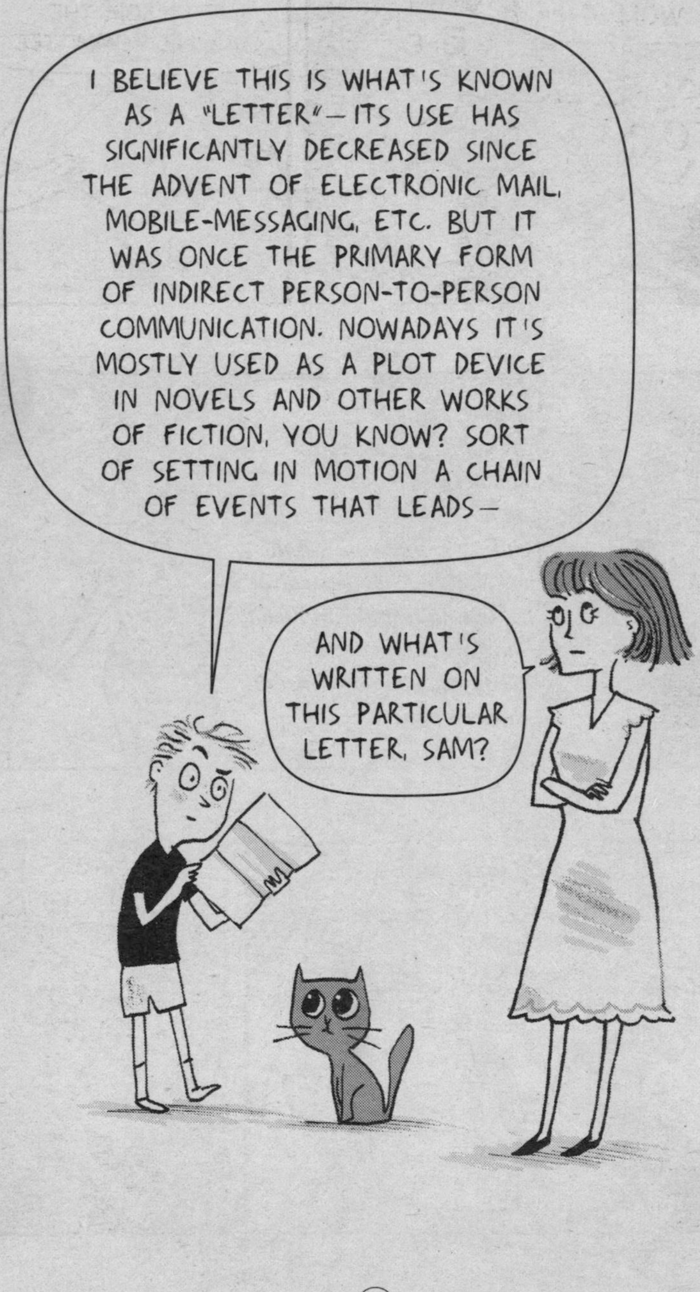
I BELIEVE THIS IS WHAT'S KNOWN AS A "LETTER"—ITS USE HAS SIGNIFICANTLY DECREASED SINCE THE ADVENT OF ELECTRONIC MAIL, MOBILE-MESSAGING, ETC. BUT IT WAS ONCE THE PRIMARY FORM OF INDIRECT PERSON-TO-PERSON COMMUNICATION. NOWADAYS IT'S MOSTLY USED AS A PLOT DEVICE IN NOVELS AND OTHER WORKS OF FICTION, YOU KNOW? SORT OF SETTING IN MOTION A CHAIN OF EVENTS THAT LEADS—
AND WHAT'S WRITTEN ON THIS PARTICULAR LETTER, SAM?

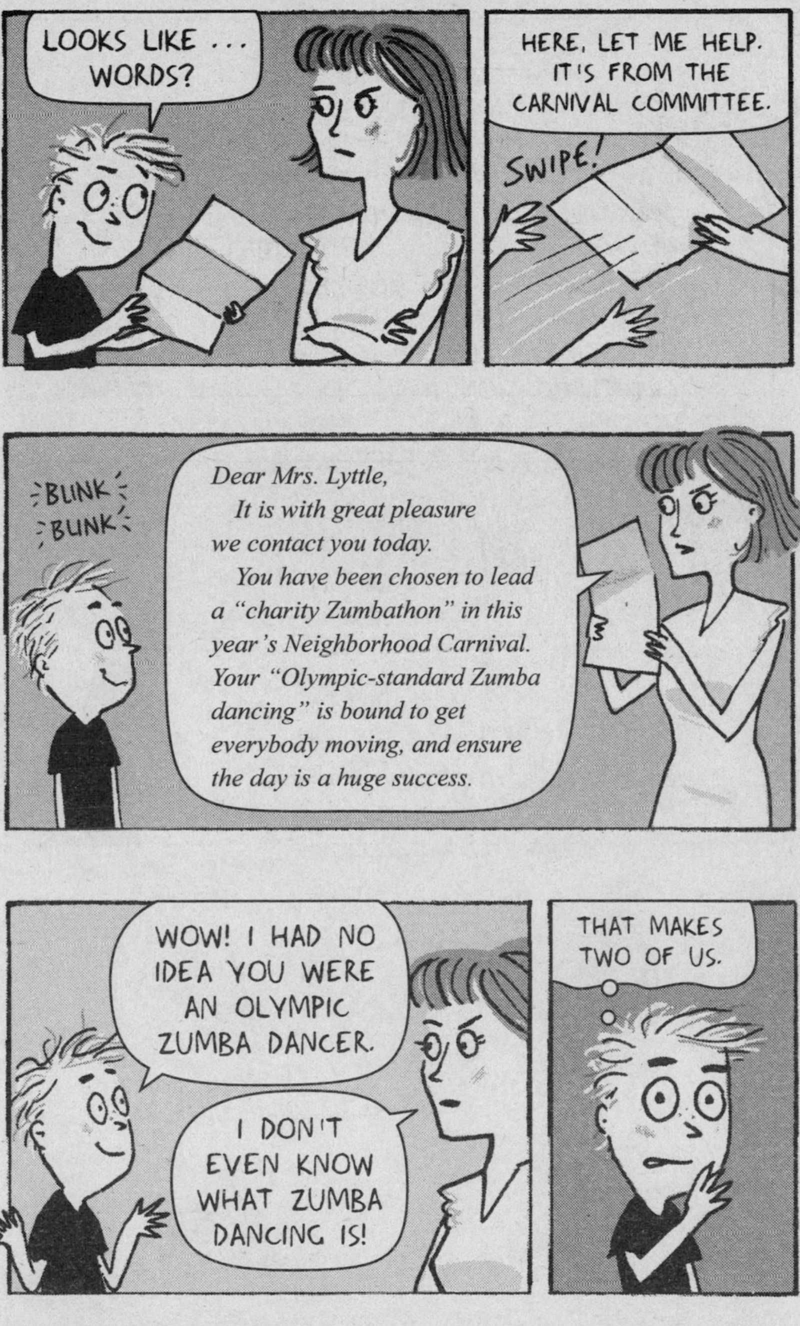
LOOKS LIKE . . . WORDS?
HERE, LET ME HELP. IT'S FROM THE CARNIVAL COMMITTEE.
SWIPE!
BLINK BLINK
Dear Mrs. Lyttle,
It is with great pleasure we contact you today.
You have been chosen to lead a "charity Zumbathon" in this year's Neighborhood Carnival. Your "Olympic-standard Zumba dancing" is bound to get everybody moving, and ensure the day is a huge success.
WOW! I HAD NO IDEA YOU WERE AN OLYMPIC ZUMBA DANCER.
I DON'T EVEN KNOW WHAT ZUMBA DANCING IS!
THAT MAKES TWO OF US.

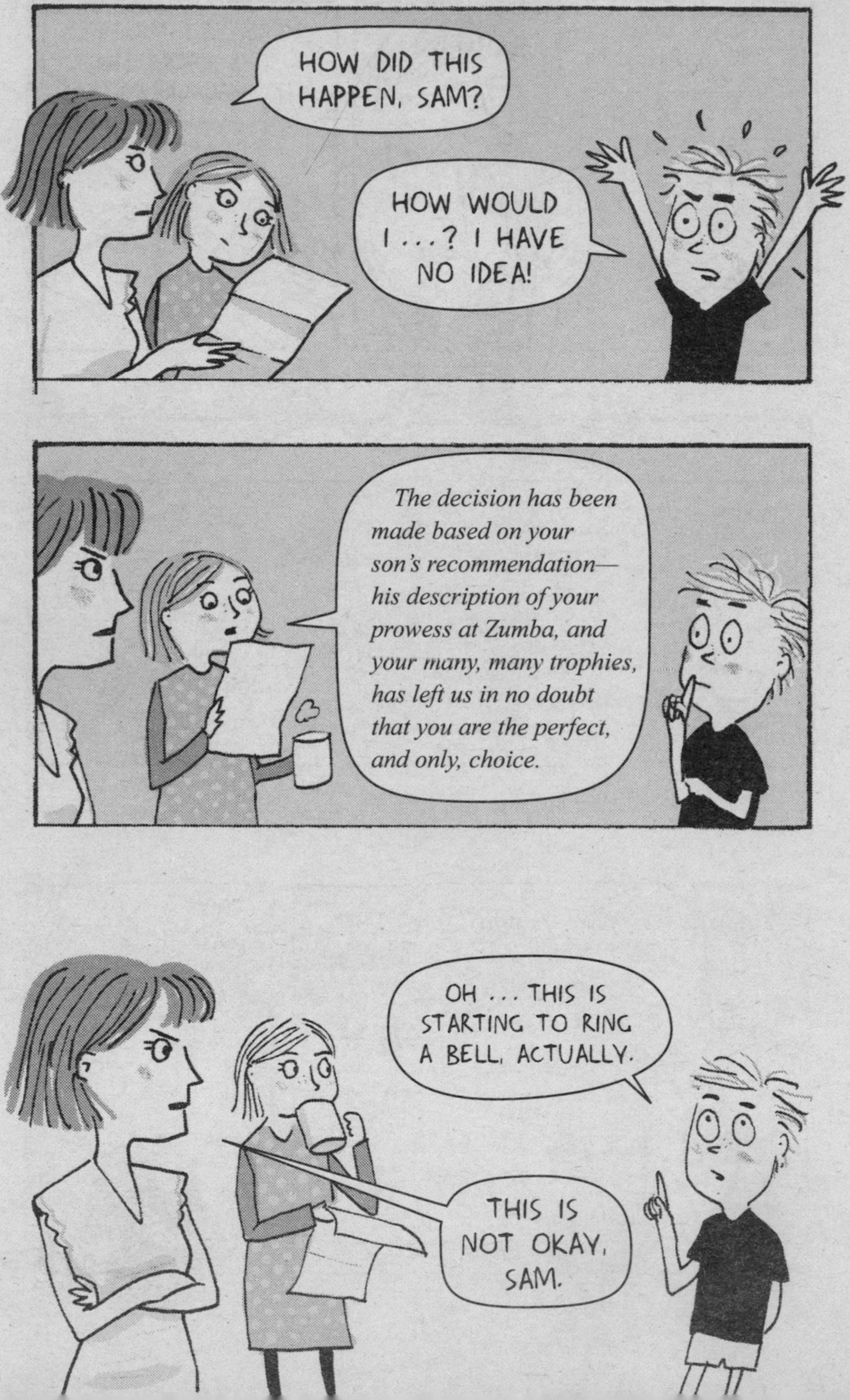
HOW DID THIS HAPPEN, SAM?
HOW WOULD I . . . ? I HAVE NO IDEA!
The decision has been made based on your son's recommendation—his description of your prowess at Zumba, and your many, many trophies, has left us in no doubt that you are the perfect, and only, choice.
OH . . . THIS IS STARTING TO RING A BELL, ACTUALLY.
THIS IS NOT OKAY, SAM.

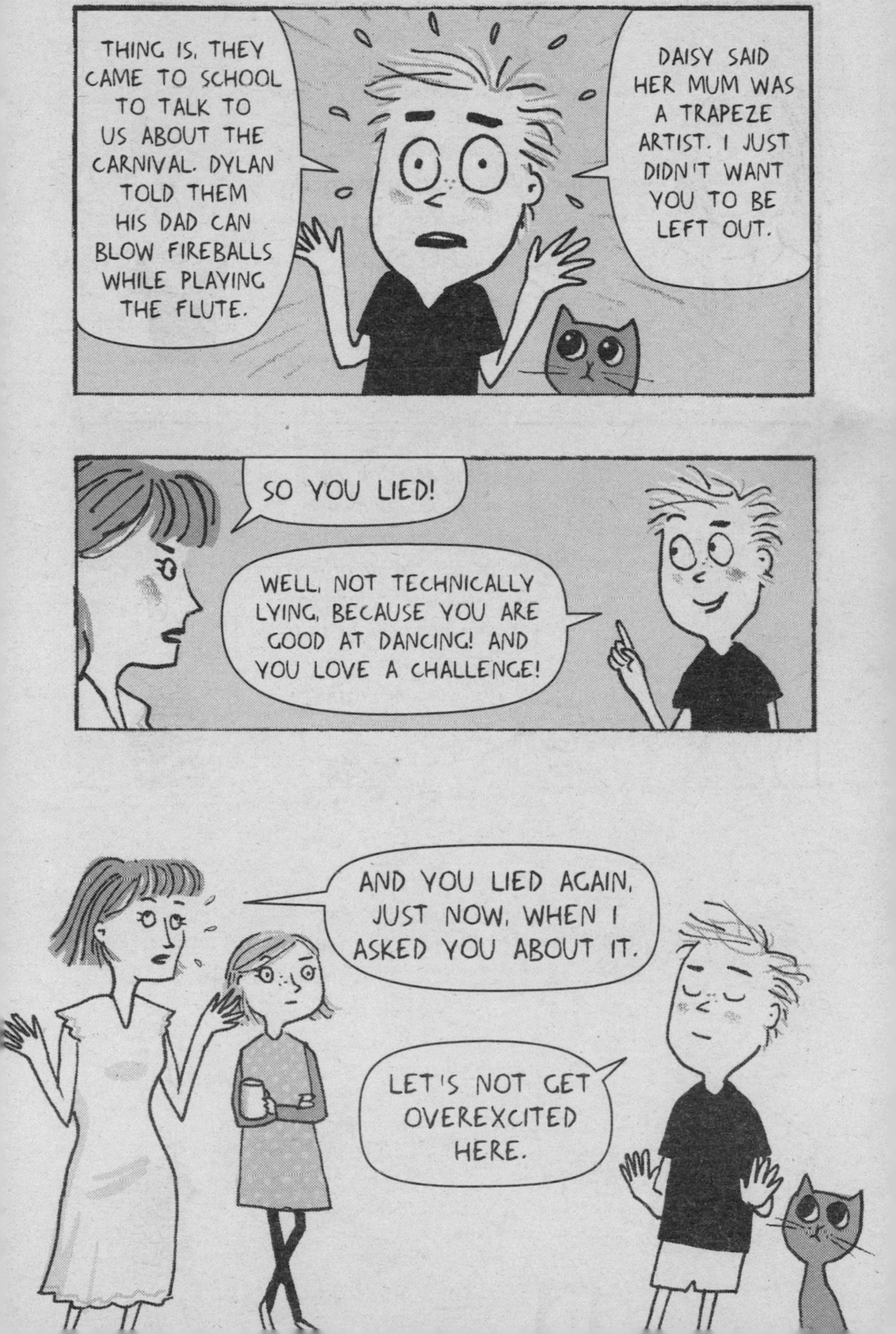
THING IS, THEY CAME TO SCHOOL TO TALK TO US ABOUT THE CARNIVAL. DYLAN TOLD THEM HIS DAD CAN BLOW FIREBALLS WHILE PLAYING THE FLUTE.
DAISY SAID HER MUM WAS A TRAPEZE ARTIST. I JUST DIDN'T WANT YOU TO BE LEFT OUT.
SO YOU LIED!
WELL, NOT TECHNICALLY LYING, BECAUSE YOU ARE GOOD AT DANCING! AND YOU LOVE A CHALLENGE!
AND YOU LIED AGAIN, JUST NOW, WHEN I ASKED YOU ABOUT IT.
LET'S NOT GET OVEREXCITED HERE.

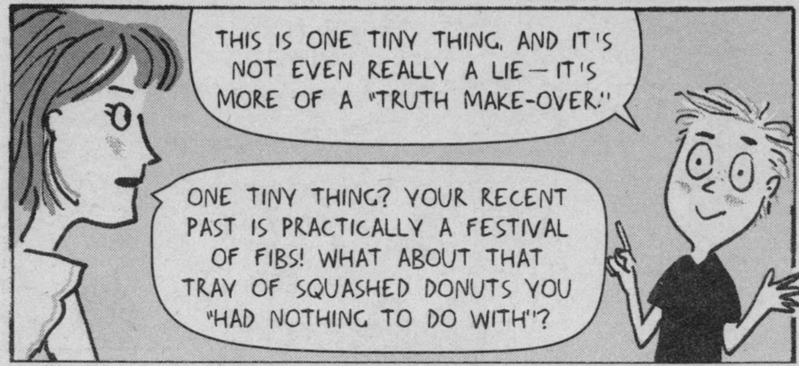
THIS IS ONE TINY THING. AND IT'S NOT EVEN REALLY A LIE—IT'S MORE OF A "TRUTH MAKE-OVER."
ONE TINY THING? YOUR RECENT PAST IS PRACTICALLY A FESTIVAL OF FIBS! WHAT ABOUT THAT TRAY OF SQUASHED DONUTS YOU "HAD NOTHING TO DO WITH"?

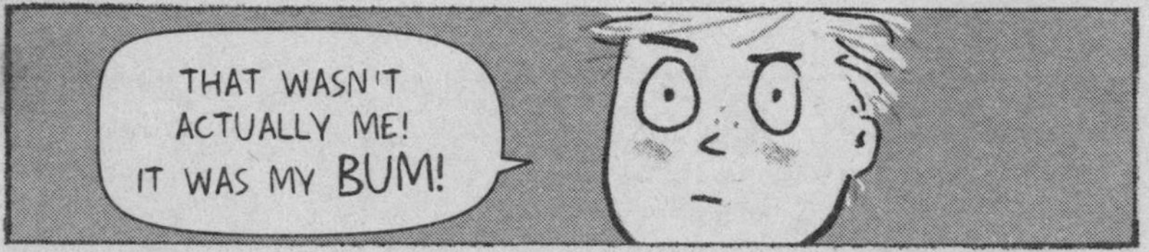
THAT WASN'T ACTUALLY ME! IT WAS MY BUM!

CAN I HELP IT IF MY BUM HEARS SOME MUSIC AND STARTS DANCING ME ALL AROUND THE KITCHEN?

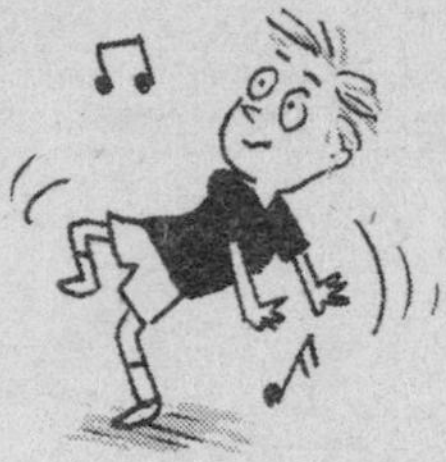

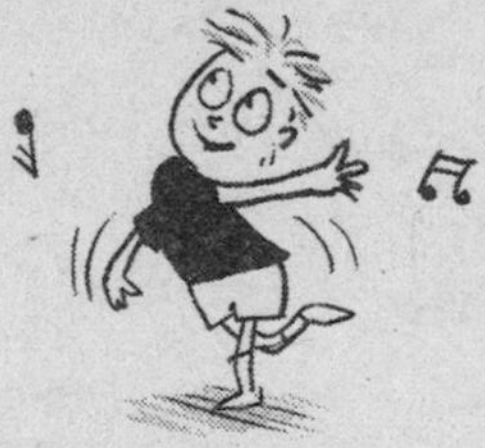

UP ONTO A CHAIR AND THEN THE COUNTERTOP?

AND THEN LANDS ME SMACK-BANG IN THE MIDDLE OF A TRAY OF DONUTS?

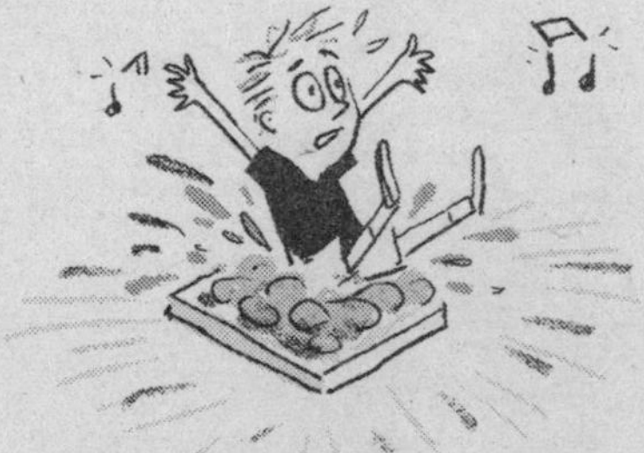

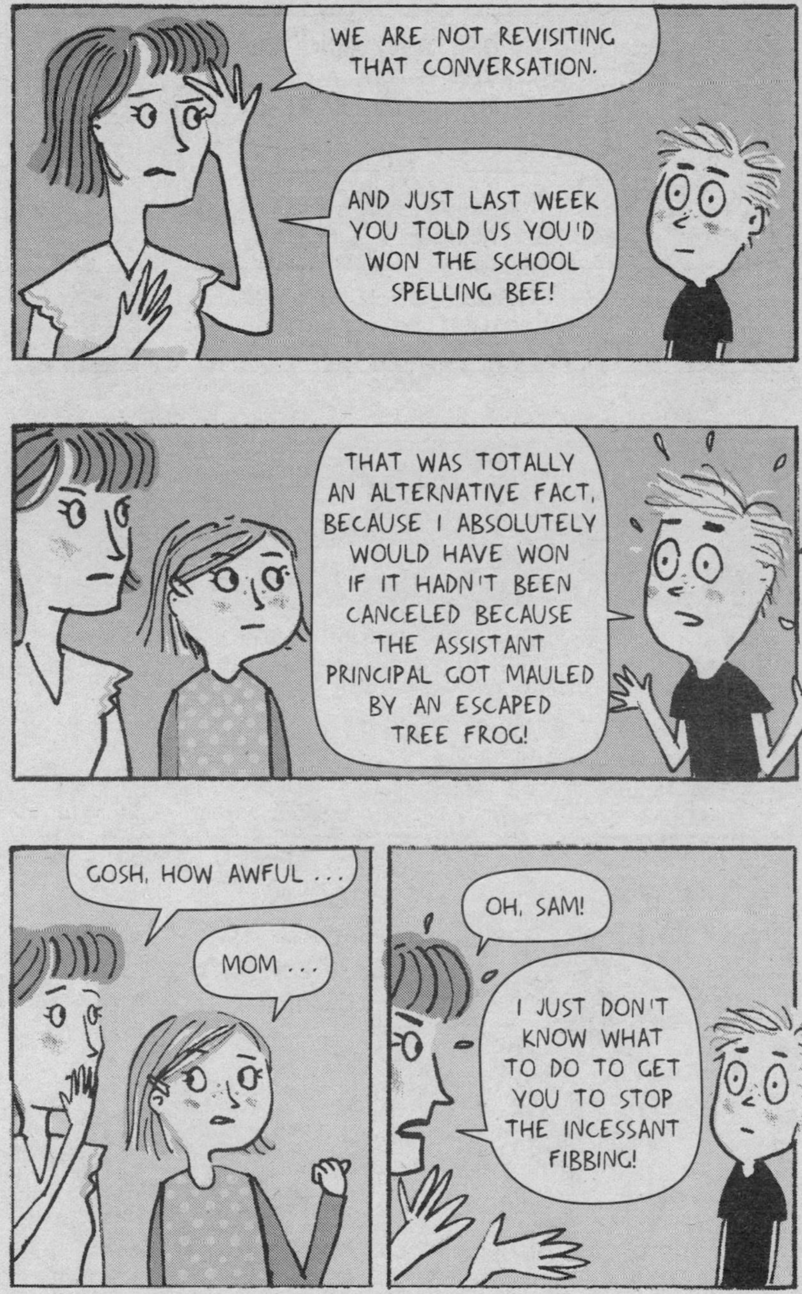
WE ARE NOT REVISITING THAT CONVERSATION.
AND JUST LAST WEEK YOU TOLD US YOU'D WON THE SCHOOL SPELLING BEE!
THAT WAS TOTALLY AN ALTERNATIVE FACT, BECAUSE I ABSOLUTELY WOULD HAVE WON IF IT HADN'T BEEN CANCELED BECAUSE THE ASSISTANT PRINCIPAL GOT MAULED BY AN ESCAPED TREE FROG!
GOSH, HOW AWFUL . . .
MOM . . .
OH, SAM!
I JUST DON'T KNOW WHAT TO DO TO GET YOU TO STOP THE INCESSANT FIBBING!

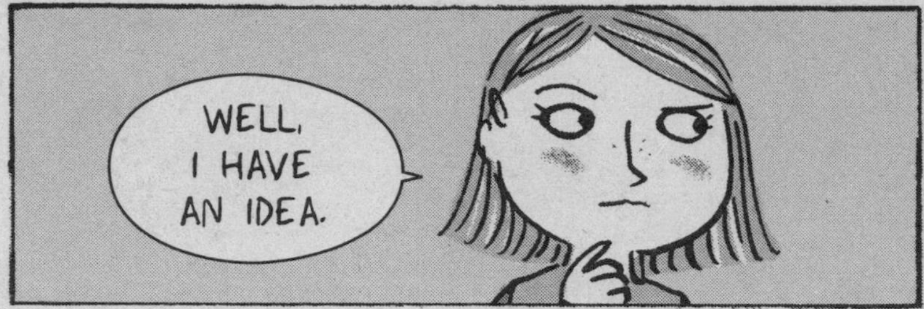
WELL, I HAVE AN IDEA.

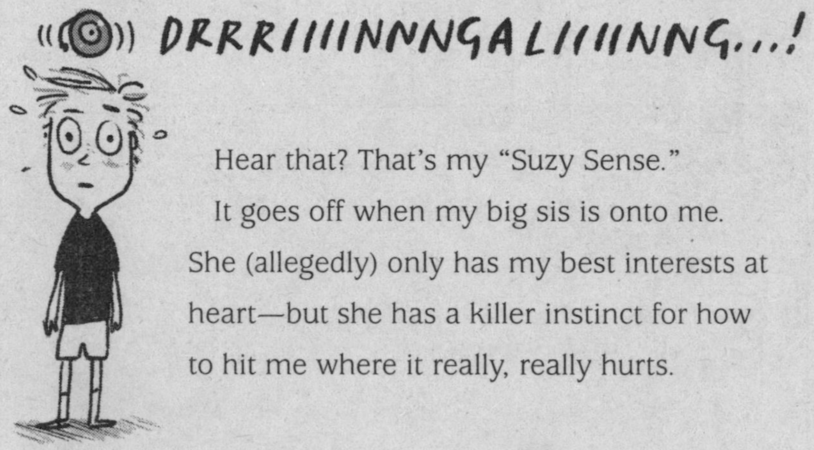
DRRRIIIINNNGALIIIINNG...!

Hear that? That's my "Suzy Sense."

It goes off when my big sis is onto me. She (allegedly) only has my best interests at heart—but she has a killer instinct for how to hit me where it really, really hurts.

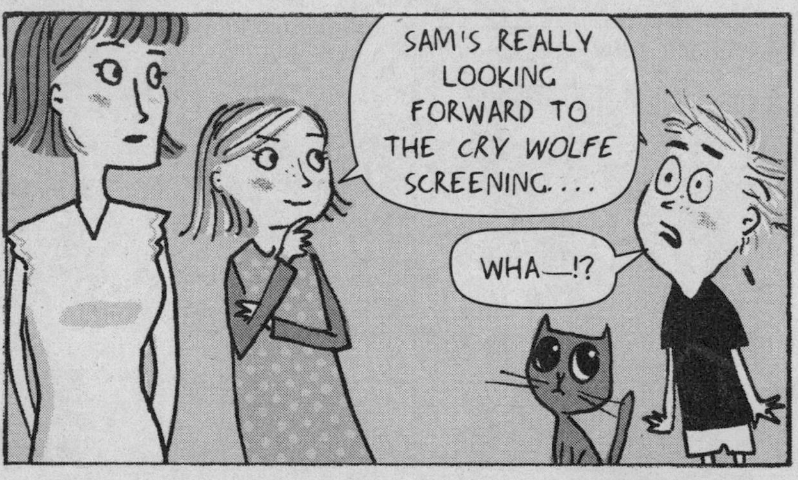
SAM'S REALLY LOOKING FORWARD TO THE *CRY WOLFE* SCREENING. . . .
WHA—!?

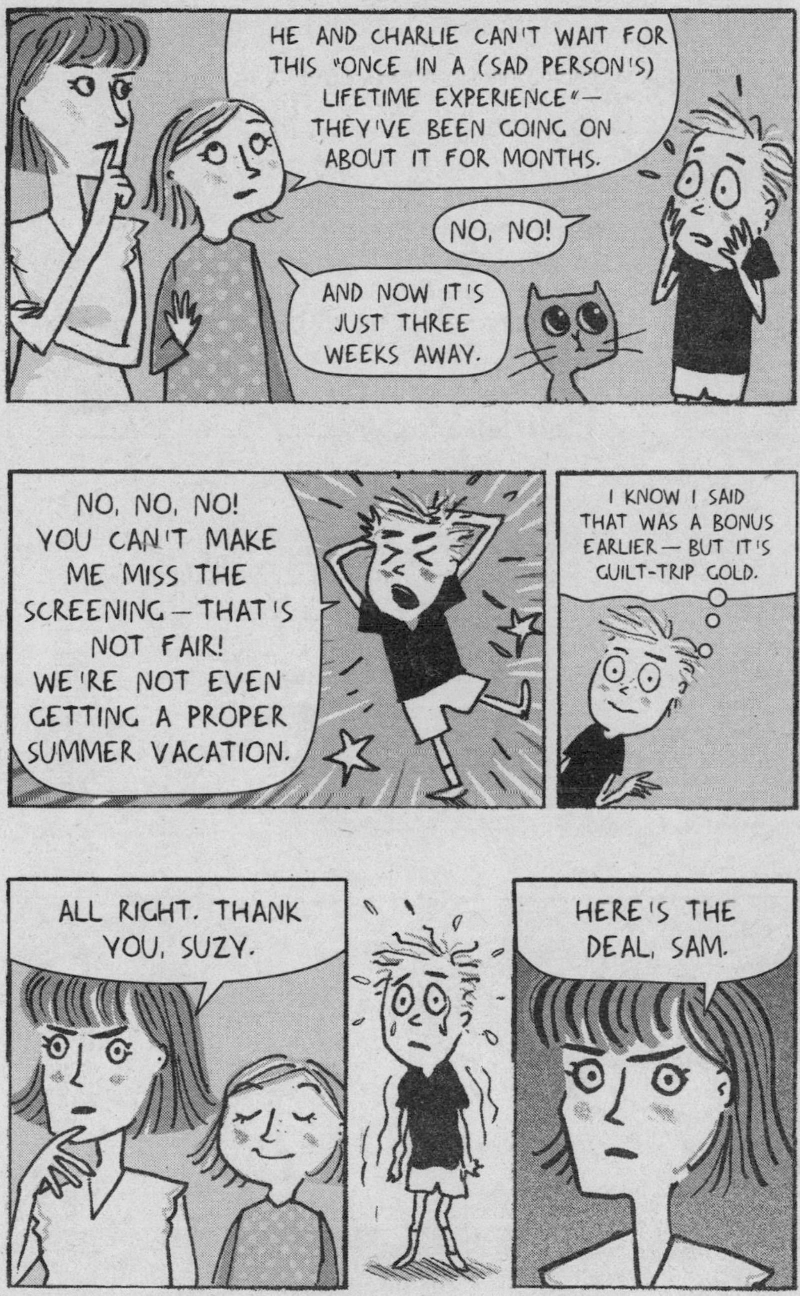
HE AND CHARLIE CAN'T WAIT FOR THIS "ONCE IN A (SAD PERSON'S) LIFETIME EXPERIENCE"— THEY'VE BEEN GOING ON ABOUT IT FOR MONTHS.
NO, NO!
AND NOW IT'S JUST THREE WEEKS AWAY.
NO, NO, NO! YOU CAN'T MAKE ME MISS THE SCREENING—THAT'S NOT FAIR! WE'RE NOT EVEN GETTING A PROPER SUMMER VACATION.
I KNOW I SAID THAT WAS A BONUS EARLIER—BUT IT'S GUILT-TRIP GOLD.
ALL RIGHT. THANK YOU, SUZY.
HERE'S THE DEAL, SAM.

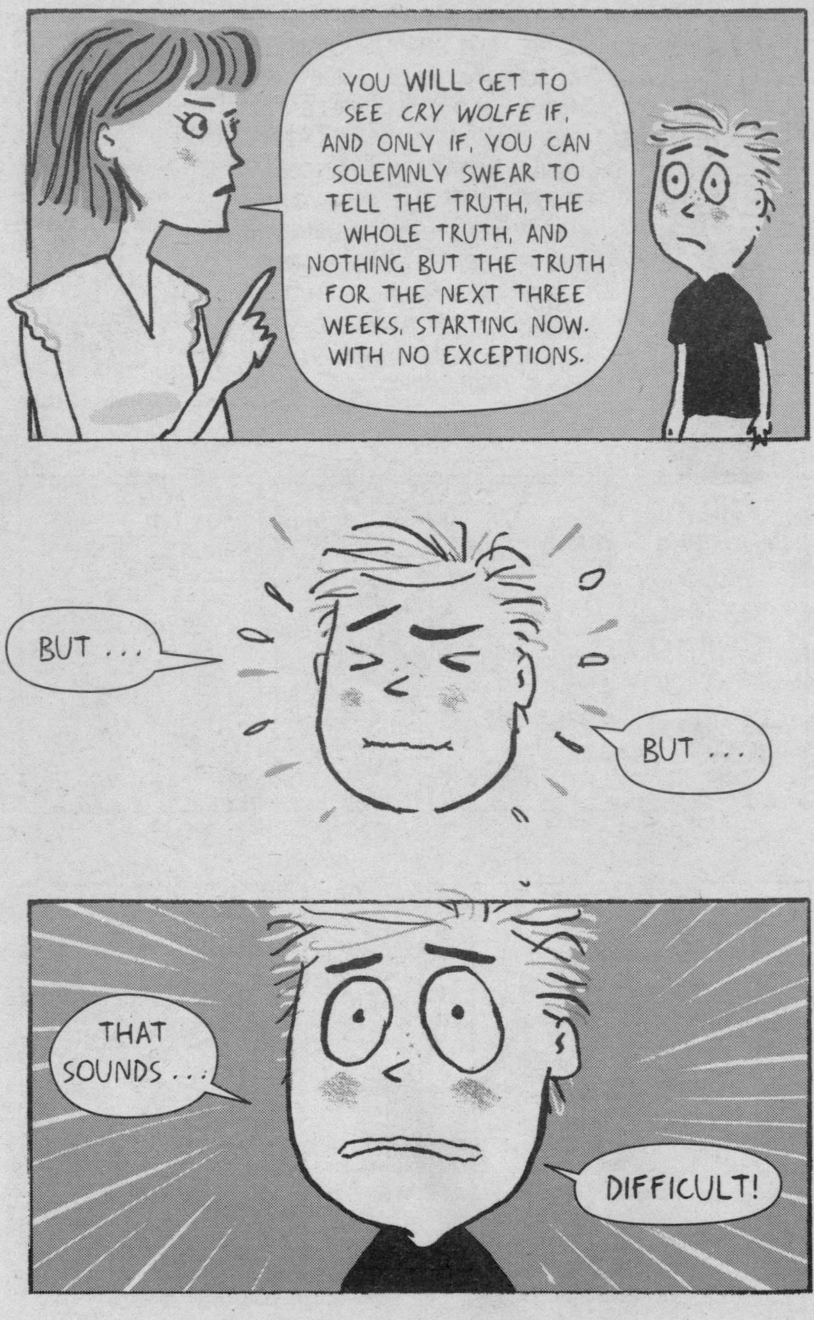
YOU WILL GET TO SEE *CRY WOLFE* IF, AND ONLY IF, YOU CAN SOLEMNLY SWEAR TO TELL THE TRUTH, THE WHOLE TRUTH, AND NOTHING BUT THE TRUTH FOR THE NEXT THREE WEEKS, STARTING NOW. WITH NO EXCEPTIONS.
BUT . . .
BUT . . .
THAT SOUNDS . . .
DIFFICULT!

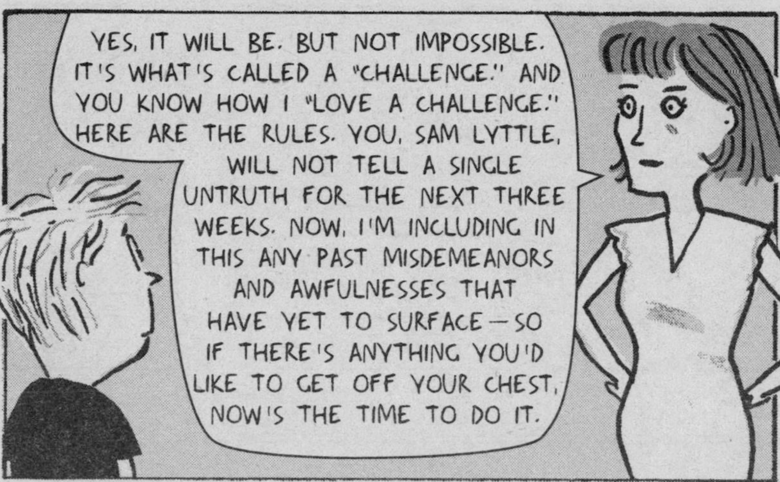
YES, IT WILL BE. BUT NOT IMPOSSIBLE. IT'S WHAT'S CALLED A "CHALLENGE." AND YOU KNOW HOW I "LOVE A CHALLENGE." HERE ARE THE RULES. YOU, SAM LYTTLE, WILL NOT TELL A SINGLE UNTRUTH FOR THE NEXT THREE WEEKS. NOW, I'M INCLUDING IN THIS ANY PAST MISDEMEANORS AND AWFULNESSES THAT HAVE YET TO SURFACE—SO IF THERE'S ANYTHING YOU'D LIKE TO GET OFF YOUR CHEST, NOW'S THE TIME TO DO IT.

Something is lurking there—something I've dumped in the deepest bargain bin of my mind . . . a faint shadow . . .

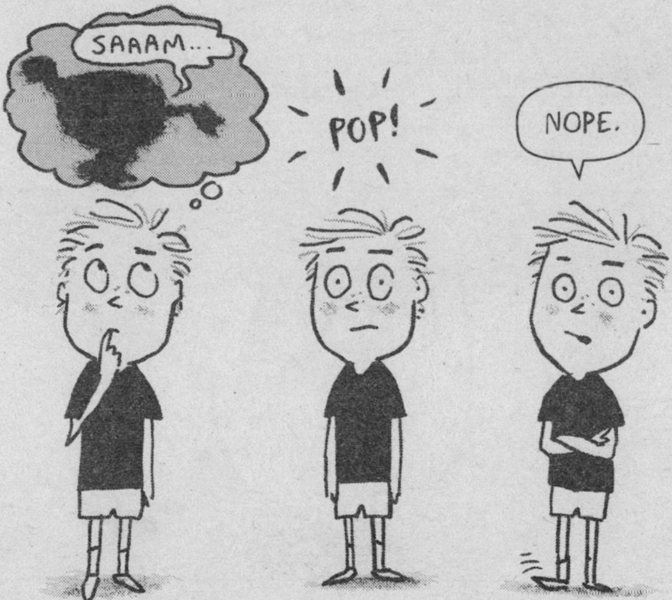
SAAAM...
POP!
NOPE.

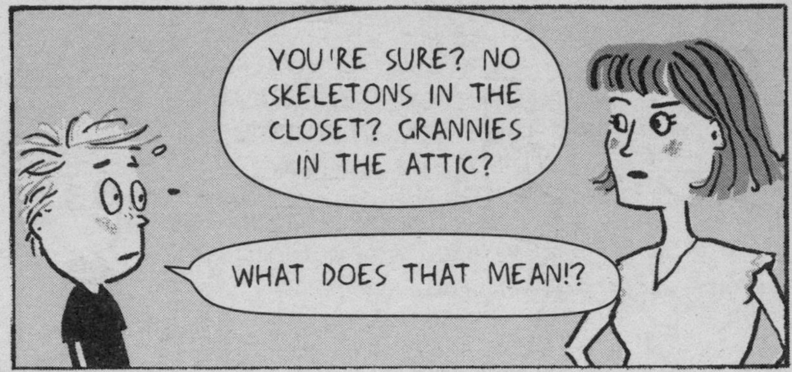
YOU'RE SURE? NO SKELETONS IN THE CLOSET? GRANNIES IN THE ATTIC?
WHAT DOES THAT MEAN!?

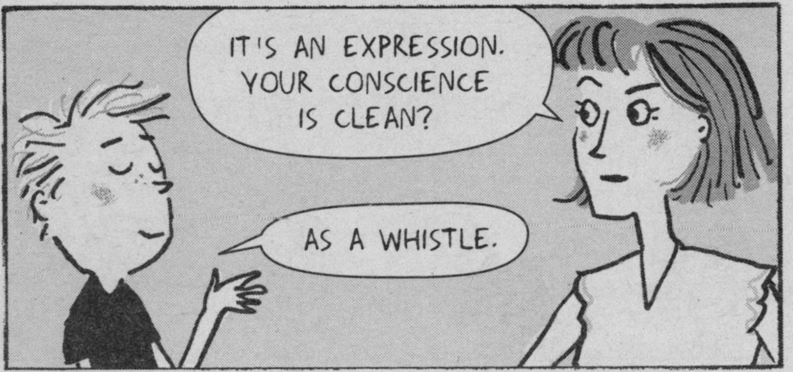
IT'S AN EXPRESSION. YOUR CONSCIENCE IS CLEAN?
AS A WHISTLE.

It never seems to occur to anyone that whistles can get grubby. . . .

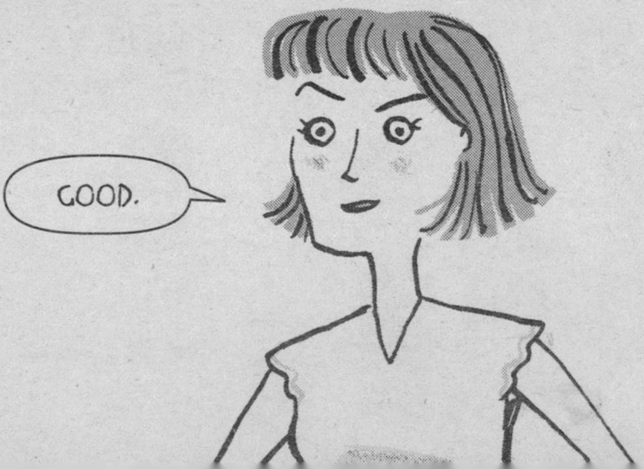
GOOD.

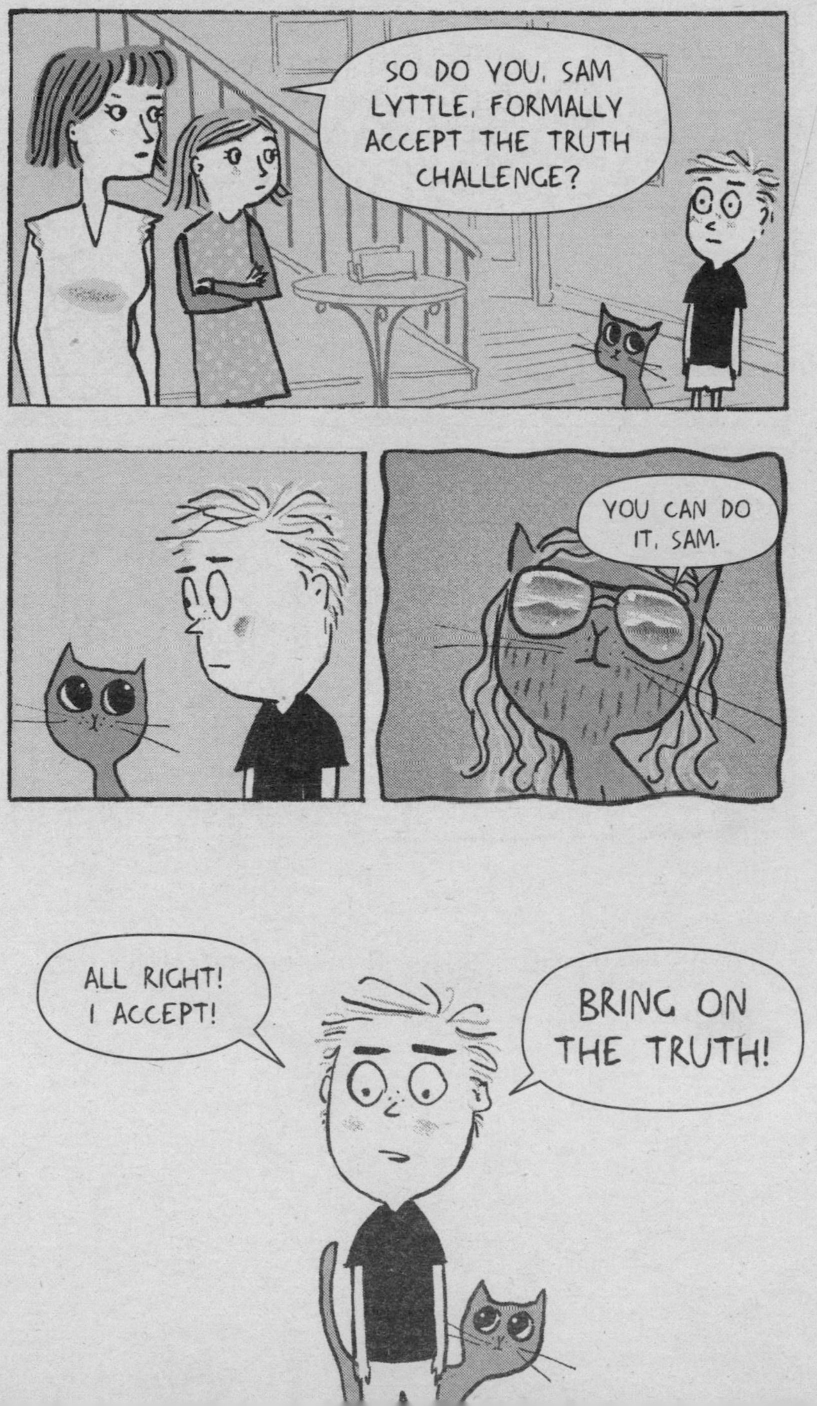
SO DO YOU, SAM LYTTLE, FORMALLY ACCEPT THE TRUTH CHALLENGE?
YOU CAN DO IT, SAM.
ALL RIGHT! I ACCEPT!
BRING ON THE TRUTH!

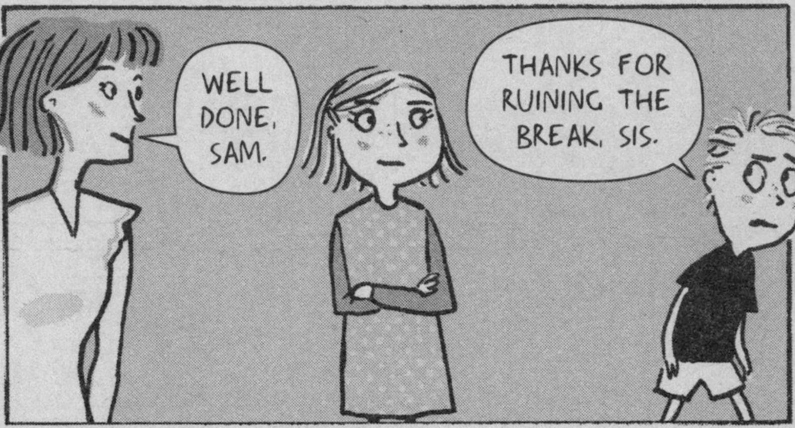
WELL DONE, SAM.
THANKS FOR RUINING THE BREAK, SIS.

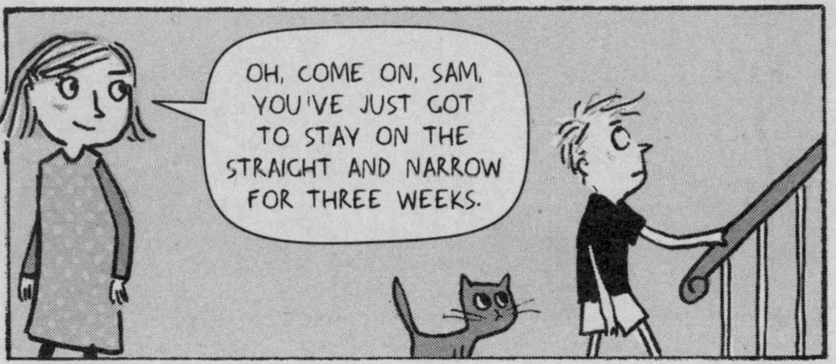
OH, COME ON, SAM. YOU'VE JUST GOT TO STAY ON THE STRAIGHT AND NARROW FOR THREE WEEKS.

That's my big sister, Suzy, always looking out for me. Apparently.

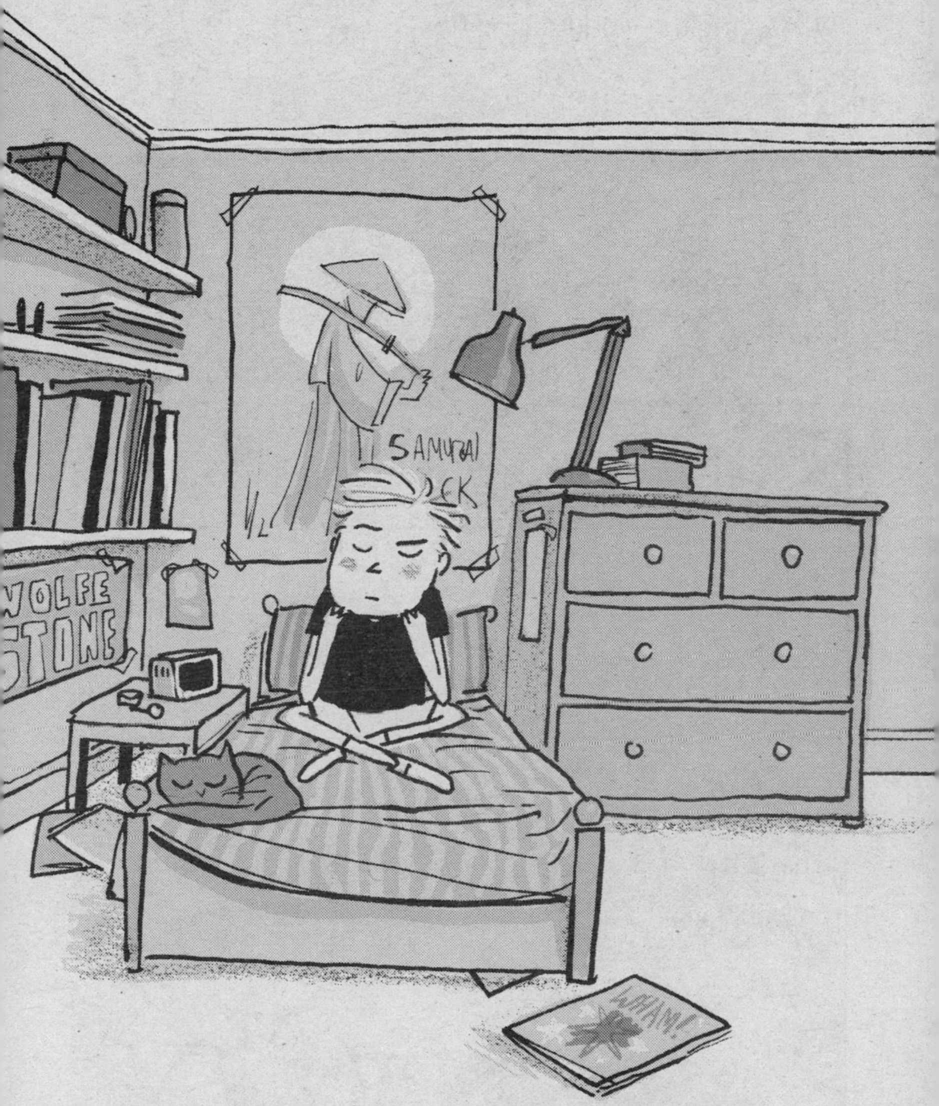
SAMURAI
OLFE
STONE
WHAM!

Here's the thing. I don't lie out of some sort of principle. I'm not, like, a warrior monk of lying, wandering the world telling fibs.

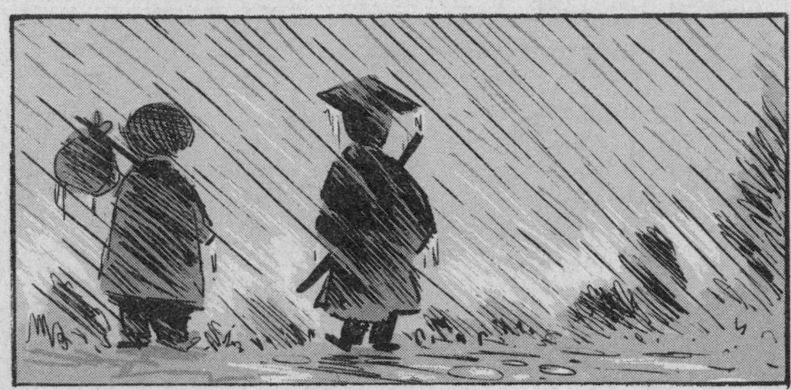

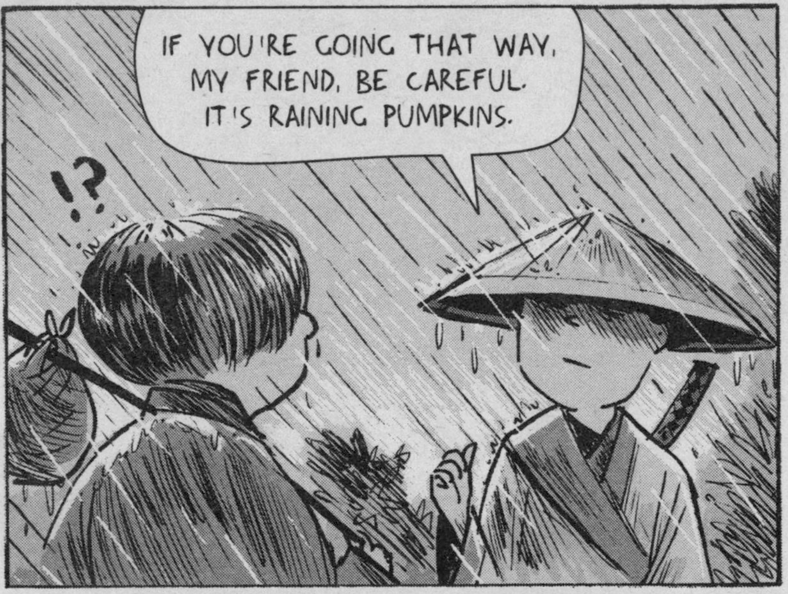
IF YOU'RE GOING THAT WAY, MY FRIEND, BE CAREFUL. IT'S RAINING PUMPKINS.
!?

Me, I'm more of a panic-liar. Accidents happen, and I don't want to get into trouble, so I have to "think on my feet."

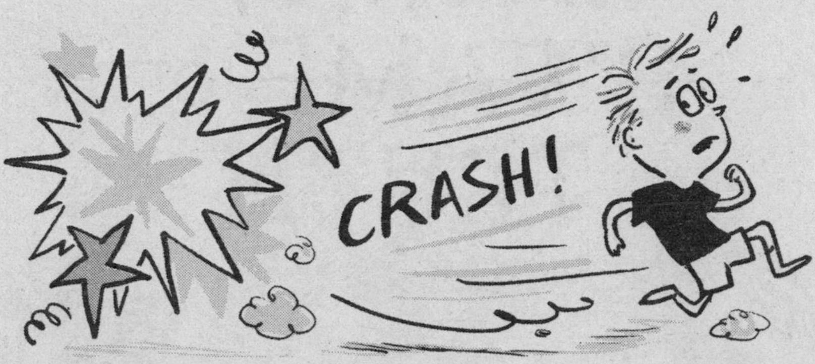
CRASH!

Which is hard when your feet are busy running away as fast as they can.

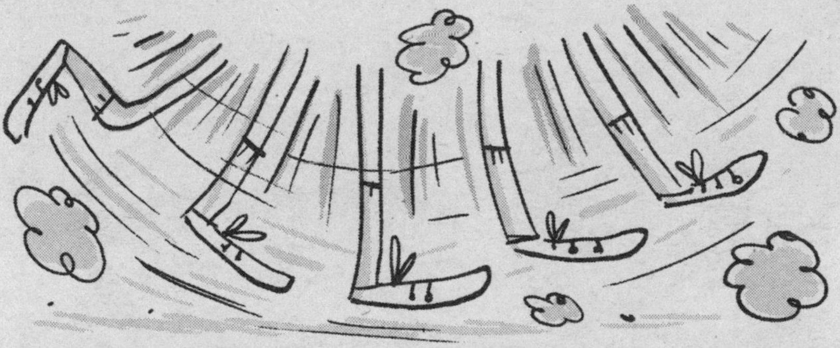

But all that has to change. No more running away.

Now I must travel the

STINKY SWAMP OF TRUTH

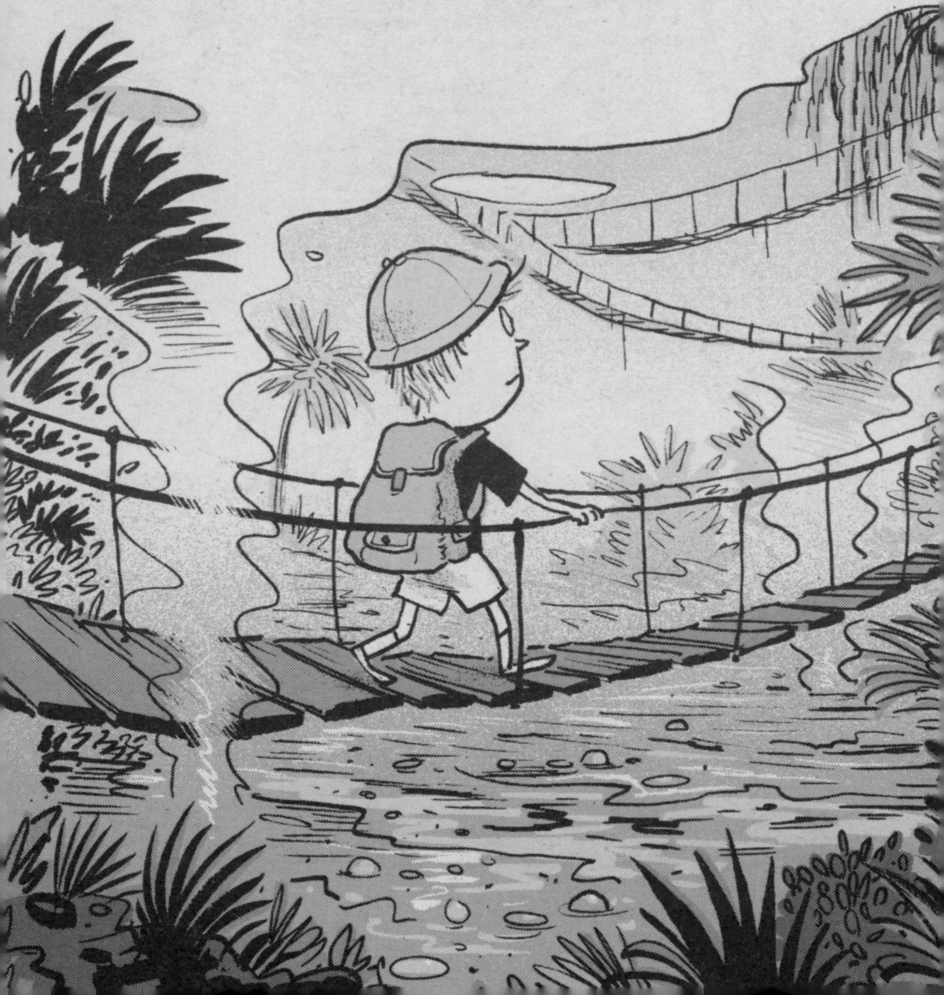

Staying on the "straight and narrow" might sound easy enough—but in fact the path of truth is a treacherous health and safety nightmare.

Every way you turn, there are gloopy, eggy bogs,

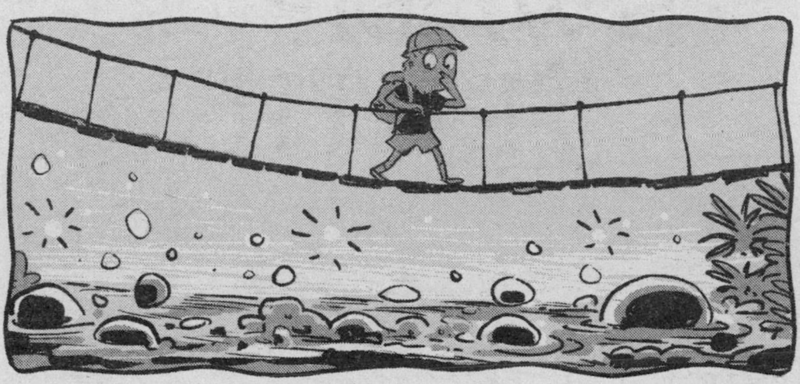

and gassy sinkholes that could do you in.

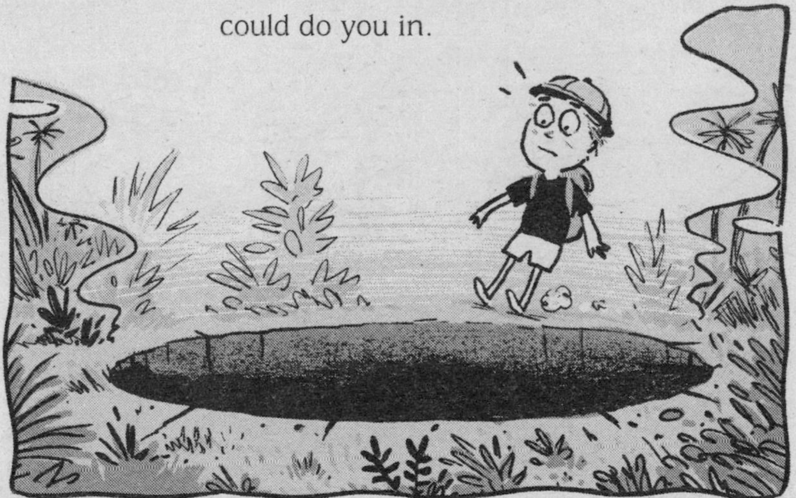

They may be narrow, but the pathways through this nightmarish swamp are anything but straight.

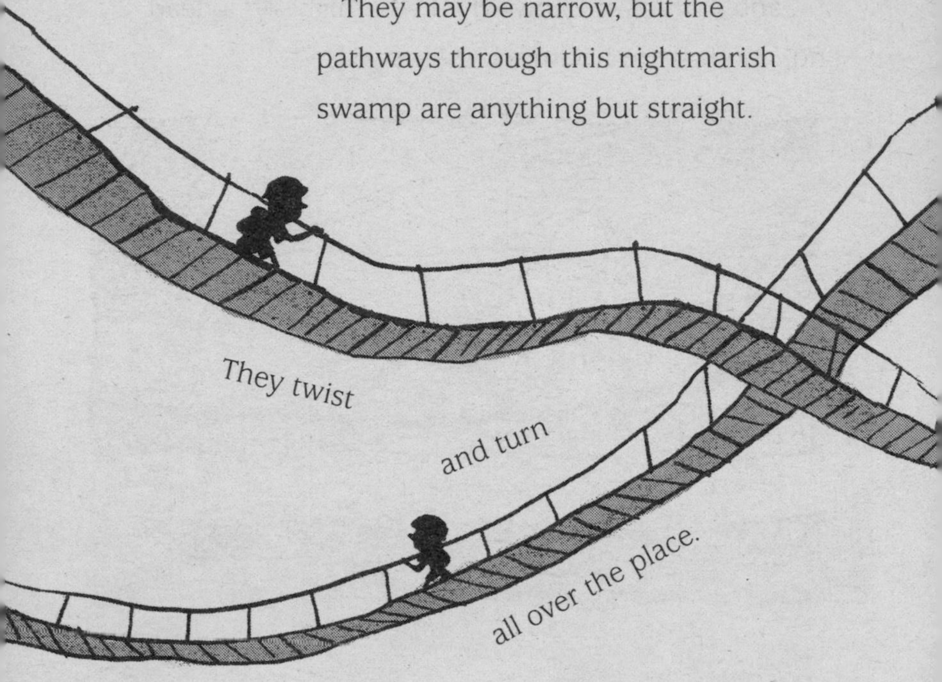

They twist

and turn

all over the place.

There are slats missing . . .

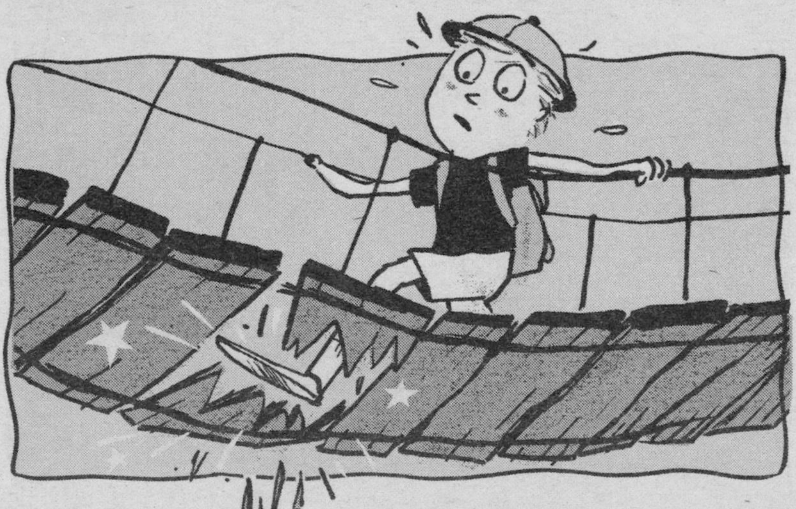

. . . and you never know when you might hit a dead end, and have to backtrack or improvise.

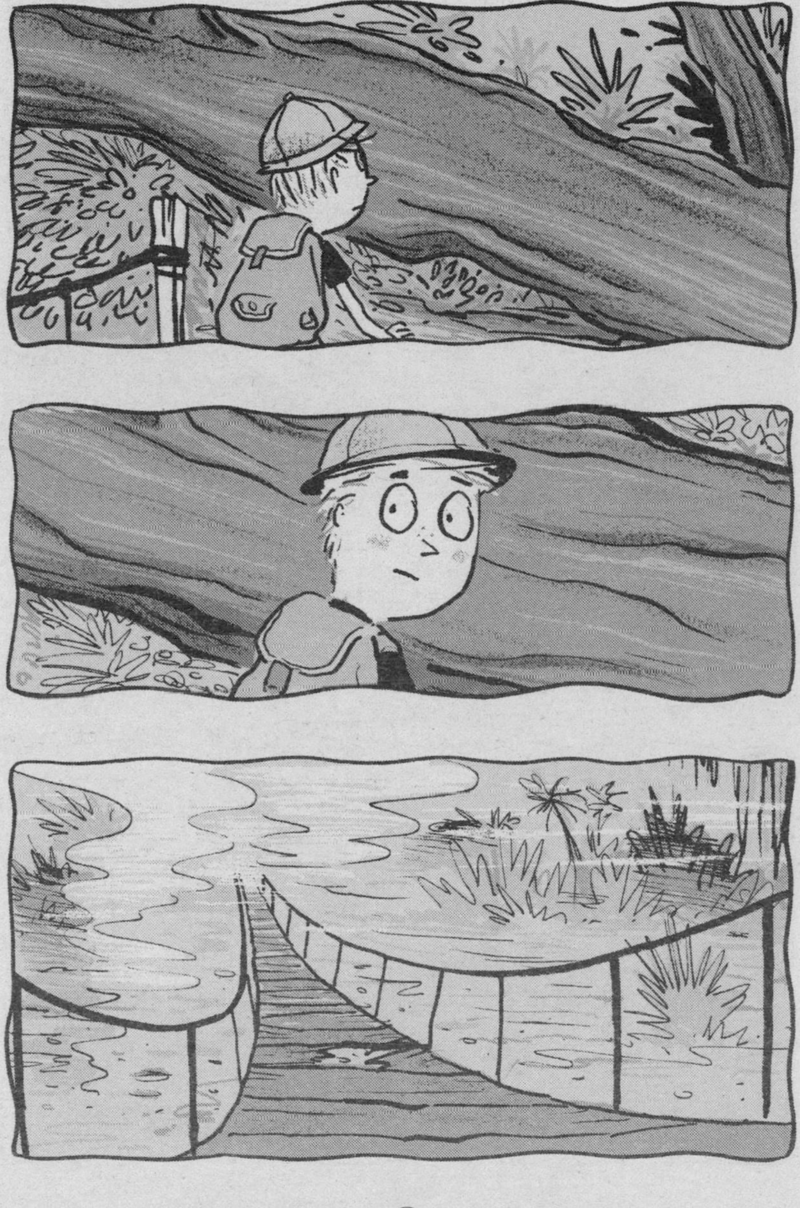

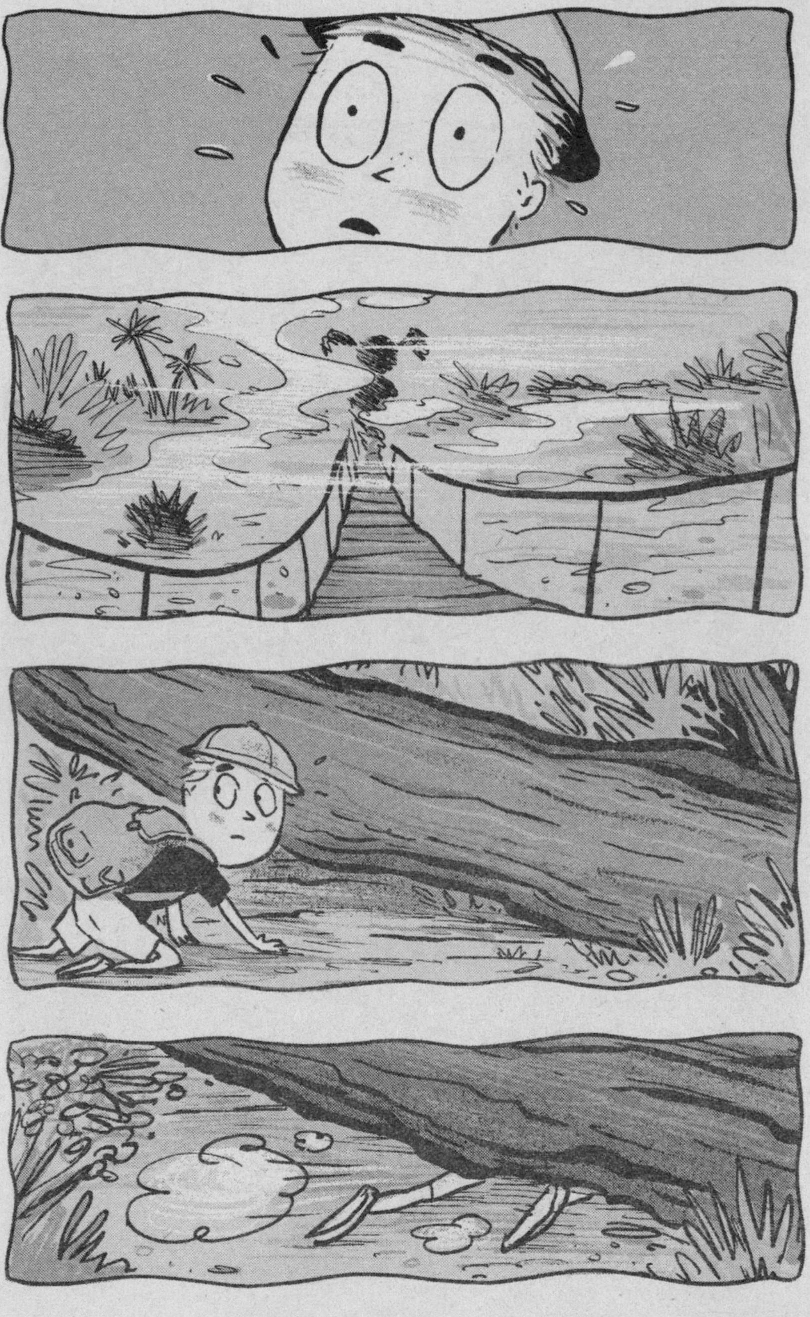

Am I prepared? Let's see . . .

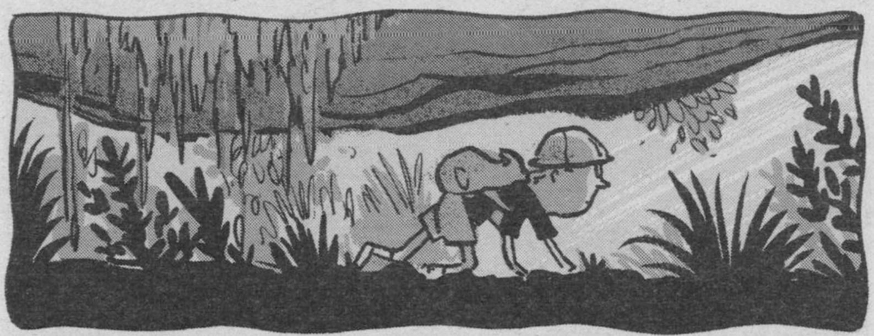

I have no compass, or torch, or noseplugs.

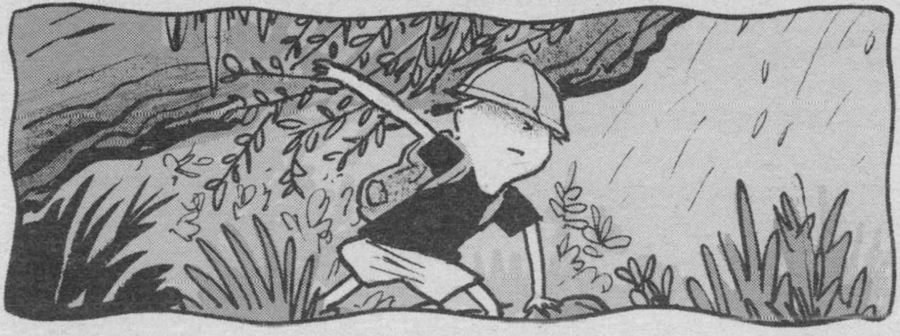

I forgot to bring a waterproof jacket in case it rains.

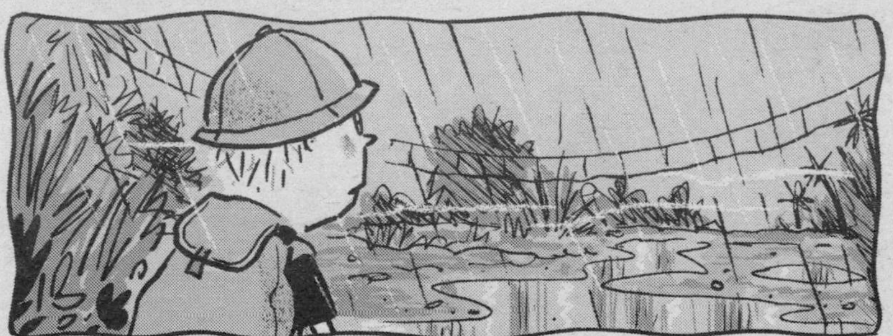

At least I have lollipops. . . .

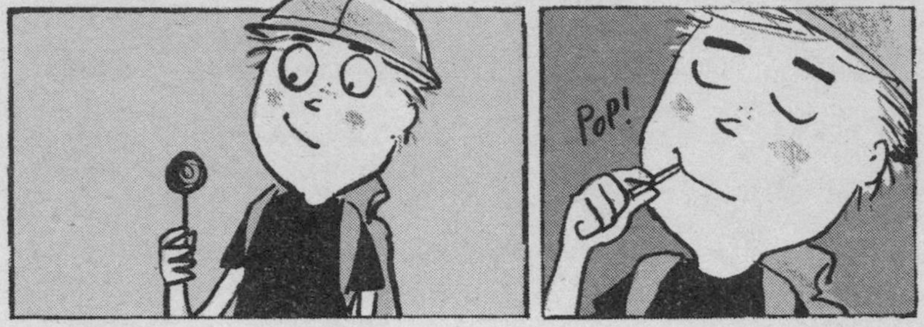
POP!

But I do know where I need to get to. Somewhere on the other side of this swamp, in three weeks' time, is a glorious fun-filled carnival, and an open-air movie-screening of the coolest crime-fighter the world has ever seen. And all I need to do is rise to the challenge before me, and stick to the truth.

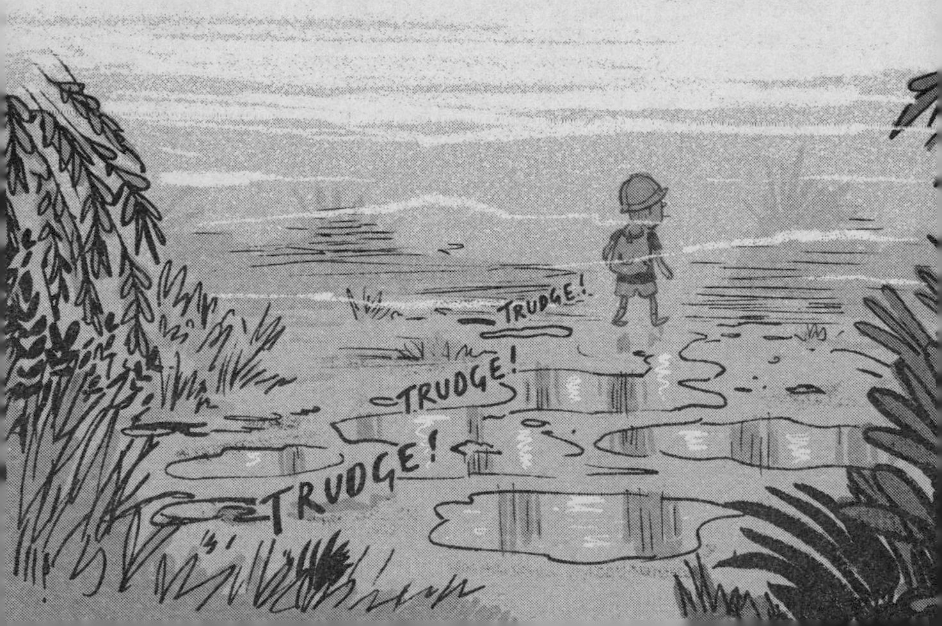
TRUDGE!
TRUDGE!
TRUDGE!

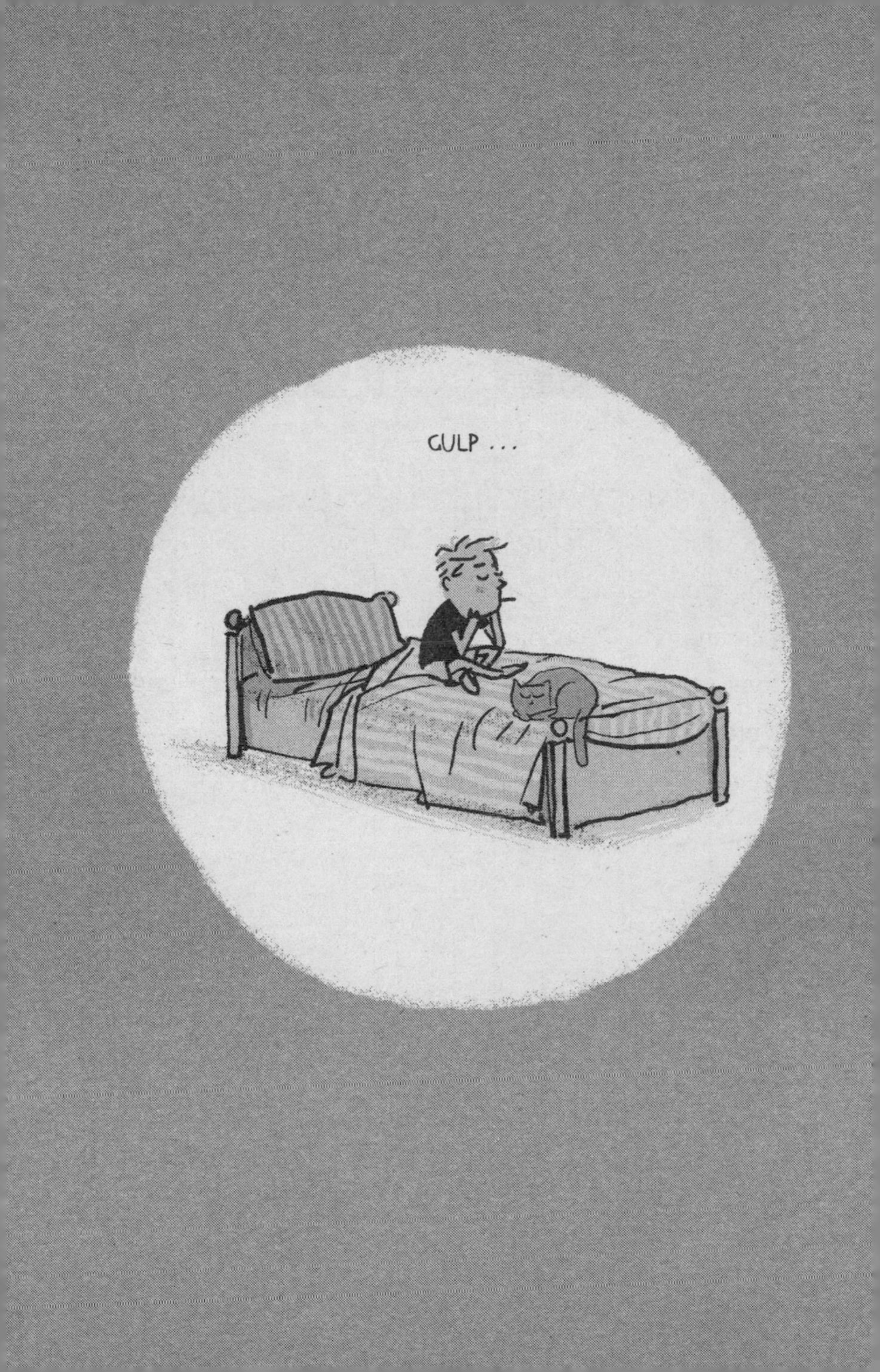
GULP . . .

TIME REMAINING TILL CARNIVAL

18 06 17

DAYS   HOURS   MINUTES

THE DEN.

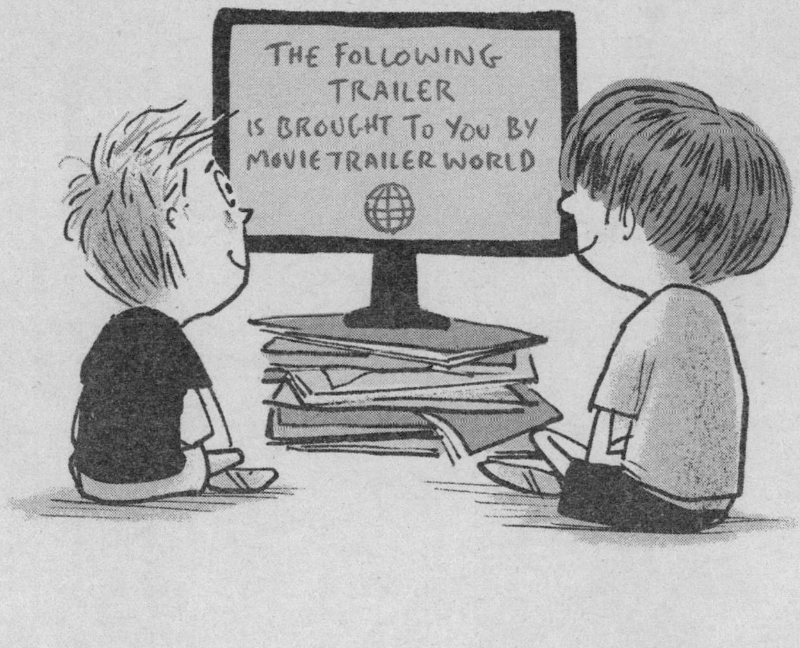
THE FOLLOWING
TRAILER
IS BROUGHT TO YOU BY
MOVIETRAILERWORLD

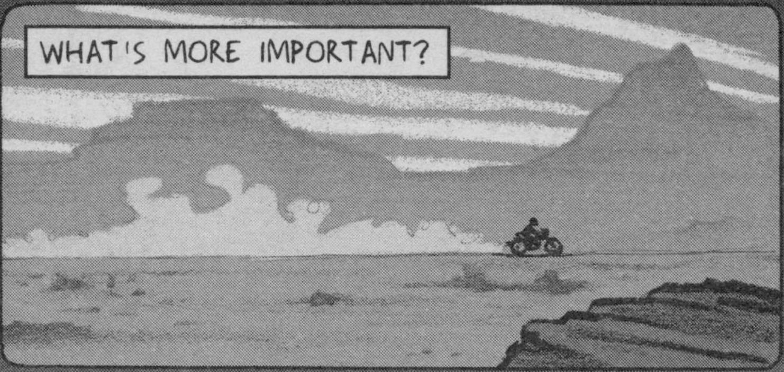
WHAT'S MORE IMPORTANT?

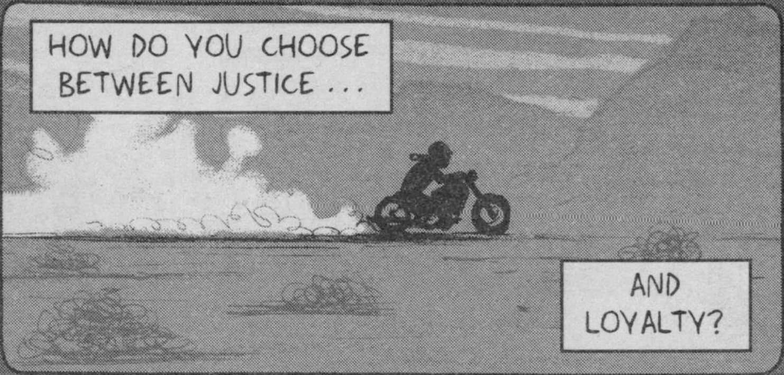
HOW DO YOU CHOOSE BETWEEN JUSTICE . . .
AND LOYALTY?

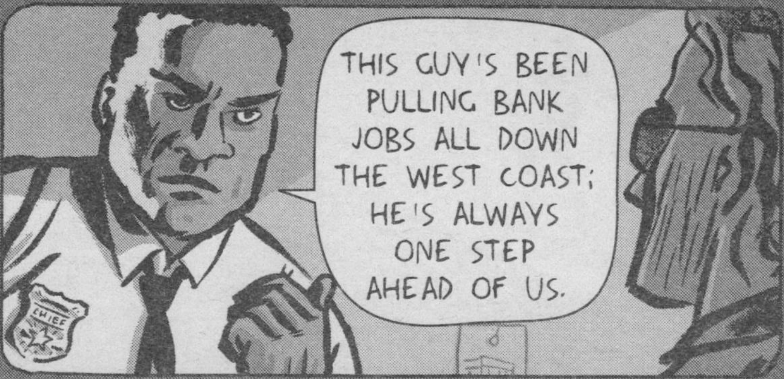
THIS GUY'S BEEN PULLING BANK JOBS ALL DOWN THE WEST COAST; HE'S ALWAYS ONE STEP AHEAD OF US.
CHIEF

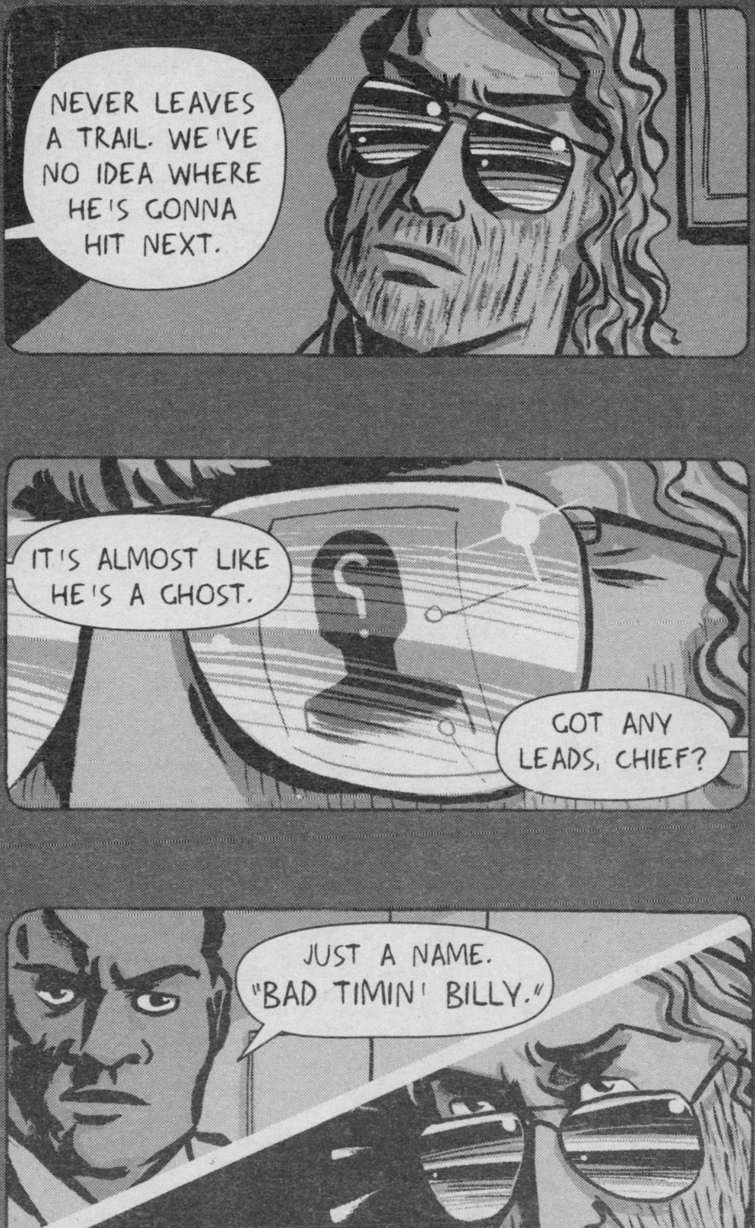
NEVER LEAVES A TRAIL. WE'VE NO IDEA WHERE HE'S GONNA HIT NEXT.
IT'S ALMOST LIKE HE'S A GHOST.
GOT ANY LEADS, CHIEF?
JUST A NAME. "BAD TIMIN' BILLY."

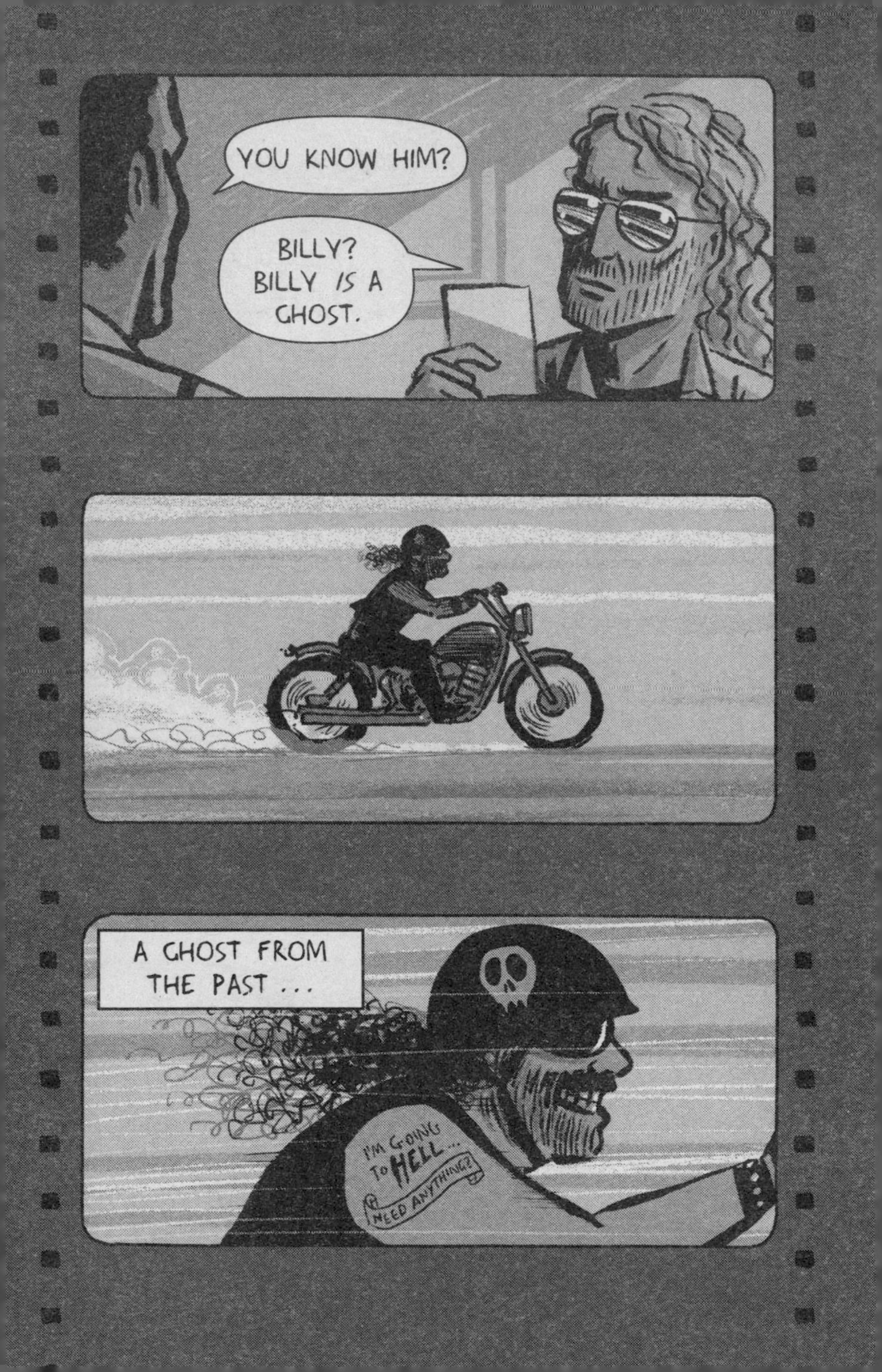
YOU KNOW HIM?
BILLY? BILLY IS A GHOST.
A GHOST FROM THE PAST . . .
I'M GOING TO HELL...
NEED ANYTHING?

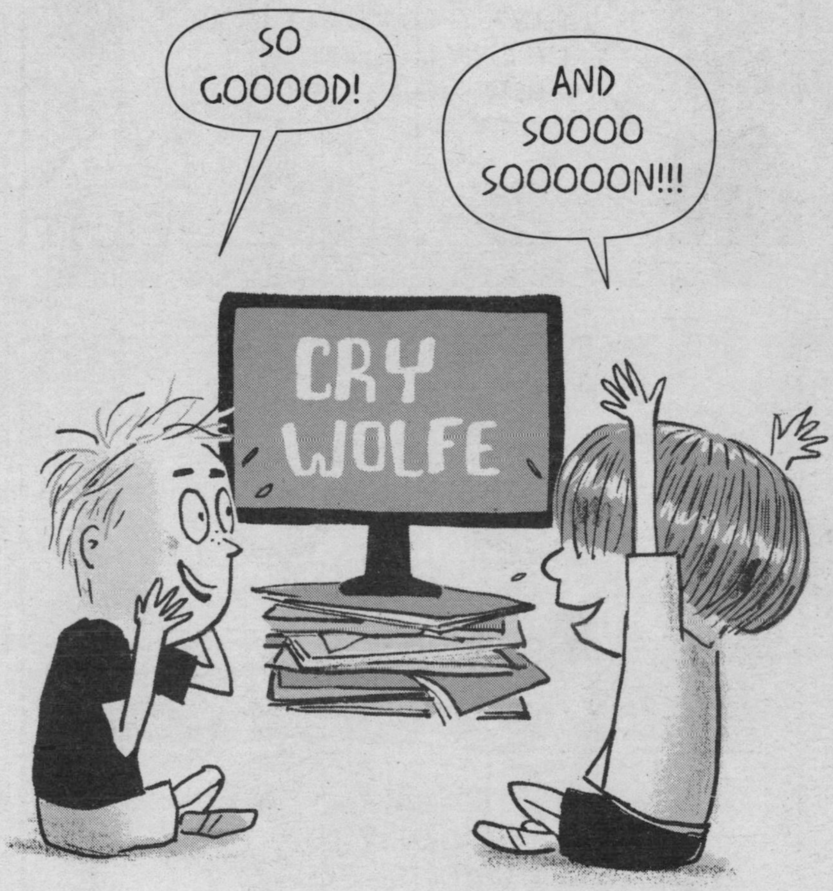
SO GOOOOD!
AND SOOOO SOOOOON!!!
CRY WOLFE

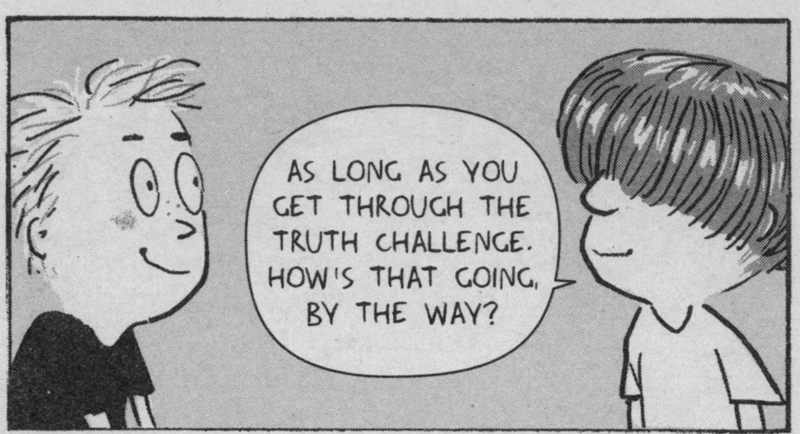
AS LONG AS YOU GET THROUGH THE TRUTH CHALLENGE. HOW'S THAT GOING, BY THE WAY?

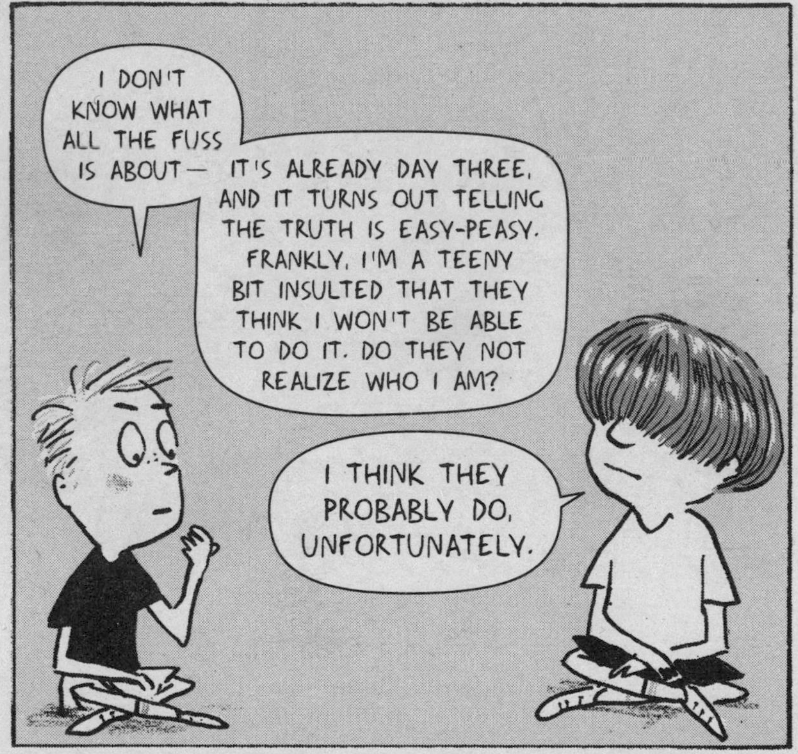
I DON'T KNOW WHAT ALL THE FUSS IS ABOUT—
IT'S ALREADY DAY THREE, AND IT TURNS OUT TELLING THE TRUTH IS EASY-PEASY. FRANKLY, I'M A TEENY BIT INSULTED THAT THEY THINK I WON'T BE ABLE TO DO IT. DO THEY NOT REALIZE WHO I AM?
I THINK THEY PROBABLY DO, UNFORTUNATELY.

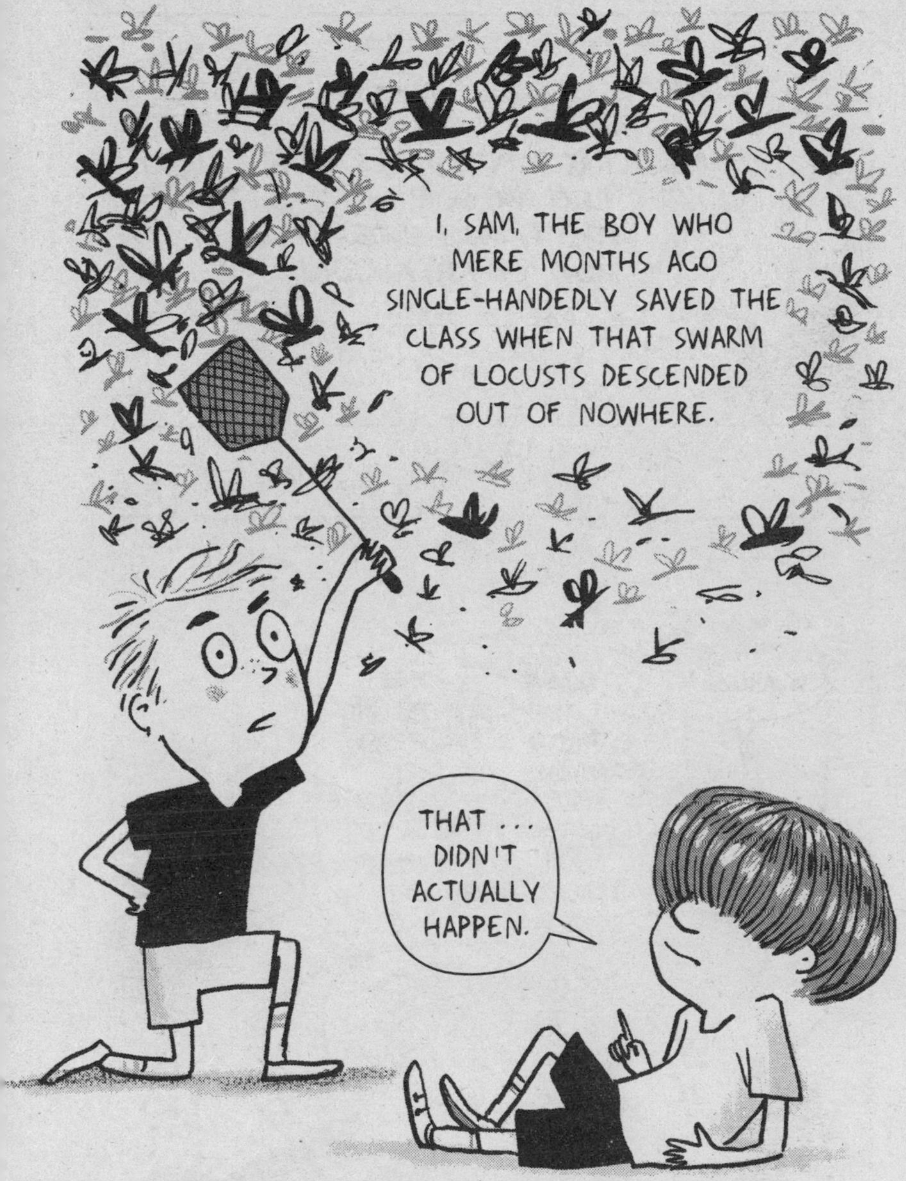
I, SAM, THE BOY WHO MERE MONTHS AGO SINGLE-HANDEDLY SAVED THE CLASS WHEN THAT SWARM OF LOCUSTS DESCENDED OUT OF NOWHERE.
THAT . . . DIDN'T ACTUALLY HAPPEN.

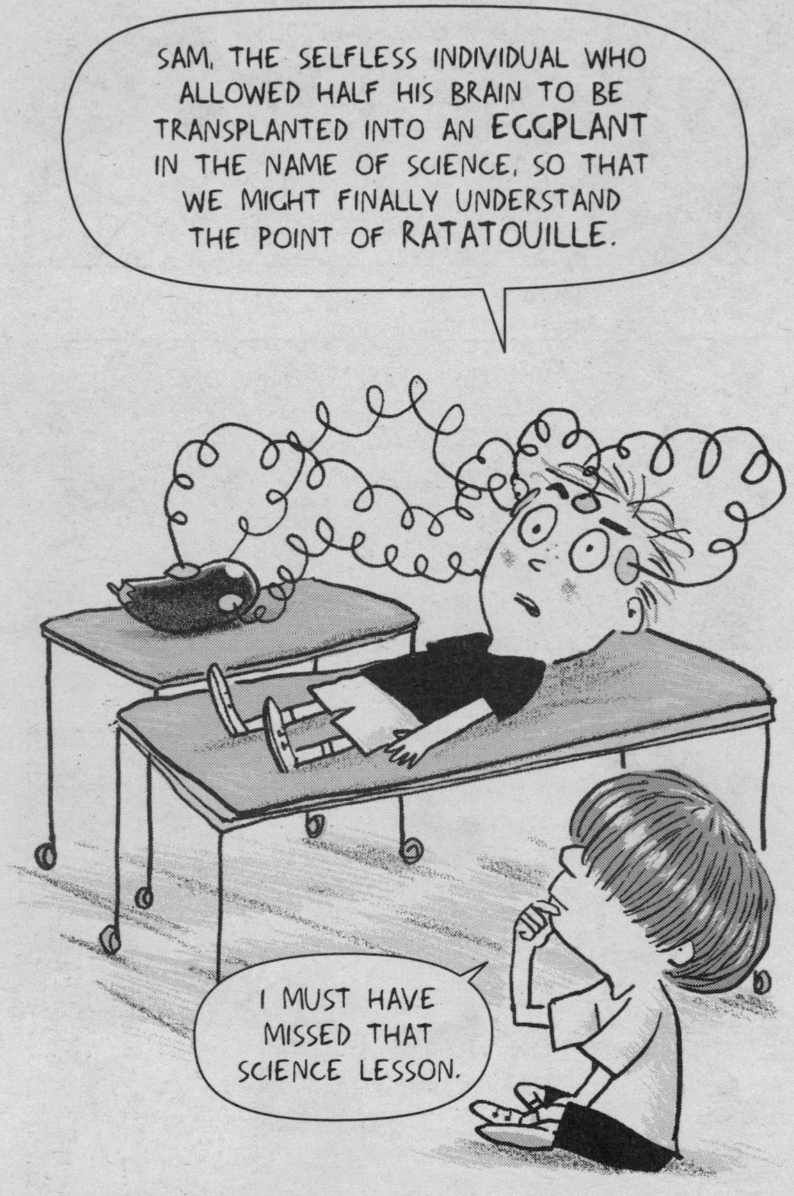
SAM, THE SELFLESS INDIVIDUAL WHO ALLOWED HALF HIS BRAIN TO BE TRANSPLANTED INTO AN EGGPLANT IN THE NAME OF SCIENCE, SO THAT WE MIGHT FINALLY UNDERSTAND THE POINT OF RATATOUILLE.
I MUST HAVE MISSED THAT SCIENCE LESSON.

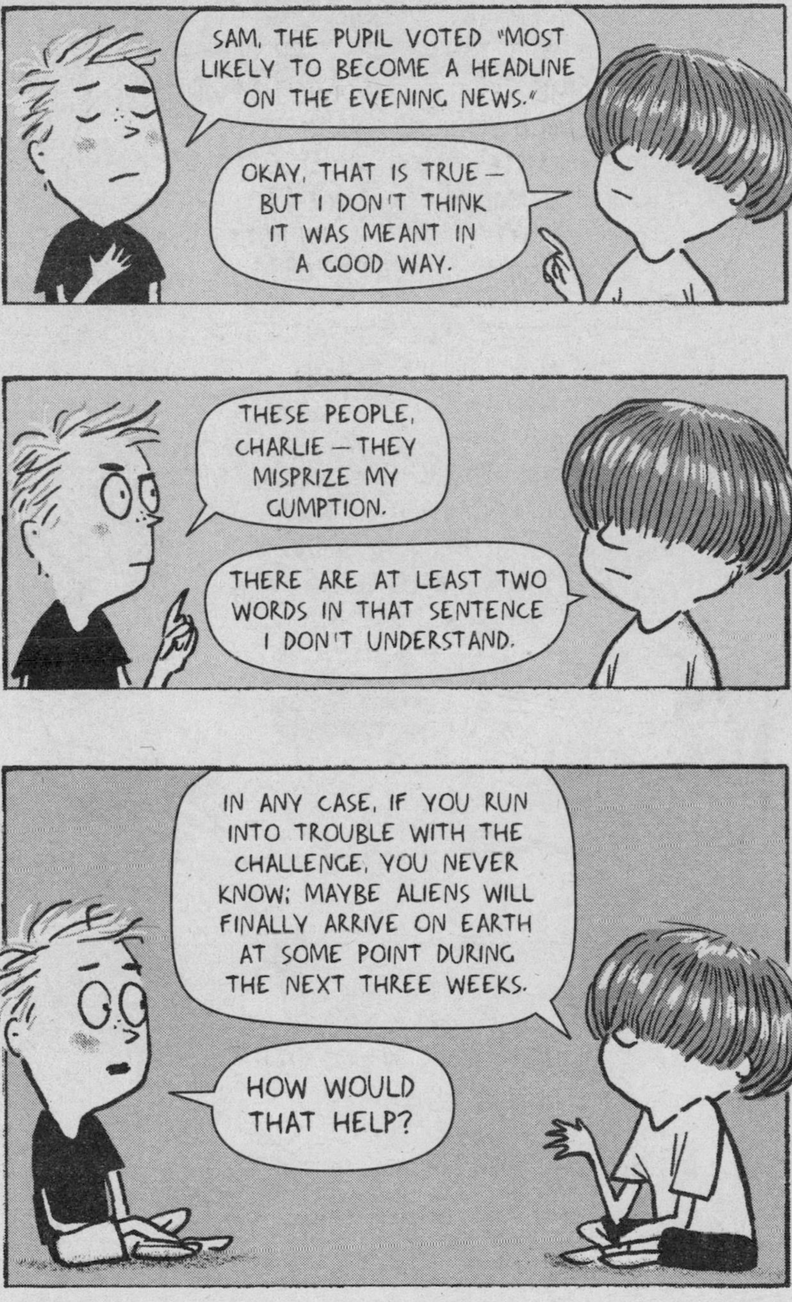
SAM, THE PUPIL VOTED "MOST LIKELY TO BECOME A HEADLINE ON THE EVENING NEWS."
OKAY, THAT IS TRUE— BUT I DON'T THINK IT WAS MEANT IN A GOOD WAY.
THESE PEOPLE, CHARLIE—THEY MISPRIZE MY GUMPTION.
THERE ARE AT LEAST TWO WORDS IN THAT SENTENCE I DON'T UNDERSTAND.
IN ANY CASE, IF YOU RUN INTO TROUBLE WITH THE CHALLENGE, YOU NEVER KNOW; MAYBE ALIENS WILL FINALLY ARRIVE ON EARTH AT SOME POINT DURING THE NEXT THREE WEEKS.
HOW WOULD THAT HELP?

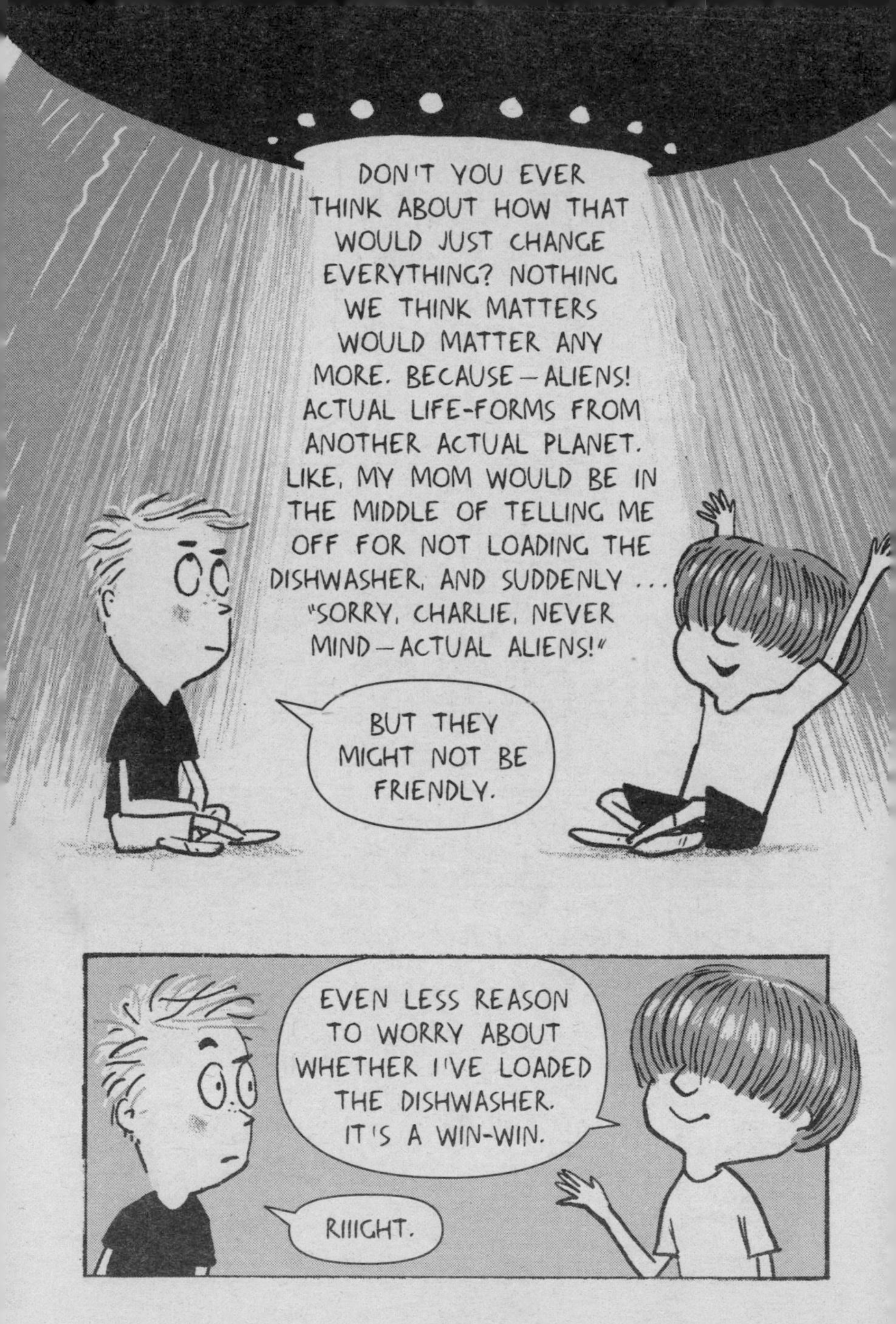
DON'T YOU EVER THINK ABOUT HOW THAT WOULD JUST CHANGE EVERYTHING? NOTHING WE THINK MATTERS WOULD MATTER ANY MORE. BECAUSE—ALIENS! ACTUAL LIFE-FORMS FROM ANOTHER ACTUAL PLANET. LIKE, MY MOM WOULD BE IN THE MIDDLE OF TELLING ME OFF FOR NOT LOADING THE DISHWASHER, AND SUDDENLY . . . "SORRY, CHARLIE, NEVER MIND—ACTUAL ALIENS!"
BUT THEY MIGHT NOT BE FRIENDLY.
EVEN LESS REASON TO WORRY ABOUT WHETHER I'VE LOADED THE DISHWASHER. IT'S A WIN-WIN.
RIIIGHT.

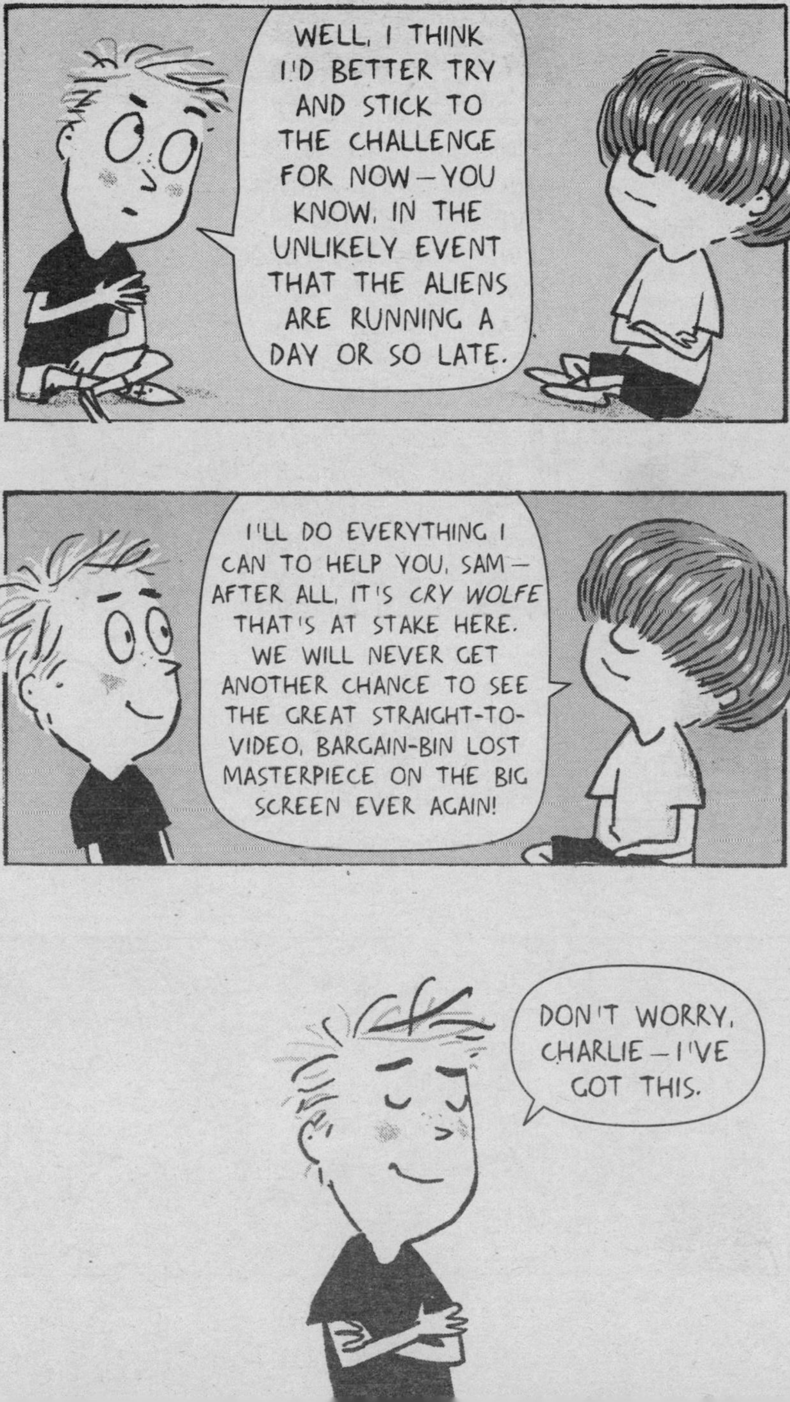
WELL, I THINK I'D BETTER TRY AND STICK TO THE CHALLENGE FOR NOW—YOU KNOW, IN THE UNLIKELY EVENT THAT THE ALIENS ARE RUNNING A DAY OR SO LATE.
I'LL DO EVERYTHING I CAN TO HELP YOU, SAM—AFTER ALL, IT'S *CRY WOLFE* THAT'S AT STAKE HERE. WE WILL NEVER GET ANOTHER CHANCE TO SEE THE GREAT STRAIGHT-TO-VIDEO, BARGAIN-BIN LOST MASTERPIECE ON THE BIG SCREEN EVER AGAIN!
DON'T WORRY, CHARLIE—I'VE GOT THIS.

TIME REMAINING TILL CARNIVAL

15 DAYS 17 HOURS 27 MINUTES

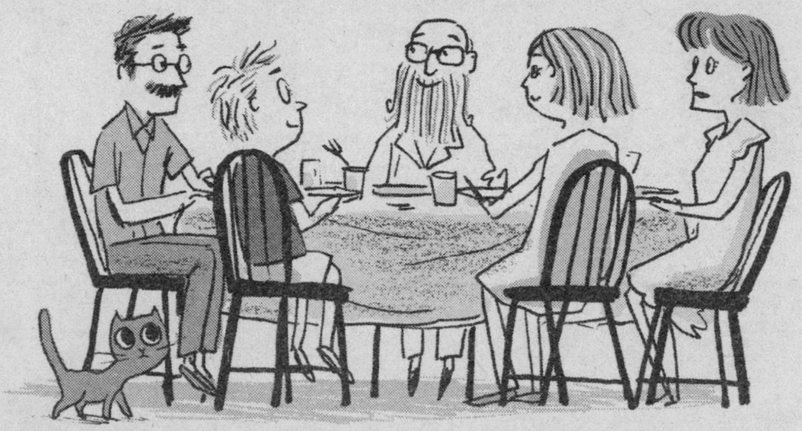

Speaking of challenges. Dinner at home has become a bit challenging in itself, since Dad moved his jazz-guitar setup down to Grandpa's plot.

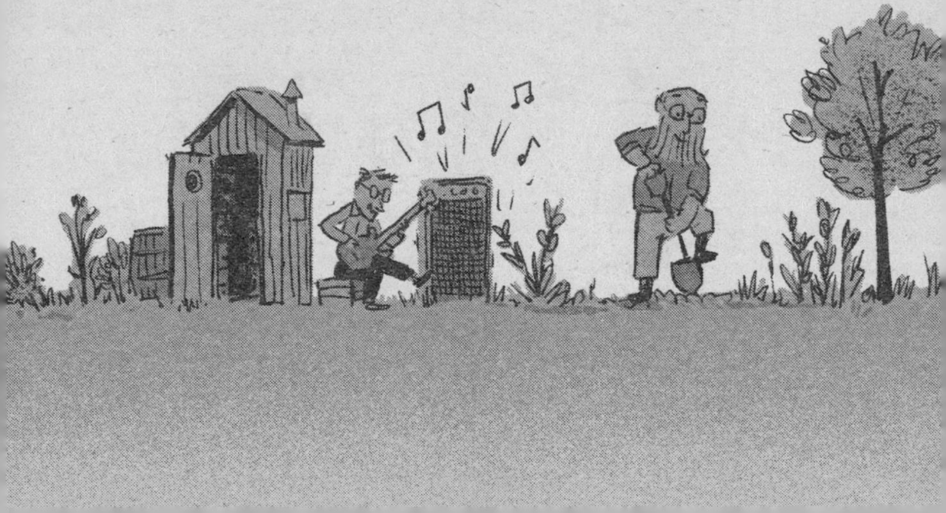

If you know my grandpa, you'll know how obsessed he is with radishes.

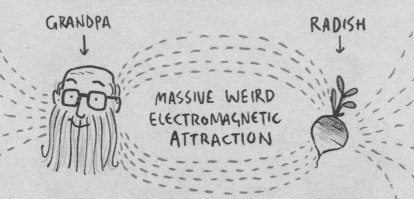

GRANDPA

RADISH

MASSIVE WEIRD ELECTROMAGNETIC ATTRACTION

Well, I'm afraid the obsession has worsened. As if raw radishes with cold butter and a pinch of salt weren't bad enough (Bleurgh!), now he also PICKLES the radishes!

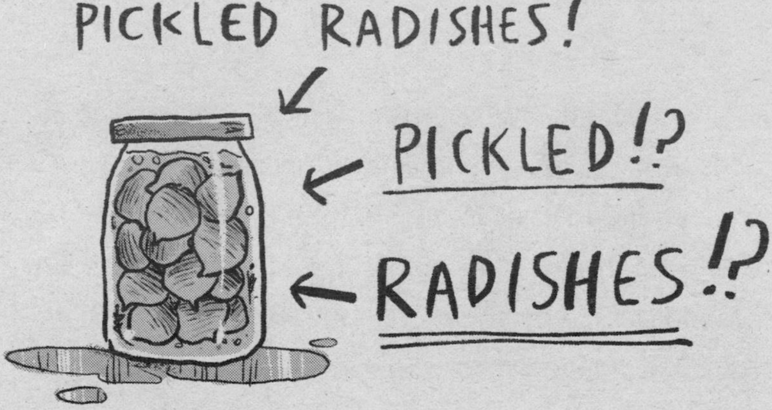

PICKLED RADISHES!

PICKLED!?

RADISHES!?

One of the peculiar things about the neighborhood carnival is how many pickle stalls there are—you'd think "none" would be the ideal number, but instead we have two.

Muriel next door always runs a pickle stall, and so does Grandpa. But every year, Muriel's pickles sell out, while Grandpa has a lot of leftovers. He's determined to sell out this year; it's kind of a pride thing. I think Grandpa's secretly sweet on Muriel, and believes she could never love a man who can't sell his own pickles.

You should see his shed on the plot. It's lined with shelves and shelves of horrifying pickling experiments.

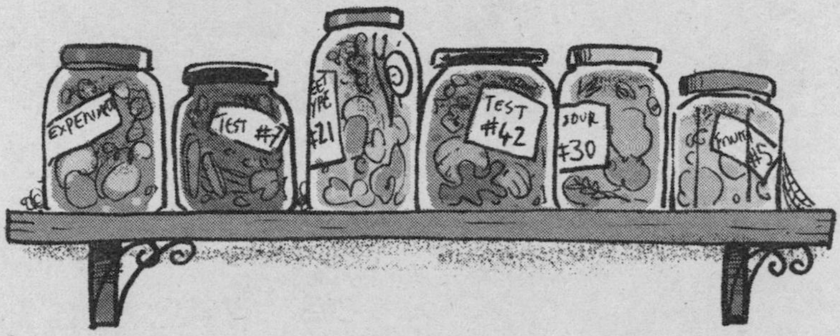
TEST #7
TEST #42

Imagine if, one night, a plucky ragtag band of radishes hauled themselves out of the ground and went looking for their comrades.

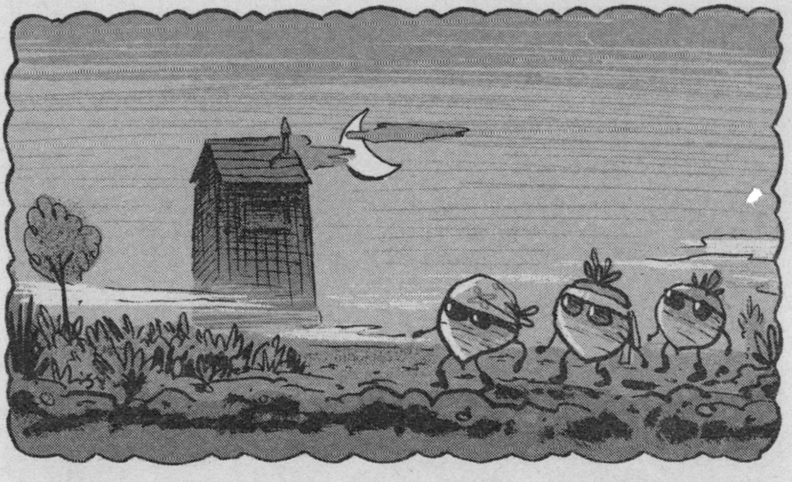

They'd creep under the door . . .

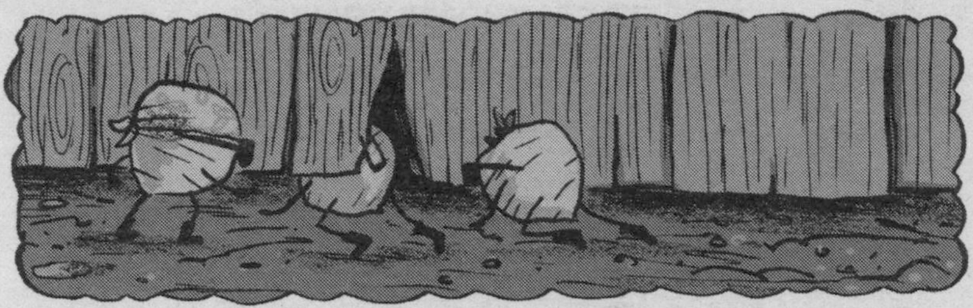

Flip on the light . . .

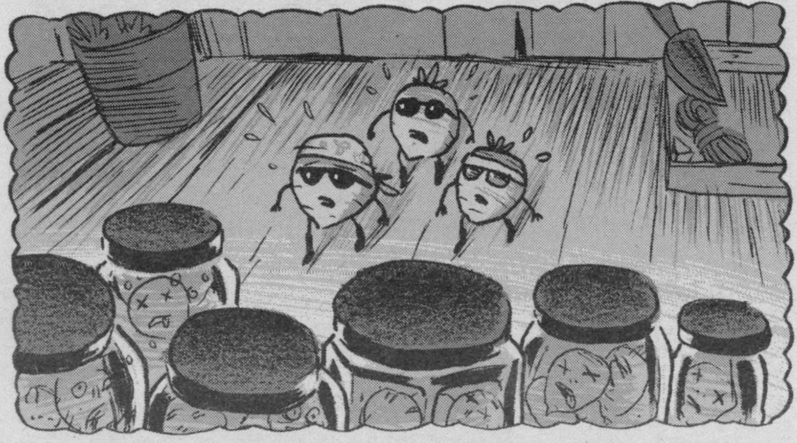

The scene that would greet them would be like something from a horror movie.

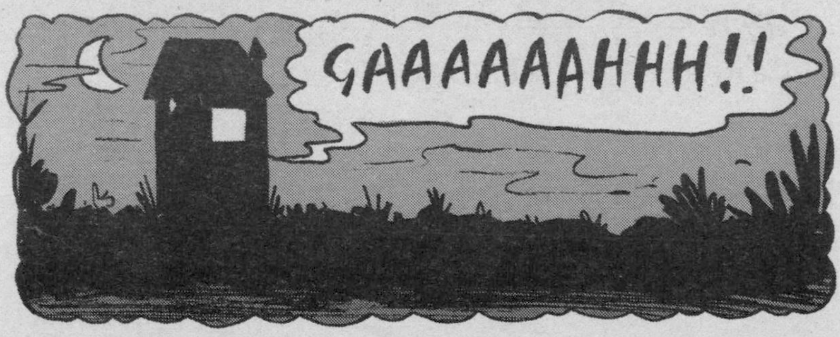
GAAAAAAHHH!!

Thing is, Grandpa's also a self-taught magician, known as "**THE GREAT WONDEROSO**."

He taught himself how to disappear a parking ticket (no one's ever found it), and how to turn an orange purple (if you ever see a purple orange, don't eat it). And he taught himself the art of hypnosis—he claims to have successfully hypnotized the slugs on his plot to despise radishes. Maybe they're hypnotized, maybe they're just sensible? Anyway, the point is, he doesn't like to learn from books. He says:

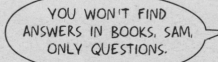

YOU WON'T FIND ANSWERS IN BOOKS, SAM, ONLY QUESTIONS.

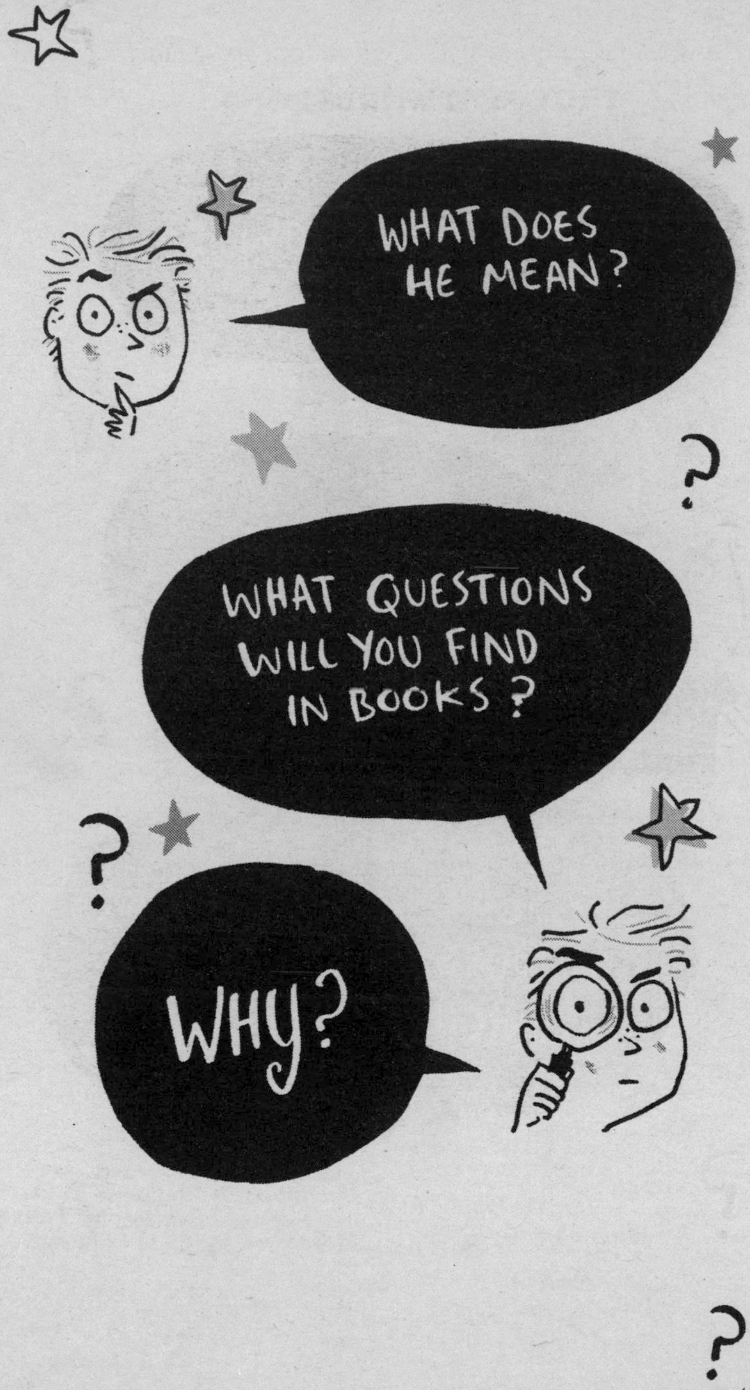
WHAT DOES HE MEAN?
WHAT QUESTIONS WILL YOU FIND IN BOOKS?
WHY?

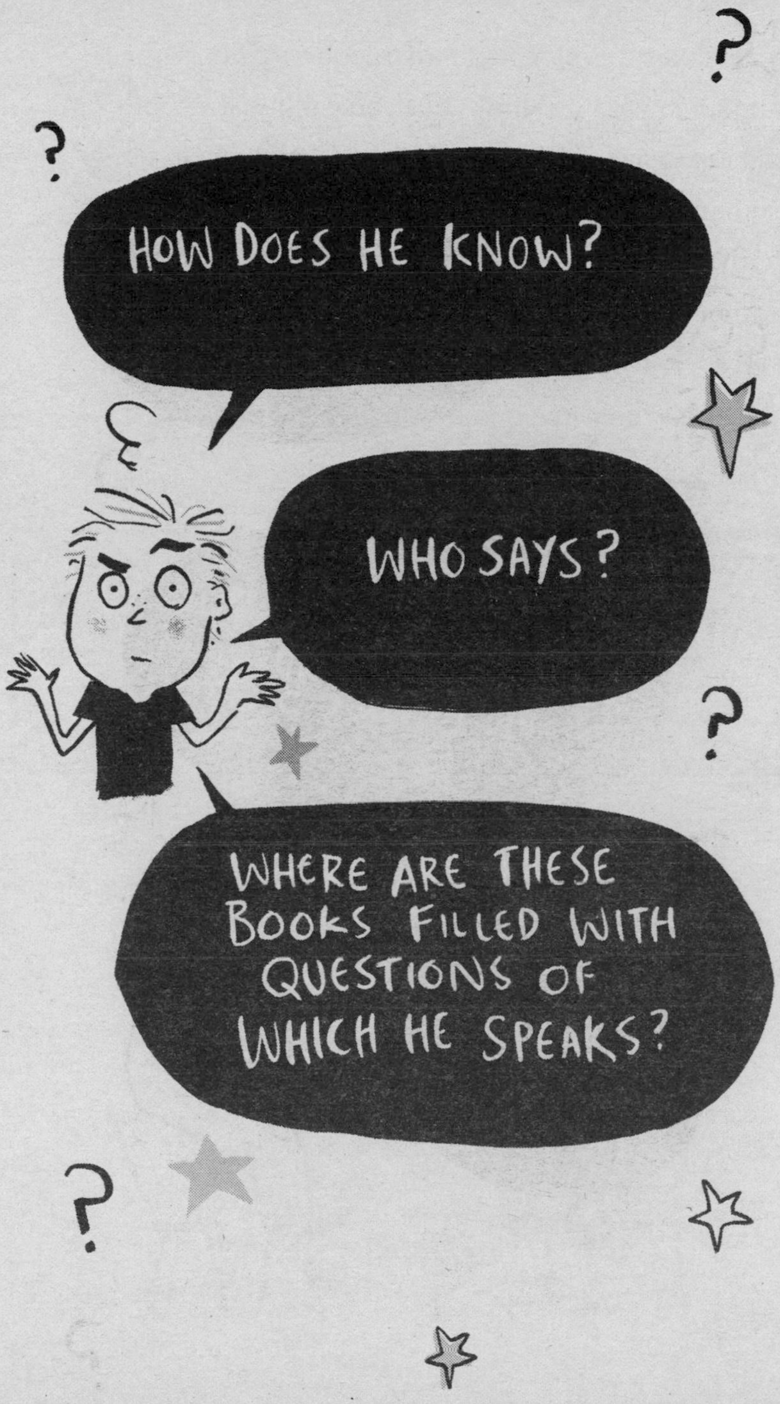
HOW DOES HE KNOW?
WHO SAYS?
WHERE ARE THESE BOOKS FILLED WITH QUESTIONS OF WHICH HE SPEAKS?

He takes this same "no-instruction-manuals" approach with pickling—but you can't learn a lot from talking to a jar of pickled radishes. You have to use something called "trial and error." And that is, I'm afraid, what makes dinner so challenging. The "error" can be quite serious when all sorts of vile herbs, spices, and sweet and sour liquids are involved, and the "trial" part involves putting these things in your poor, unsuspecting mouth.

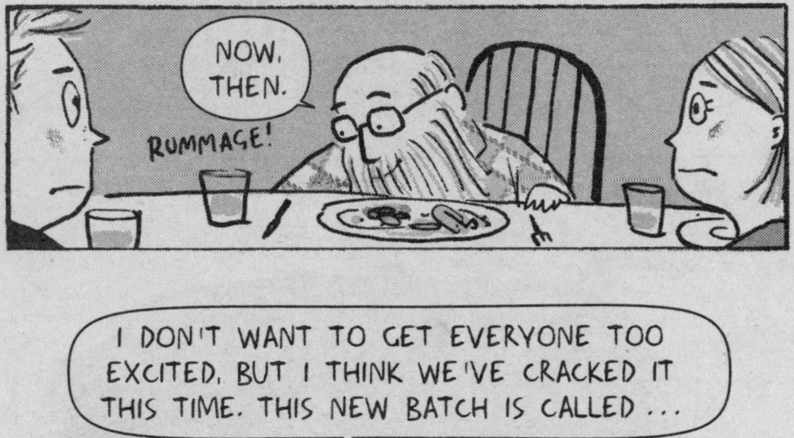
NOW, THEN.
RUMMAGE!

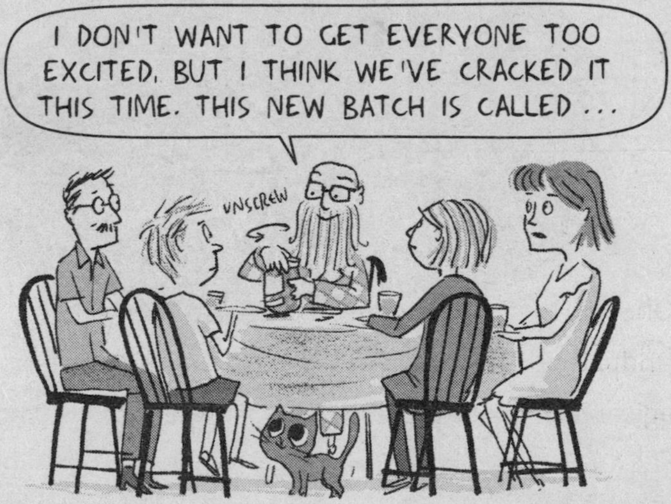
I DON'T WANT TO GET EVERYONE TOO EXCITED, BUT I THINK WE'VE CRACKED IT THIS TIME. THIS NEW BATCH IS CALLED . . .
UNSCREW

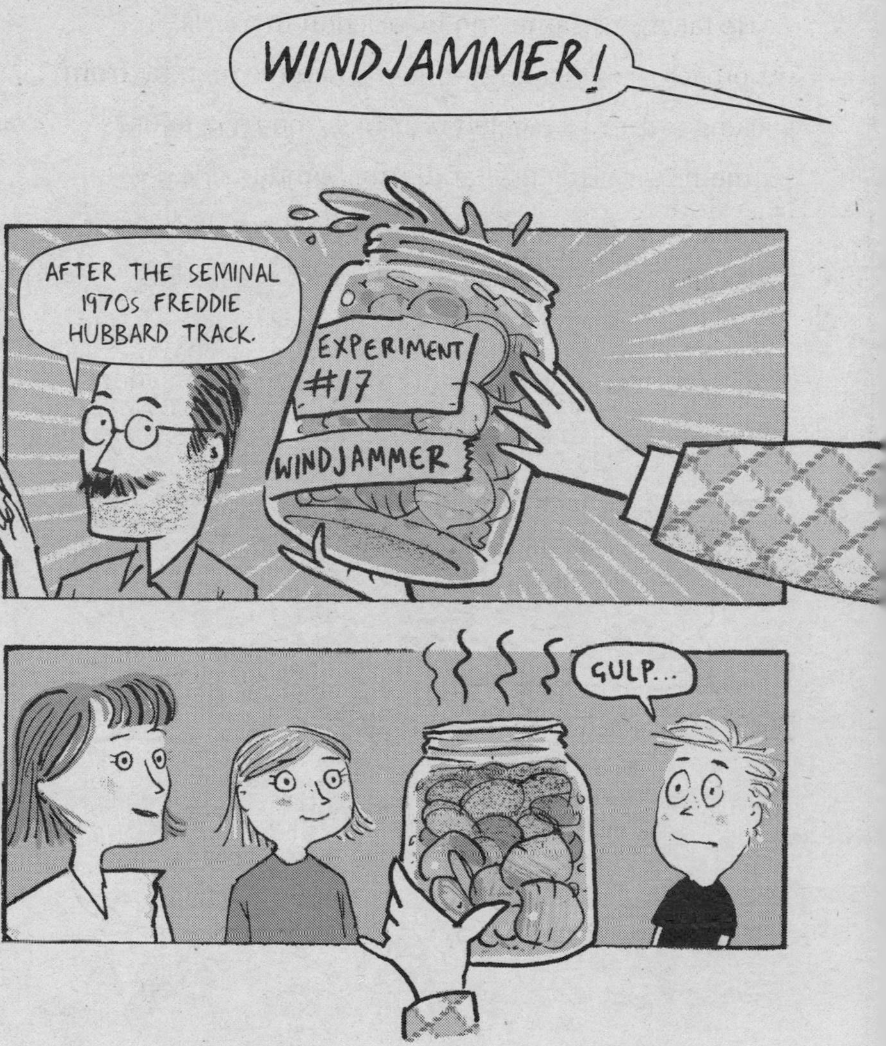
WINDJAMMER!
AFTER THE SEMINAL 1970s FREDDIE HUBBARD TRACK.
EXPERIMENT #17
WINDJAMMER
GULP...

Oh, yes, there's something I forgot to mention. Grandpa's convinced that the secret to the elusive magical pickling formula is Dad's jazz-guitar noodling.

Since Dad moved his sound system down to the plot, the vegetables are growing bigger and faster and, apparently, tastier than ever before. Each batch of pickles is named after the tune that Dad was jamming whilst Grandpa tossed random stinky nasties into the pickling vat.

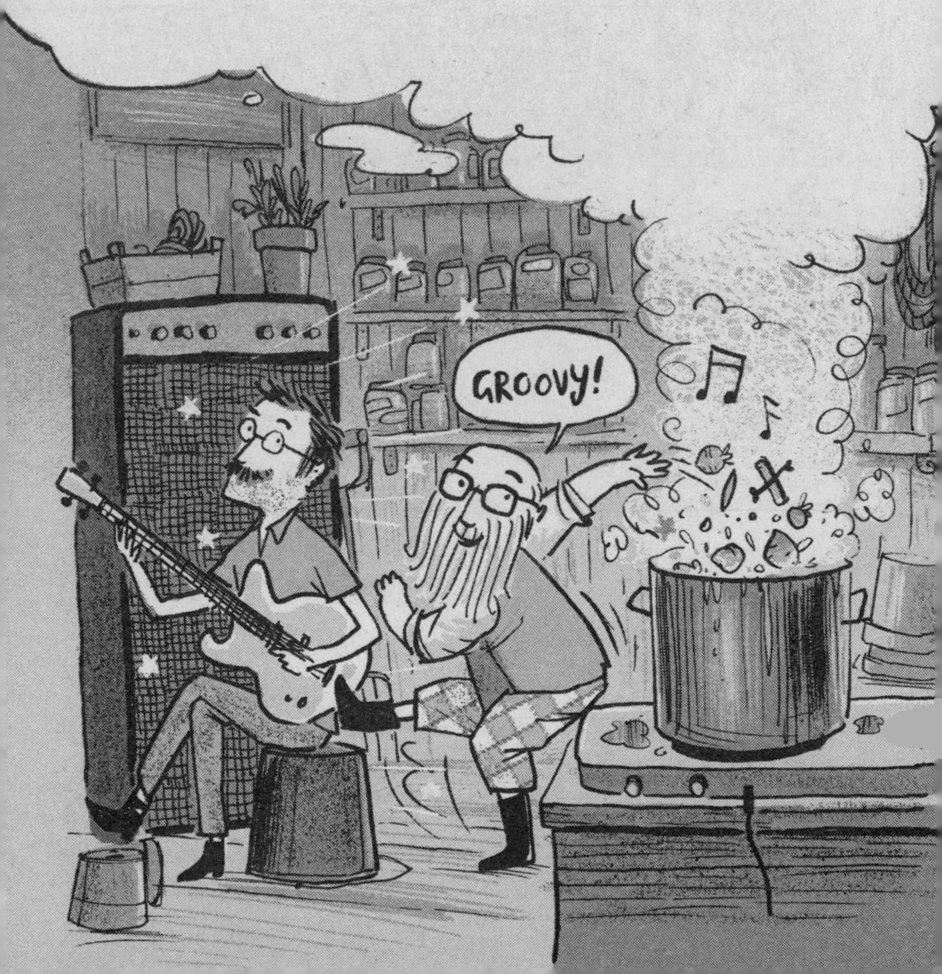
GROOVY!

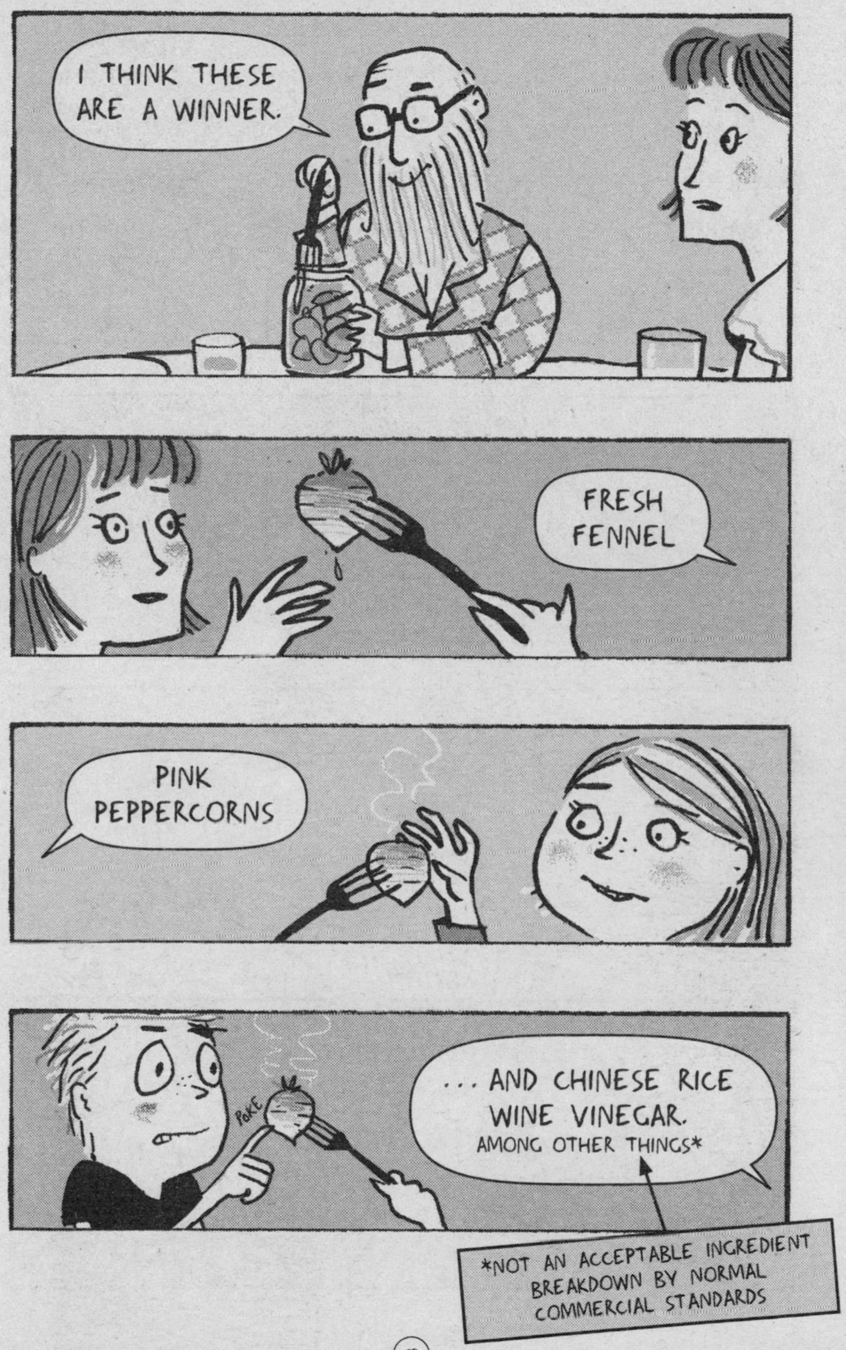
I THINK THESE ARE A WINNER.
FRESH FENNEL
PINK PEPPERCORNS
POKE
. . . AND CHINESE RICE WINE VINEGAR.
AMONG OTHER THINGS*
*NOT AN ACCEPTABLE INGREDIENT BREAKDOWN BY NORMAL COMMERCIAL STANDARDS

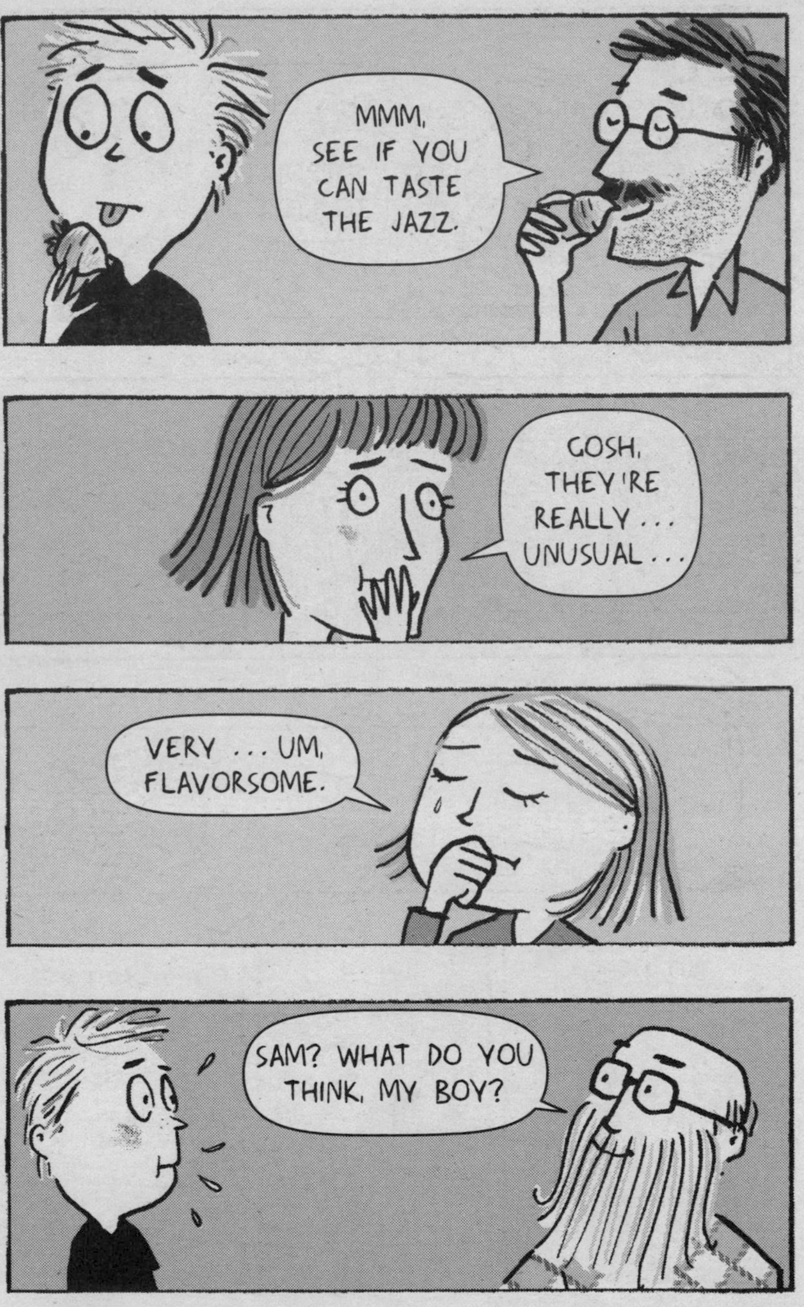
MMM, SEE IF YOU CAN TASTE THE JAZZ.
GOSH, THEY'RE REALLY ... UNUSUAL ...
VERY ... UM, FLAVORSOME.
SAM? WHAT DO YOU THINK, MY BOY?

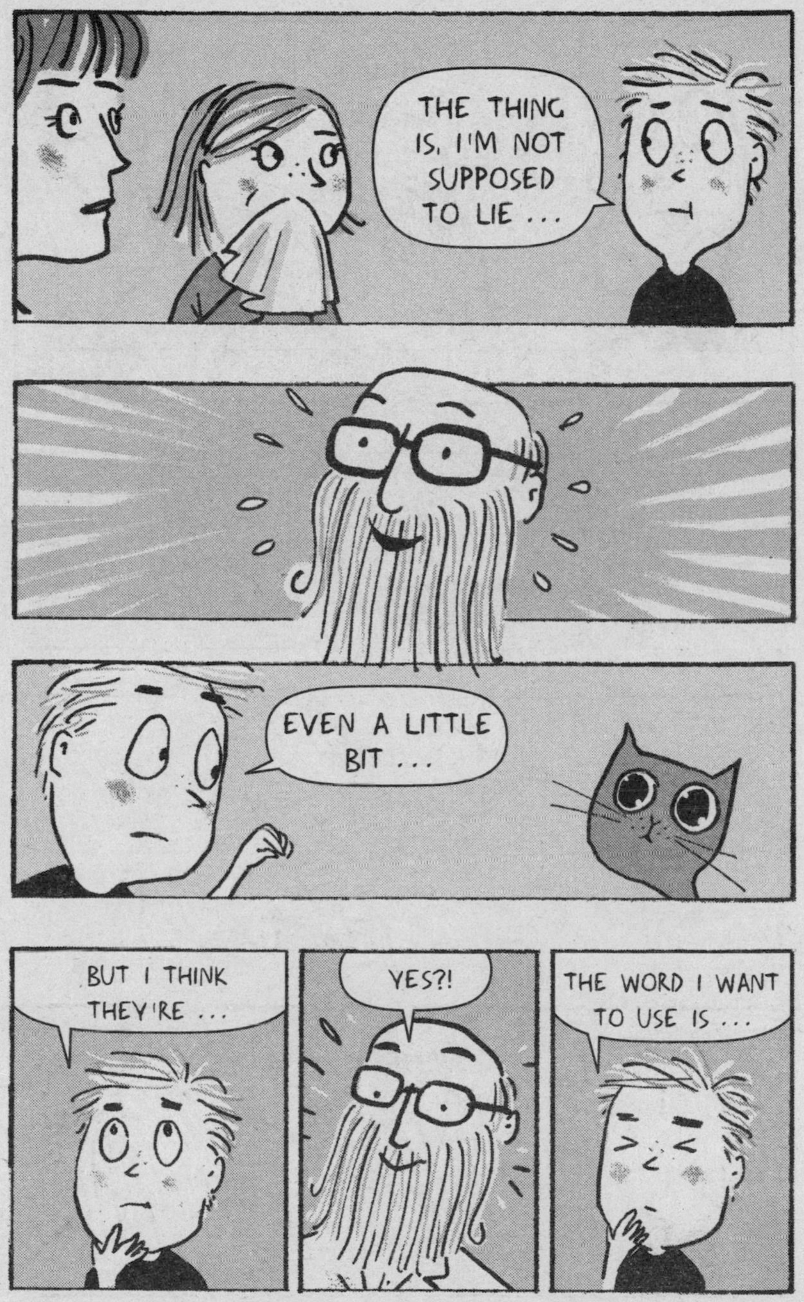
THE THING IS, I'M NOT SUPPOSED TO LIE . . .
EVEN A LITTLE BIT . . .
BUT I THINK THEY'RE . . .
YES?!
THE WORD I WANT TO USE IS . . .

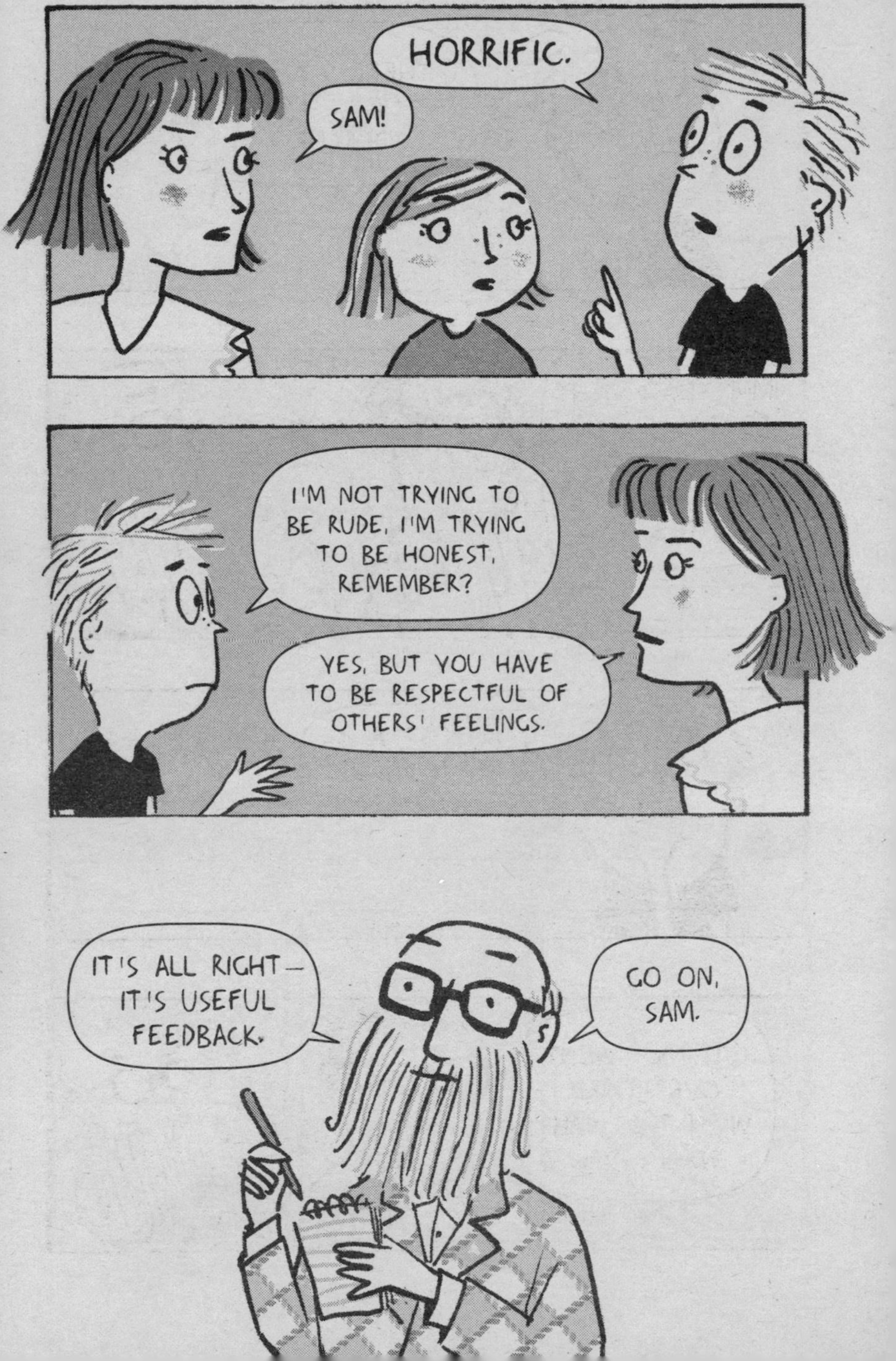
HORRIFIC.
SAM!
I'M NOT TRYING TO BE RUDE, I'M TRYING TO BE HONEST, REMEMBER?
YES, BUT YOU HAVE TO BE RESPECTFUL OF OTHERS' FEELINGS.
IT'S ALL RIGHT— IT'S USEFUL FEEDBACK.
GO ON, SAM.

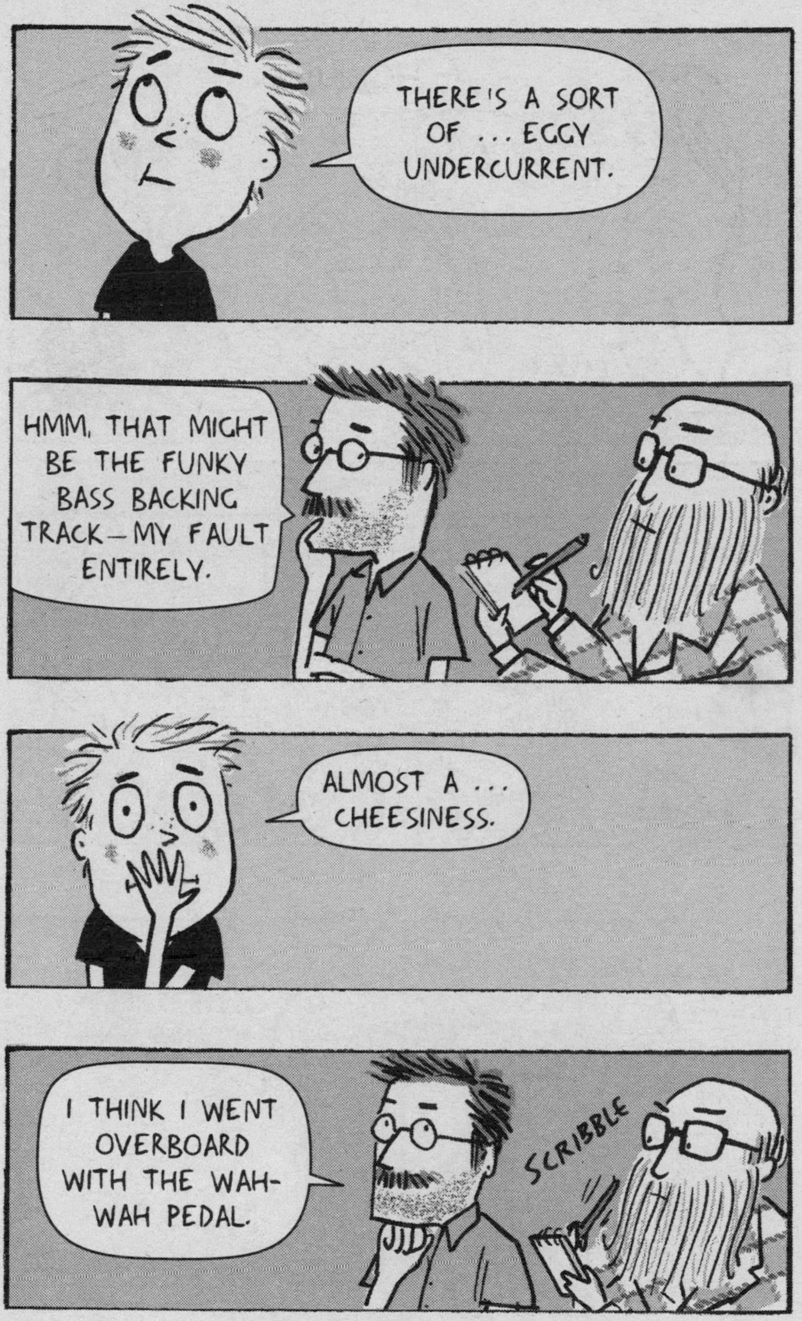
THERE'S A SORT OF ... EGGY UNDERCURRENT.
HMM, THAT MIGHT BE THE FUNKY BASS BACKING TRACK—MY FAULT ENTIRELY.
ALMOST A ... CHEESINESS.
I THINK I WENT OVERBOARD WITH THE WAH-WAH PEDAL.
SCRIBBLE

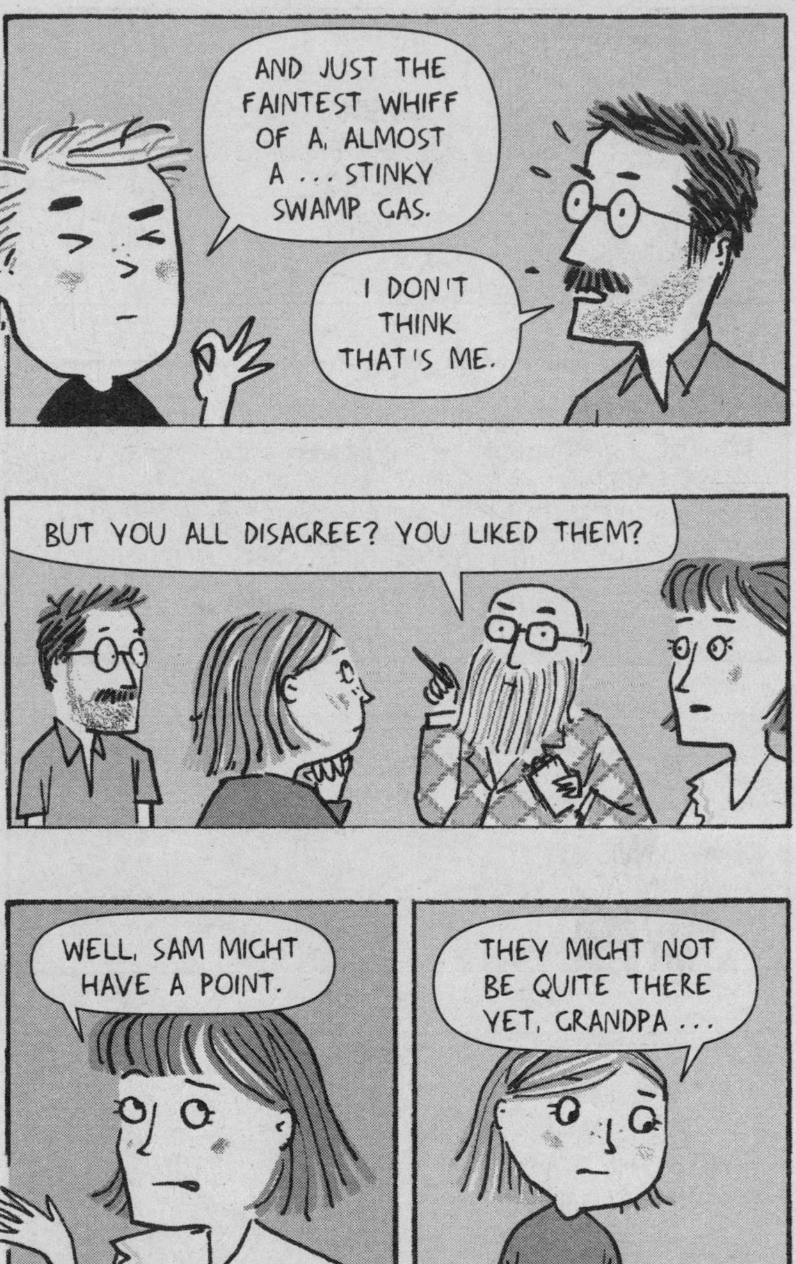
AND JUST THE FAINTEST WHIFF OF A, ALMOST A . . . STINKY SWAMP GAS.
I DON'T THINK THAT'S ME.
BUT YOU ALL DISAGREE? YOU LIKED THEM?
WELL, SAM MIGHT HAVE A POINT.
THEY MIGHT NOT BE QUITE THERE YET, GRANDPA . . .

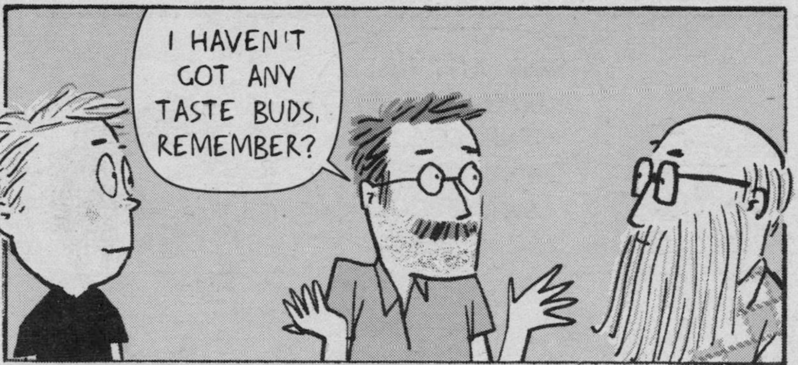
I HAVEN'T GOT ANY TASTE BUDS, REMEMBER?

This is true—Dad's taste buds were zapped in a bizarre accident involving a faulty guitar amp and a lightning storm in the late 1990s. Which does make me question his usefulness as a pickling partner—no one else seems to be bothered, though.

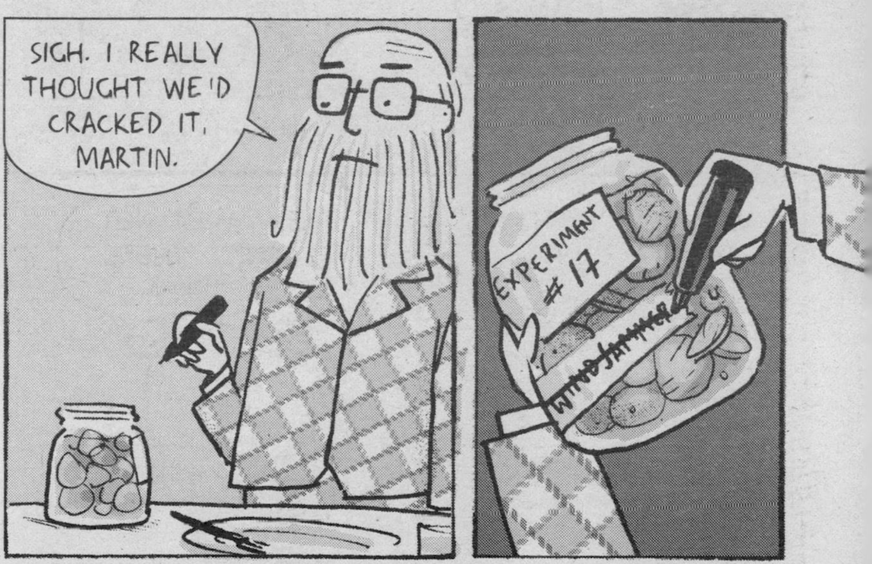
SIGH. I REALLY THOUGHT WE'D CRACKED IT, MARTIN.
EXPERIMENT #17

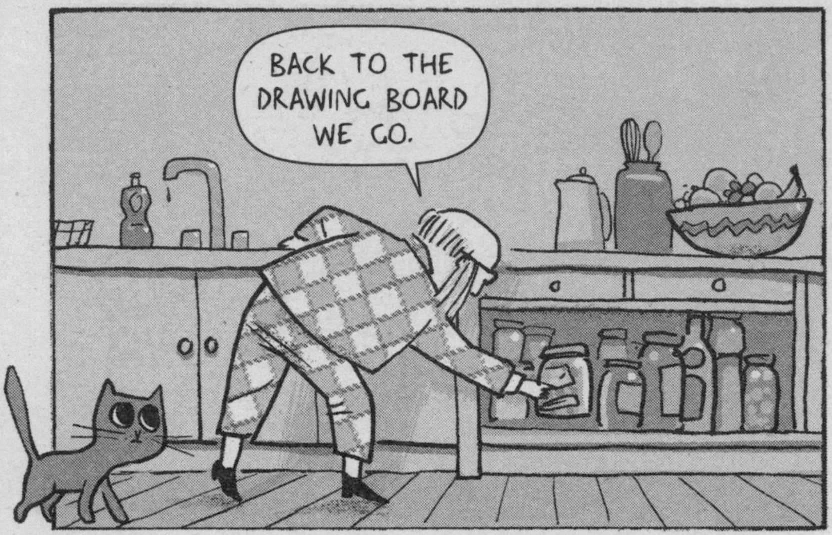
BACK TO THE DRAWING BOARD WE GO.

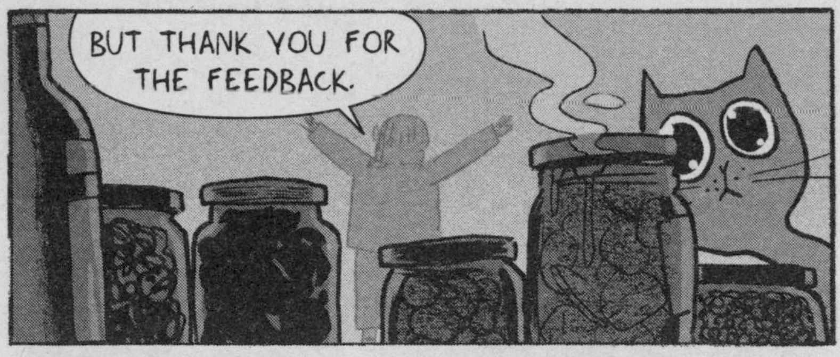
BUT THANK YOU FOR THE FEEDBACK.

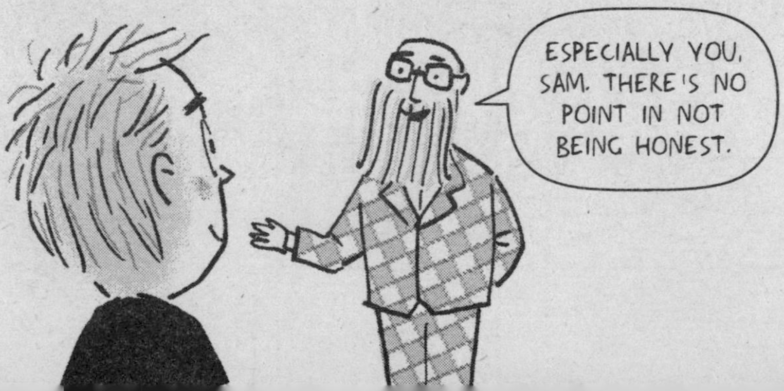
ESPECIALLY YOU, SAM. THERE'S NO POINT IN NOT BEING HONEST.

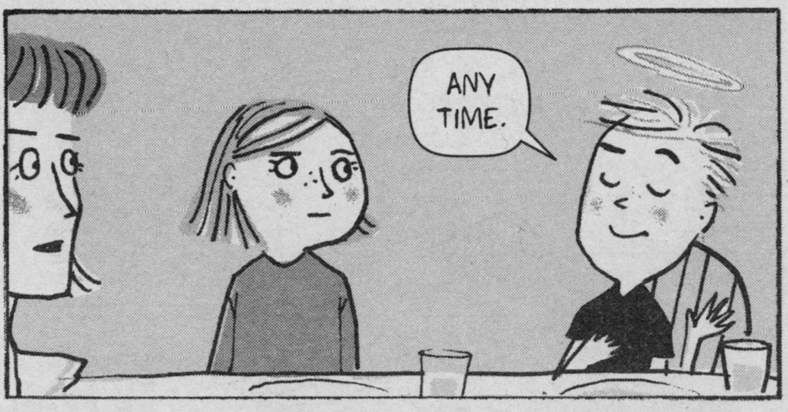
ANY TIME.

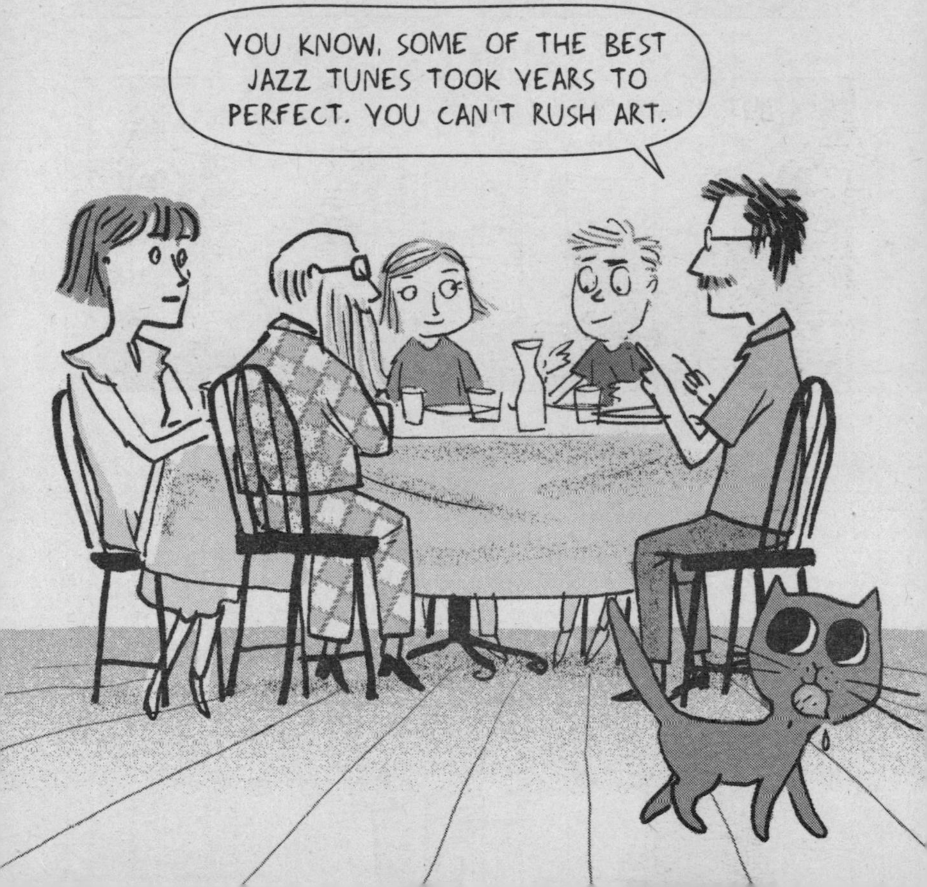
YOU KNOW, SOME OF THE BEST JAZZ TUNES TOOK YEARS TO PERFECT. YOU CAN'T RUSH ART.

So I'm off and running. . . .

Let's just hope this **STINKY SWAMP OF TRUTH** doesn't have too many creepy surprises in it.

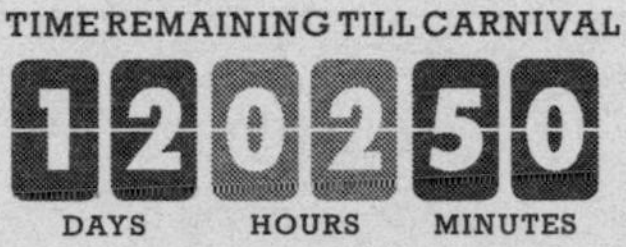
TIME REMAINING TILL CARNIVAL
12 02 50
DAYS
HOURS
MINUTES

If I'm honest . . .

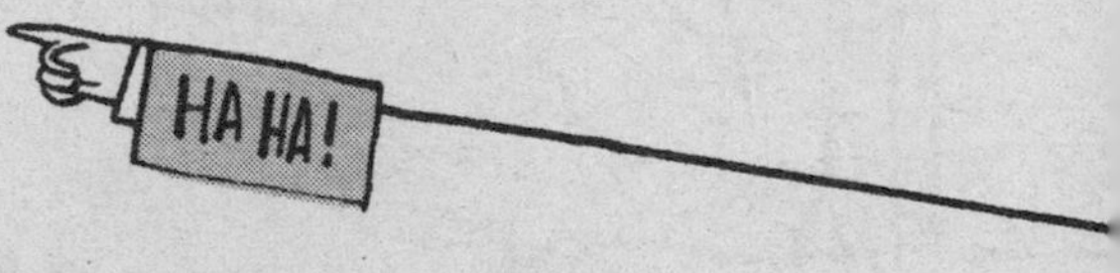
HA HA!

. . . this "telling the truth" lark is actually pretty straightforward once you get into the swing of it.

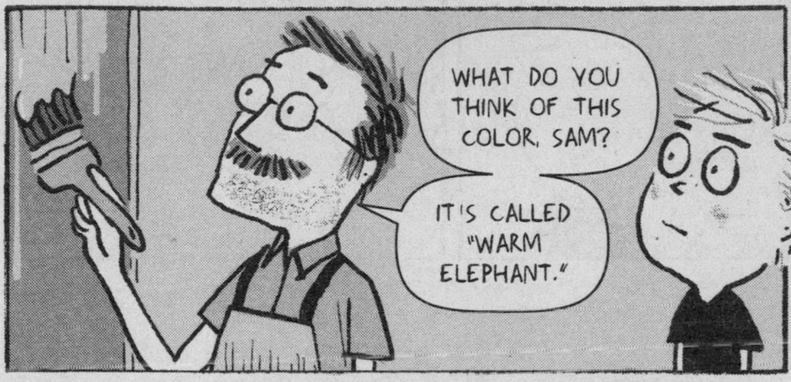
WHAT DO YOU THINK OF THIS COLOR, SAM?
IT'S CALLED "WARM ELEPHANT."

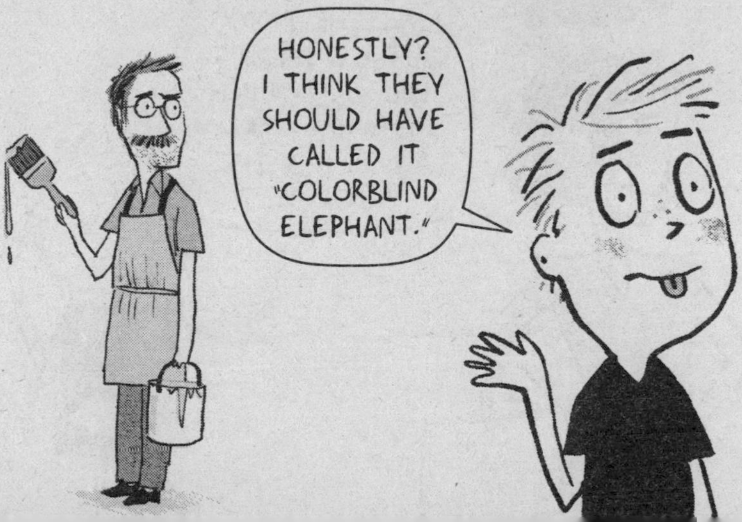
HONESTLY? I THINK THEY SHOULD HAVE CALLED IT "COLORBLIND ELEPHANT."

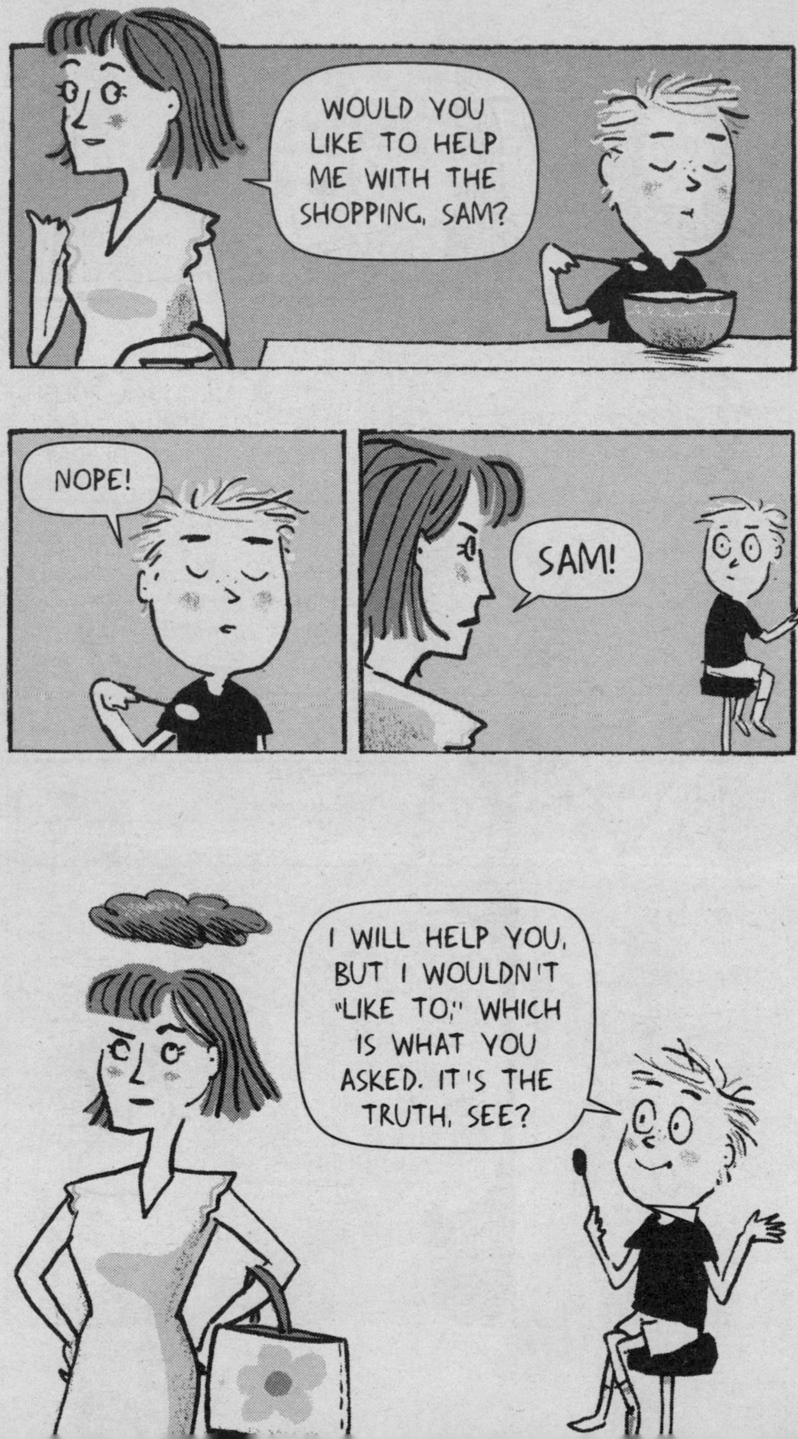
WOULD YOU LIKE TO HELP ME WITH THE SHOPPING, SAM?
NOPE!
SAM!
I WILL HELP YOU, BUT I WOULDN'T "LIKE TO," WHICH IS WHAT YOU ASKED. IT'S THE TRUTH, SEE?

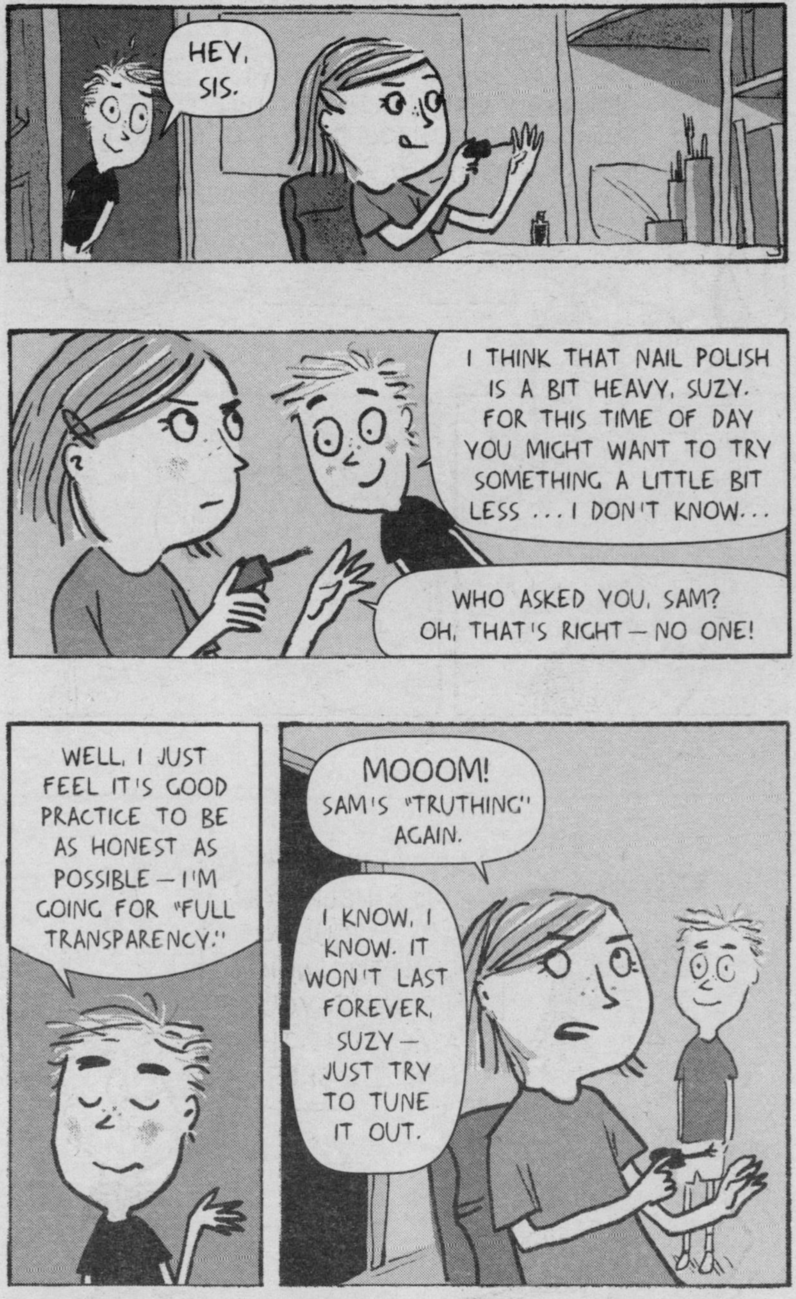
HEY, SIS.
I THINK THAT NAIL POLISH IS A BIT HEAVY, SUZY. FOR THIS TIME OF DAY YOU MIGHT WANT TO TRY SOMETHING A LITTLE BIT LESS . . . I DON'T KNOW. . .
WHO ASKED YOU, SAM? OH, THAT'S RIGHT—NO ONE!
WELL, I JUST FEEL IT'S GOOD PRACTICE TO BE AS HONEST AS POSSIBLE—I'M GOING FOR "FULL TRANSPARENCY."
MOOOM! SAM'S "TRUTHING" AGAIN.
I KNOW, I KNOW. IT WON'T LAST FOREVER, SUZY—JUST TRY TO TUNE IT OUT.

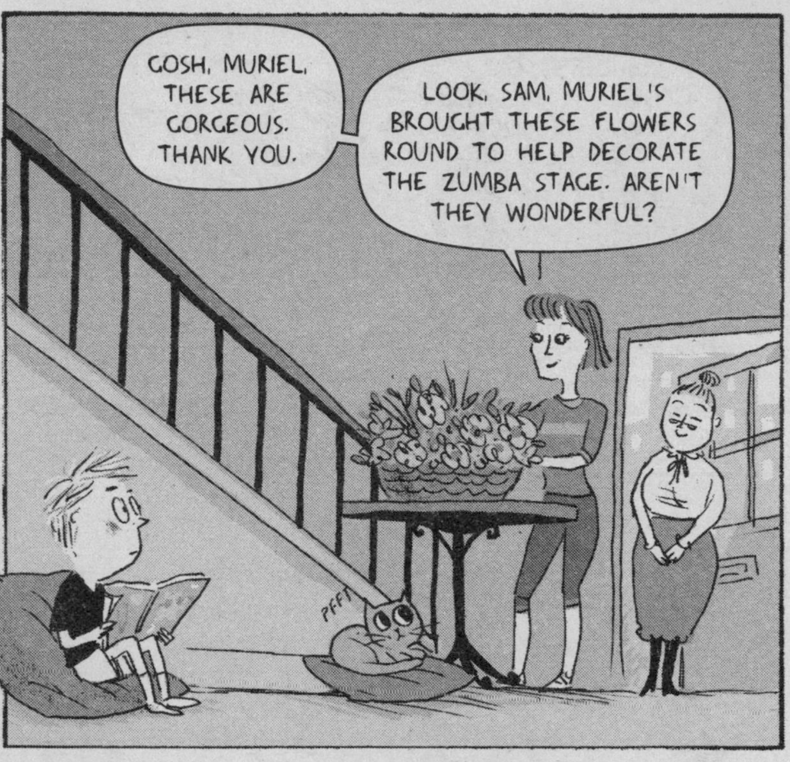
GOSH, MURIEL, THESE ARE GORGEOUS. THANK YOU.
LOOK, SAM, MURIEL'S BROUGHT THESE FLOWERS ROUND TO HELP DECORATE THE ZUMBA STAGE. AREN'T THEY WONDERFUL?
PFFT

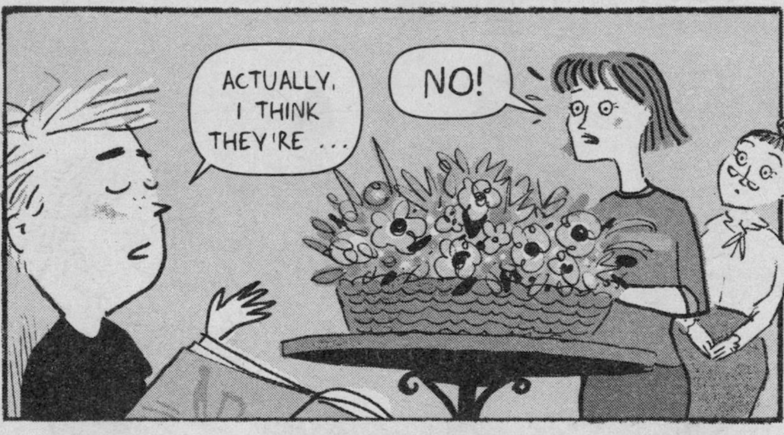
ACTUALLY, I THINK THEY'RE . . .
NO!

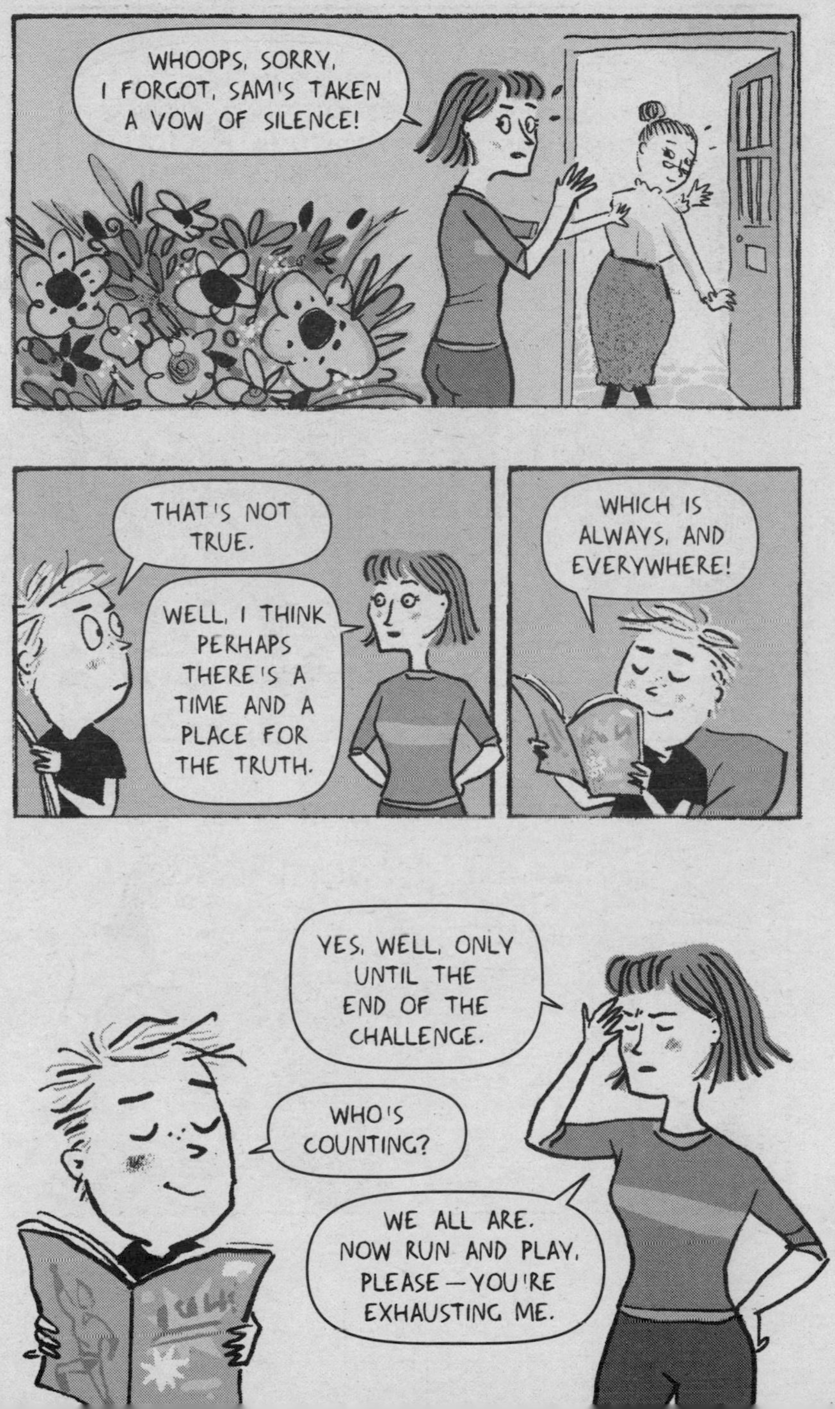
WHOOPS, SORRY, I FORGOT, SAM'S TAKEN A VOW OF SILENCE!
THAT'S NOT TRUE.
WELL, I THINK PERHAPS THERE'S A TIME AND A PLACE FOR THE TRUTH.
WHICH IS ALWAYS, AND EVERYWHERE!
YES, WELL, ONLY UNTIL THE END OF THE CHALLENGE.
WHO'S COUNTING?
WE ALL ARE. NOW RUN AND PLAY, PLEASE—YOU'RE EXHAUSTING ME.

TIME REMAINING TILL CARNIVAL

0 9 0 2 2 2

DAYS   HOURS   MINUTES

Telling the truth may be easy, but staying out of trouble can be harder—especially when you've got so much "nothing" to do.

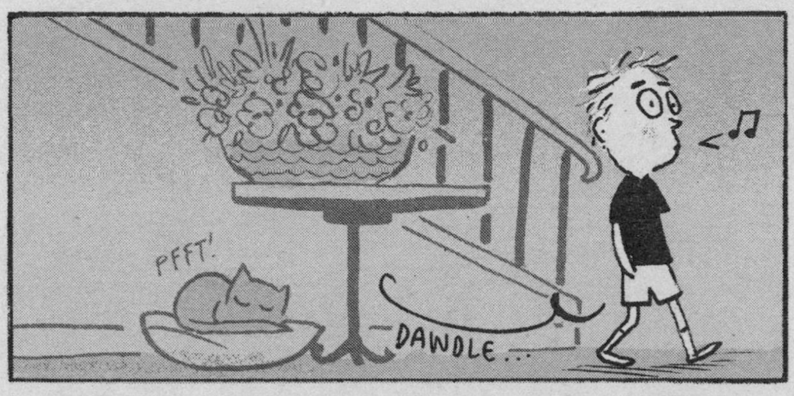
PFFT!
DAWDLE...

I know, I know, I said I was really looking forward to doing nothing all summer—but that's only fun when it happens together with Charlie. And when he's not around because he's got to buy shoes or go to a silly wedding or whatever, time really starts to drag. And that's when accidents happen.

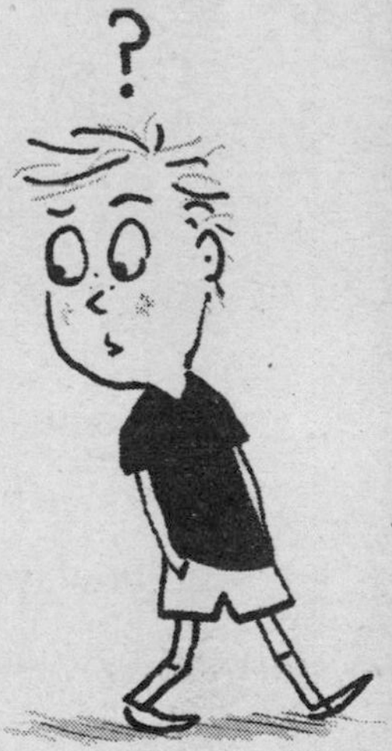
?

For instance, who could have foreseen that a simple piece of plastic tubing would create untold havoc?

Not me.

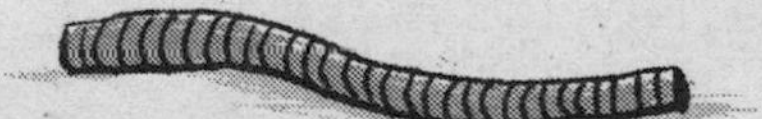

All I did was pick it up and whoosh it round my head a couple of times, and discover that it made a marvelous low, droning, whooshy sound.

LOW DRONING WHOOSHY WHOOSH...

(Well, actually, I did know this would happen. I have tried it once before.)

And how was I supposed to know that doing this in the living room would be a BIG mistake?

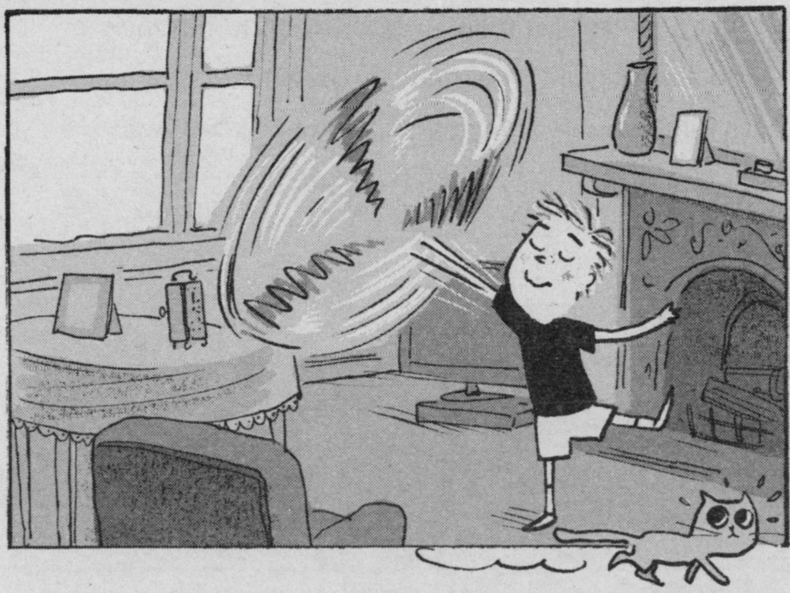

(Again, now that I think about it, that is what I did last time.)

But honestly—who would leave that stupid clock on the side table AGAIN where it could get knocked off onto the floor AGAIN and the glass face broken AGAIN?

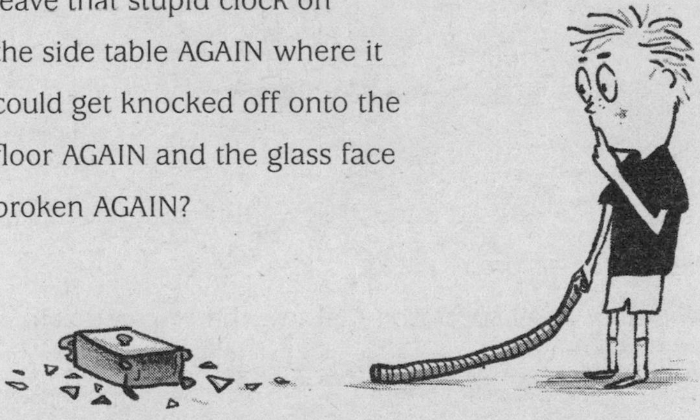

Okay, the last time this happened I put the clock back on the table and ran away. When it was discovered, I denied any involvement. Which was "lying." So this time, when the exact same thing happens, I have a careful think.

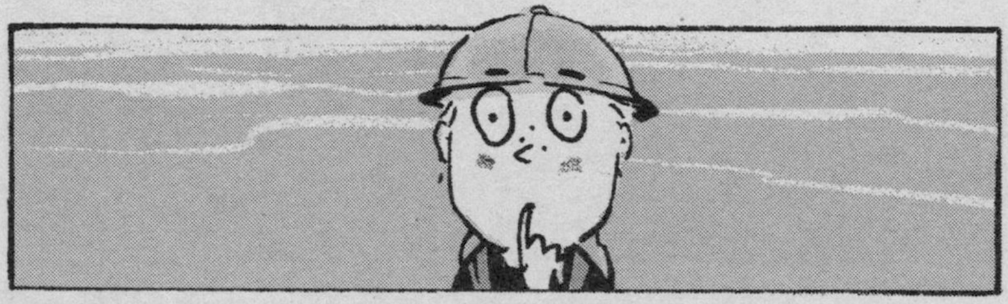

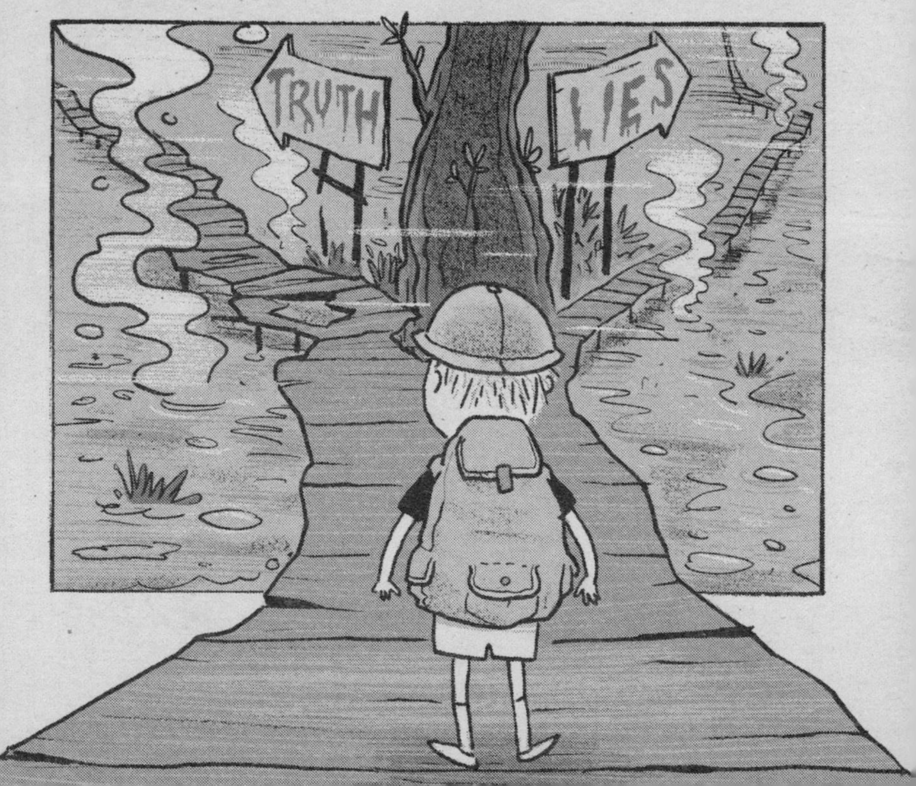
TRUTH
LIES

I go to Mom, and explain what happened. Mom is very cross, and I will have to pay for the damage to the clock from my pocket money. But I have told the truth! I stayed on the right path.

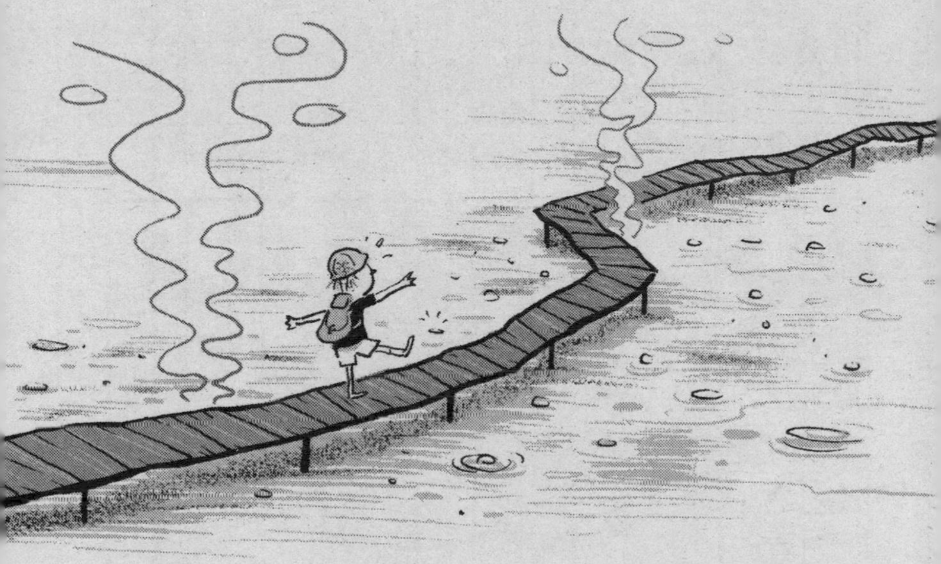

TIME REMAINING TILL CARNIVAL

06	17	19
DAYS	HOURS	MINUTES

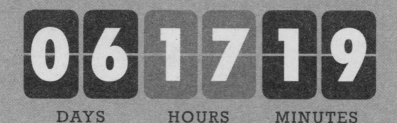

Meanwhile, everyone else is so busy that they keep out of my way.

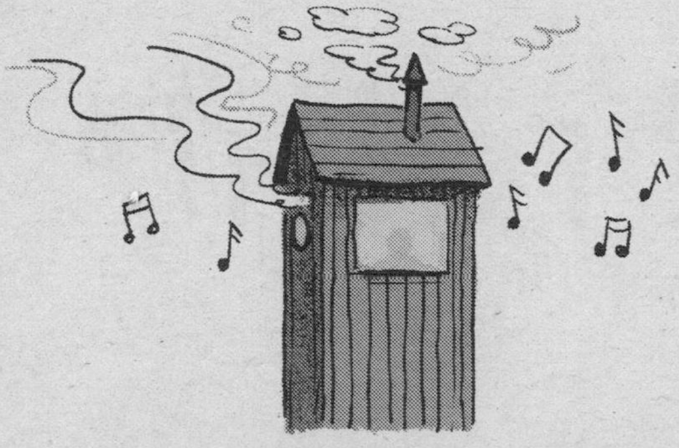

Grandpa and Dad are rattling through many further iterations of pickle disaster,

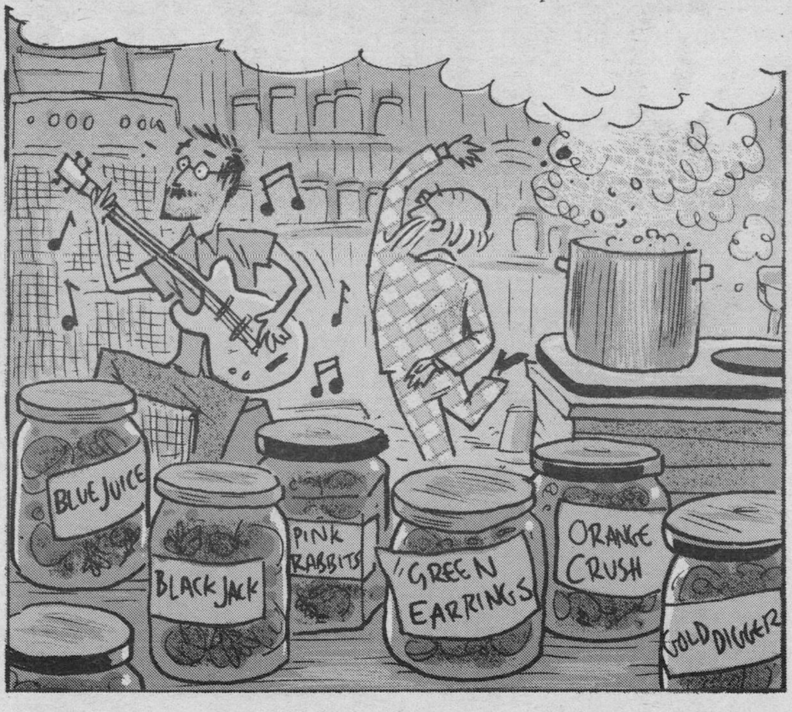
BLUE JUICE
BLACK JACK
PINK RABBITS
GREEN EARRINGS
ORANGE CRUSH
GOLD DIGGER

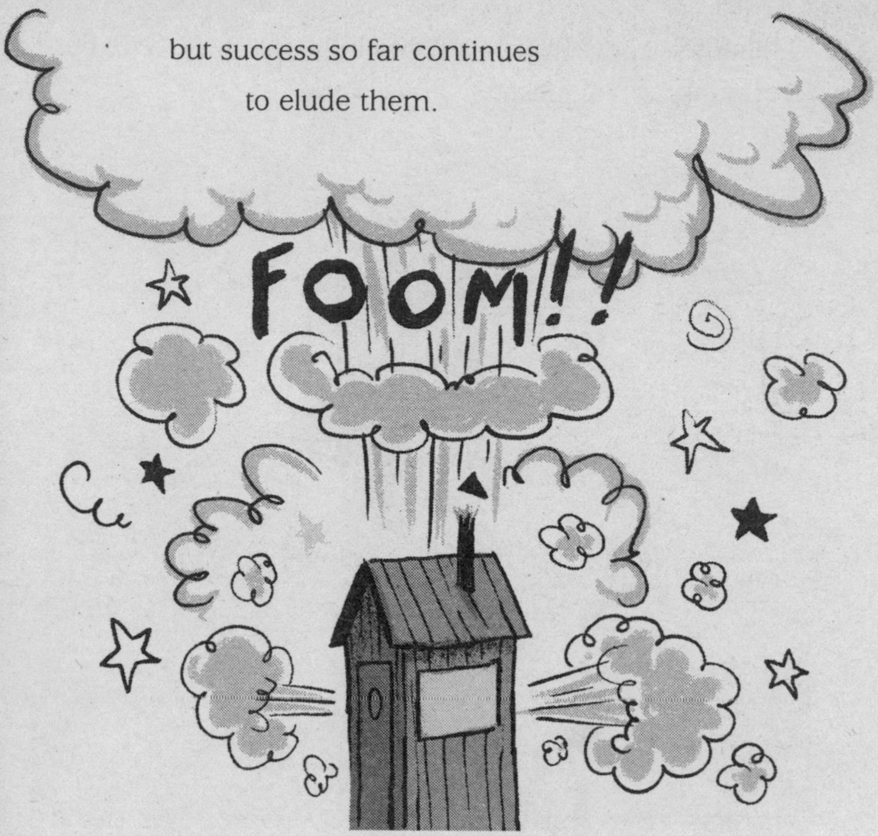
but success so far continues
to elude them.
FOOM!!

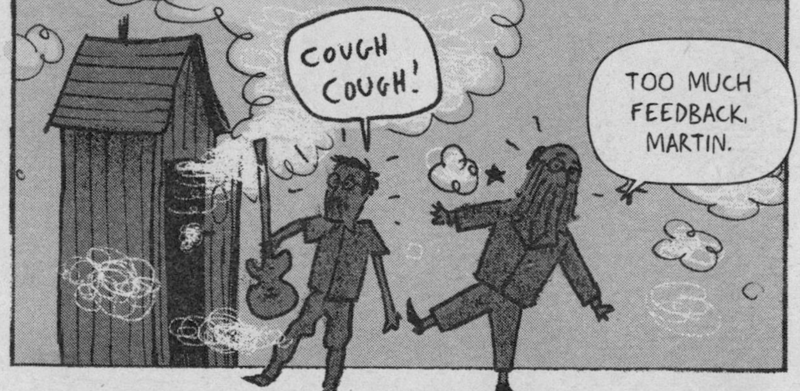
COUGH
COUGH!
TOO MUCH
FEEDBACK,
MARTIN.

Mom is rising to the Zumba challenge.

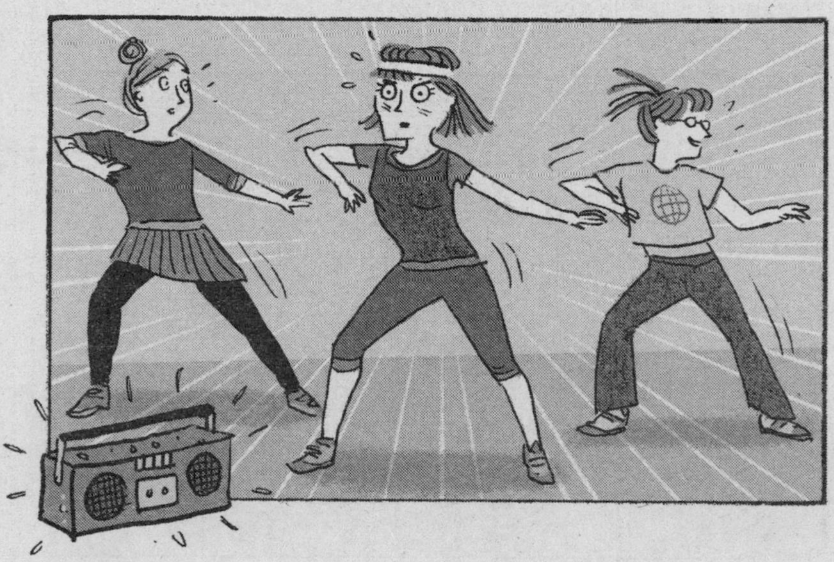

She's co-opted several of my friends' moms (including Charlie's) to join the Zumba Moms charity Zumbathon.

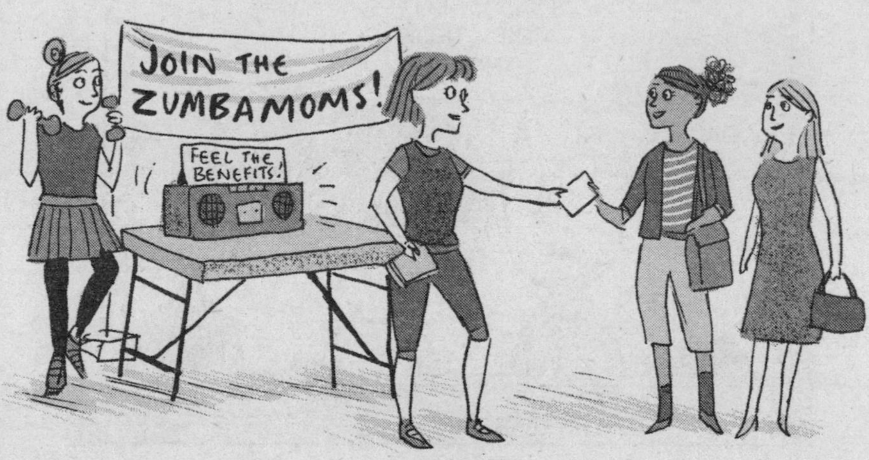
JOIN THE ZUMBAMOMS!
FEEL THE BENEFITS!

It is a little more ambitious than I had in mind when I mentioned it to the committee.

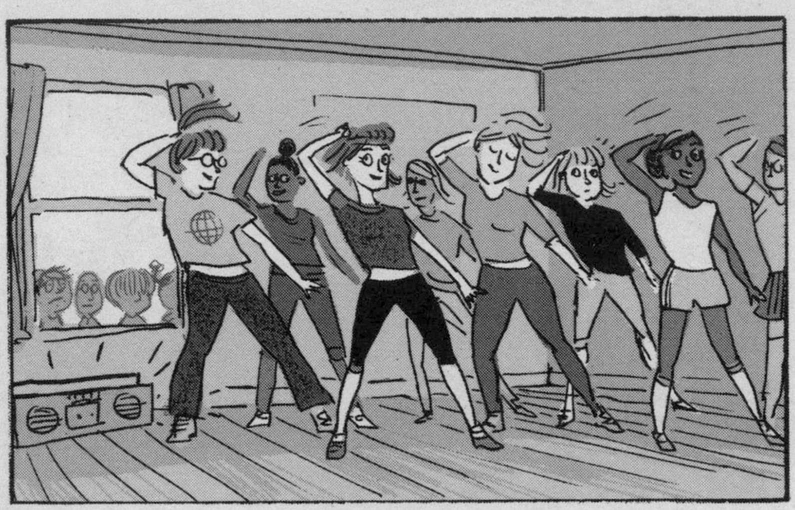

My friends are not thrilled about this.

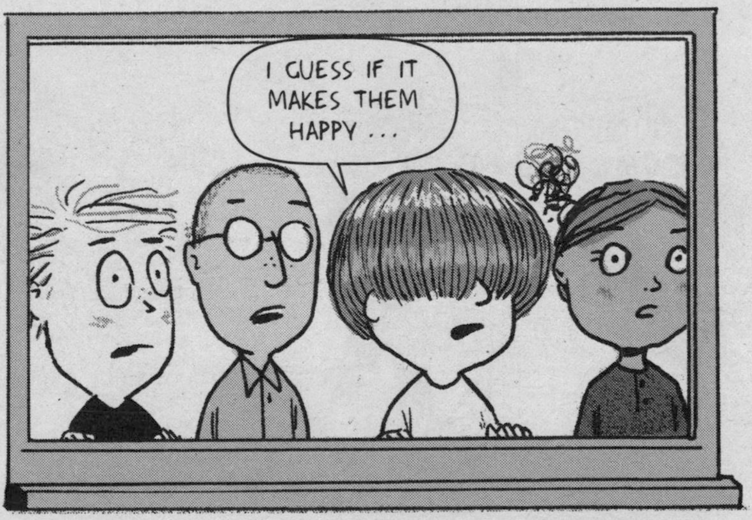
I GUESS IF IT MAKES THEM HAPPY . . .

Even Suzy's got the carnival bug. She's running a stall selling all her old toys—it's almost like she *wants* to grow up or something. Weirdo.

She's canvasing the neighborhood for old toys and games to sell at her charity stall—I imagine the spiel goes something like this:

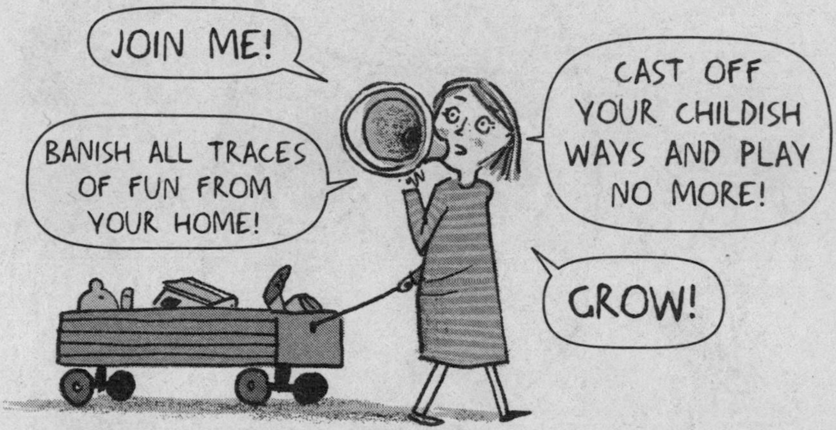
JOIN ME!
BANISH ALL TRACES OF FUN FROM YOUR HOME!
CAST OFF YOUR CHILDISH WAYS AND PLAY NO MORE!
GROW!

Pudding, on the other hand, is not faring quite so well.

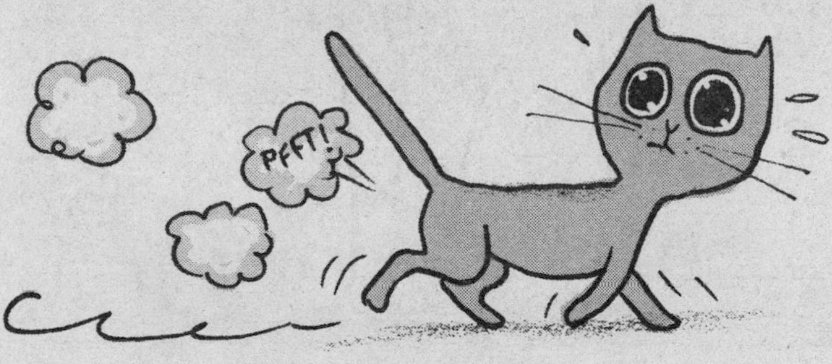
PFFT!

She has begun to produce the most heinous noxious gases, and her fur seems to be getting visibly lighter.

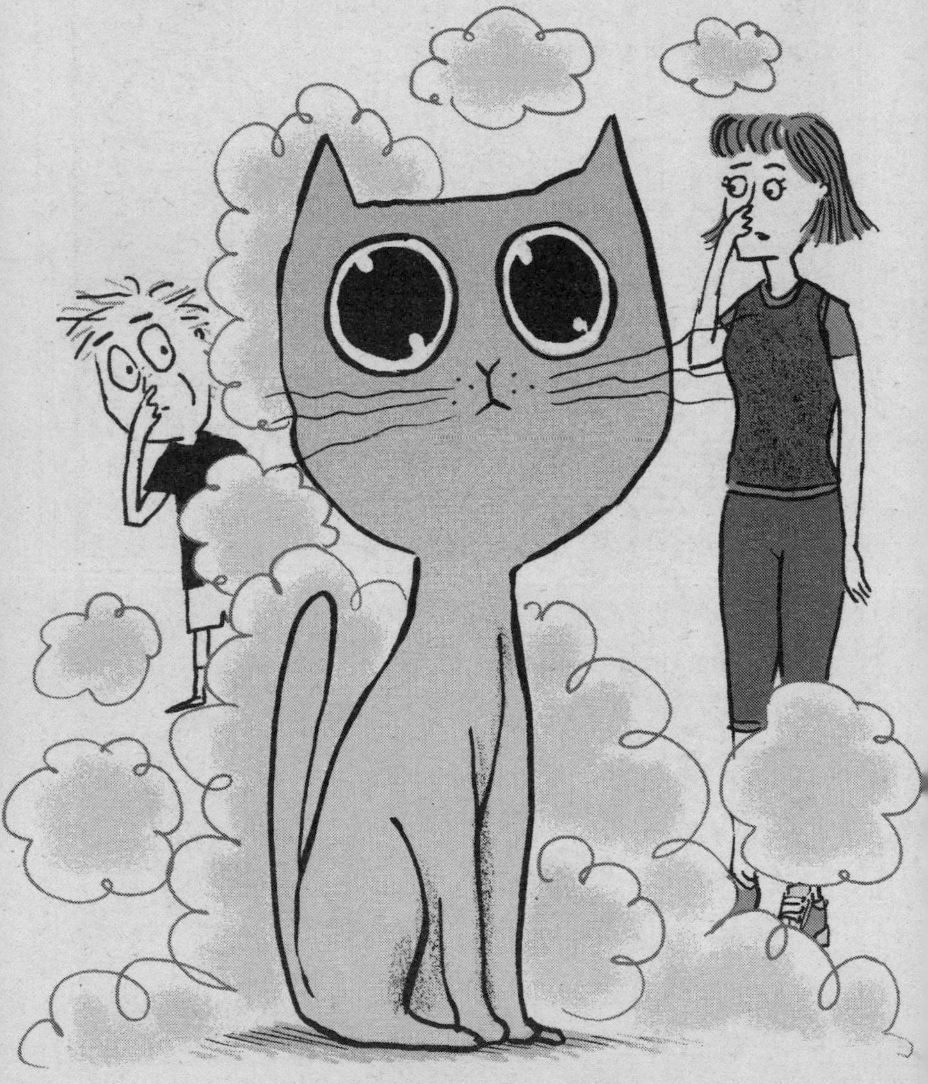

Mom takes her to the vet but she gets a clean bill of health.

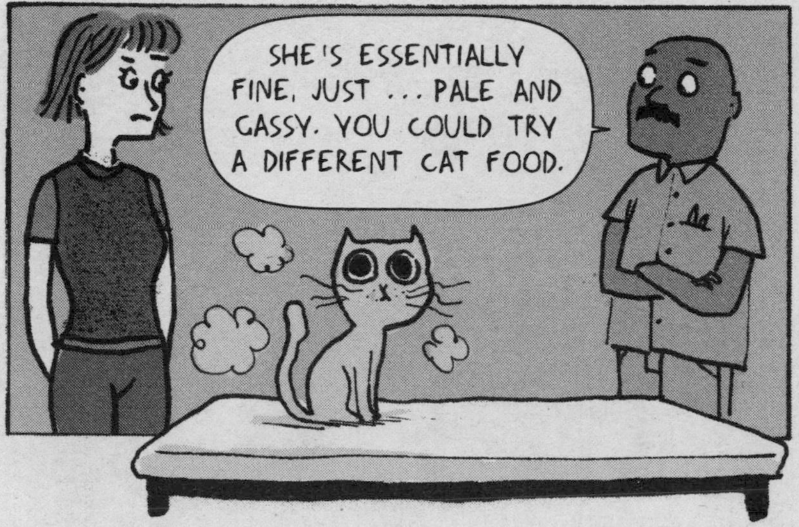
SHE'S ESSENTIALLY FINE, JUST . . . PALE AND GASSY. YOU COULD TRY A DIFFERENT CAT FOOD.

I've even had to ban her from the den, which is where Charlie and I go to watch more excerpts from *Cry Wolfe*. . . .

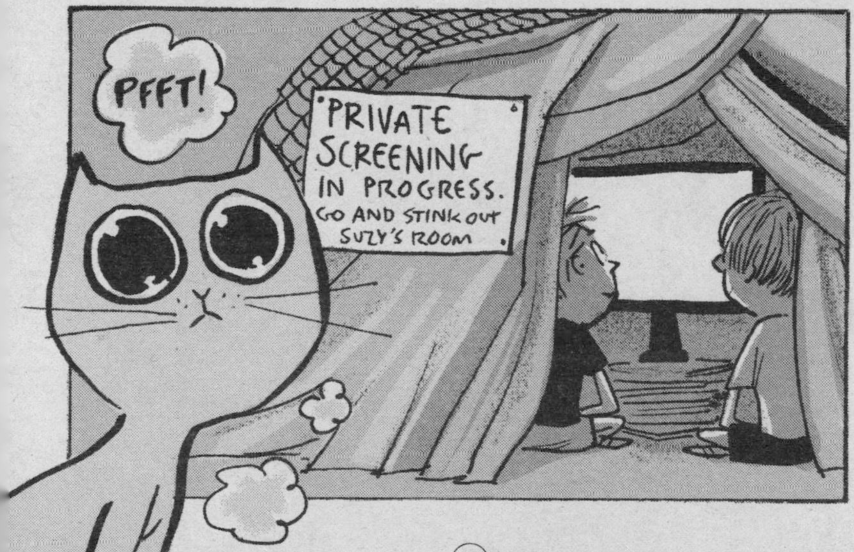
PFFT!
PRIVATE SCREENING IN PROGRESS. GO AND STINK OUT SUZY'S ROOM

The Following Preview Has Been
Approved for All Audiences

CRY WOLFE

Contains mild peril,
threat of acting, and
frequent bad hair

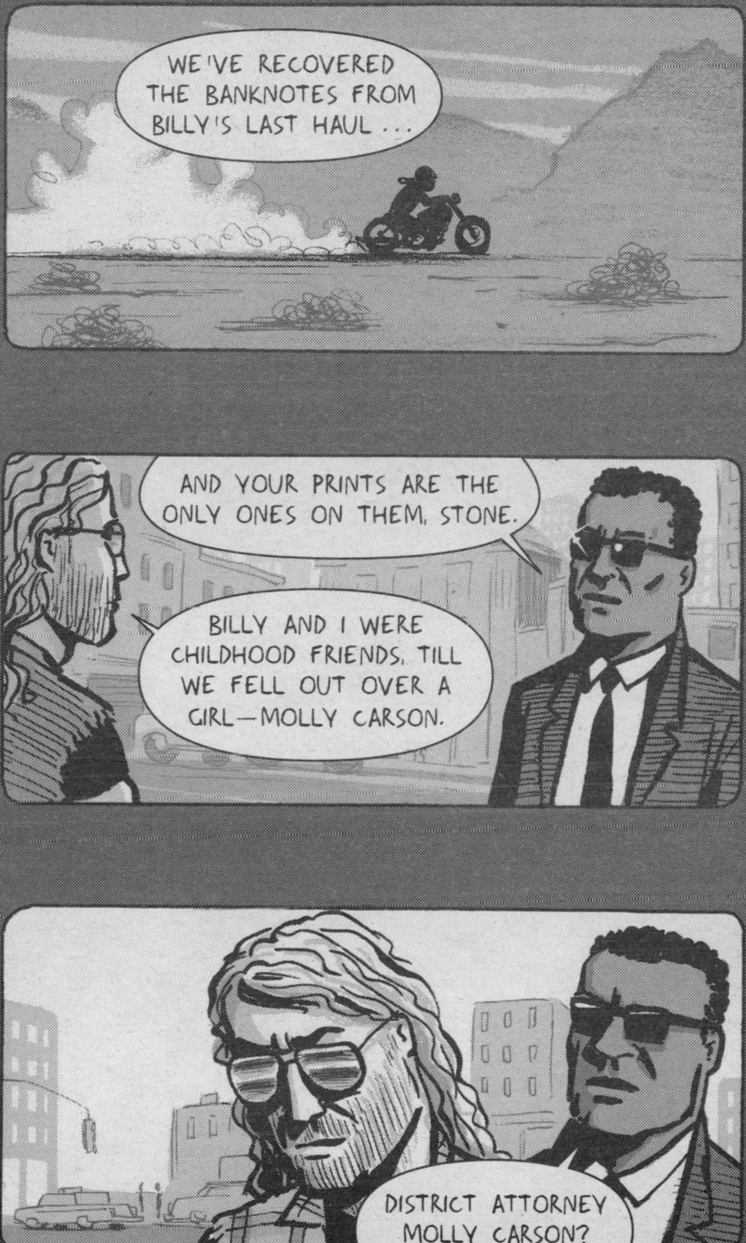
WE'VE RECOVERED THE BANKNOTES FROM BILLY'S LAST HAUL . . .
AND YOUR PRINTS ARE THE ONLY ONES ON THEM, STONE.
BILLY AND I WERE CHILDHOOD FRIENDS, TILL WE FELL OUT OVER A GIRL—MOLLY CARSON.
DISTRICT ATTORNEY MOLLY CARSON?

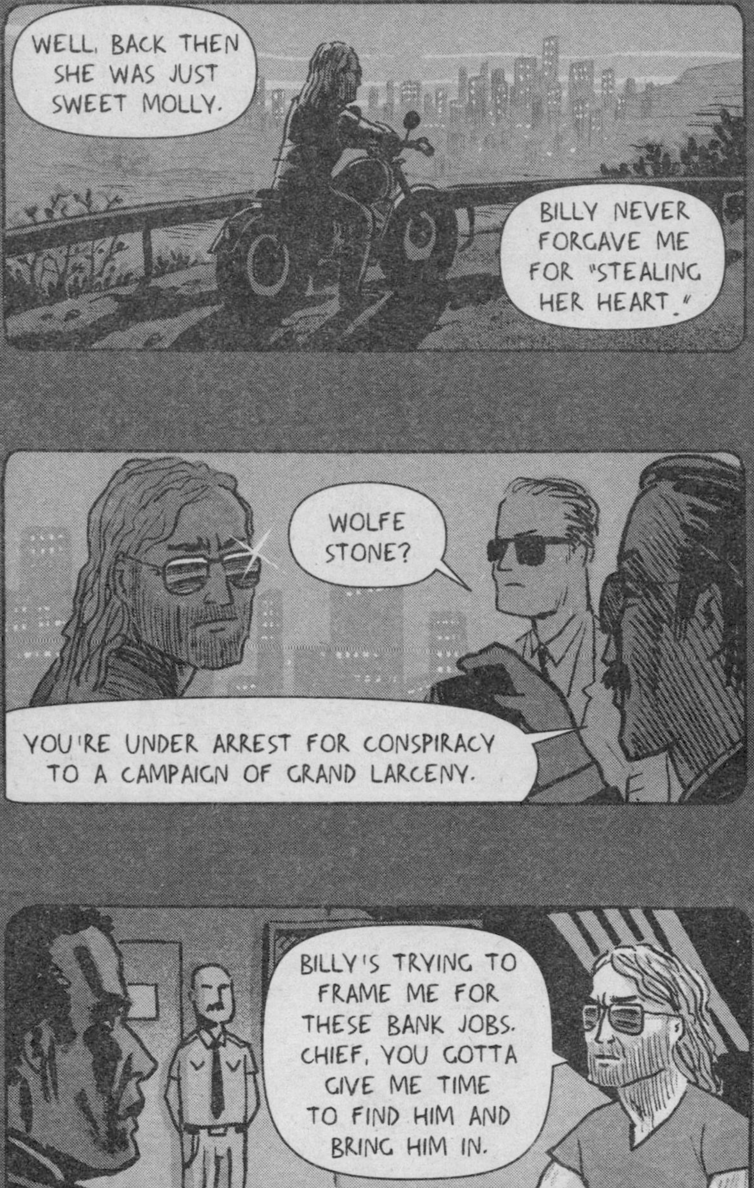
WELL, BACK THEN SHE WAS JUST SWEET MOLLY.
BILLY NEVER FORGAVE ME FOR "STEALING HER HEART."
WOLFE STONE?
YOU'RE UNDER ARREST FOR CONSPIRACY TO A CAMPAIGN OF GRAND LARCENY.
BILLY'S TRYING TO FRAME ME FOR THESE BANK JOBS. CHIEF, YOU GOTTA GIVE ME TIME TO FIND HIM AND BRING HIM IN.

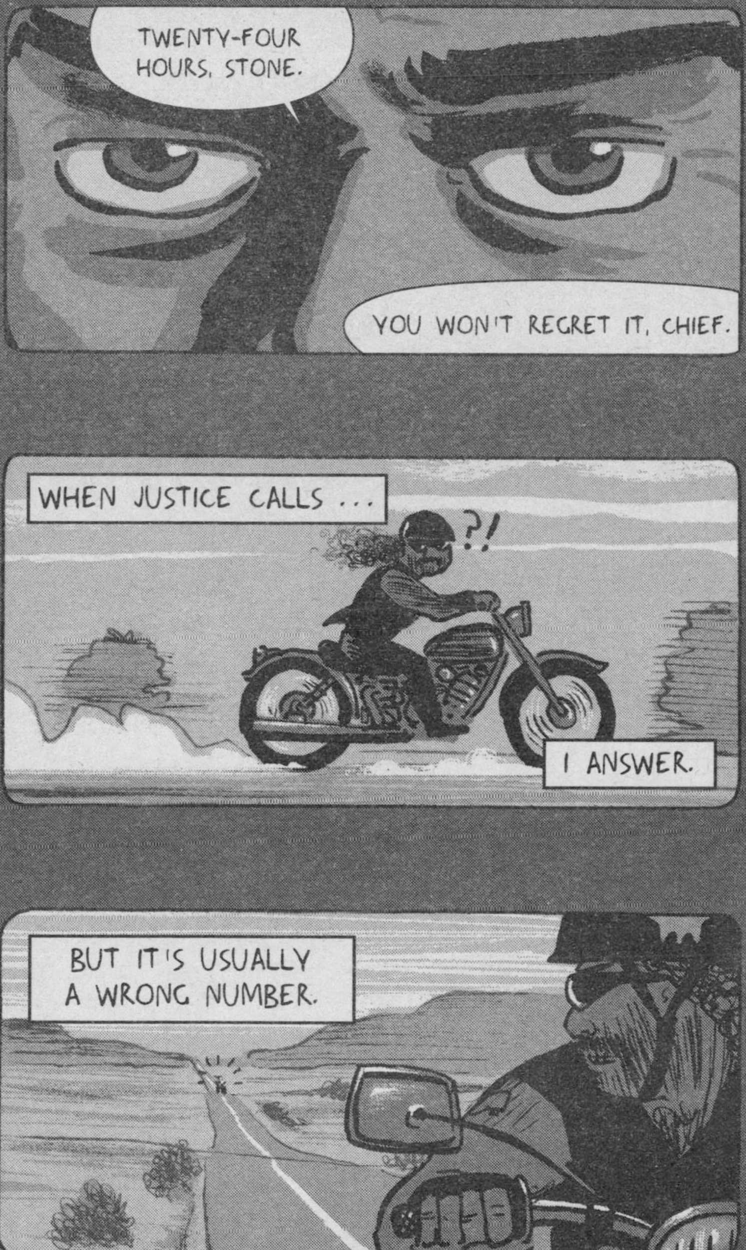
TWENTY-FOUR HOURS, STONE.
YOU WON'T REGRET IT, CHIEF.
WHEN JUSTICE CALLS ...
?!
I ANSWER.
BUT IT'S USUALLY A WRONG NUMBER.

TIME REMAINING TILL CARNIVAL

0 3 1 6 0 6

DAYS   HOURS   MINUTES

The days are ticking by, but my troubled relationship with the truth continues to be put to the test. Even when Charlie is around, problems can still occur.

For instance . . .

Mr. EG (our name for him) is the old man who lives in the green house at the top of the road.

It's not an actual greenhouse—in fact it's not even green anymore, it's pale orange. But when it was green we called it "the green house"—"the pale orange house" doesn't sound right so we still call it the green house . . . we know what we mean.

We have long suspected him of being an Evil Genius (which is what "EG" stands for), so when we see him taking delivery of a sinister-shaped box . . .

. . . it's pretty obvious that it will contain components for a giant death ray.

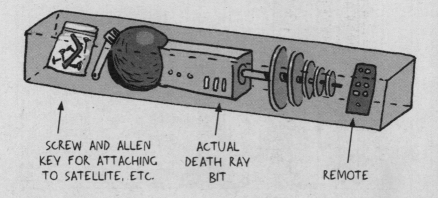

SCREW AND ALLEN KEY FOR ATTACHING TO SATELLITE, ETC.

ACTUAL DEATH RAY BIT

REMOTE

All the signs are there:

SIGN 1:

The box says,

AUDIO/VISUAL PROJECTOR SCREEN

on the side, which is EXACTLY what you'd write on it if you didn't want people to know it was components for a giant death ray.

SIGN 2:

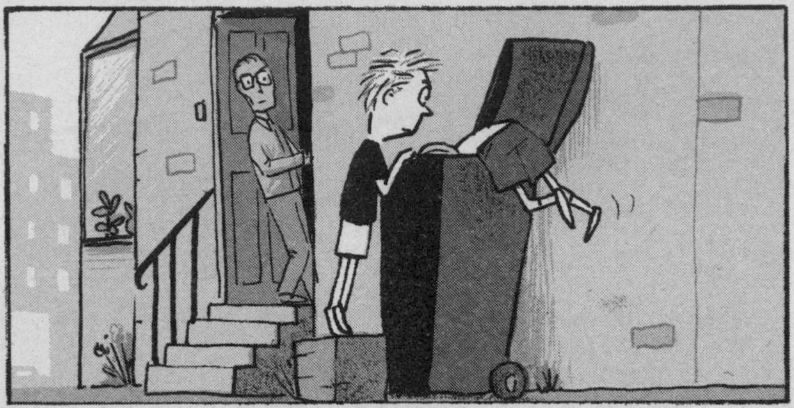

While we're going through his trash cans looking for evidence of evil plans, he jumps out at us and chases us away.

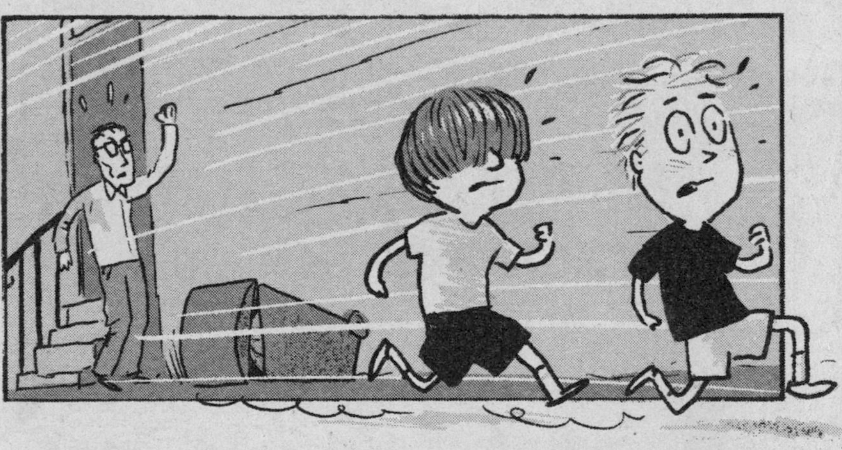

What's he trying to hide?

SIGN 3:

He somehow (spy satellite? network of informants (including my sister, perhaps)?) knows where I live, and comes to speak to my mom.

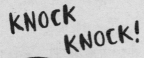

SIGN 4:

He is irrationally angry and upset about the mess we've made, another clear sign that he is up to no good.

My mom calls me and Charlie . . .

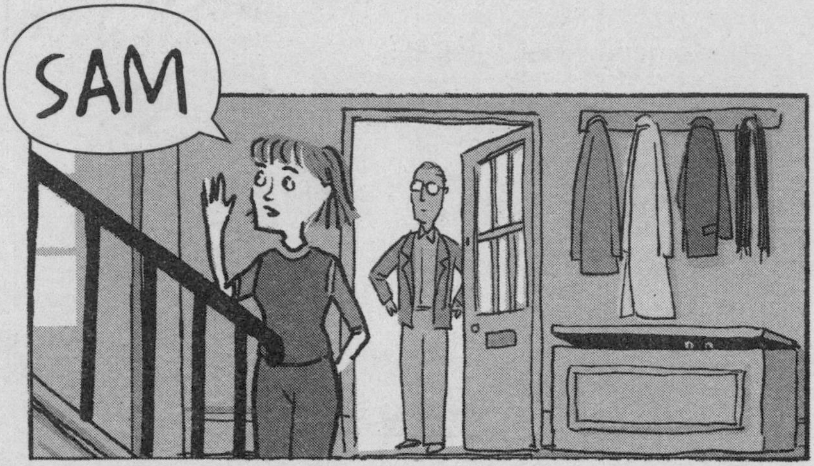
SAM

. . . we are hiding in a shoe chest at this point, listening in on the conversation to see if we have enough evidence to warn the government.

That's when Mom spots us. It's embarassing. It's awkward.

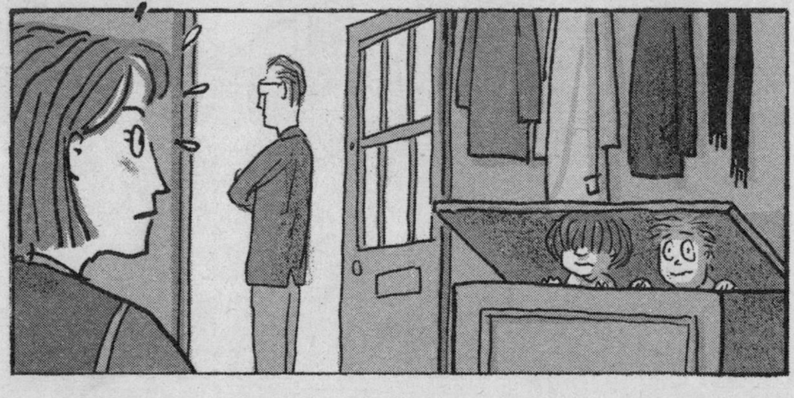

The old me would have tried to lie my way out.

I SWEAR—WE ONLY WENT IN HIS TRASH CAN BECAUSE WE SAW A LEPRECHAUN HIDING IN IT, AND I JUST WANTED TO RETURN THE POT OF GOLD TO ITS RIGHTFUL OWNER....

The new me, the one who desperately wants to win the challenge, apologizes.

SORRY.

My mom is, again, fairly grumpy about the whole thing, but I did tell the truth. In any case, she's got more important things to do, like work out how to Zumba dance for three hours straight, in a week's time.

I'm pretty proud of her, actually—she's really going for it with the Zumba. She's so excited about it she's keeping a calendar where she marks off the days to the big event. At least I think that's what it's about.

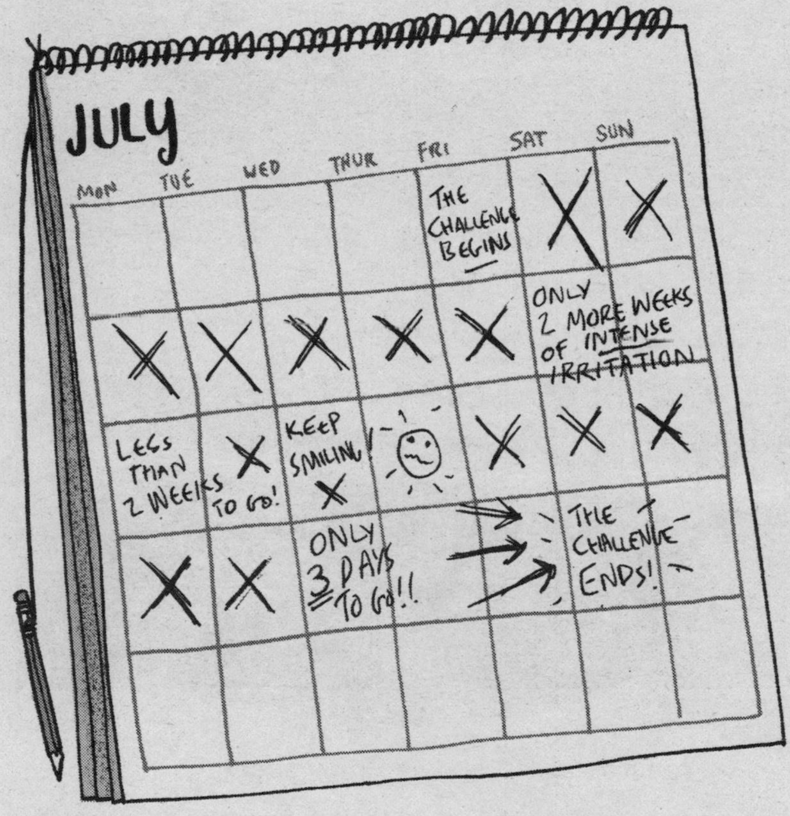
JULY
MON
TUE
WED
THUR
FRI
SAT
SUN
THE CHALLENGE BEGINS
ONLY 2 MORE WEEKS OF INTENSE IRRITATION
LESS THAN 2 WEEKS TO GO!
KEEP SMILING!
ONLY 3 DAYS TO GO!!
THE CHALLENGE ENDS!

So onward I plod through the bog, keeping my head down and my eyes on the prize.

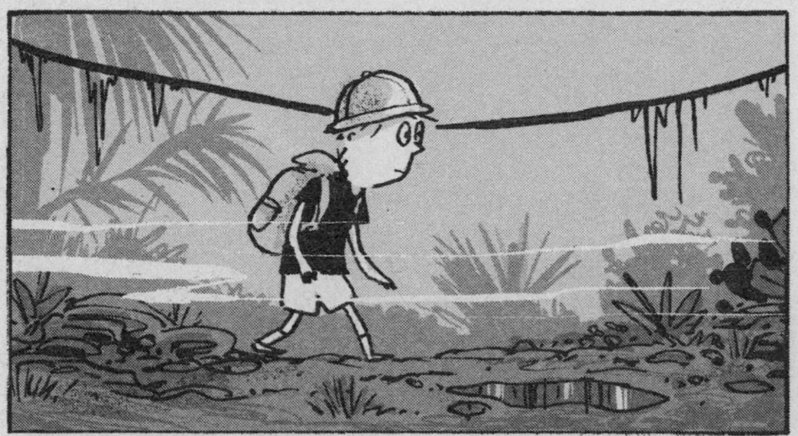

And almost before you can say

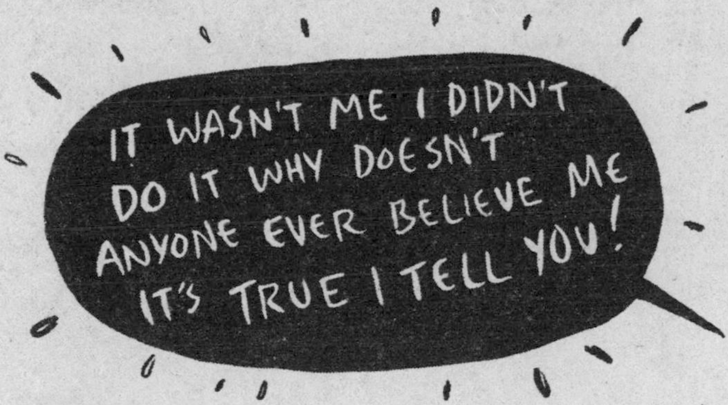
IT WASN'T ME I DIDN'T DO IT WHY DOESN'T ANYONE EVER BELIEVE ME IT'S TRUE I TELL YOU!

it's the eve of the big day itself.

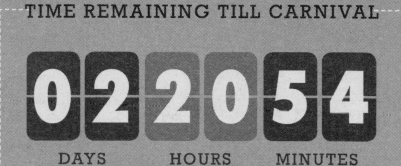

TIME REMAINING TILL CARNIVAL

0 2 2 0 5 4

DAYS   HOURS   MINUTES

I've nearly done it. I've navigated a tricky path through the stinky swamp of truth; the mists are clearing, the bogs are drying out, and success is within sight.

Which is, of course, when it all goes horribly wrong.

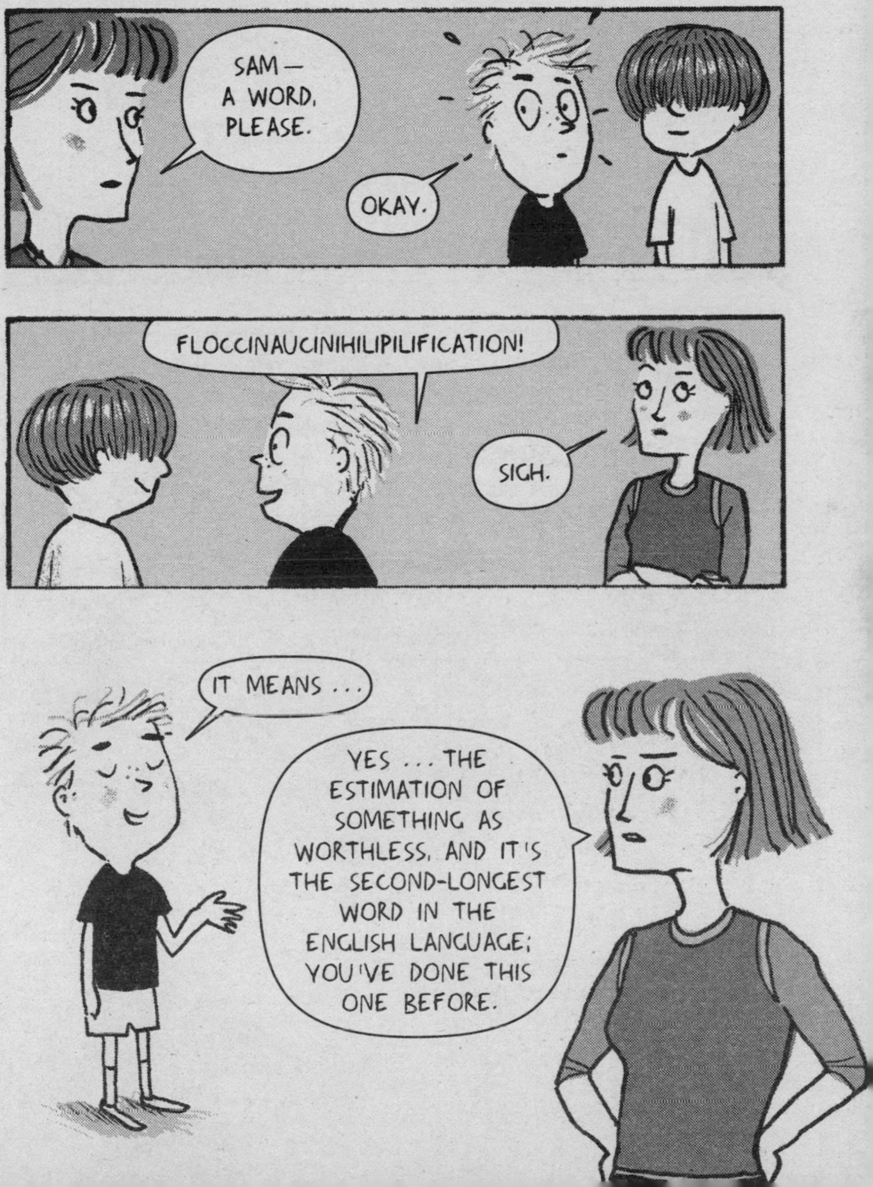
SAM — A WORD, PLEASE.
OKAY.
FLOCCINAUCINIHILIPILIFICATION!
SIGH.
IT MEANS . . .
YES . . . THE ESTIMATION OF SOMETHING AS WORTHLESS, AND IT'S THE SECOND-LONGEST WORD IN THE ENGLISH LANGUAGE; YOU'VE DONE THIS ONE BEFORE.

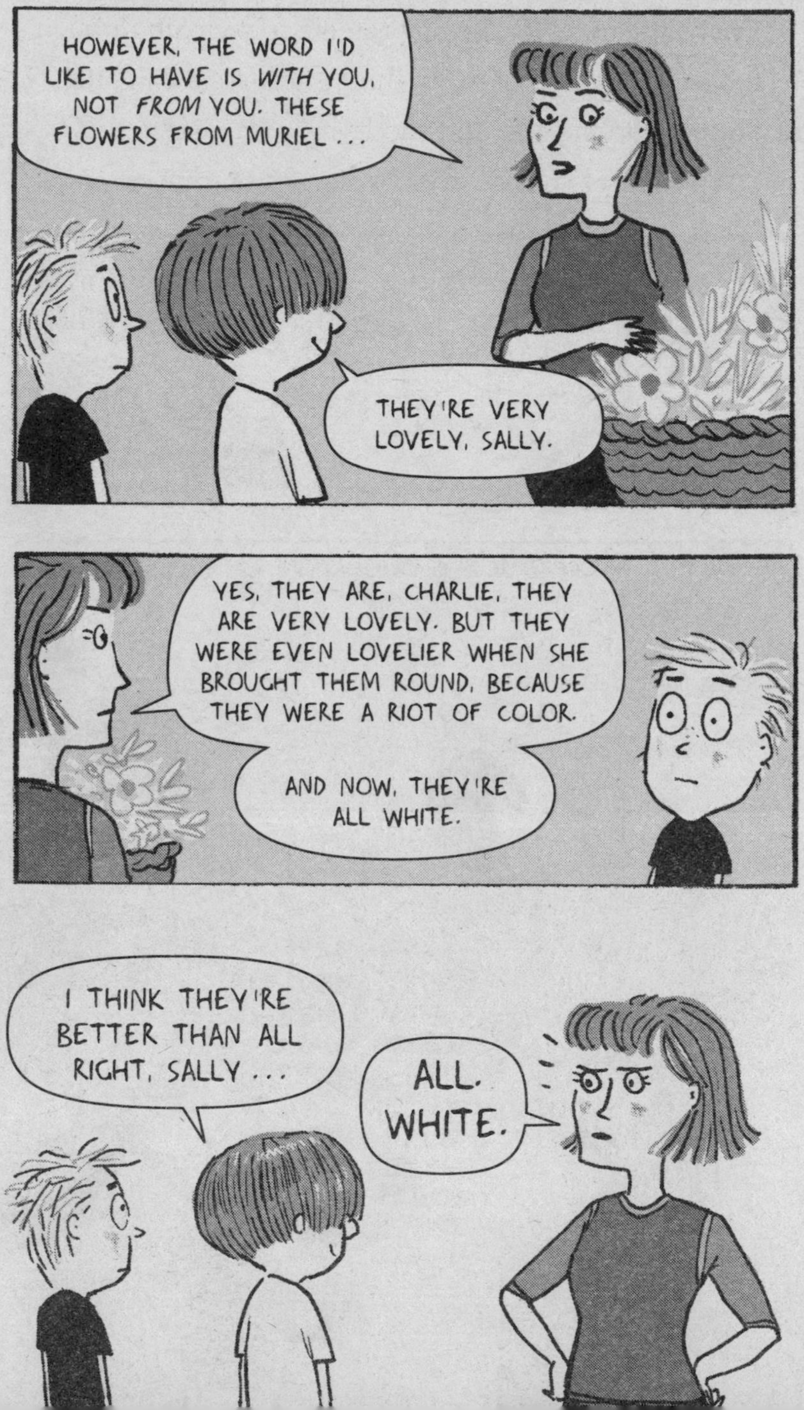
HOWEVER, THE WORD I'D LIKE TO HAVE IS *WITH* YOU, NOT *FROM* YOU. THESE FLOWERS FROM MURIEL . . .
THEY'RE VERY LOVELY, SALLY.
YES, THEY ARE, CHARLIE, THEY ARE VERY LOVELY. BUT THEY WERE EVEN LOVELIER WHEN SHE BROUGHT THEM ROUND, BECAUSE THEY WERE A RIOT OF COLOR.
AND NOW, THEY'RE ALL WHITE.
I THINK THEY'RE BETTER THAN ALL RIGHT, SALLY . . .
ALL. WHITE.

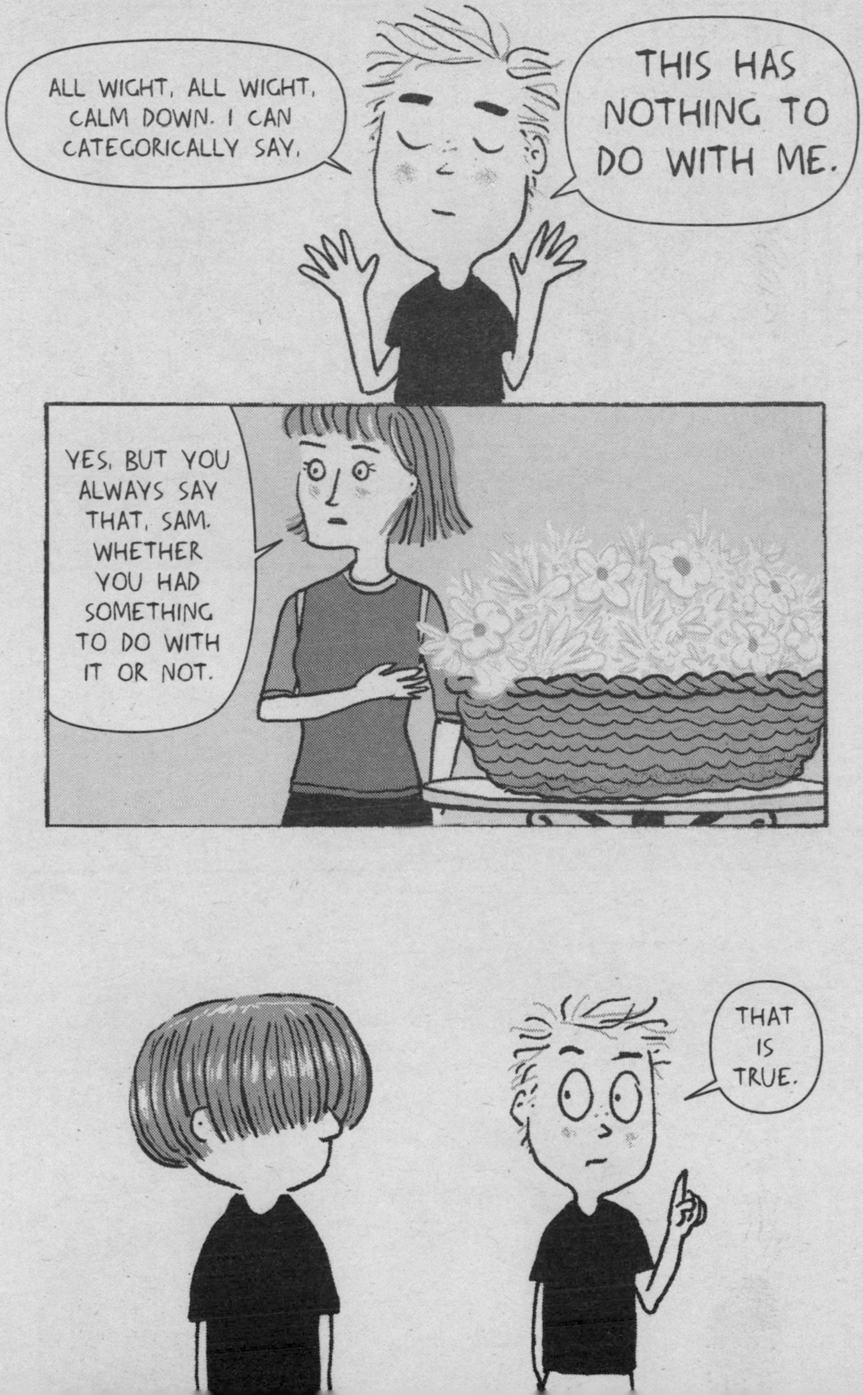
ALL WIGHT, ALL WIGHT, CALM DOWN. I CAN CATEGORICALLY SAY,
THIS HAS NOTHING TO DO WITH ME.
YES, BUT YOU ALWAYS SAY THAT, SAM. WHETHER YOU HAD SOMETHING TO DO WITH IT OR NOT.
THAT IS TRUE.

BUT I HAVEN'T ALWAYS DONE SO AFTER TAKING A TRUTH CHALLENGE. MOM, THIS IS THE EXACT SAME THING THAT HAPPENS TO WOLFE STONE IN *CRY WOLFE.* HE GETS ACCUSED OF SOMETHING HE DIDN'T DO. SEE, WHEN SOMEONE TELLS LOTS OF LIES . . .
YES I KNOW WHAT CRYING WOLF IS. WITHOUT AN "E." AND I WILL HAVE TO TAKE YOUR WORD FOR IT. THIS TIME.

SAM, YOU'RE SO NEARLY THERE— THE CARNIVAL IS TOMORROW. HOW ABOUT YOU AND CHARLIE RUN AN ERRAND FOR ME RIGHT NOW, TO HELP KEEP YOU OUT OF TROUBLE?
DO YOU WANT AN HONEST ANSWER?

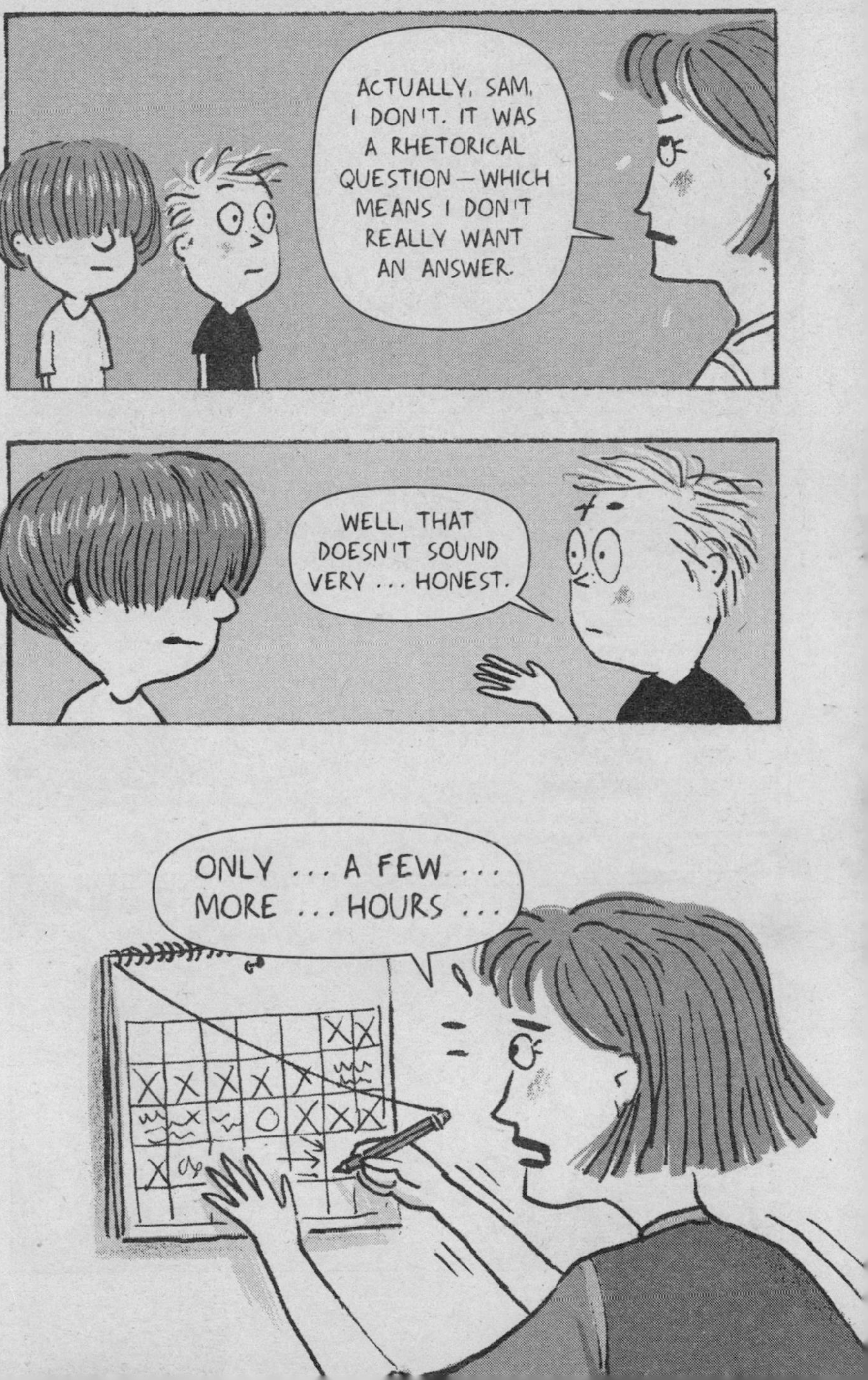
ACTUALLY, SAM, I DON'T. IT WAS A RHETORICAL QUESTION—WHICH MEANS I DON'T REALLY WANT AN ANSWER.
WELL, THAT DOESN'T SOUND VERY . . . HONEST.
ONLY . . . A FEW . . . MORE . . . HOURS . . .

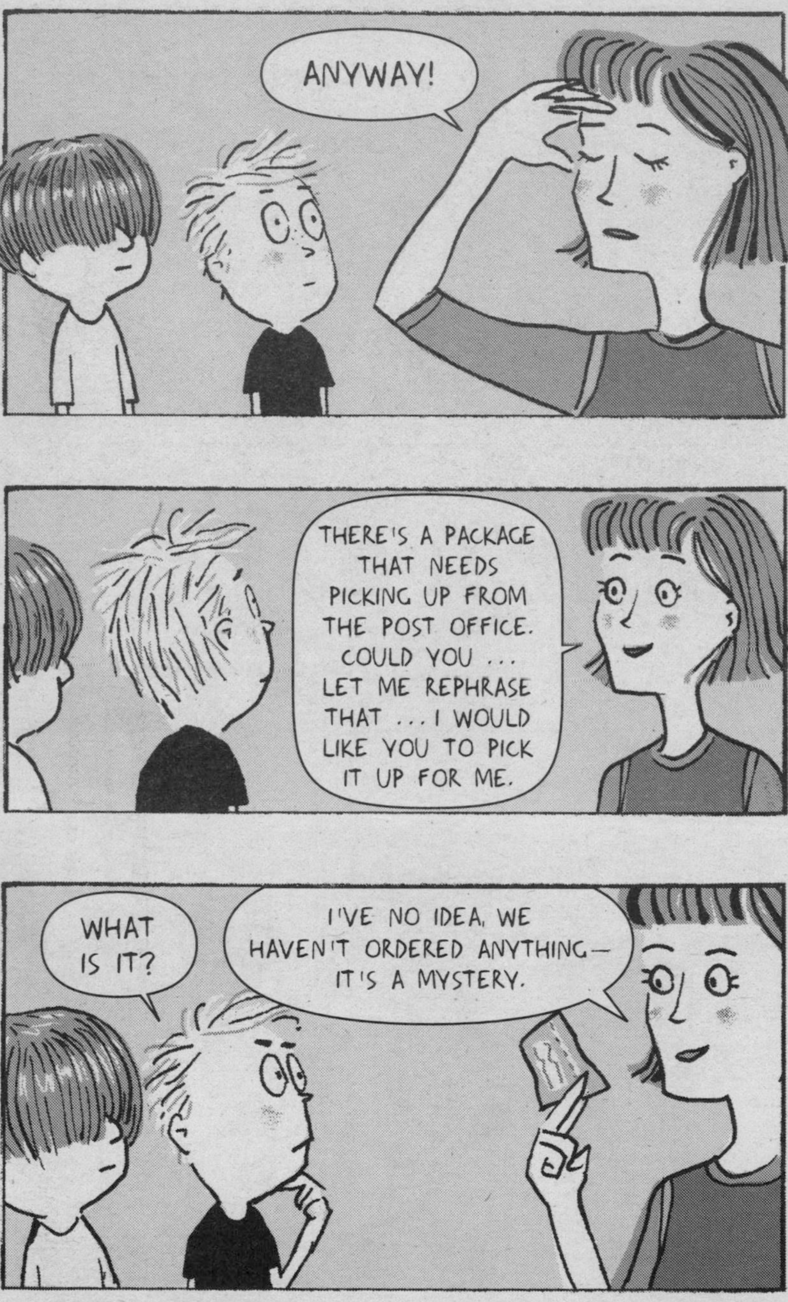
ANYWAY!
THERE'S A PACKAGE THAT NEEDS PICKING UP FROM THE POST OFFICE. COULD YOU ... LET ME REPHRASE THAT ... I WOULD LIKE YOU TO PICK IT UP FOR ME.
WHAT IS IT?
I'VE NO IDEA. WE HAVEN'T ORDERED ANYTHING— IT'S A MYSTERY.

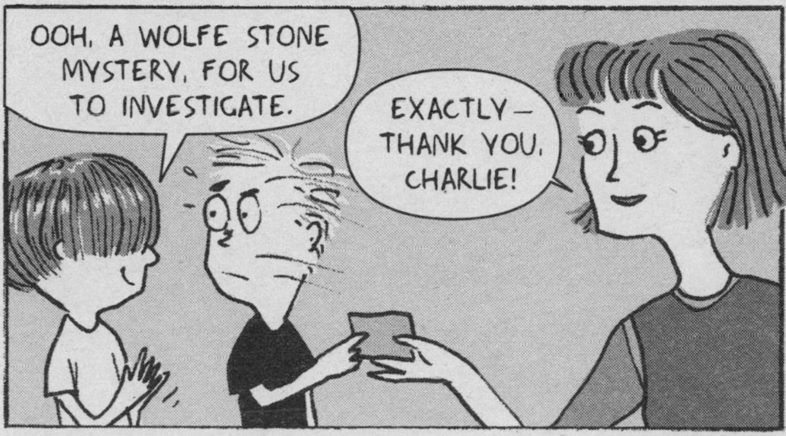
OOH, A WOLFE STONE MYSTERY, FOR US TO INVESTIGATE.
EXACTLY— THANK YOU, CHARLIE!

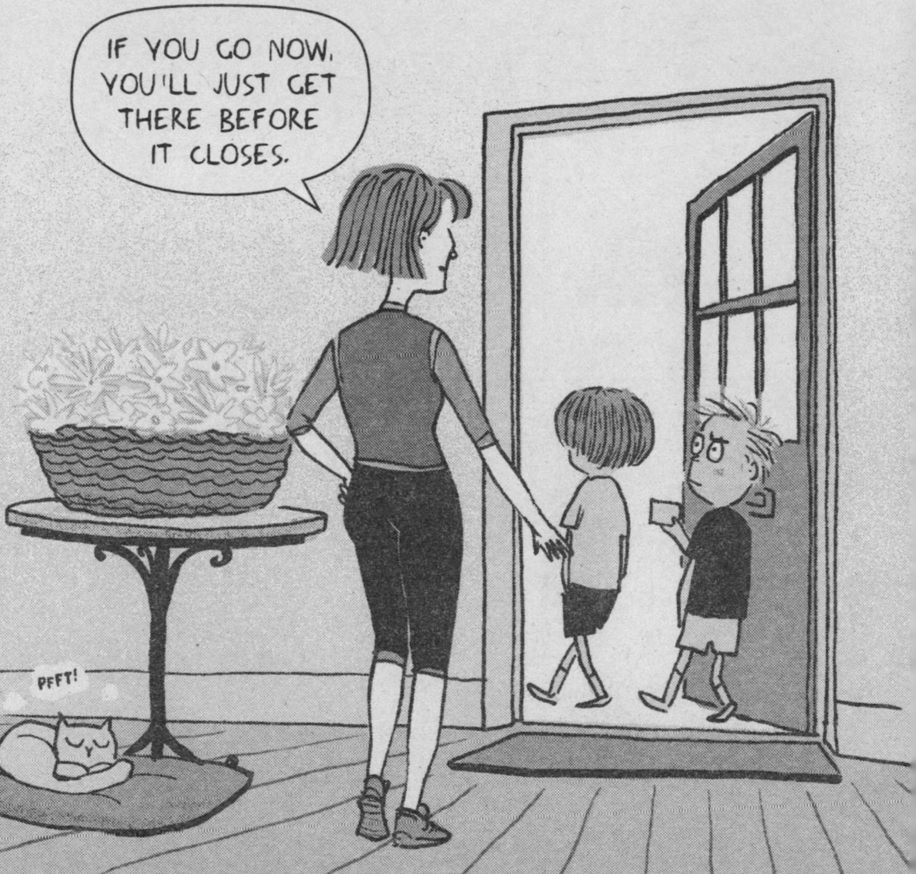
IF YOU GO NOW, YOU'LL JUST GET THERE BEFORE IT CLOSES.
PFFT!

So Charlie and I go to pick up the package, little suspecting the disaster that awaits. . . .

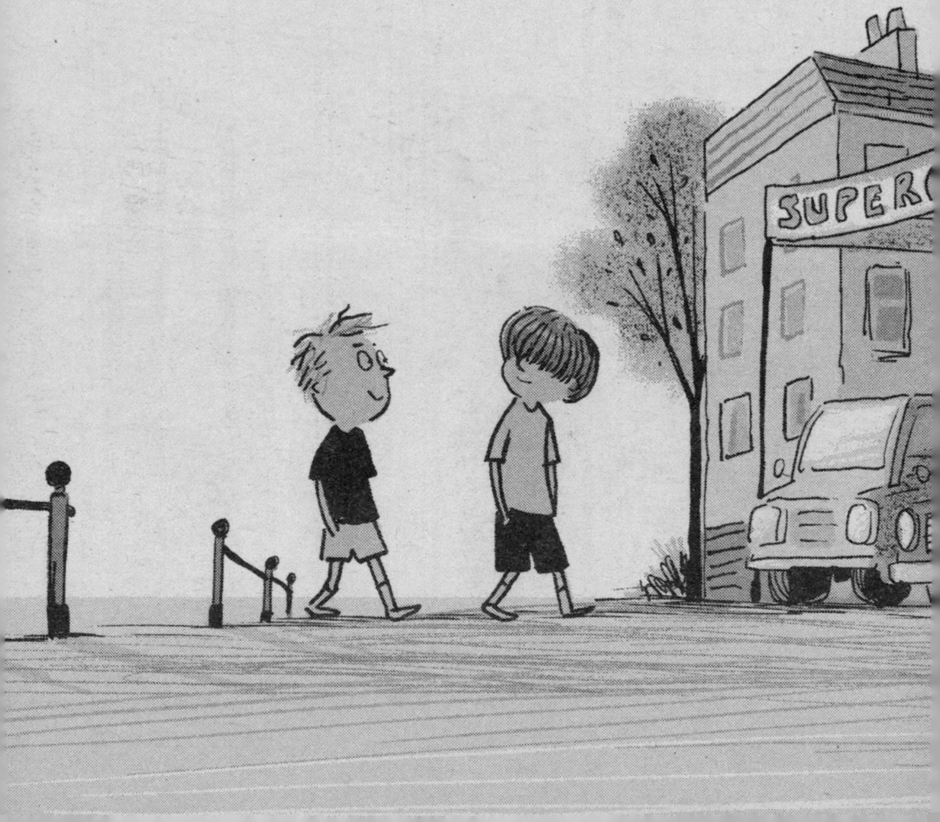
SUPER

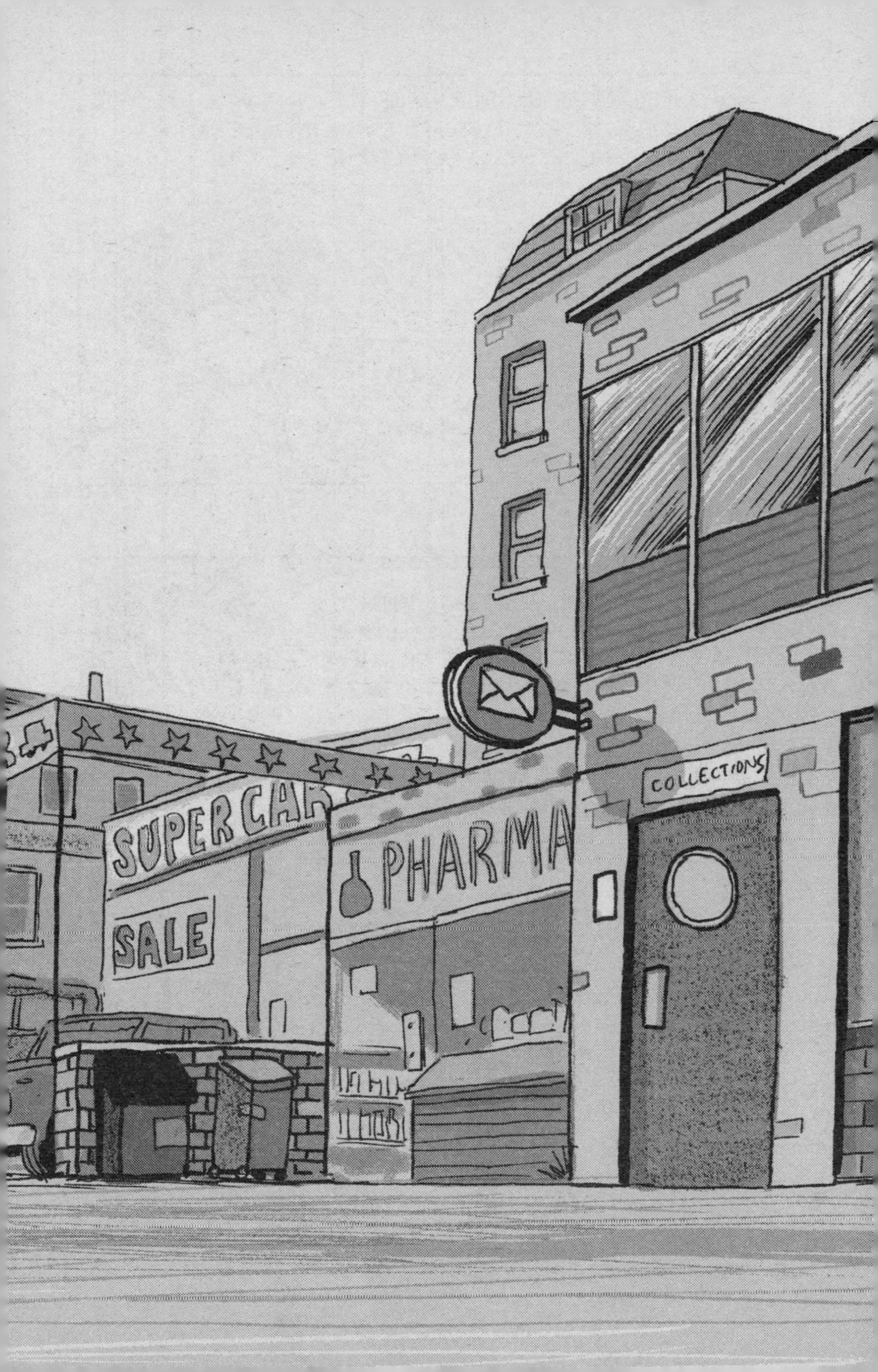
SUPERCAR
SALE
PHARMA
COLLECTIONS

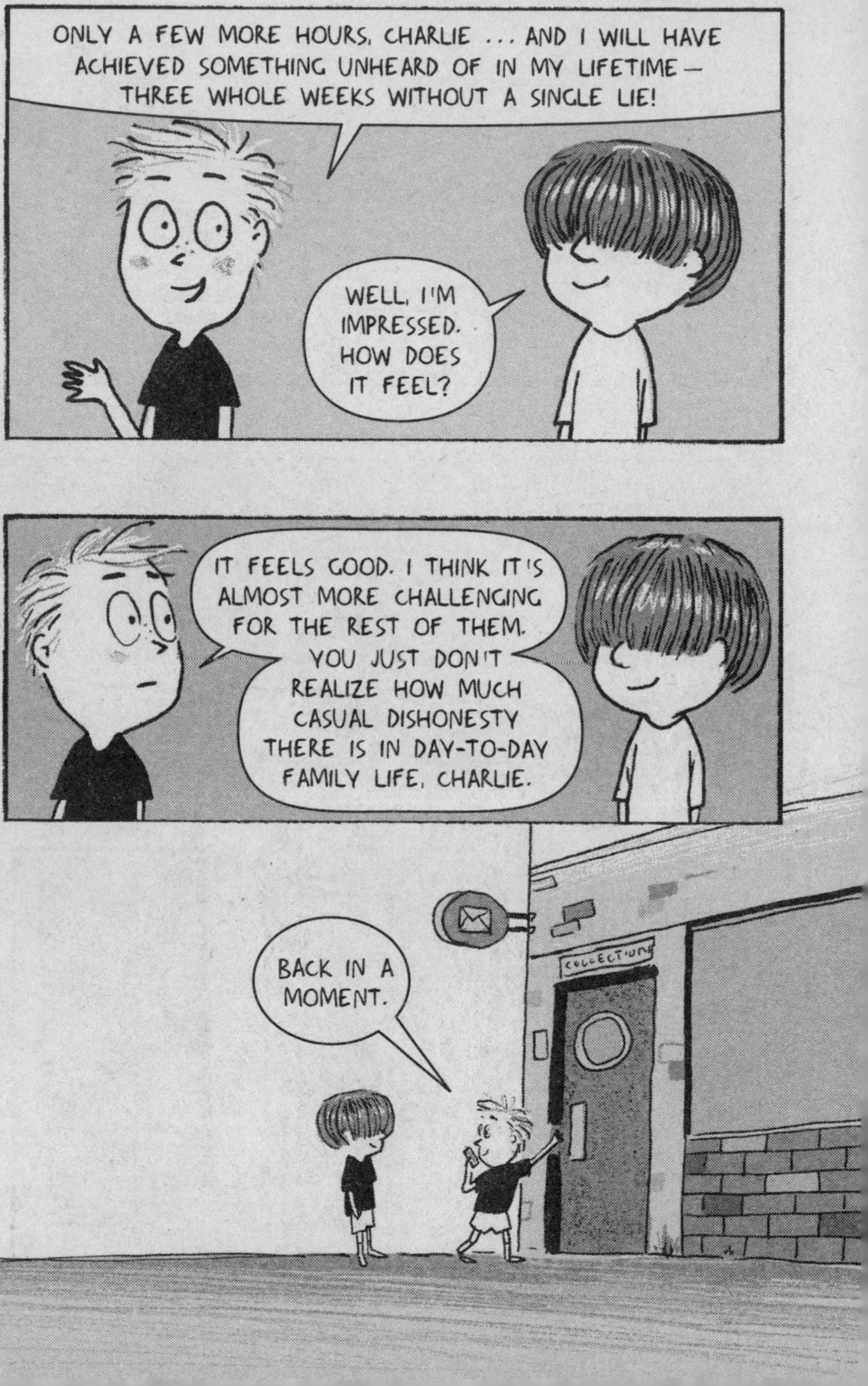
ONLY A FEW MORE HOURS, CHARLIE . . . AND I WILL HAVE ACHIEVED SOMETHING UNHEARD OF IN MY LIFETIME— THREE WHOLE WEEKS WITHOUT A SINGLE LIE!
WELL, I'M IMPRESSED. HOW DOES IT FEEL?
IT FEELS GOOD. I THINK IT'S ALMOST MORE CHALLENGING FOR THE REST OF THEM.
YOU JUST DON'T REALIZE HOW MUCH CASUAL DISHONESTY THERE IS IN DAY-TO-DAY FAMILY LIFE, CHARLIE.
BACK IN A MOMENT.

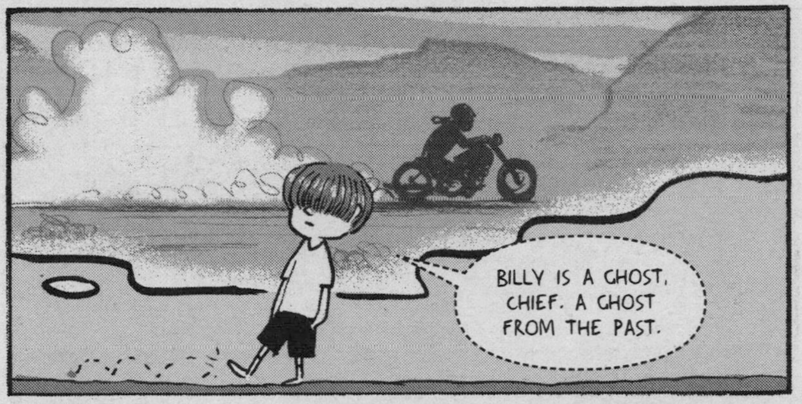
BILLY IS A GHOST, CHIEF. A GHOST FROM THE PAST.

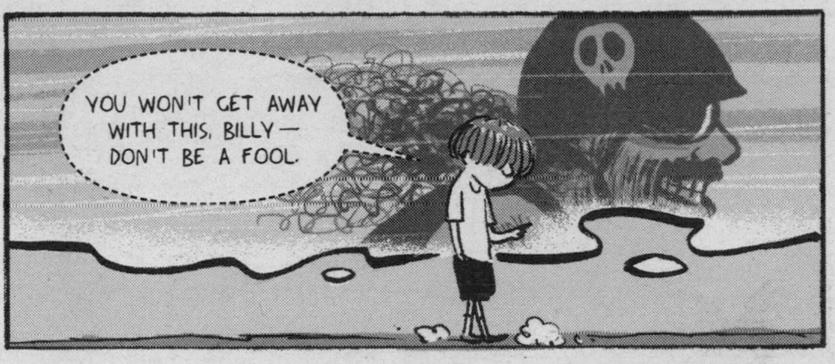
YOU WON'T GET AWAY WITH THIS, BILLY— DON'T BE A FOOL.

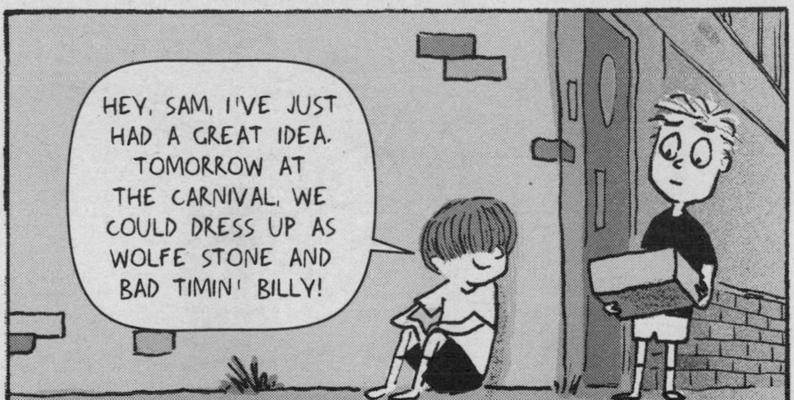
HEY, SAM, I'VE JUST HAD A GREAT IDEA. TOMORROW AT THE CARNIVAL, WE COULD DRESS UP AS WOLFE STONE AND BAD TIMIN' BILLY!

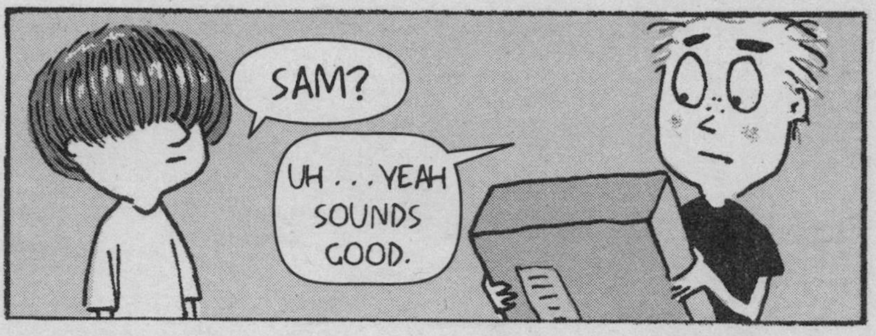
SAM?
UH . . . YEAH SOUNDS GOOD.

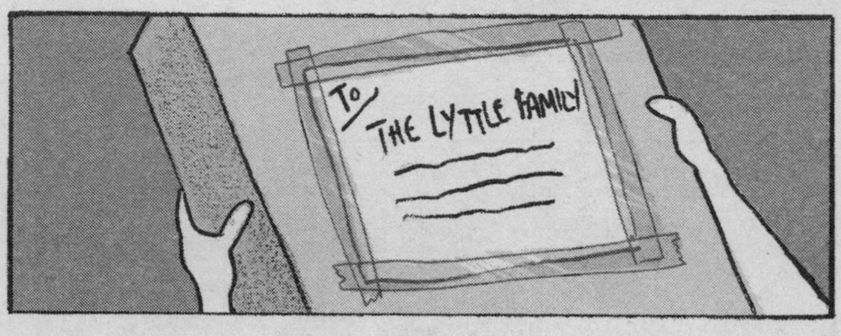
TO/ THE LYTTLE FAMILY

On the reverse of this mystery package is the return address—a vacation house we stayed at ages ago.

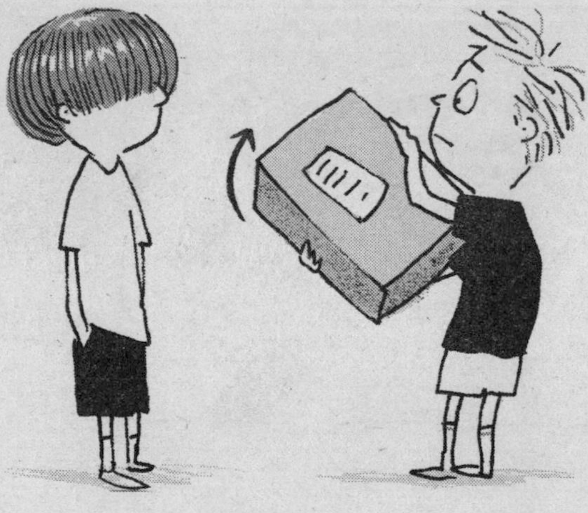

When I see it, a tiny alarm bell goes off in my head.

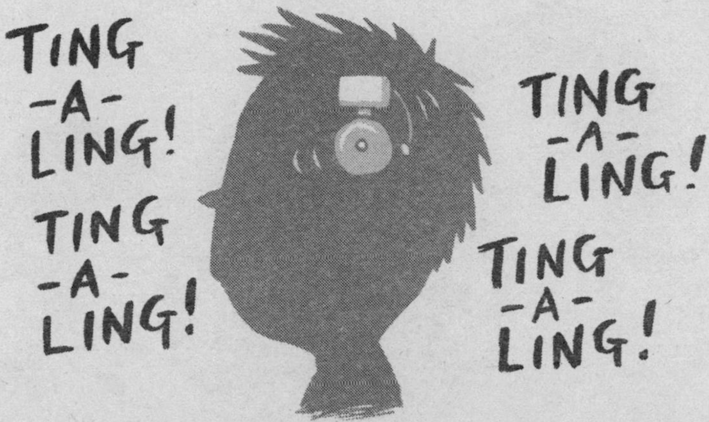
TING -A- LING!
TING -A- LING!
TING -A- LING!
TING -A- LING!

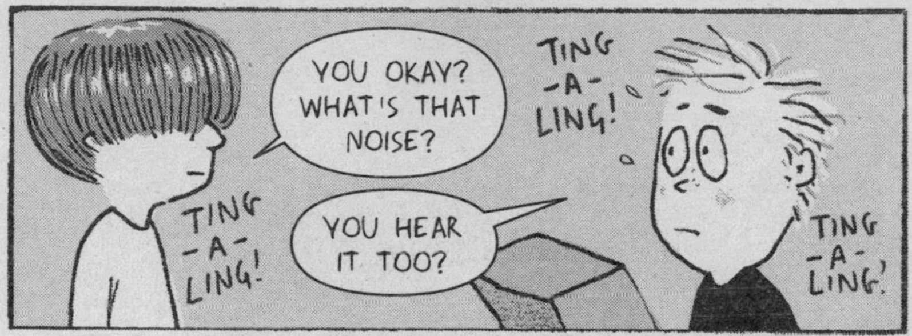
YOU OKAY? WHAT'S THAT NOISE?
TING -A- LING!
TING -A- LING!
YOU HEAR IT TOO?
TING -A- LING!

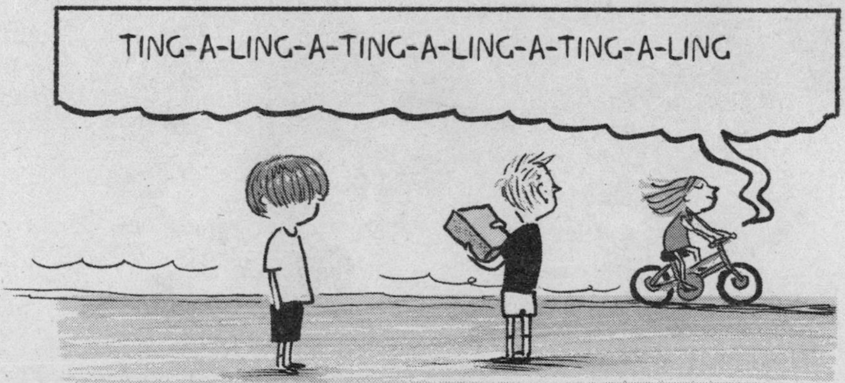
TING-A-LING-A-TING-A-LING-A-TING-A-LING

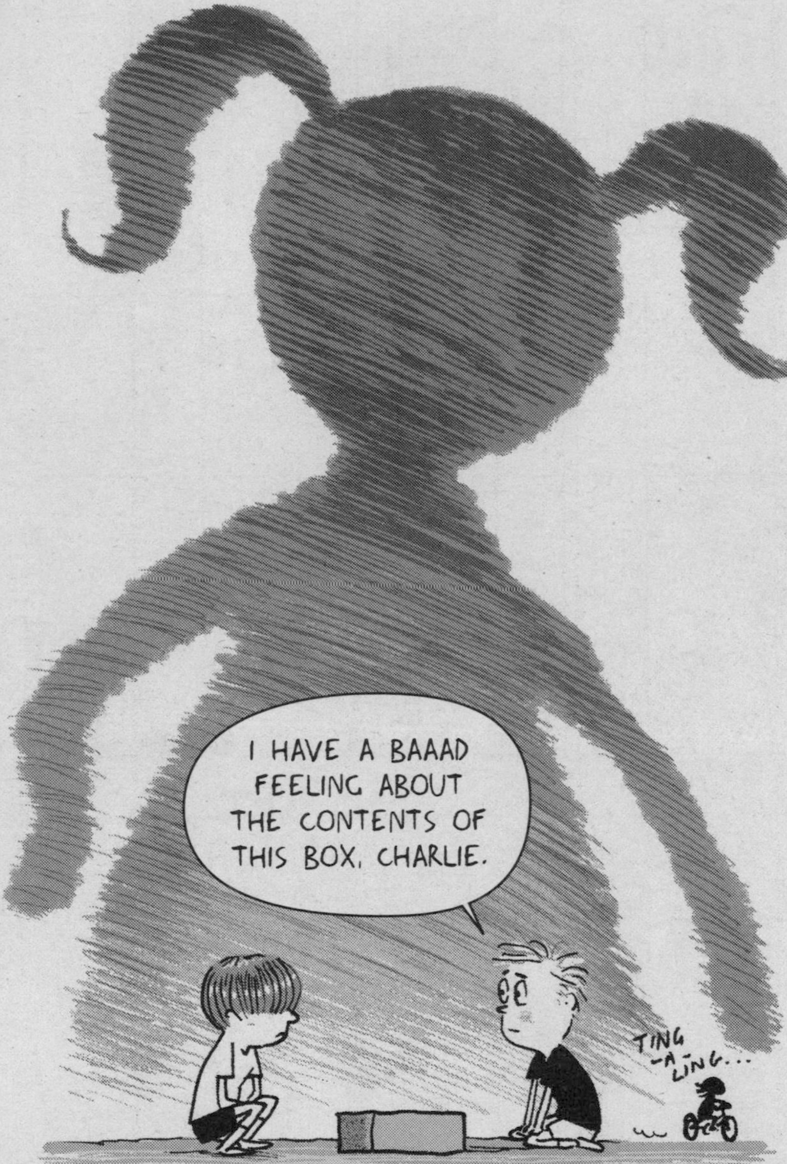
I HAVE A BAAAD FEELING ABOUT THE CONTENTS OF THIS BOX, CHARLIE.
TING -A- LING...

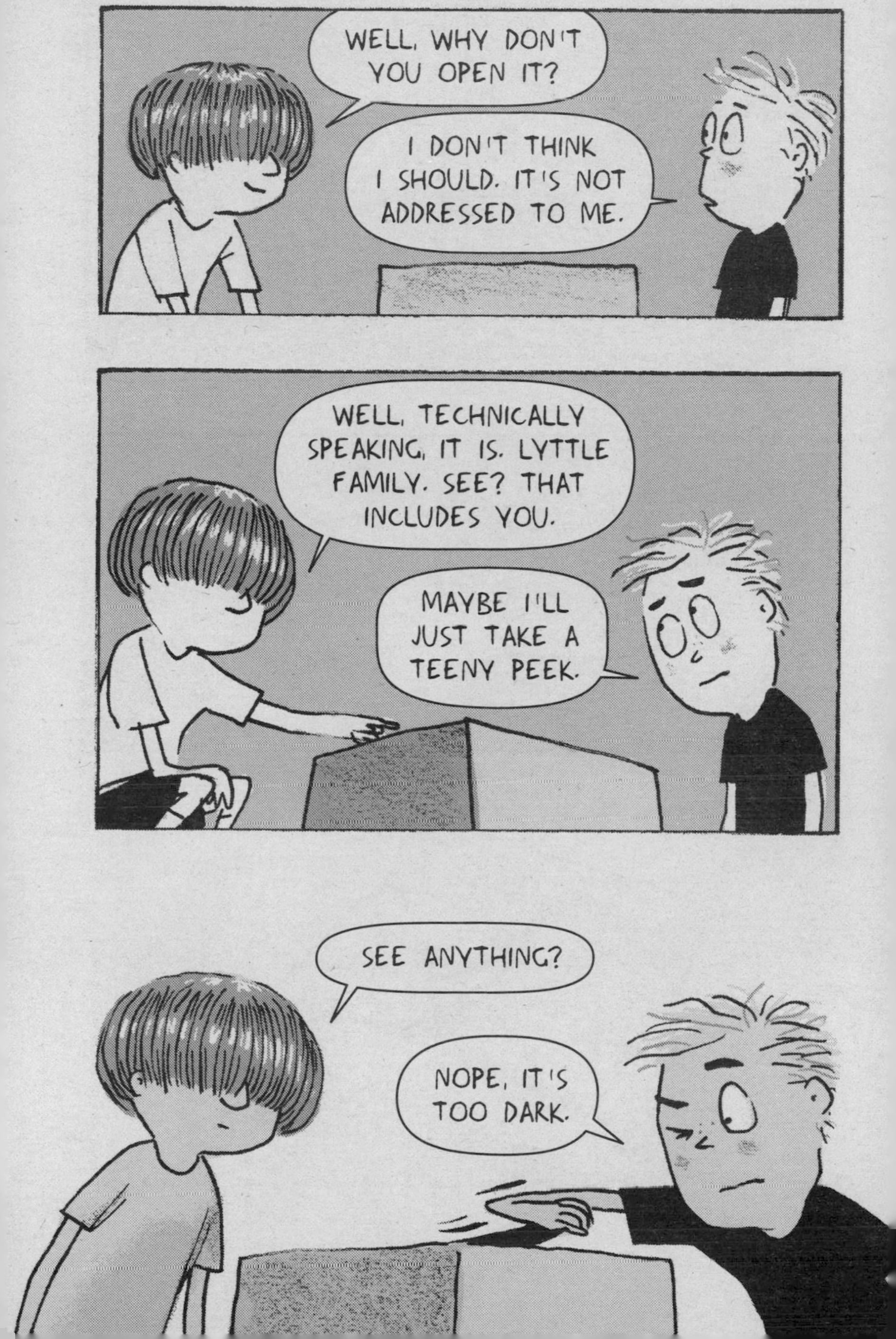
WELL, WHY DON'T YOU OPEN IT?
I DON'T THINK I SHOULD. IT'S NOT ADDRESSED TO ME.
WELL, TECHNICALLY SPEAKING, IT IS. LYTTLE FAMILY. SEE? THAT INCLUDES YOU.
MAYBE I'LL JUST TAKE A TEENY PEEK.
SEE ANYTHING?
NOPE, IT'S TOO DARK.

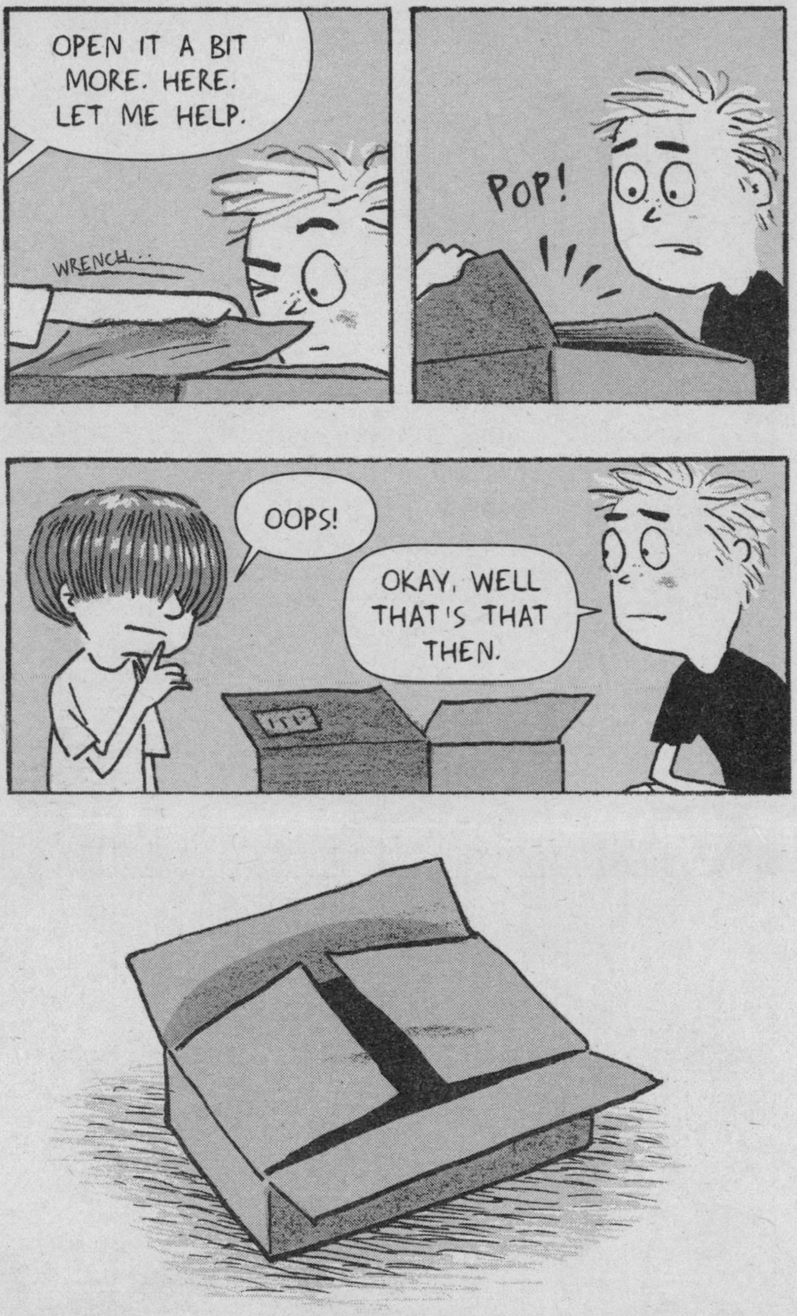
OPEN IT A BIT MORE. HERE. LET ME HELP.
WRENCH...
POP!
OOPS!
OKAY. WELL THAT'S THAT THEN.

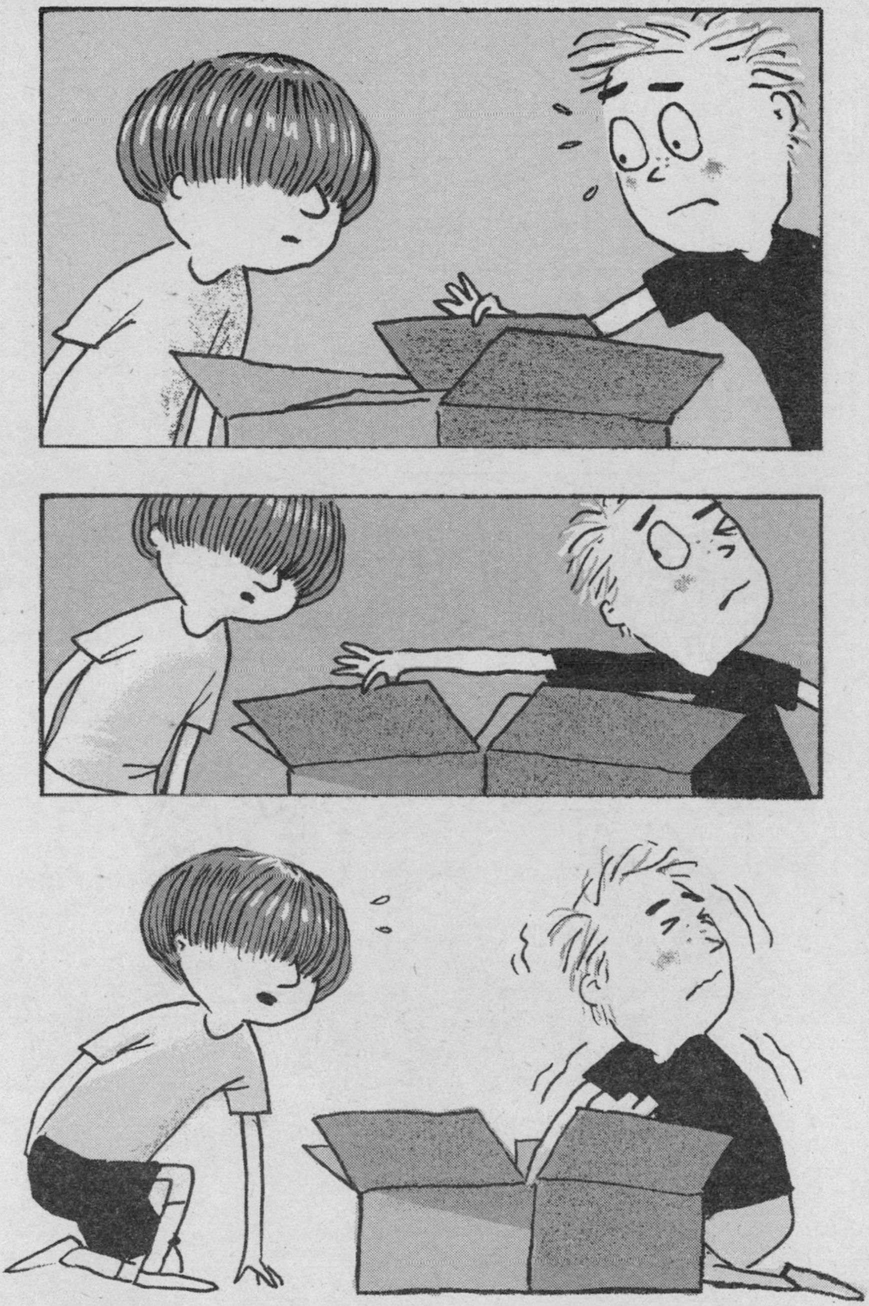

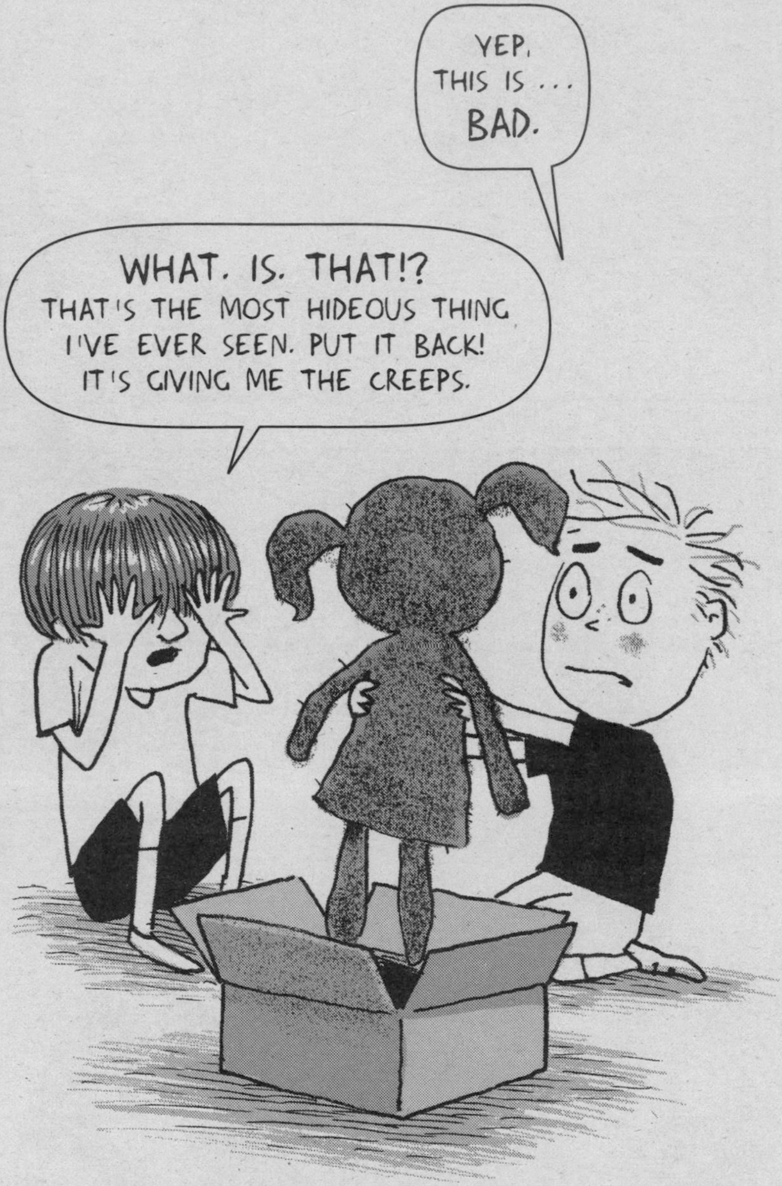
YEP. THIS IS . . . BAD.
WHAT. IS. THAT!? THAT'S THE MOST HIDEOUS THING I'VE EVER SEEN. PUT IT BACK! IT'S GIVING ME THE CREEPS.

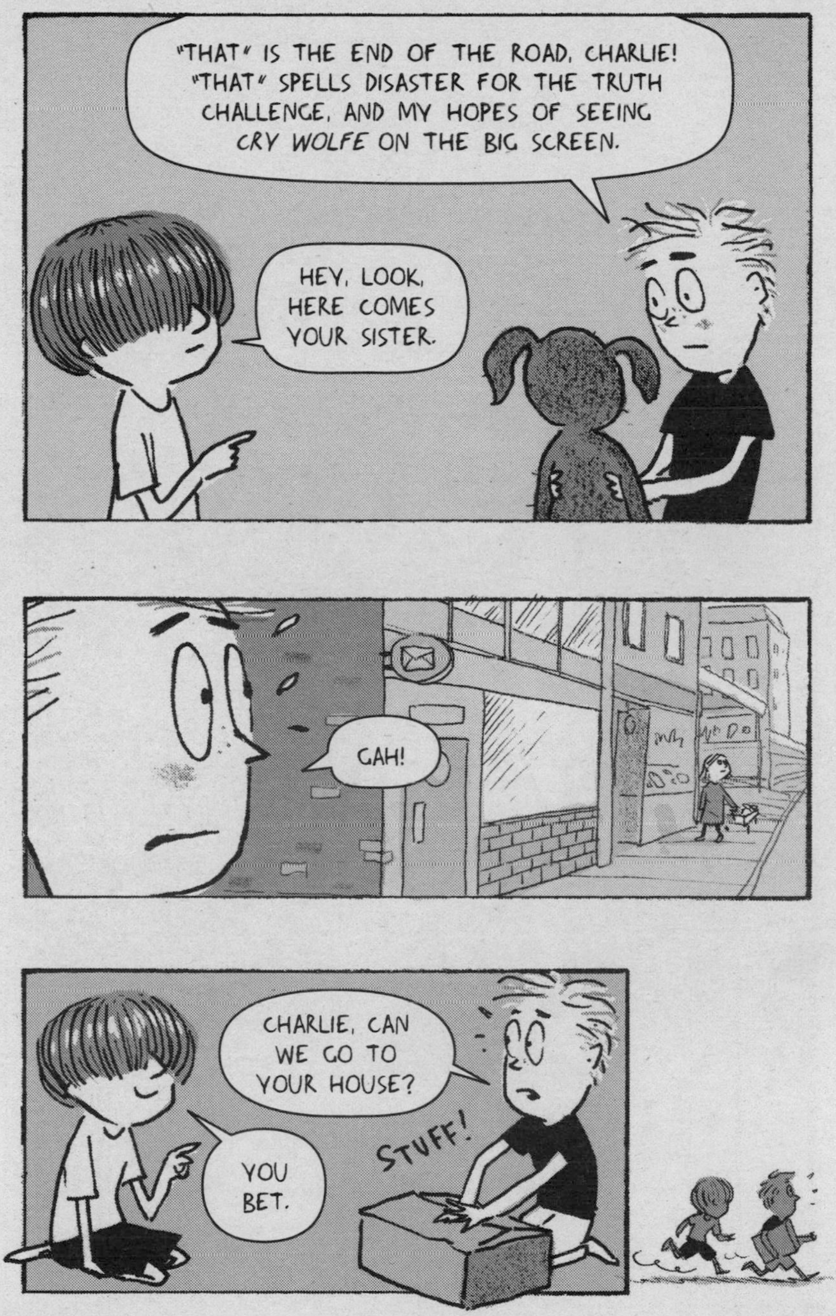
"THAT" IS THE END OF THE ROAD, CHARLIE! "THAT" SPELLS DISASTER FOR THE TRUTH CHALLENGE, AND MY HOPES OF SEEING CRY WOLFE ON THE BIG SCREEN.
HEY, LOOK, HERE COMES YOUR SISTER.
GAH!
CHARLIE, CAN WE GO TO YOUR HOUSE?
YOU BET.
STUFF!

CHARLIE'S BEDROOM.

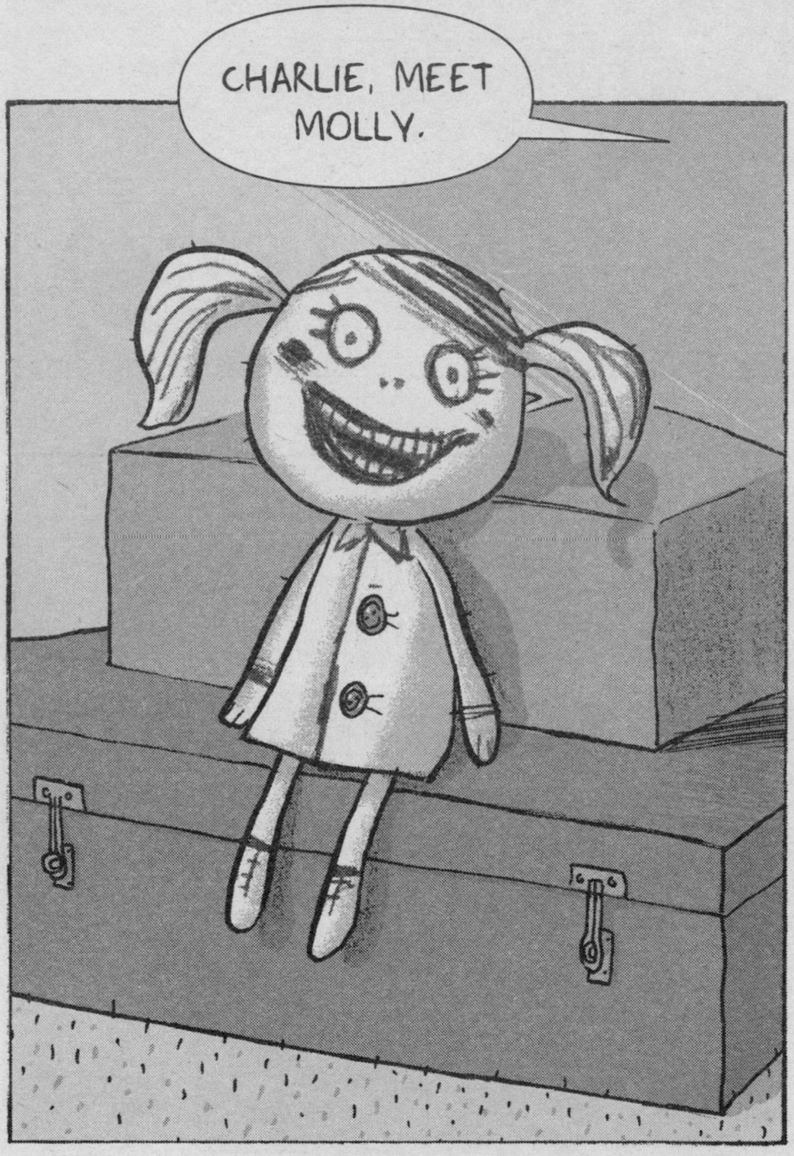
CHARLIE, MEET MOLLY.

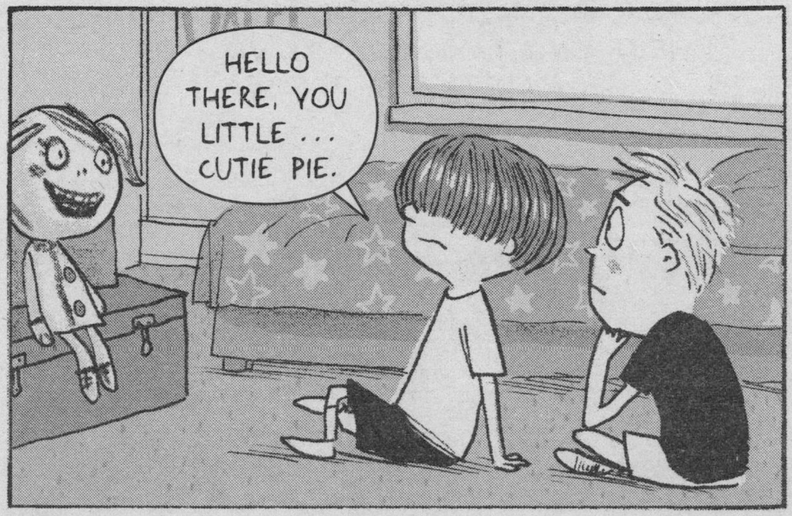
HELLO THERE, YOU LITTLE . . . CUTIE PIE.

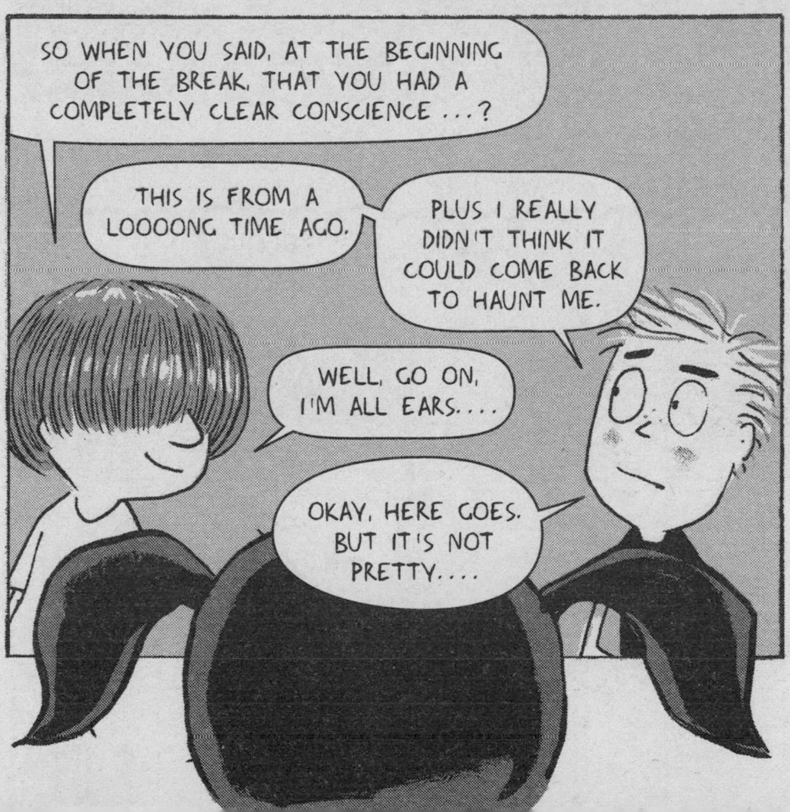
SO WHEN YOU SAID, AT THE BEGINNING OF THE BREAK, THAT YOU HAD A COMPLETELY CLEAR CONSCIENCE . . . ?
THIS IS FROM A LOOOONG TIME AGO.
PLUS I REALLY DIDN'T THINK IT COULD COME BACK TO HAUNT ME.
WELL, GO ON, I'M ALL EARS. . . .
OKAY, HERE GOES. BUT IT'S NOT PRETTY. . . .

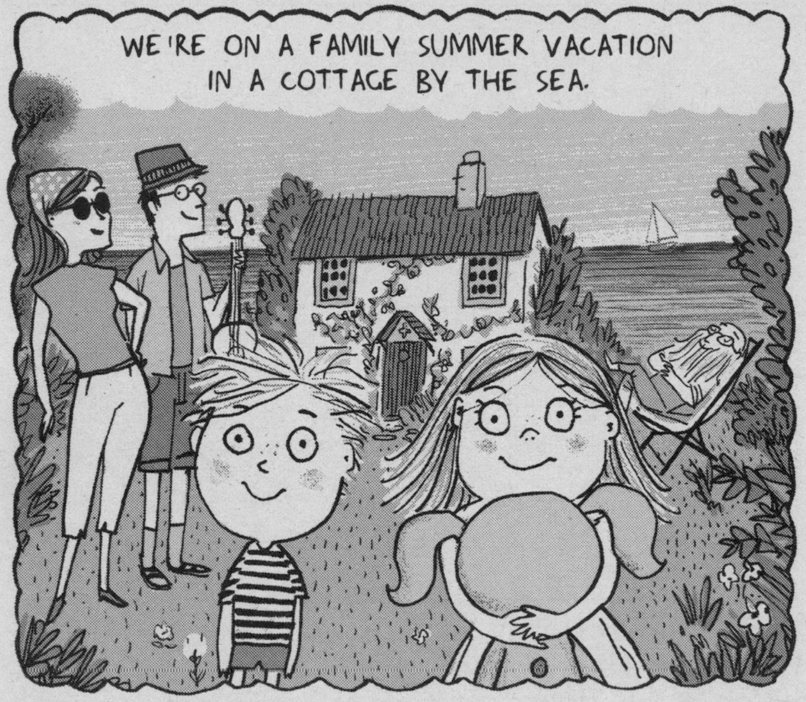
WE'RE ON A FAMILY SUMMER VACATION
IN A COTTAGE BY THE SEA.

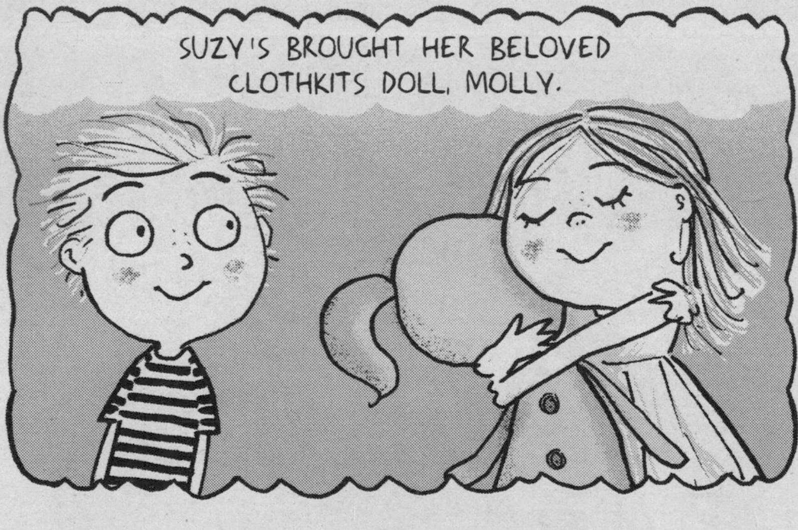
SUZY'S BROUGHT HER BELOVED
CLOTHKITS DOLL, MOLLY.

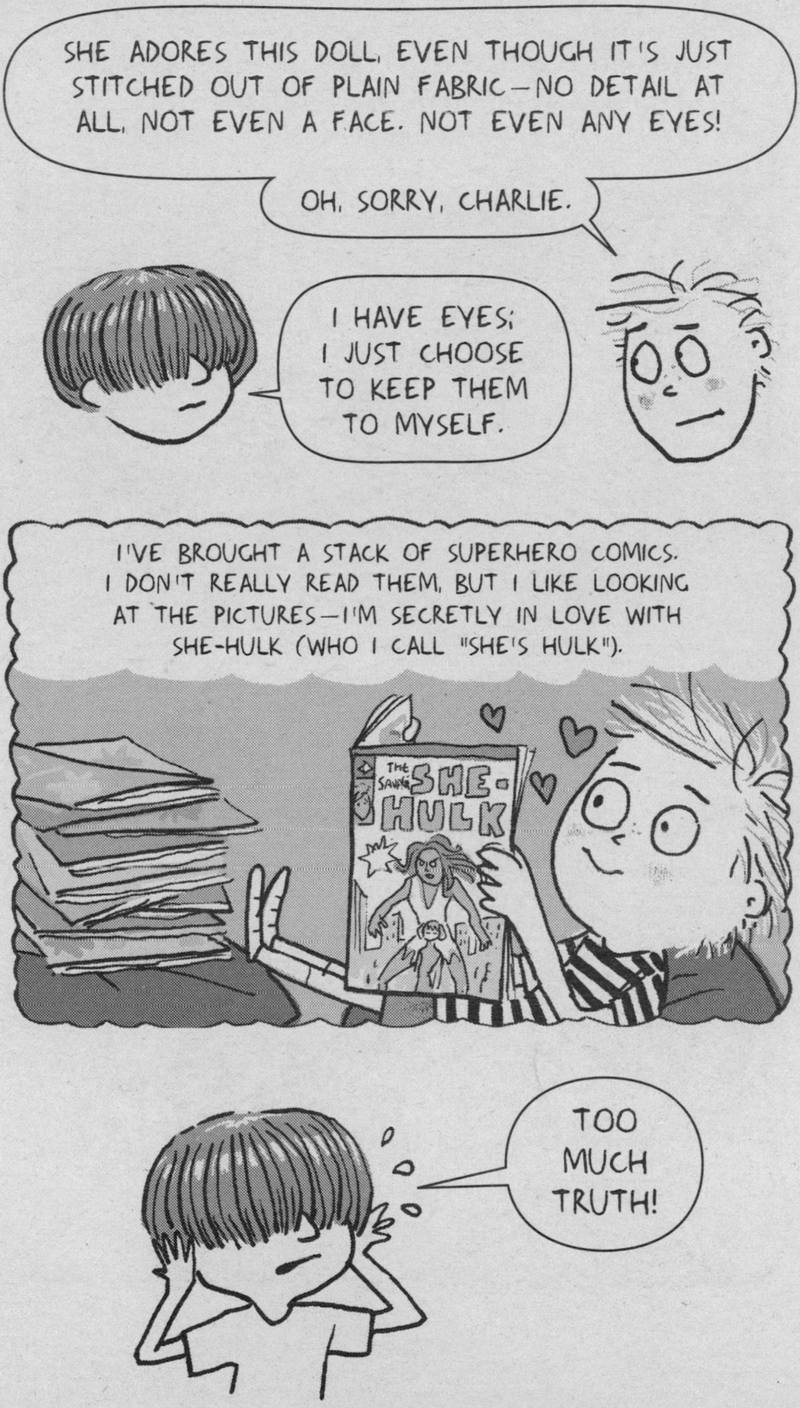
SHE ADORES THIS DOLL, EVEN THOUGH IT'S JUST STITCHED OUT OF PLAIN FABRIC—NO DETAIL AT ALL, NOT EVEN A FACE. NOT EVEN ANY EYES!
OH, SORRY, CHARLIE.
I HAVE EYES; I JUST CHOOSE TO KEEP THEM TO MYSELF.
I'VE BROUGHT A STACK OF SUPERHERO COMICS. I DON'T REALLY READ THEM, BUT I LIKE LOOKING AT THE PICTURES—I'M SECRETLY IN LOVE WITH SHE-HULK (WHO I CALL "SHE'S HULK").
SHE-HULK
TOO MUCH TRUTH!

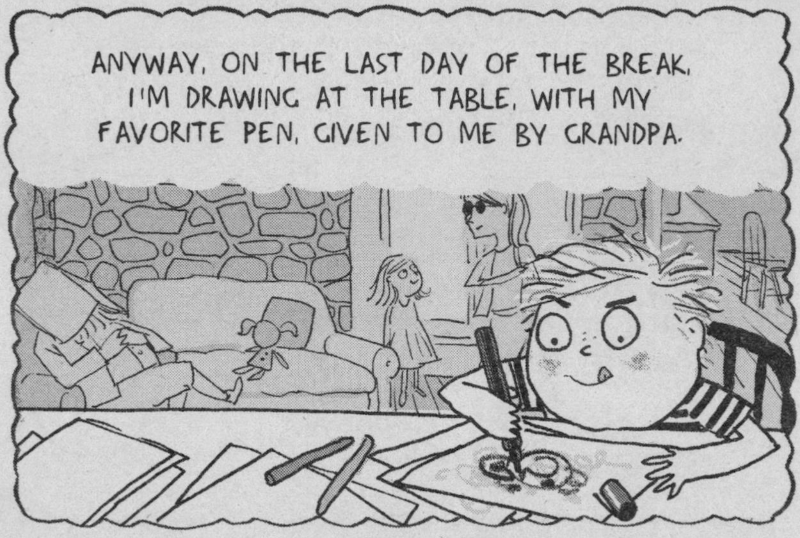
ANYWAY, ON THE LAST DAY OF THE BREAK, I'M DRAWING AT THE TABLE, WITH MY FAVORITE PEN, GIVEN TO ME BY GRANDPA.

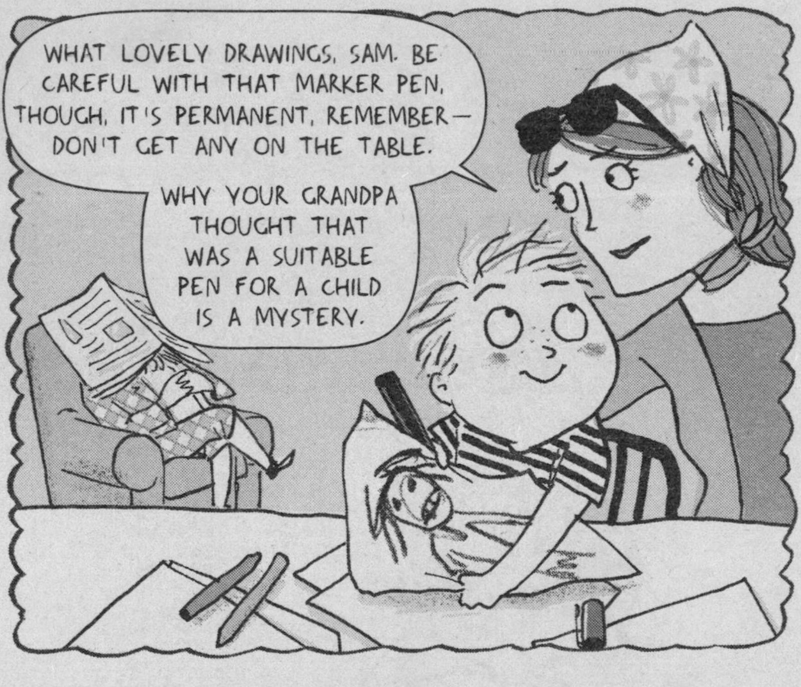
WHAT LOVELY DRAWINGS, SAM. BE CAREFUL WITH THAT MARKER PEN, THOUGH, IT'S PERMANENT, REMEMBER—DON'T GET ANY ON THE TABLE.
WHY YOUR GRANDPA THOUGHT THAT WAS A SUITABLE PEN FOR A CHILD IS A MYSTERY.

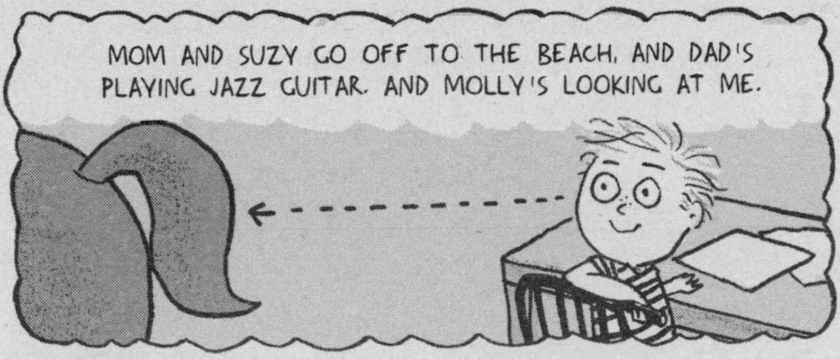
MOM AND SUZY GO OFF TO THE BEACH, AND DAD'S PLAYING JAZZ GUITAR. AND MOLLY'S LOOKING AT ME.

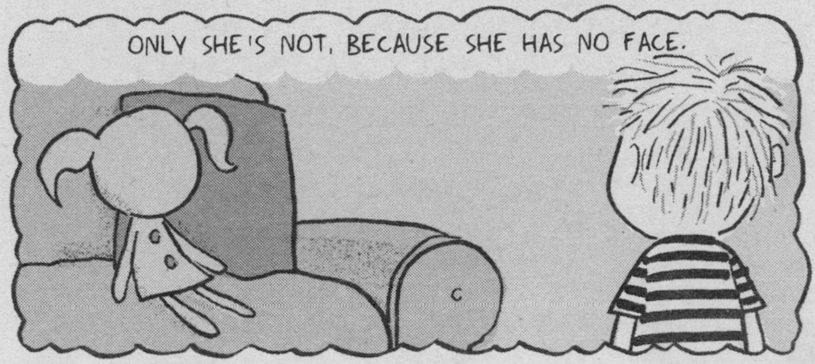
ONLY SHE'S NOT, BECAUSE SHE HAS NO FACE.

AND I SUDDENLY HAVE A BRILLIANT IDEA.

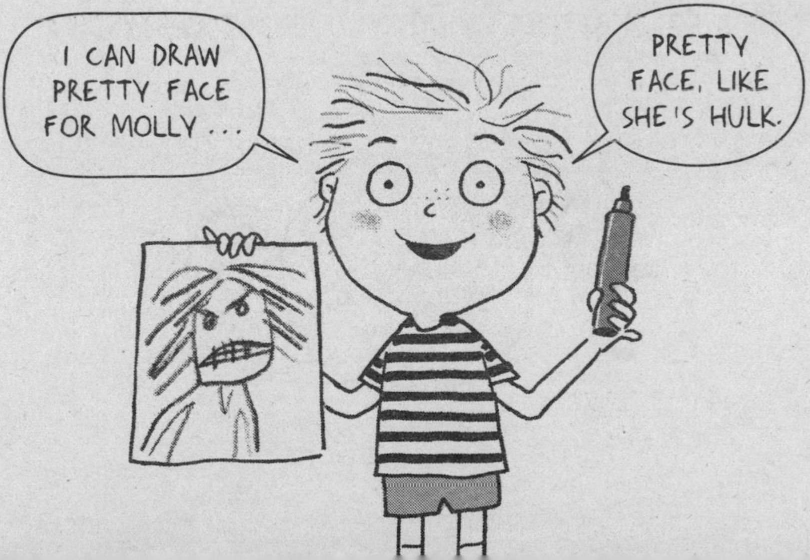
I CAN DRAW PRETTY FACE FOR MOLLY . . .
PRETTY FACE, LIKE SHE'S HULK.

IT'S POSSIBLE I HAVE AN INFLATED
SENSE OF MY ARTISTIC ABILITY....

I'M NOT TOTALLY HAPPY WITH THE SMILE—
SO I HAVE ANOTHER GO AT THE MOUTH....

THEN THE EYES SEEM A BIT PENSIVE, SO I ADD
A BIT MORE LIFE TO THEM, AND THE CHEEKS....

AND THEN I THINK MAYBE THE FACE IS NOW A LITTLE OUT OF KEEPING WITH THE REST OF THE DOLL, SO I ADD A BIT OF DETAIL TO MAKE IT ALL FIT....

Sam Lyttle

All artistic commissions undertaken

No job too ambitious!

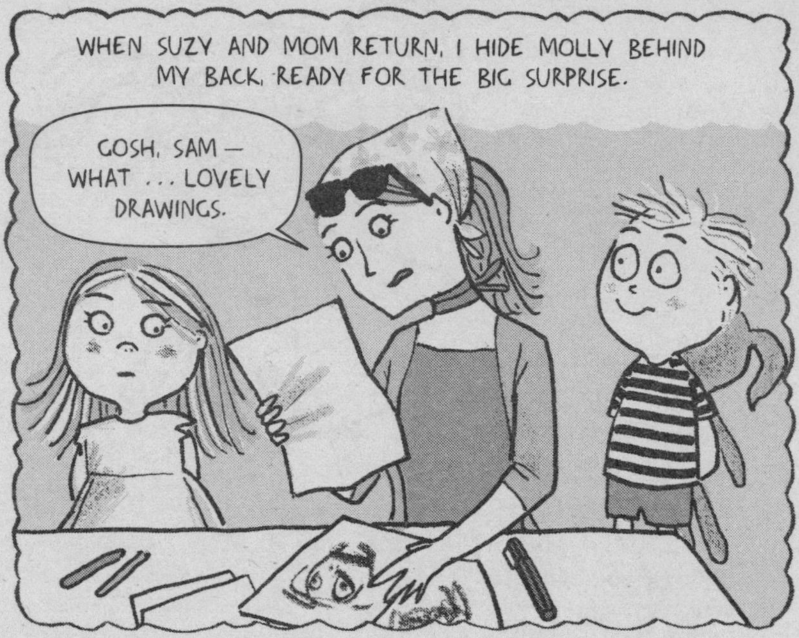
WHEN SUZY AND MOM RETURN, I HIDE MOLLY BEHIND MY BACK, READY FOR THE BIG SURPRISE.
GOSH, SAM — WHAT . . . LOVELY DRAWINGS.

AND I SAY . . .

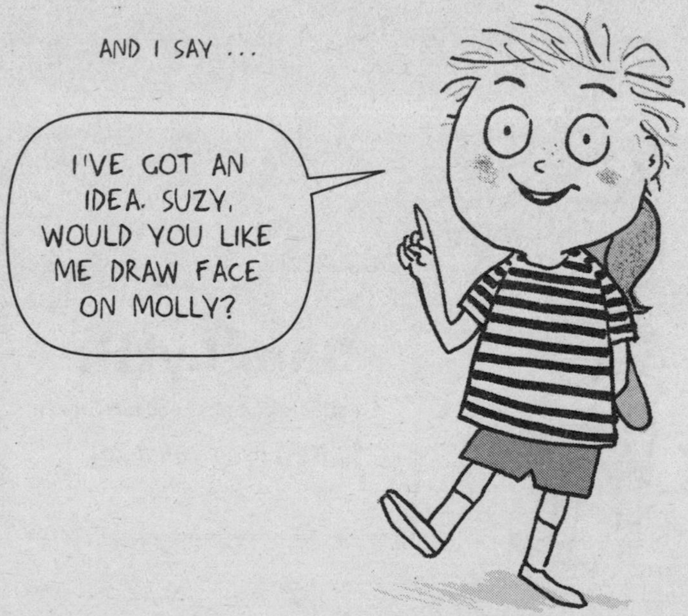
I'VE GOT AN IDEA. SUZY, WOULD YOU LIKE ME DRAW FACE ON MOLLY?

AND SUZY SAYS ...

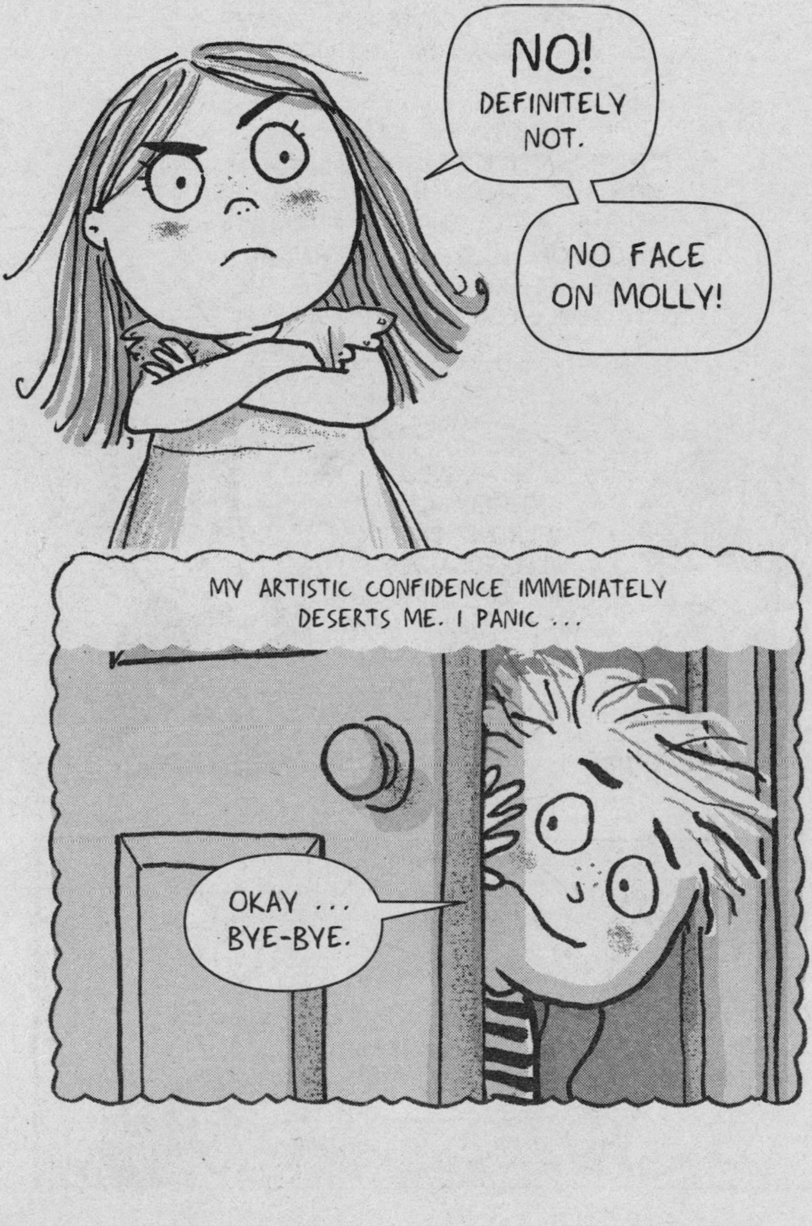
NO!
DEFINITELY NOT.
NO FACE ON MOLLY!
MY ARTISTIC CONFIDENCE IMMEDIATELY DESERTS ME. I PANIC ...
OKAY ... BYE-BYE.

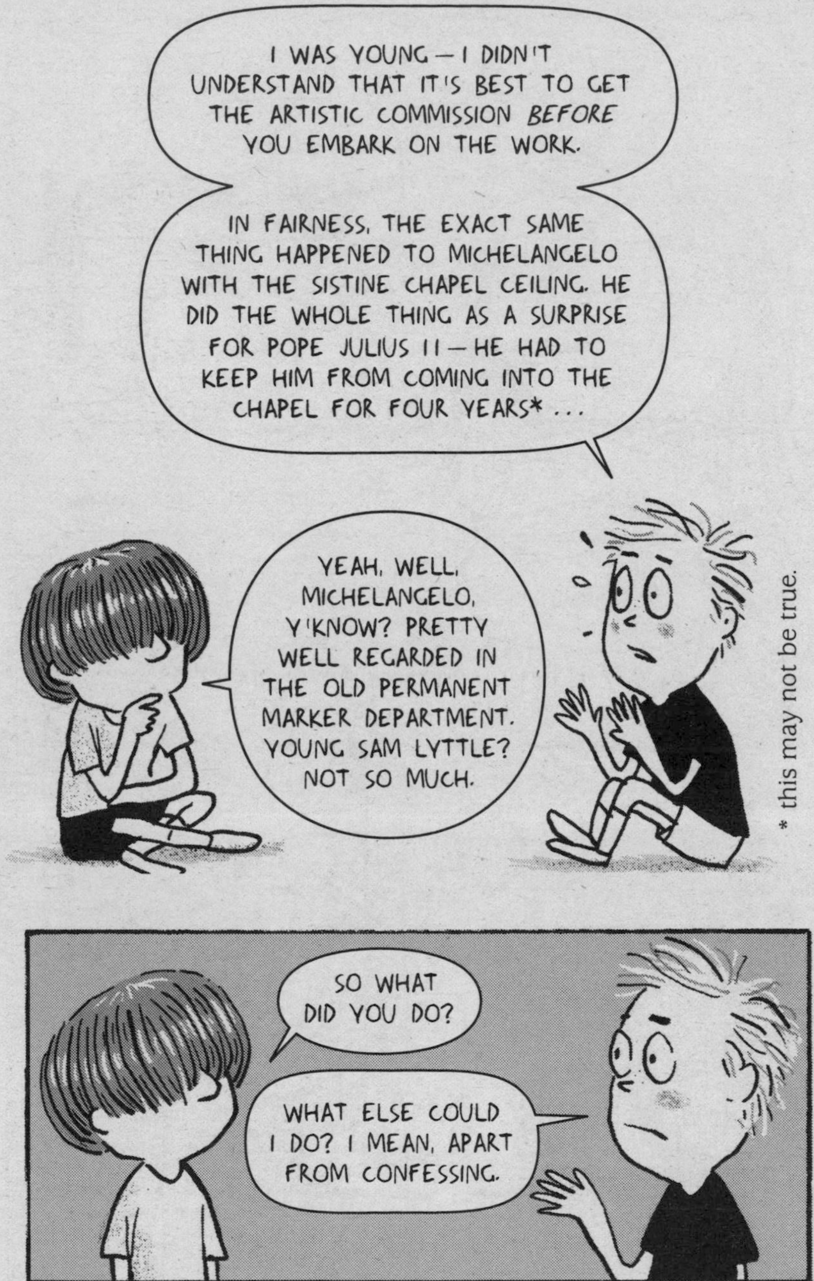
I WAS YOUNG — I DIDN'T UNDERSTAND THAT IT'S BEST TO GET THE ARTISTIC COMMISSION *BEFORE* YOU EMBARK ON THE WORK.
IN FAIRNESS, THE EXACT SAME THING HAPPENED TO MICHELANGELO WITH THE SISTINE CHAPEL CEILING. HE DID THE WHOLE THING AS A SURPRISE FOR POPE JULIUS II — HE HAD TO KEEP HIM FROM COMING INTO THE CHAPEL FOR FOUR YEARS* ...
YEAH, WELL, MICHELANGELO, Y'KNOW? PRETTY WELL REGARDED IN THE OLD PERMANENT MARKER DEPARTMENT. YOUNG SAM LYTTLE? NOT SO MUCH.
* this may not be true.
SO WHAT DID YOU DO?
WHAT ELSE COULD I DO? I MEAN, APART FROM CONFESSING.

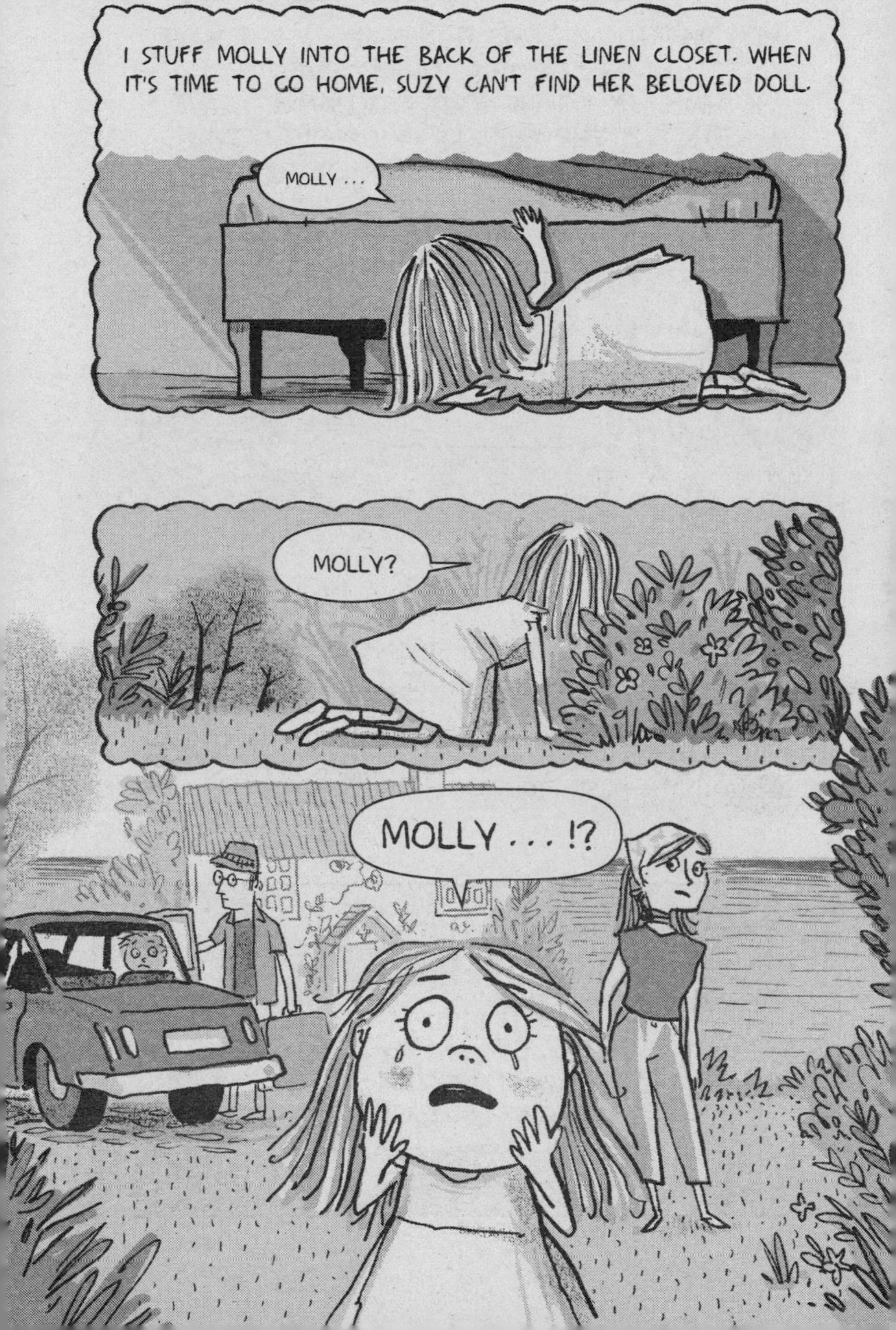
I STUFF MOLLY INTO THE BACK OF THE LINEN CLOSET. WHEN IT'S TIME TO GO HOME, SUZY CAN'T FIND HER BELOVED DOLL.
MOLLY . . .
MOLLY?
MOLLY . . . !?

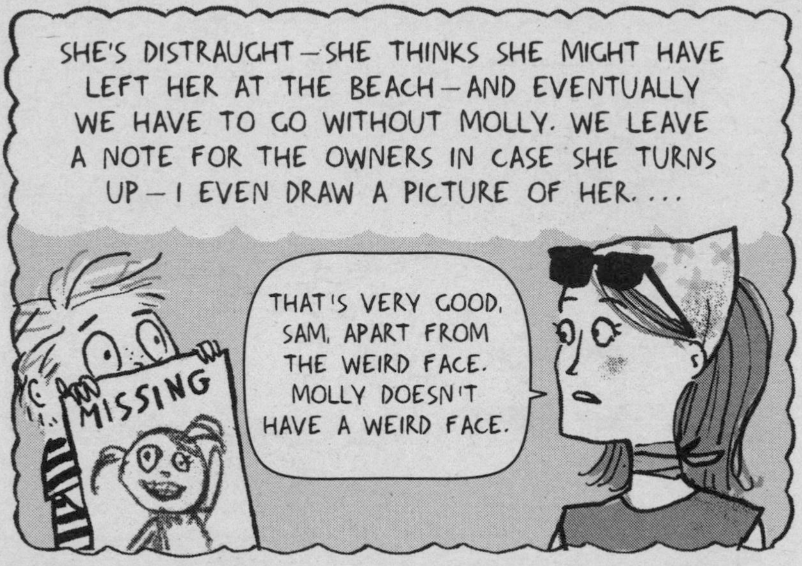
SHE'S DISTRAUGHT—SHE THINKS SHE MIGHT HAVE LEFT HER AT THE BEACH—AND EVENTUALLY WE HAVE TO GO WITHOUT MOLLY. WE LEAVE A NOTE FOR THE OWNERS IN CASE SHE TURNS UP—I EVEN DRAW A PICTURE OF HER. . . .
MISSING
THAT'S VERY GOOD, SAM, APART FROM THE WEIRD FACE. MOLLY DOESN'T HAVE A WEIRD FACE.

Over time, Suzy forgot about Molly, and no one ever suspected I had anything to do with the disappearance—I gradually buried the awful thing I did in the deepest recesses of my mind. And now, like a ghost from the past, Molly has found her way home.

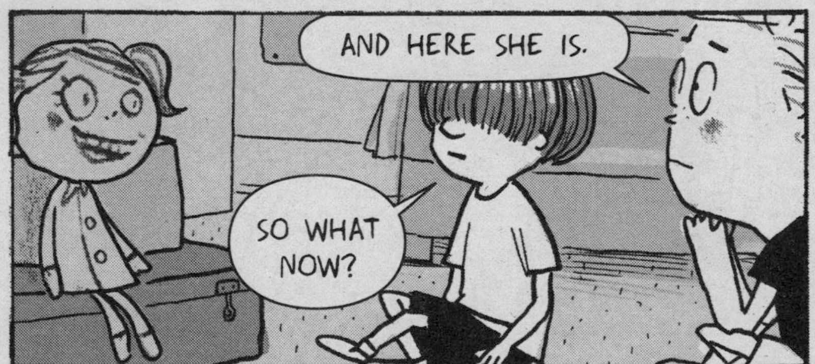
AND HERE SHE IS.
SO WHAT NOW?

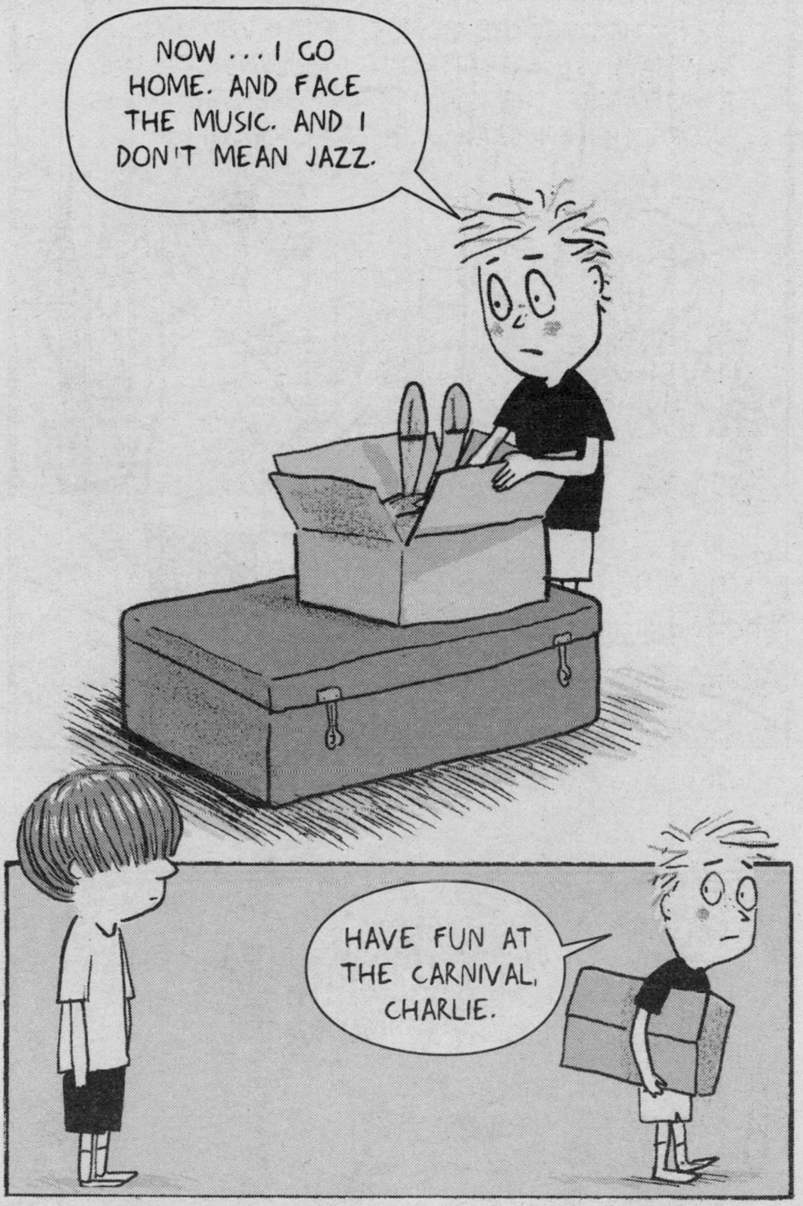
NOW ... I GO HOME. AND FACE THE MUSIC. AND I DON'T MEAN JAZZ.
HAVE FUN AT THE CARNIVAL, CHARLIE.

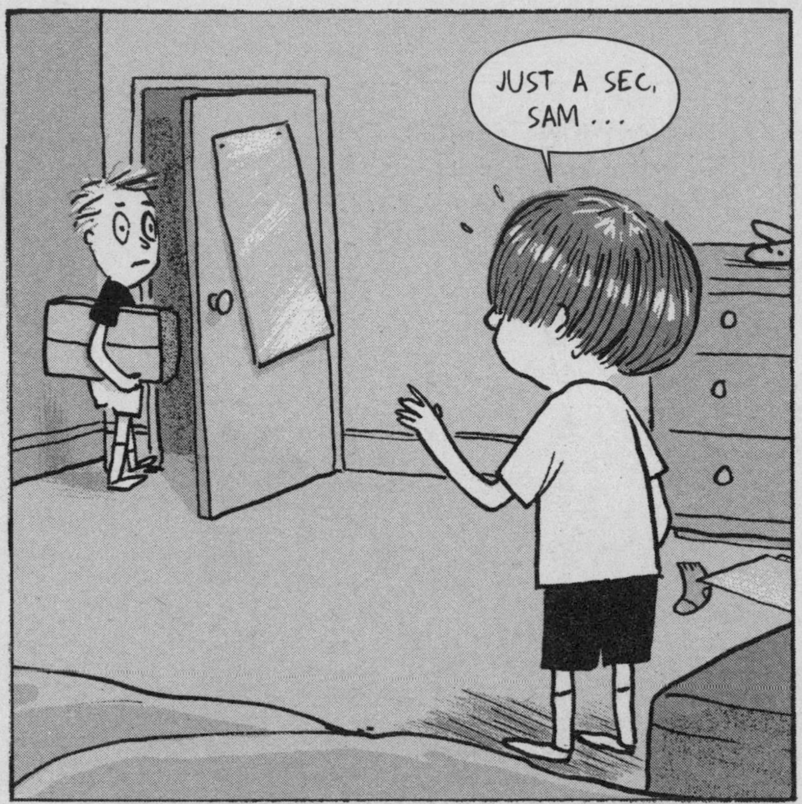
JUST A SEC, SAM . . .

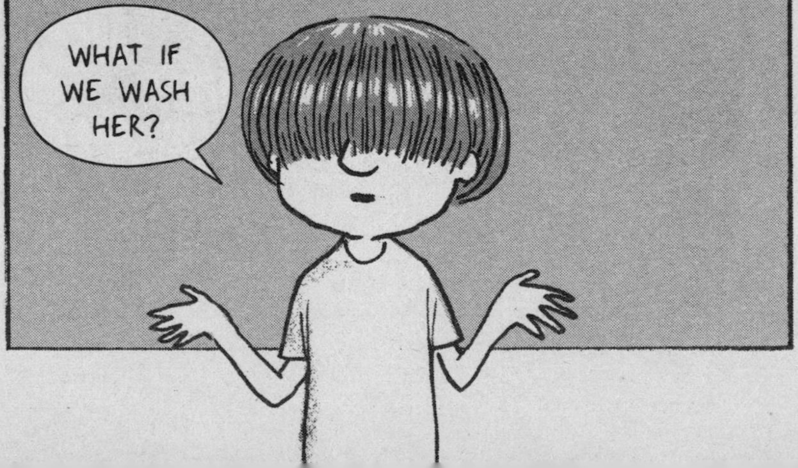
WHAT IF WE WASH HER?

I KNOW HOW TO WORK THE MACHINE. AND THE DRYER. MY MOM GETS ME TO HELP WITH THE WASHING SOMETIMES.
THAT'S GOING TO TAKE AGES . . . AND, ANYWAY, IT'S PERMANENT MARKER.

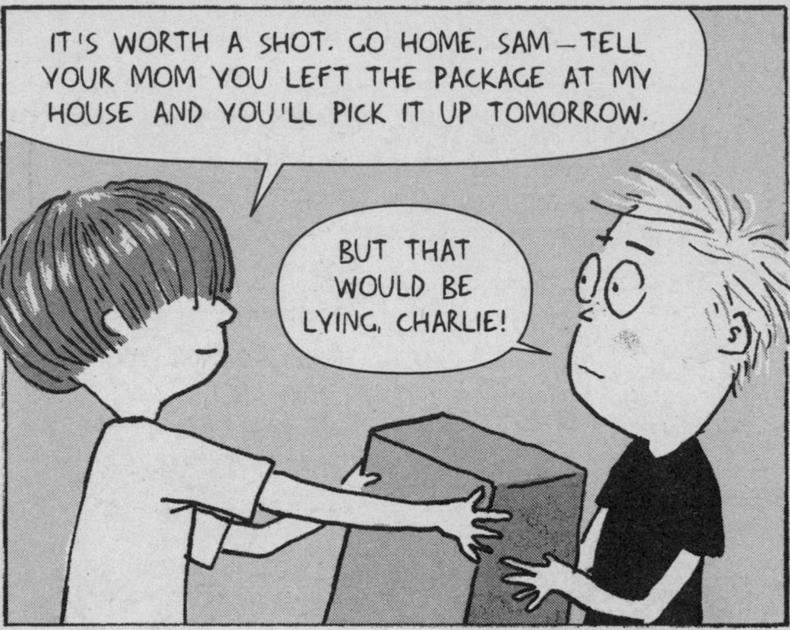
IT'S WORTH A SHOT. GO HOME, SAM—TELL YOUR MOM YOU LEFT THE PACKAGE AT MY HOUSE AND YOU'LL PICK IT UP TOMORROW.
BUT THAT WOULD BE LYING, CHARLIE!

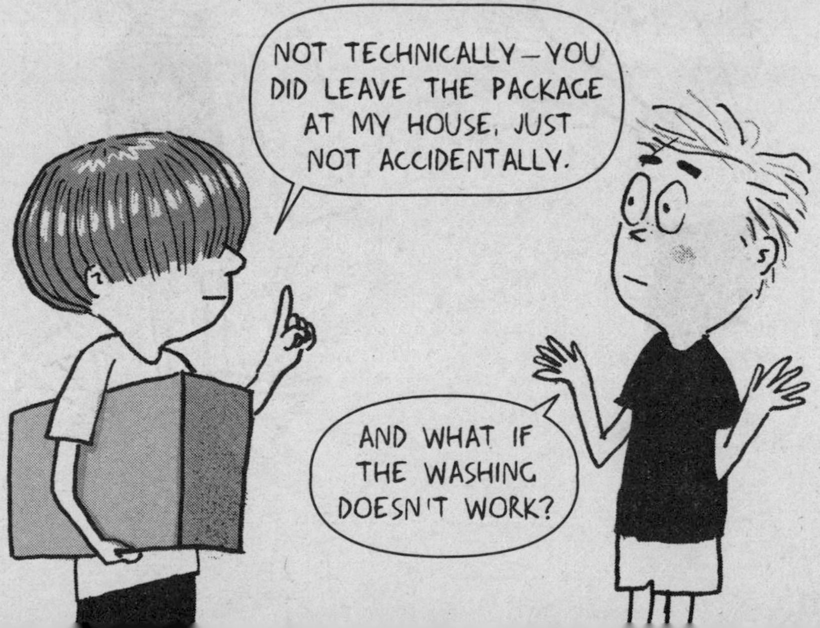
NOT TECHNICALLY—YOU DID LEAVE THE PACKAGE AT MY HOUSE, JUST NOT ACCIDENTALLY.
AND WHAT IF THE WASHING DOESN'T WORK?

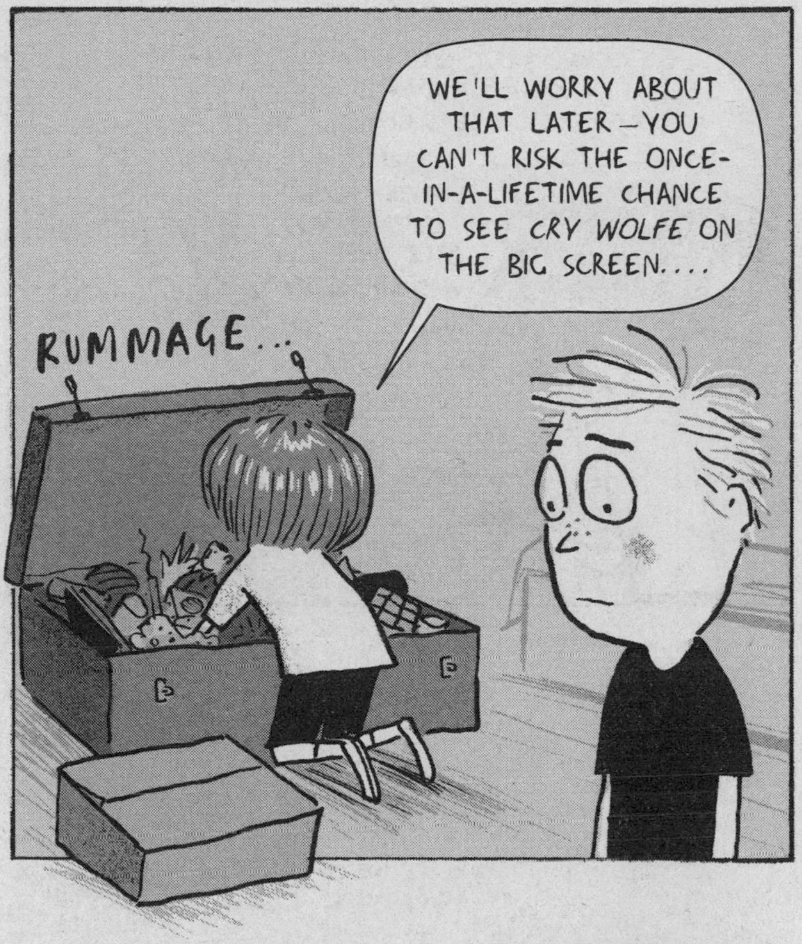
WE'LL WORRY ABOUT THAT LATER—YOU CAN'T RISK THE ONCE-IN-A-LIFETIME CHANCE TO SEE *CRY WOLFE* ON THE BIG SCREEN. . . .
RUMMAGE . . .

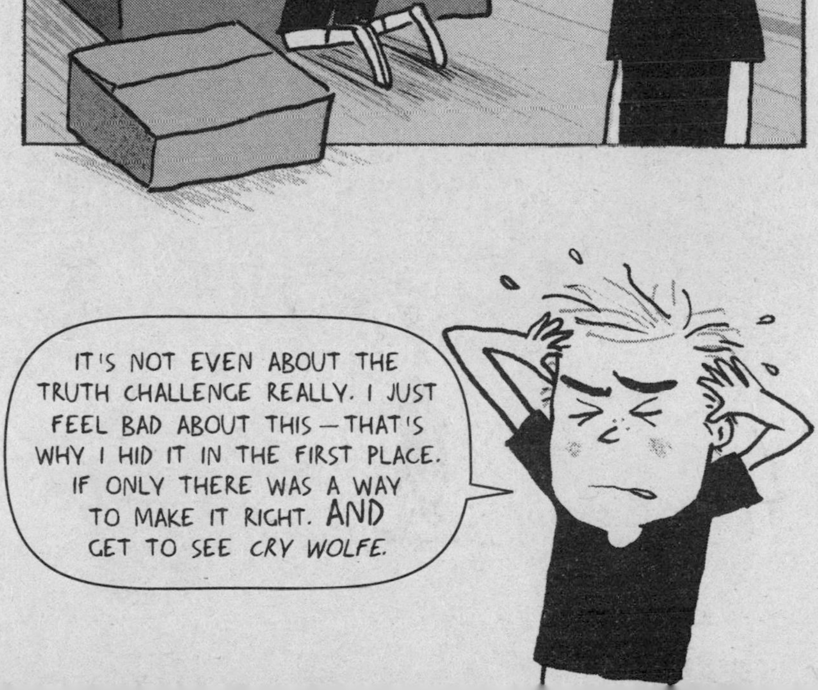
IT'S NOT EVEN ABOUT THE TRUTH CHALLENGE REALLY. I JUST FEEL BAD ABOUT THIS—THAT'S WHY I HID IT IN THE FIRST PLACE. IF ONLY THERE WAS A WAY TO MAKE IT RIGHT. AND GET TO SEE *CRY WOLFE*.

GO, QUICKLY! I'VE GOT TO GET HER WASHED AND DRIED BEFORE MY MOM GETS HOME.
TAKE THIS WALKIE-TALKIE— I'LL BUZZ YOU LATER ONCE I'VE WASHED MOLLY.

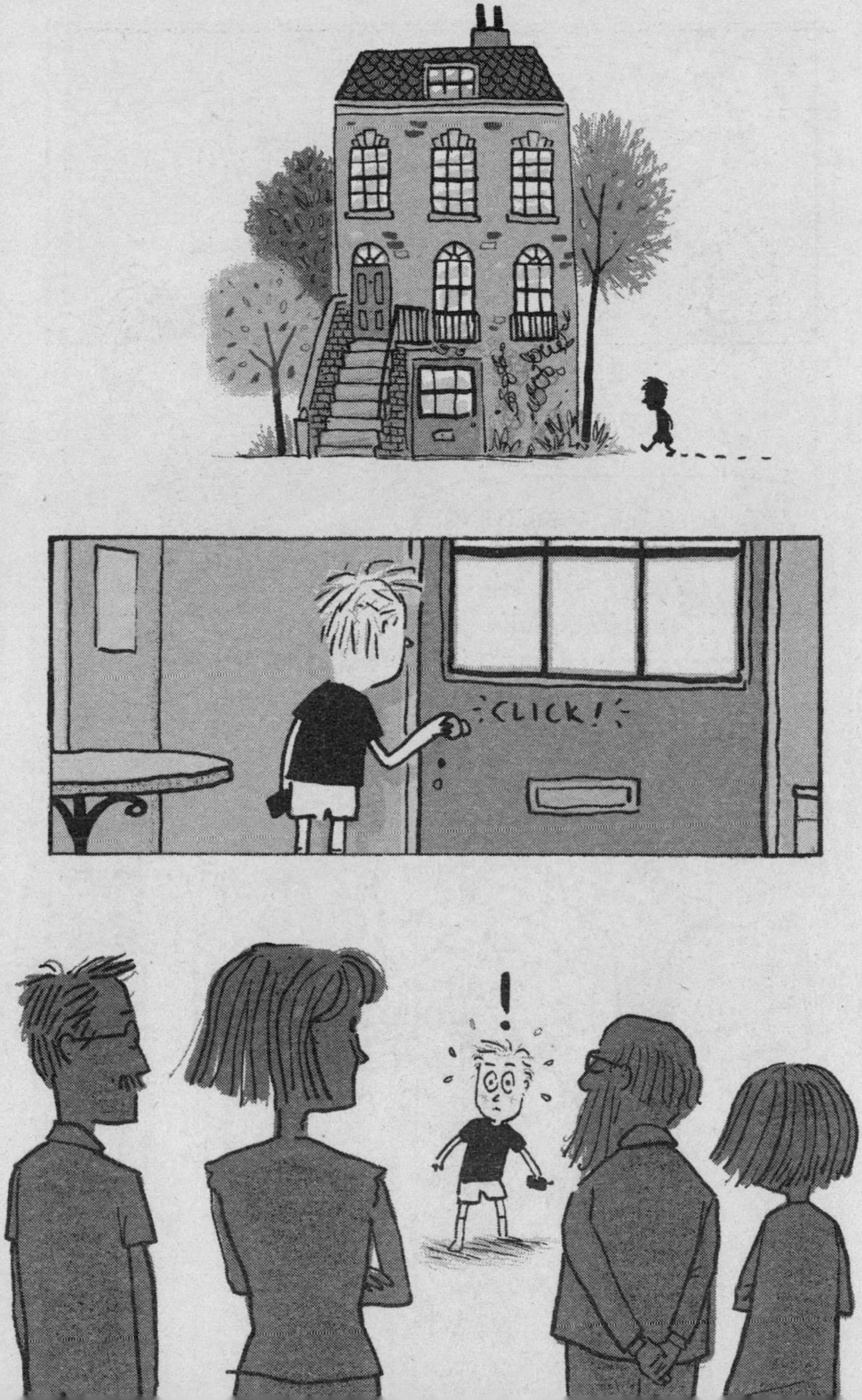
CLICK!
!

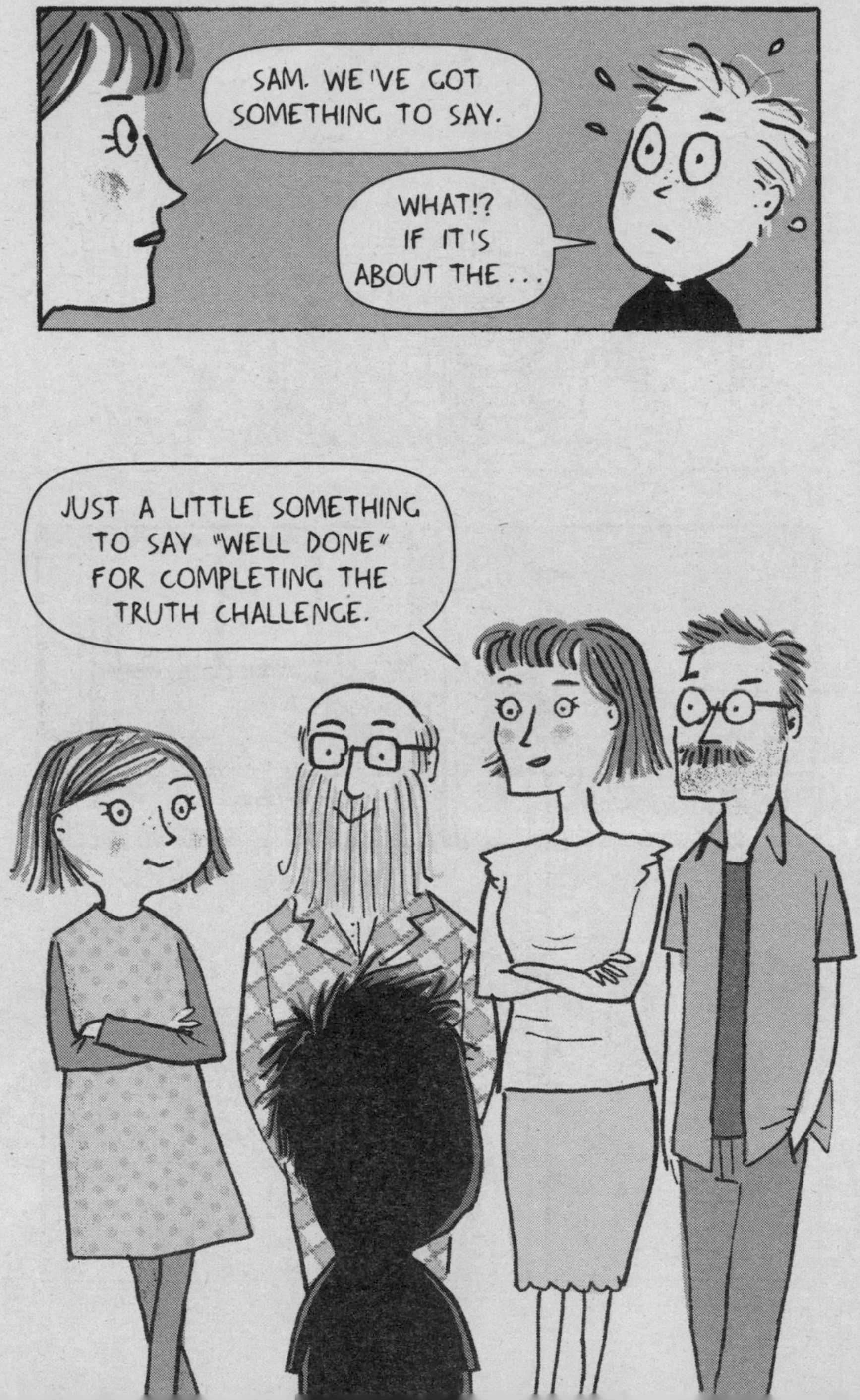
SAM. WE'VE GOT SOMETHING TO SAY.
WHAT!? IF IT'S ABOUT THE . . .
JUST A LITTLE SOMETHING TO SAY "WELL DONE" FOR COMPLETING THE TRUTH CHALLENGE.

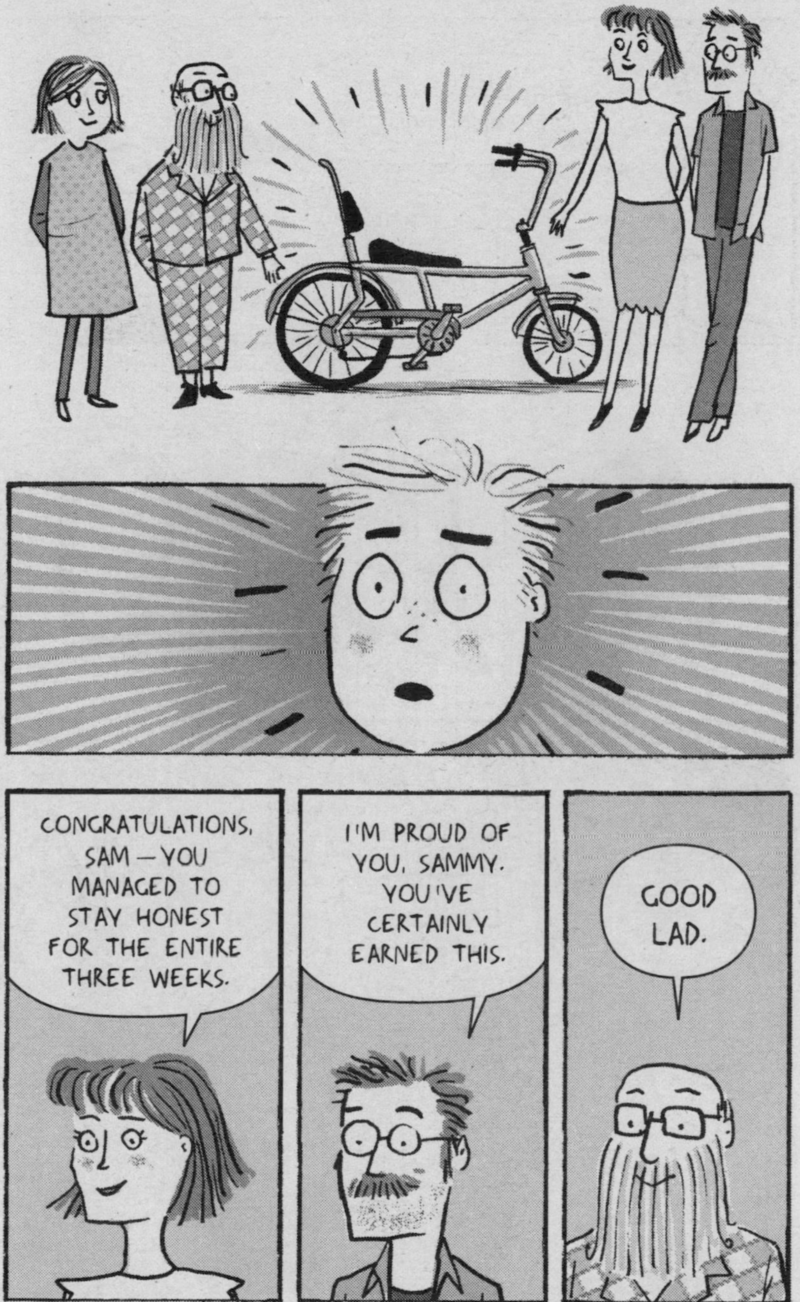
CONGRATULATIONS, SAM — YOU MANAGED TO STAY HONEST FOR THE ENTIRE THREE WEEKS.
I'M PROUD OF YOU, SAMMY. YOU'VE CERTAINLY EARNED THIS.
GOOD LAD.

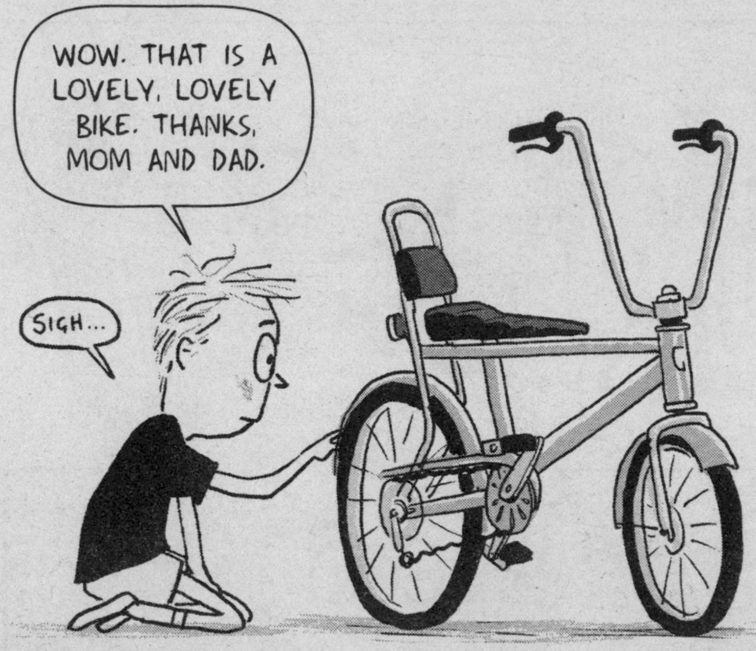
WOW. THAT IS A LOVELY, LOVELY BIKE. THANKS, MOM AND DAD.
SIGH...

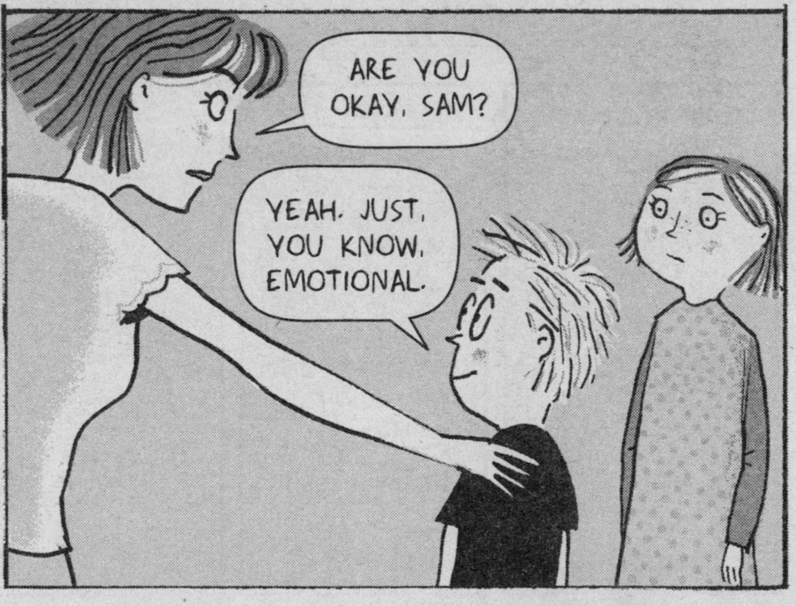
ARE YOU OKAY, SAM?
YEAH. JUST, YOU KNOW, EMOTIONAL.

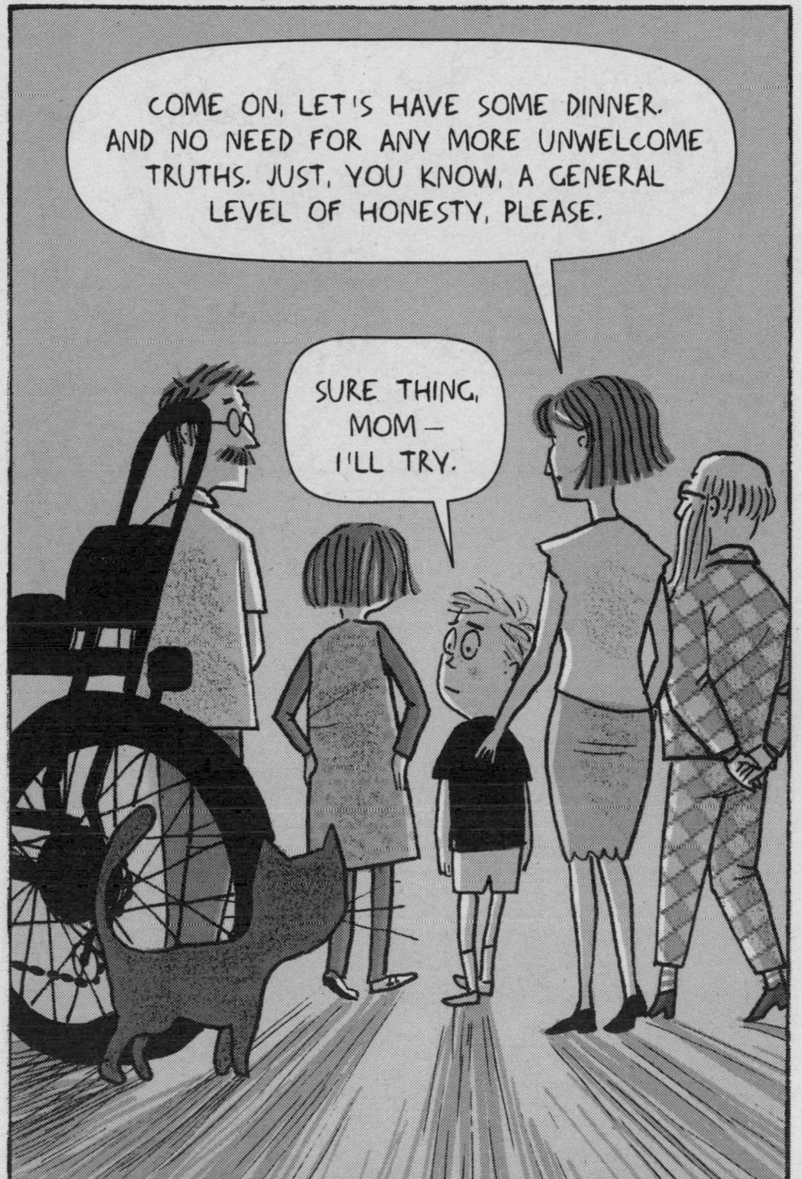
COME ON, LET'S HAVE SOME DINNER. AND NO NEED FOR ANY MORE UNWELCOME TRUTHS. JUST, YOU KNOW, A GENERAL LEVEL OF HONESTY, PLEASE.
SURE THING, MOM— I'LL TRY.

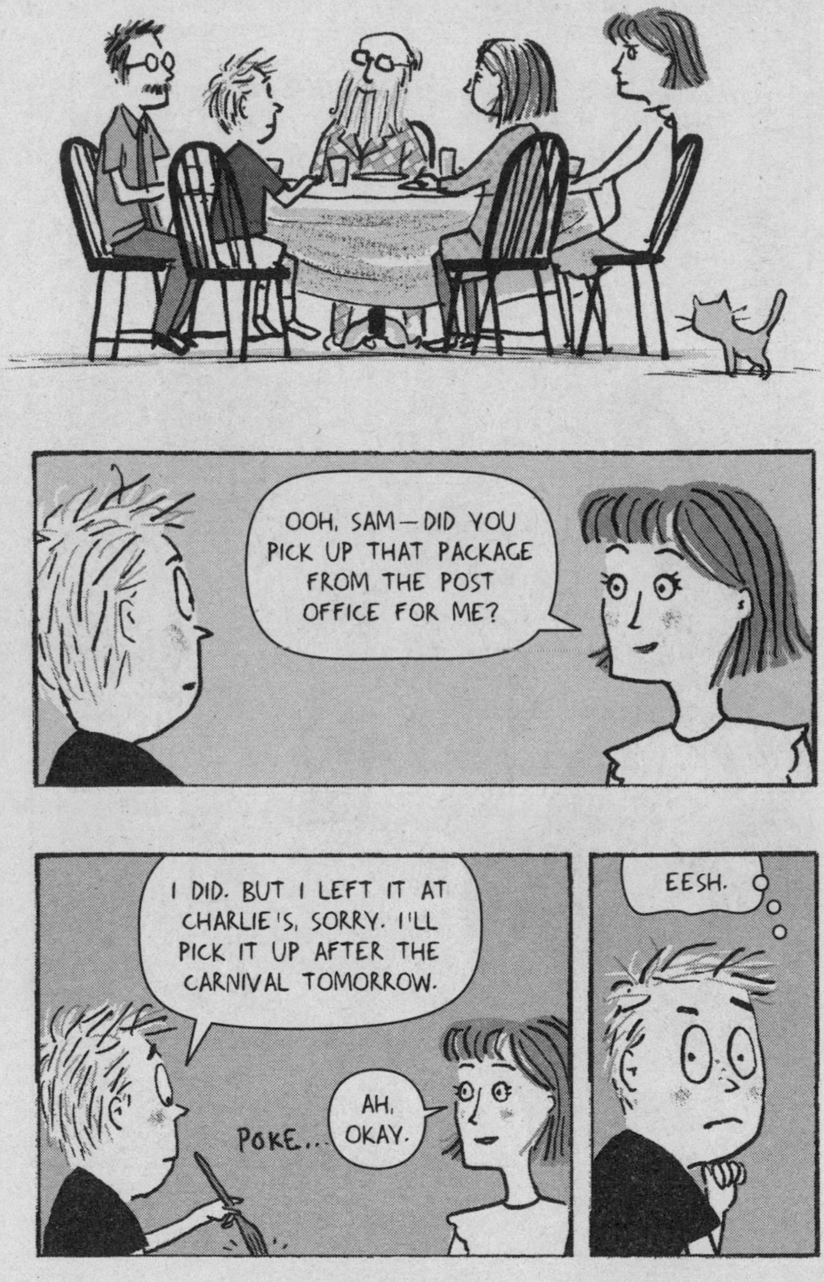
OOH, SAM—DID YOU PICK UP THAT PACKAGE FROM THE POST OFFICE FOR ME?
I DID. BUT I LEFT IT AT CHARLIE'S, SORRY. I'LL PICK IT UP AFTER THE CARNIVAL TOMORROW.
POKE...
AH, OKAY.
EESH.

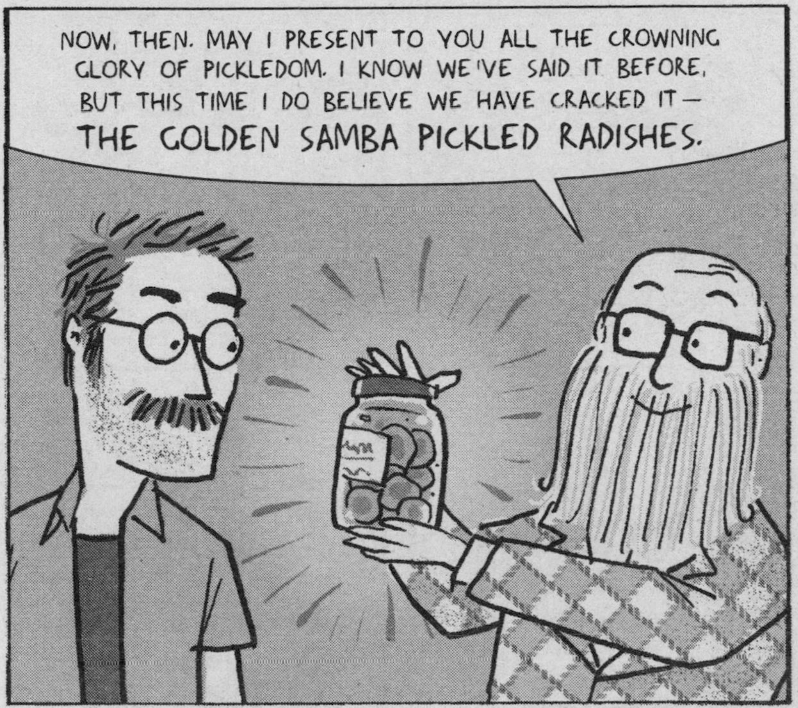
NOW, THEN. MAY I PRESENT TO YOU ALL THE CROWNING GLORY OF PICKLEDOM. I KNOW WE'VE SAID IT BEFORE, BUT THIS TIME I DO BELIEVE WE HAVE CRACKED IT—
THE GOLDEN SAMBA PICKLED RADISHES.

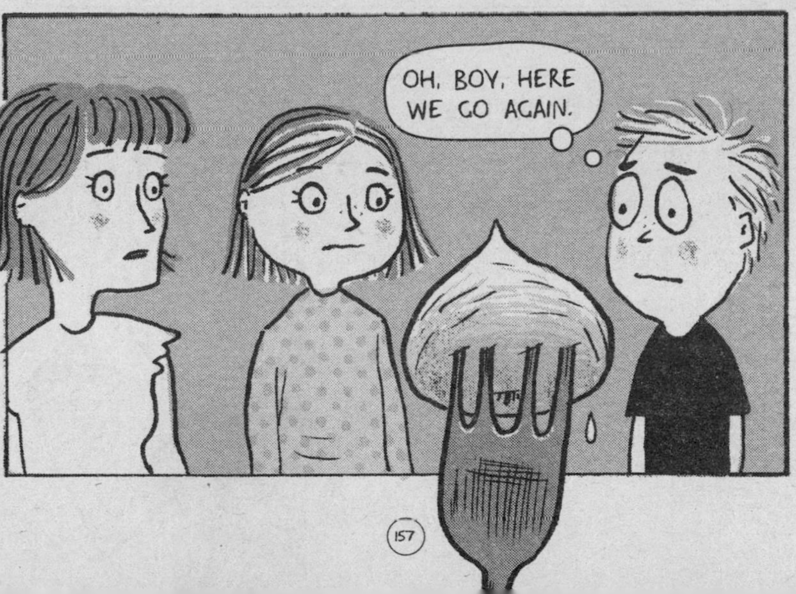
OH, BOY, HERE WE GO AGAIN.

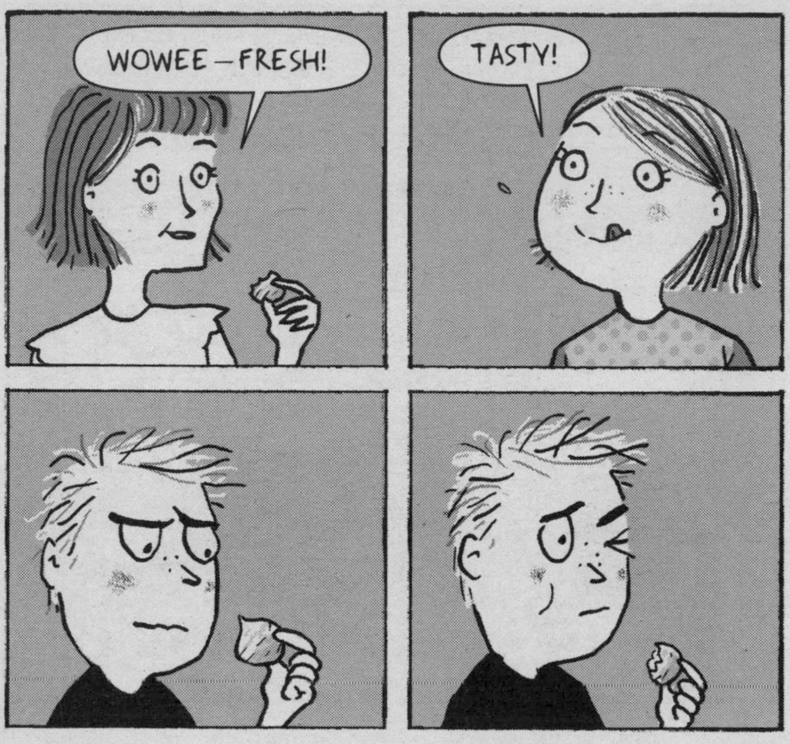
WOWEE—FRESH!
TASTY!

You know that bit in commercials on TV, when the person takes a bite of food they're not expecting to be nice and it actually is. They make a certain kind of face, like:

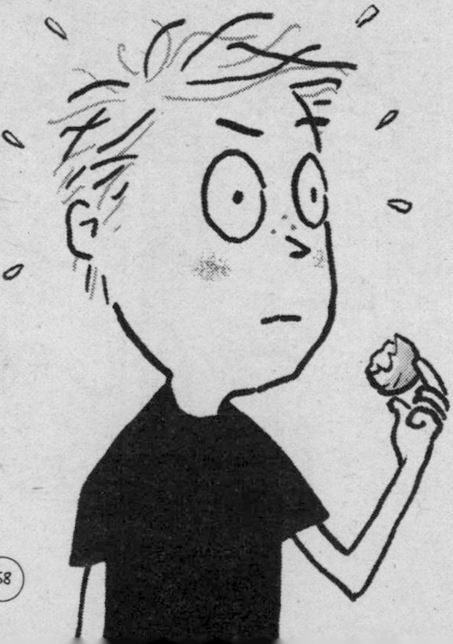

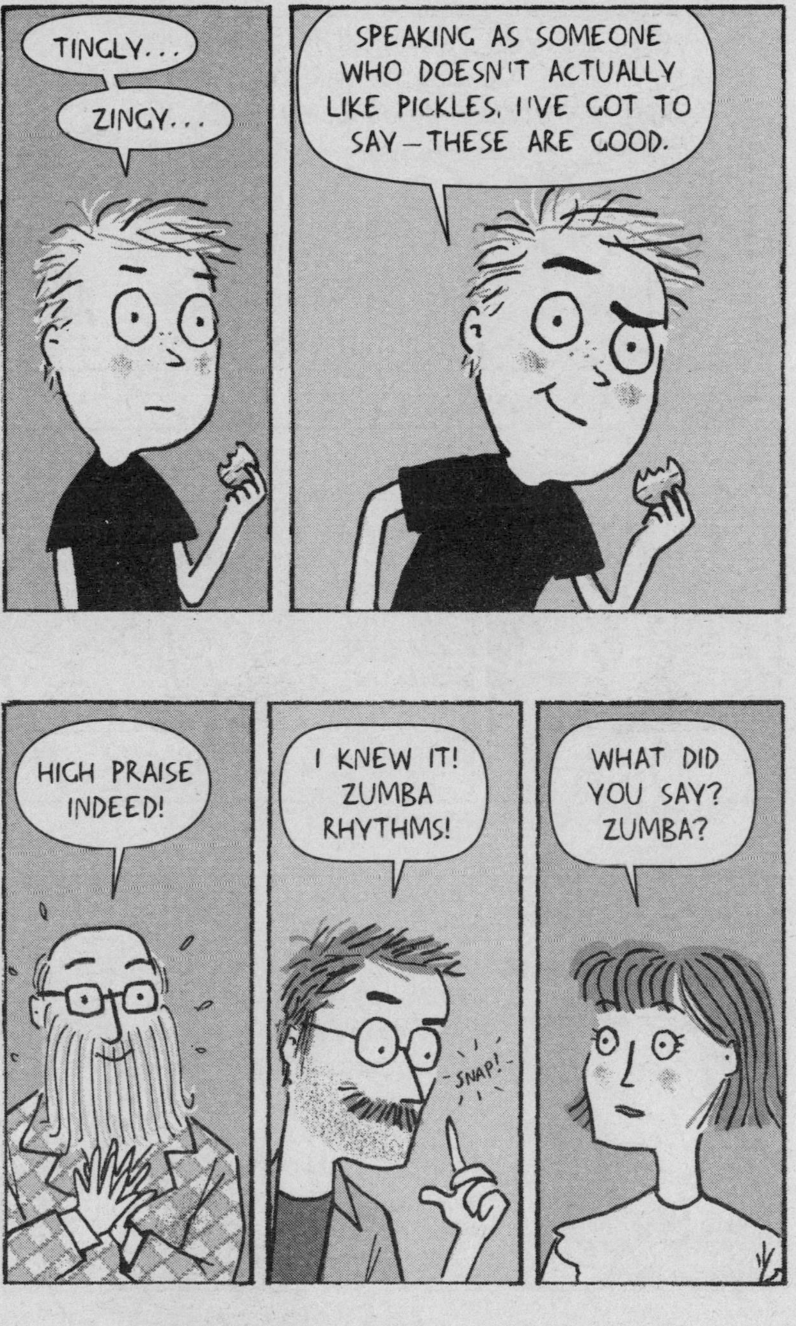
TINGLY...
ZINGY...
SPEAKING AS SOMEONE WHO DOESN'T ACTUALLY LIKE PICKLES, I'VE GOT TO SAY—THESE ARE GOOD.
HIGH PRAISE INDEED!
I KNEW IT! ZUMBA RHYTHMS!
SNAP!
WHAT DID YOU SAY? ZUMBA?

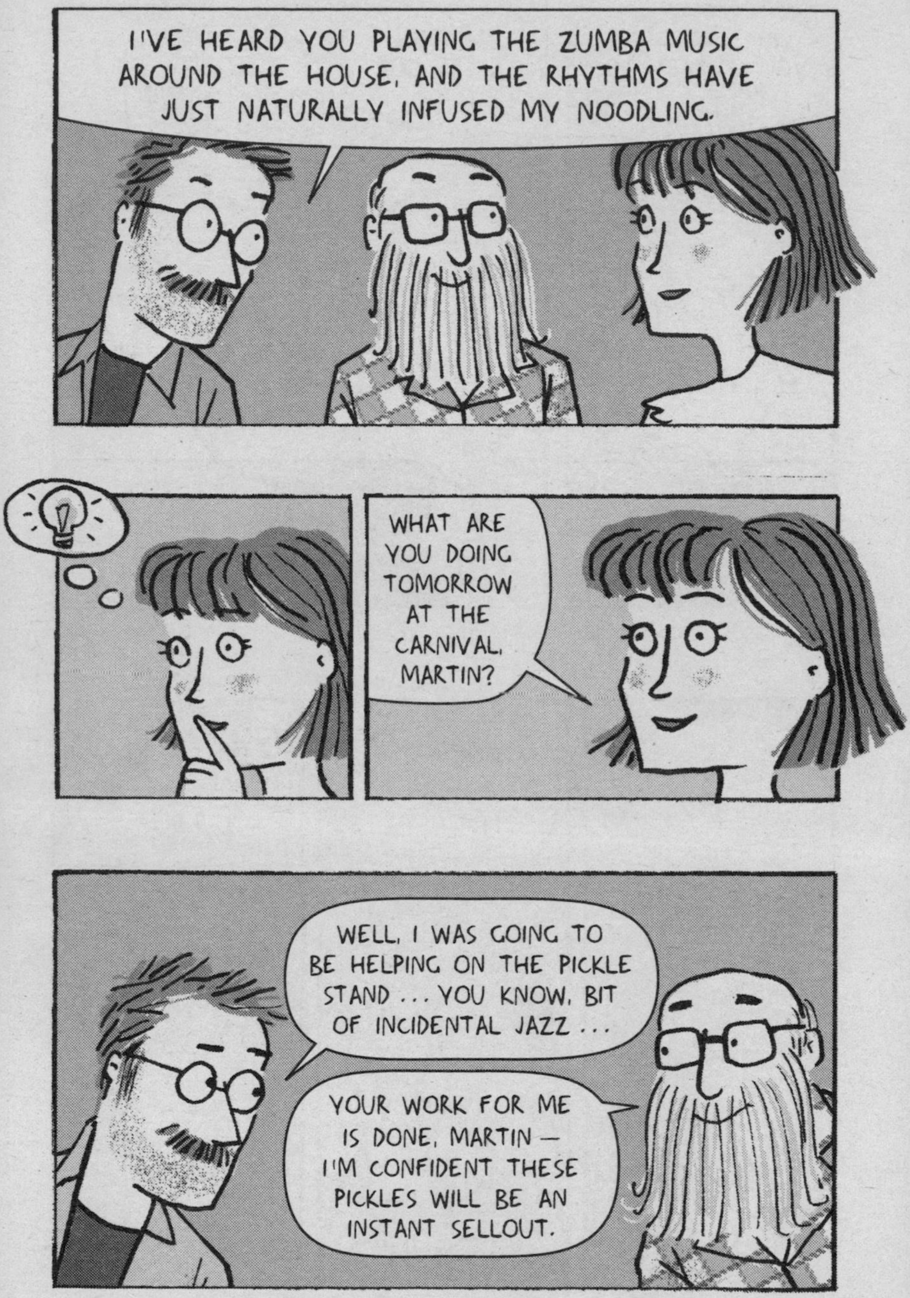
I'VE HEARD YOU PLAYING THE ZUMBA MUSIC AROUND THE HOUSE, AND THE RHYTHMS HAVE JUST NATURALLY INFUSED MY NOODLING.
WHAT ARE YOU DOING TOMORROW AT THE CARNIVAL, MARTIN?
WELL, I WAS GOING TO BE HELPING ON THE PICKLE STAND . . . YOU KNOW, BIT OF INCIDENTAL JAZZ . . .
YOUR WORK FOR ME IS DONE, MARTIN — I'M CONFIDENT THESE PICKLES WILL BE AN INSTANT SELLOUT.

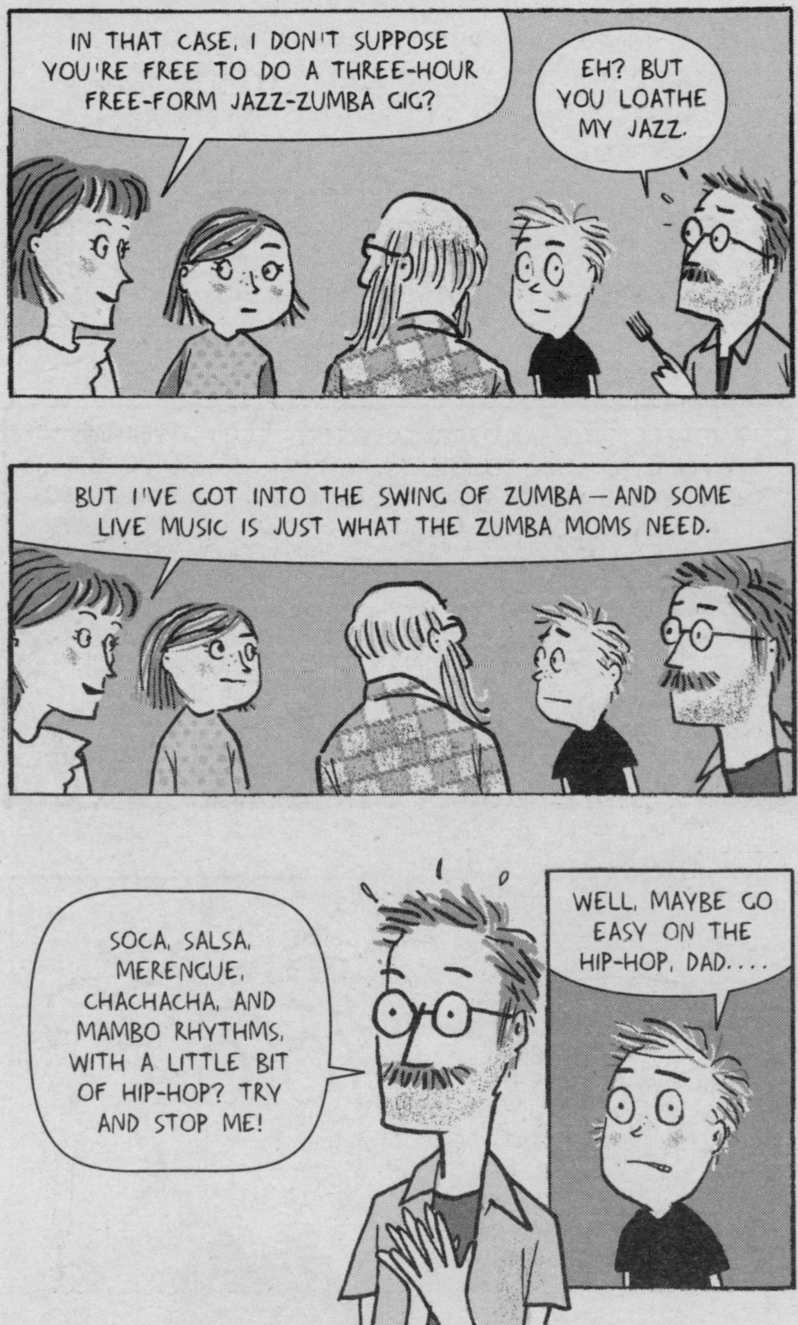
IN THAT CASE, I DON'T SUPPOSE YOU'RE FREE TO DO A THREE-HOUR FREE-FORM JAZZ-ZUMBA GIG?
EH? BUT YOU LOATHE MY JAZZ.
BUT I'VE GOT INTO THE SWING OF ZUMBA—AND SOME LIVE MUSIC IS JUST WHAT THE ZUMBA MOMS NEED.
SOCA, SALSA, MERENGUE, CHACHACHA, AND MAMBO RHYTHMS, WITH A LITTLE BIT OF HIP-HOP? TRY AND STOP ME!
WELL, MAYBE GO EASY ON THE HIP-HOP, DAD. . . .

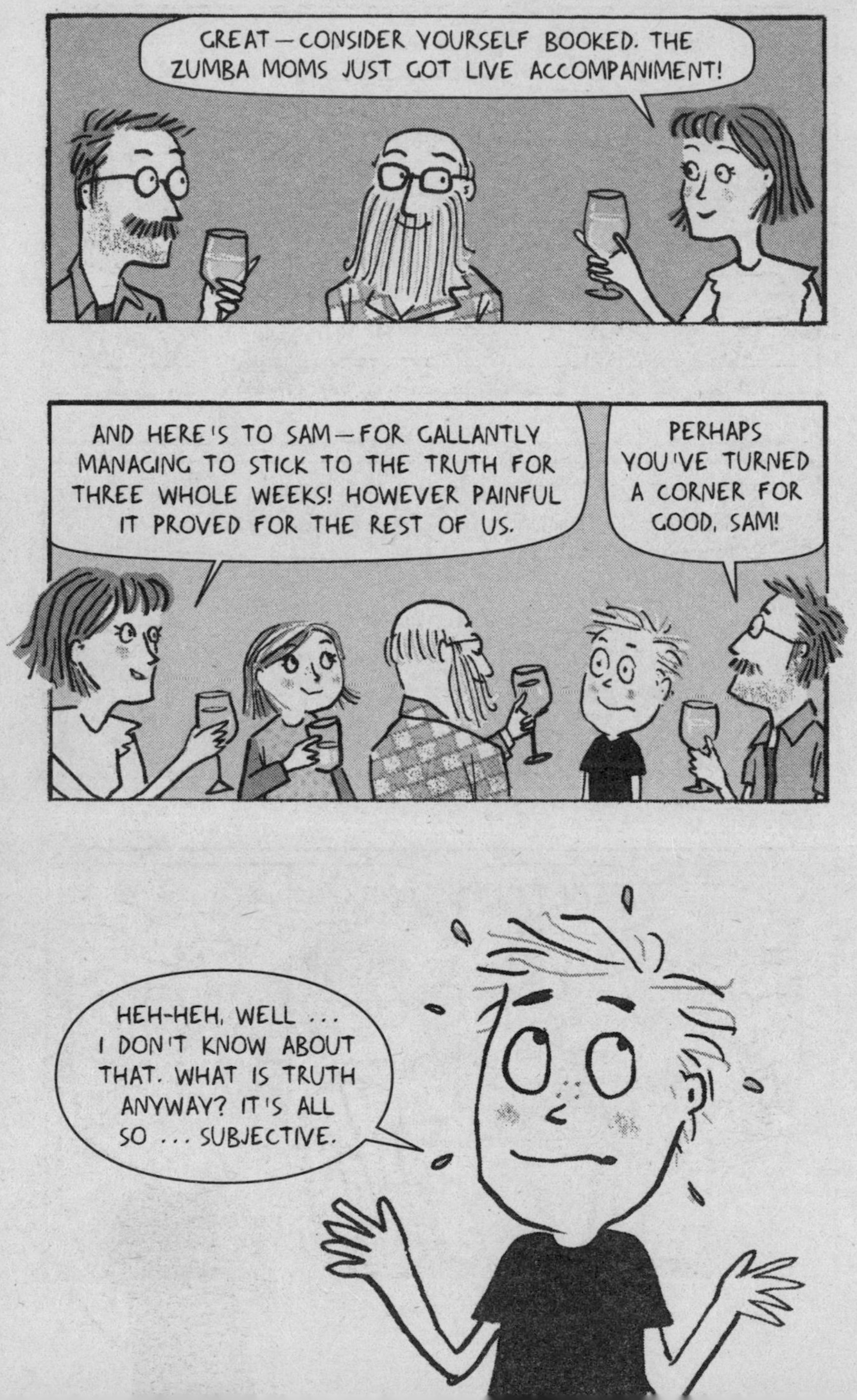
GREAT—CONSIDER YOURSELF BOOKED. THE ZUMBA MOMS JUST GOT LIVE ACCOMPANIMENT!
AND HERE'S TO SAM—FOR GALLANTLY MANAGING TO STICK TO THE TRUTH FOR THREE WHOLE WEEKS! HOWEVER PAINFUL IT PROVED FOR THE REST OF US.
PERHAPS YOU'VE TURNED A CORNER FOR GOOD, SAM!
HEH-HEH, WELL . . . I DON'T KNOW ABOUT THAT. WHAT IS TRUTH ANYWAY? IT'S ALL SO . . . SUBJECTIVE.

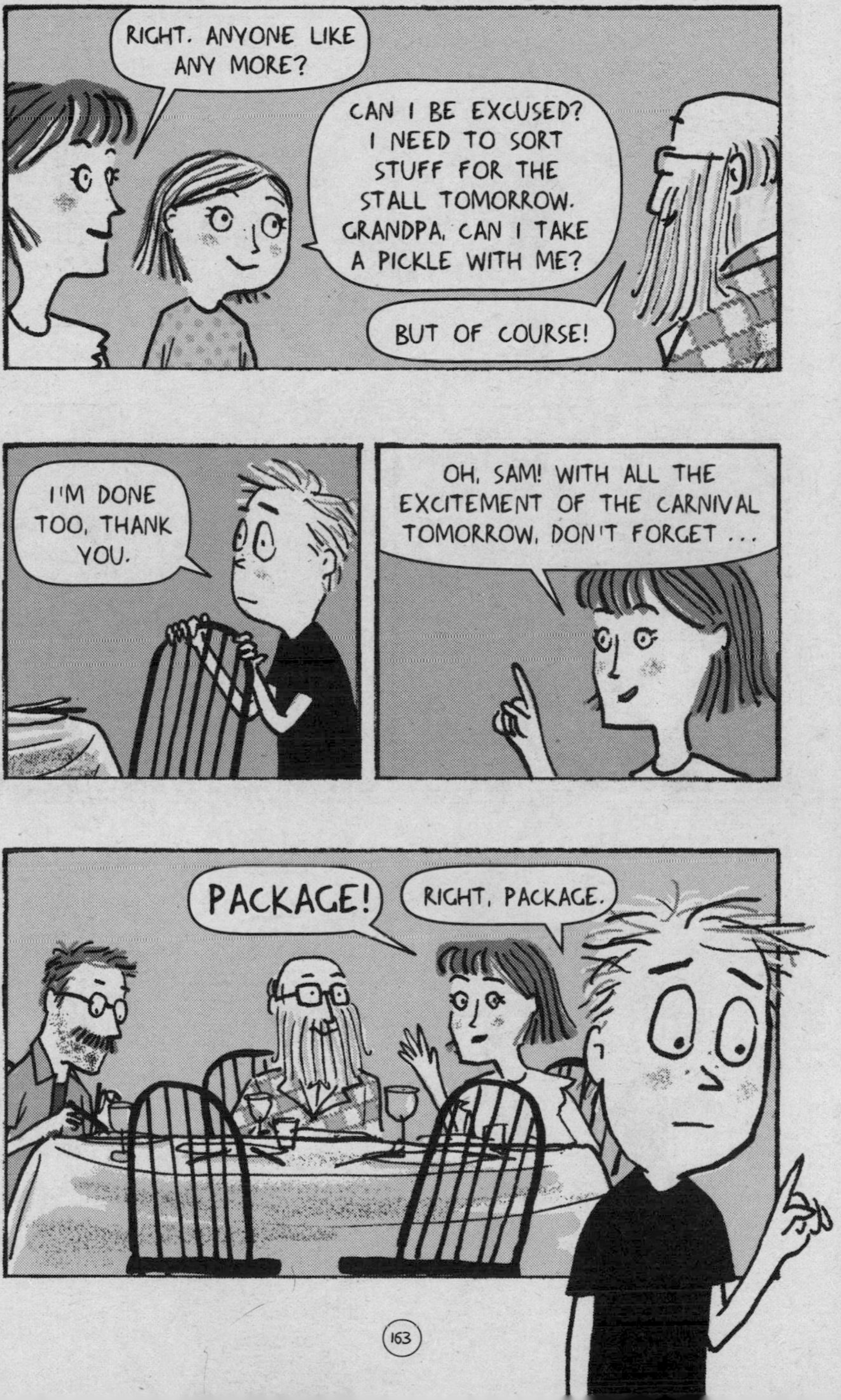
RIGHT. ANYONE LIKE ANY MORE?
CAN I BE EXCUSED? I NEED TO SORT STUFF FOR THE STALL TOMORROW. GRANDPA, CAN I TAKE A PICKLE WITH ME?
BUT OF COURSE!
I'M DONE TOO, THANK YOU.
OH, SAM! WITH ALL THE EXCITEMENT OF THE CARNIVAL TOMORROW, DON'T FORGET . . .
PACKAGE!
RIGHT, PACKAGE.

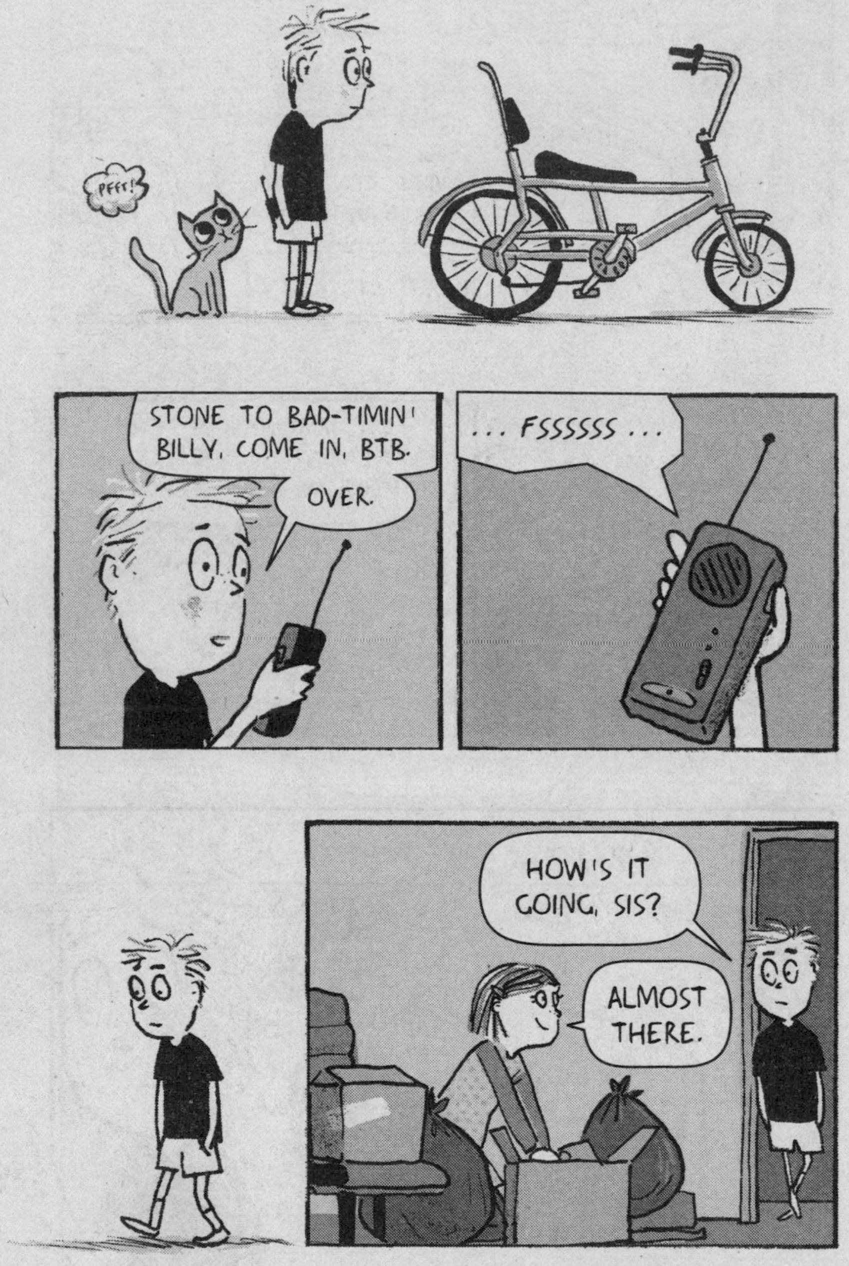
PFFT!
STONE TO BAD-TIMIN' BILLY. COME IN, BTB.
OVER.
... FSSSSSS ...
HOW'S IT GOING, SIS?
ALMOST THERE.

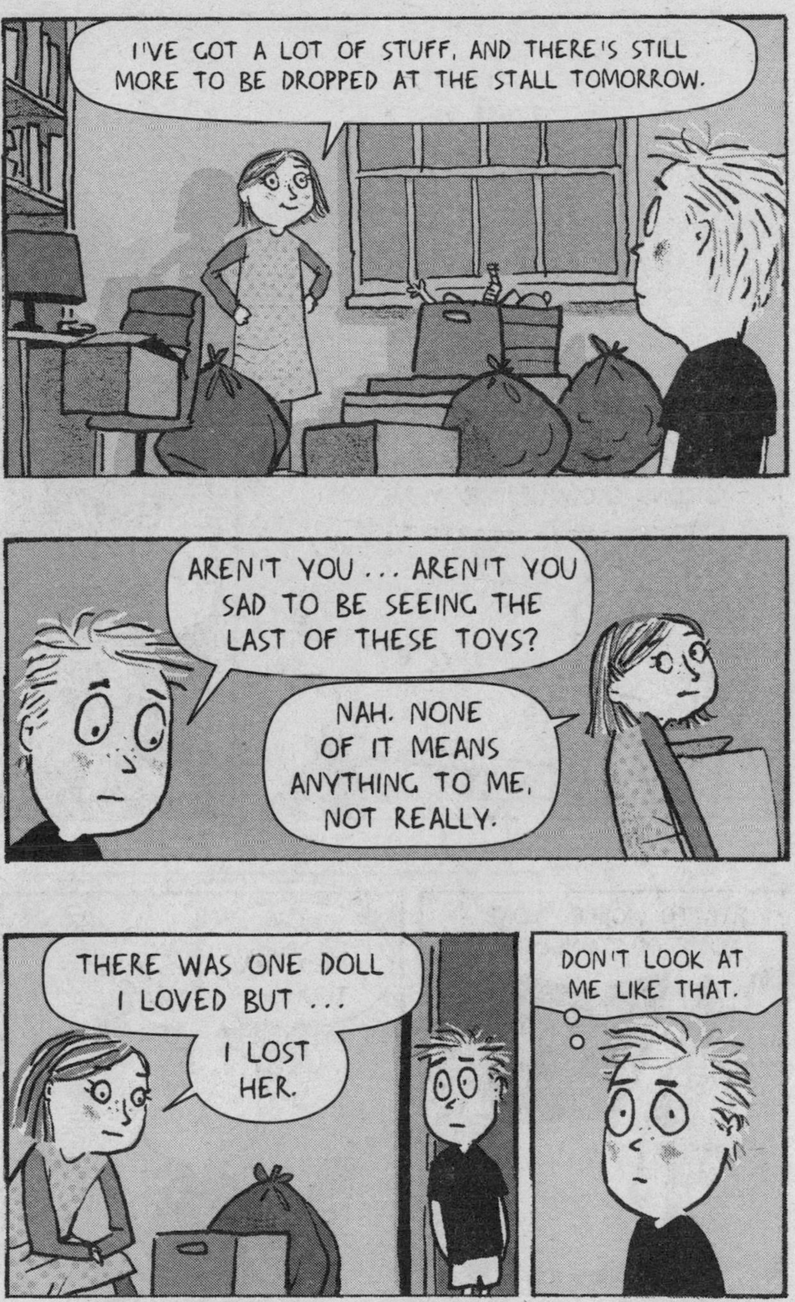
I'VE GOT A LOT OF STUFF, AND THERE'S STILL MORE TO BE DROPPED AT THE STALL TOMORROW.
AREN'T YOU ... AREN'T YOU SAD TO BE SEEING THE LAST OF THESE TOYS?
NAH. NONE OF IT MEANS ANYTHING TO ME, NOT REALLY.
THERE WAS ONE DOLL I LOVED BUT ...
I LOST HER.
DON'T LOOK AT ME LIKE THAT.

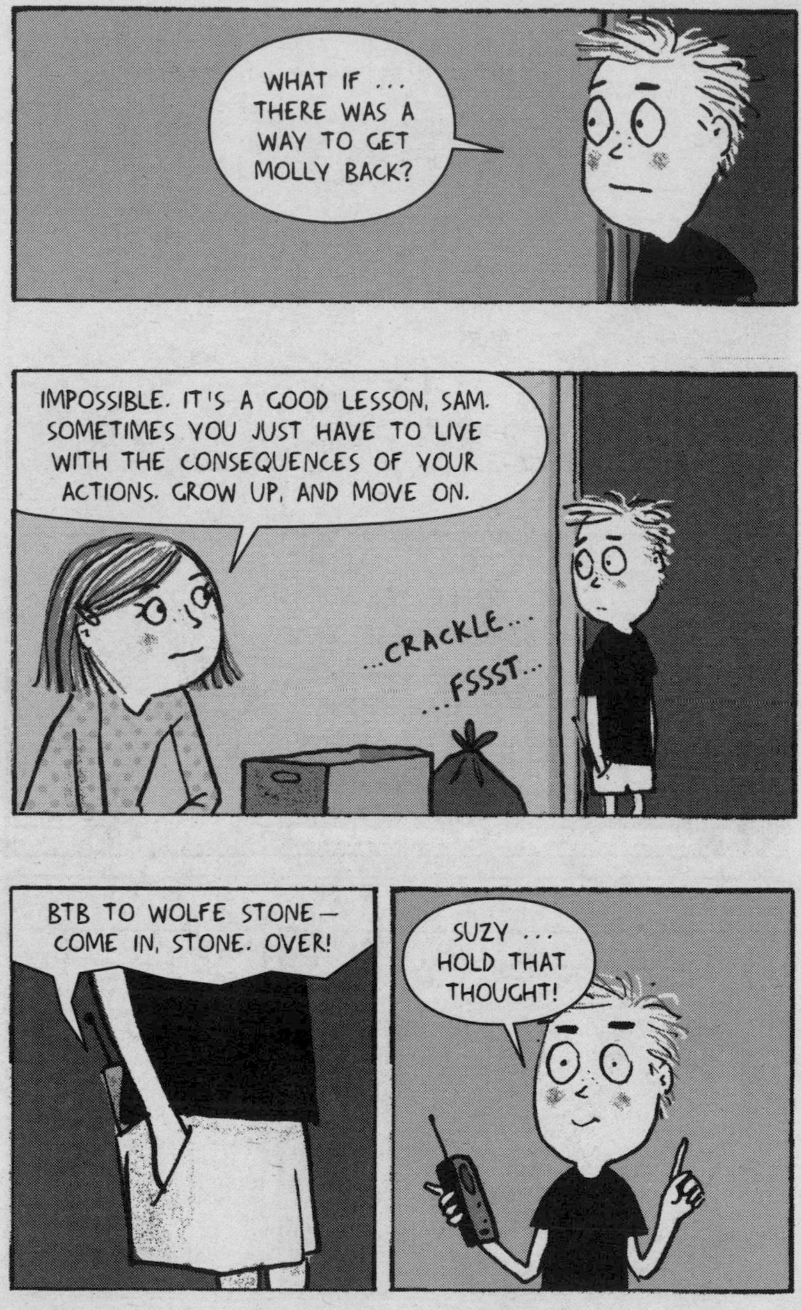
WHAT IF ... THERE WAS A WAY TO GET MOLLY BACK?
IMPOSSIBLE. IT'S A GOOD LESSON, SAM. SOMETIMES YOU JUST HAVE TO LIVE WITH THE CONSEQUENCES OF YOUR ACTIONS. GROW UP, AND MOVE ON.
...CRACKLE...
...FSSST...
BTB TO WOLFE STONE— COME IN, STONE. OVER!
SUZY ... HOLD THAT THOUGHT!

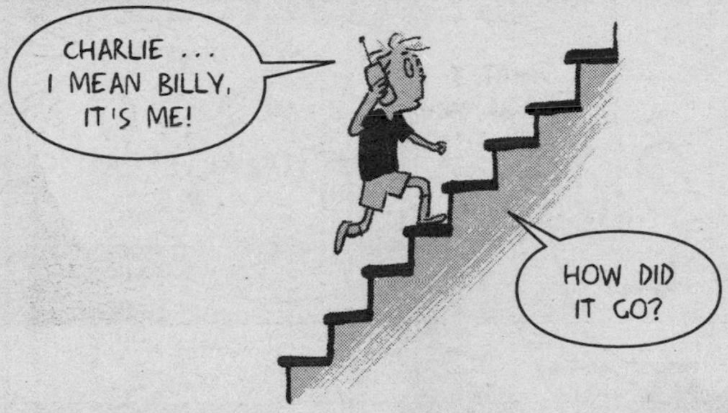
CHARLIE ... I MEAN BILLY, IT'S ME!
HOW DID IT GO?

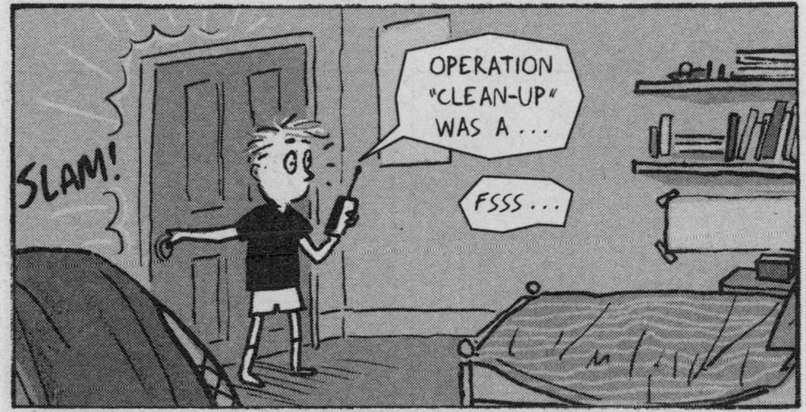
SLAM!
OPERATION "CLEAN-UP" WAS A ...
FSSS ...

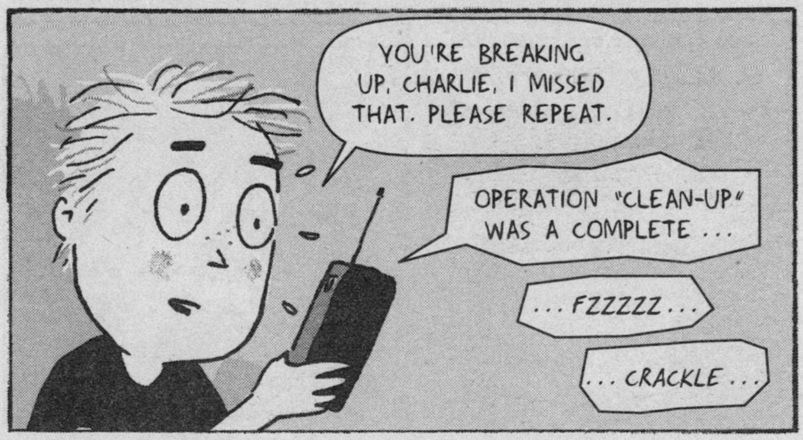
YOU'RE BREAKING UP, CHARLIE, I MISSED THAT. PLEASE REPEAT.
OPERATION "CLEAN-UP" WAS A COMPLETE ...
... FZZZZZ ...
... CRACKLE ...

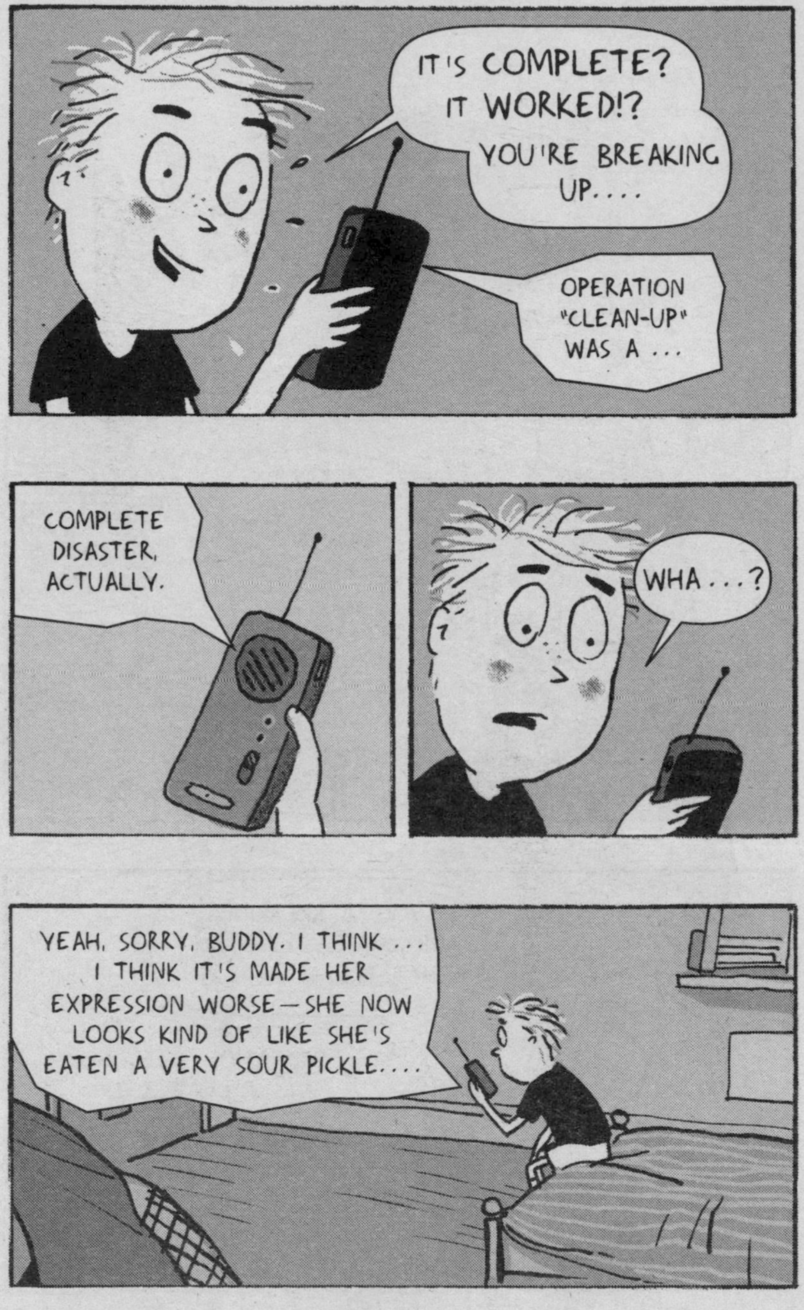
IT'S COMPLETE? IT WORKED!? YOU'RE BREAKING UP....
OPERATION "CLEAN-UP" WAS A ...
COMPLETE DISASTER, ACTUALLY.
WHA...?
YEAH, SORRY, BUDDY. I THINK ... I THINK IT'S MADE HER EXPRESSION WORSE—SHE NOW LOOKS KIND OF LIKE SHE'S EATEN A VERY SOUR PICKLE....

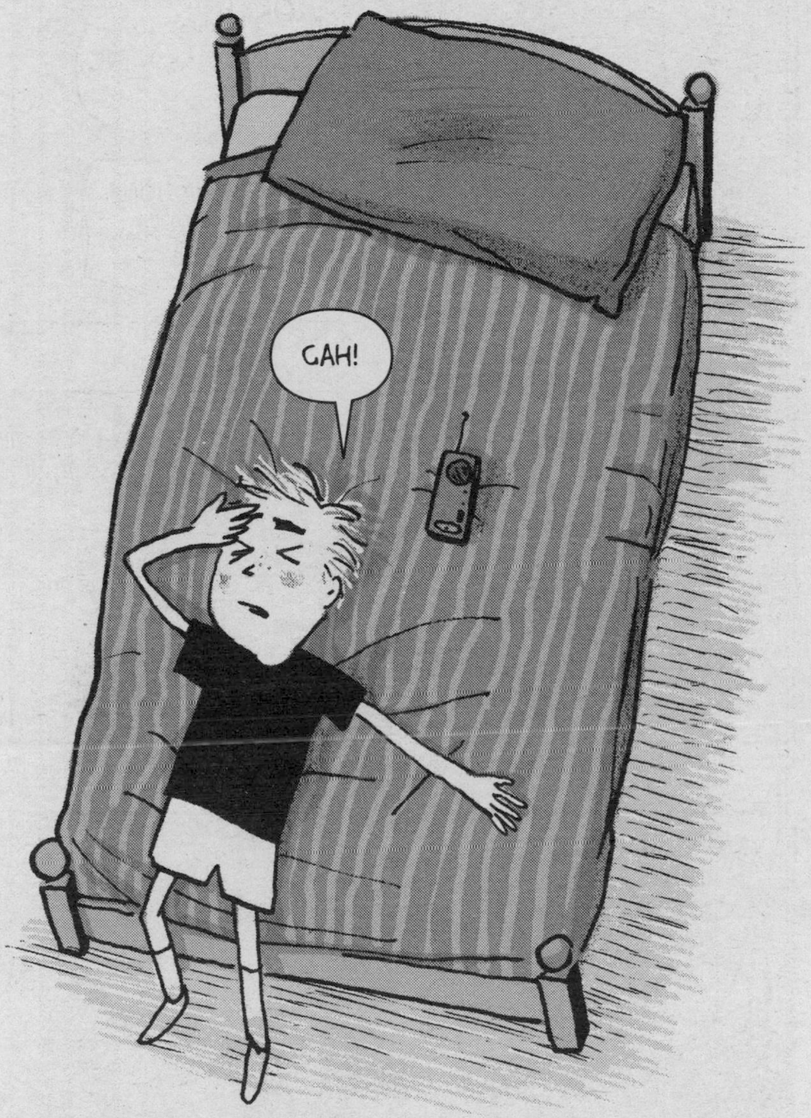
GAH!

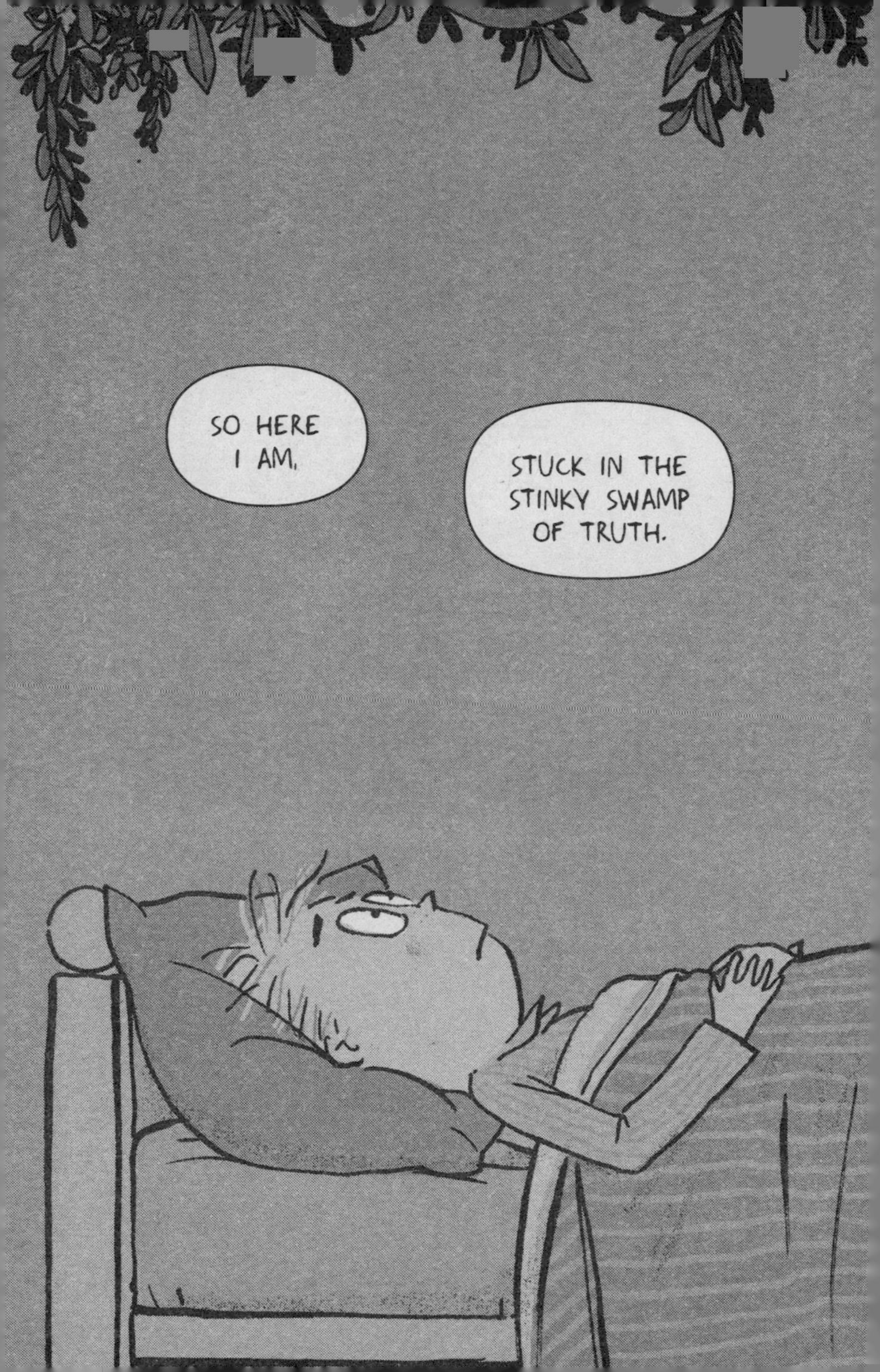
SO HERE I AM.
STUCK IN THE STINKY SWAMP OF TRUTH.

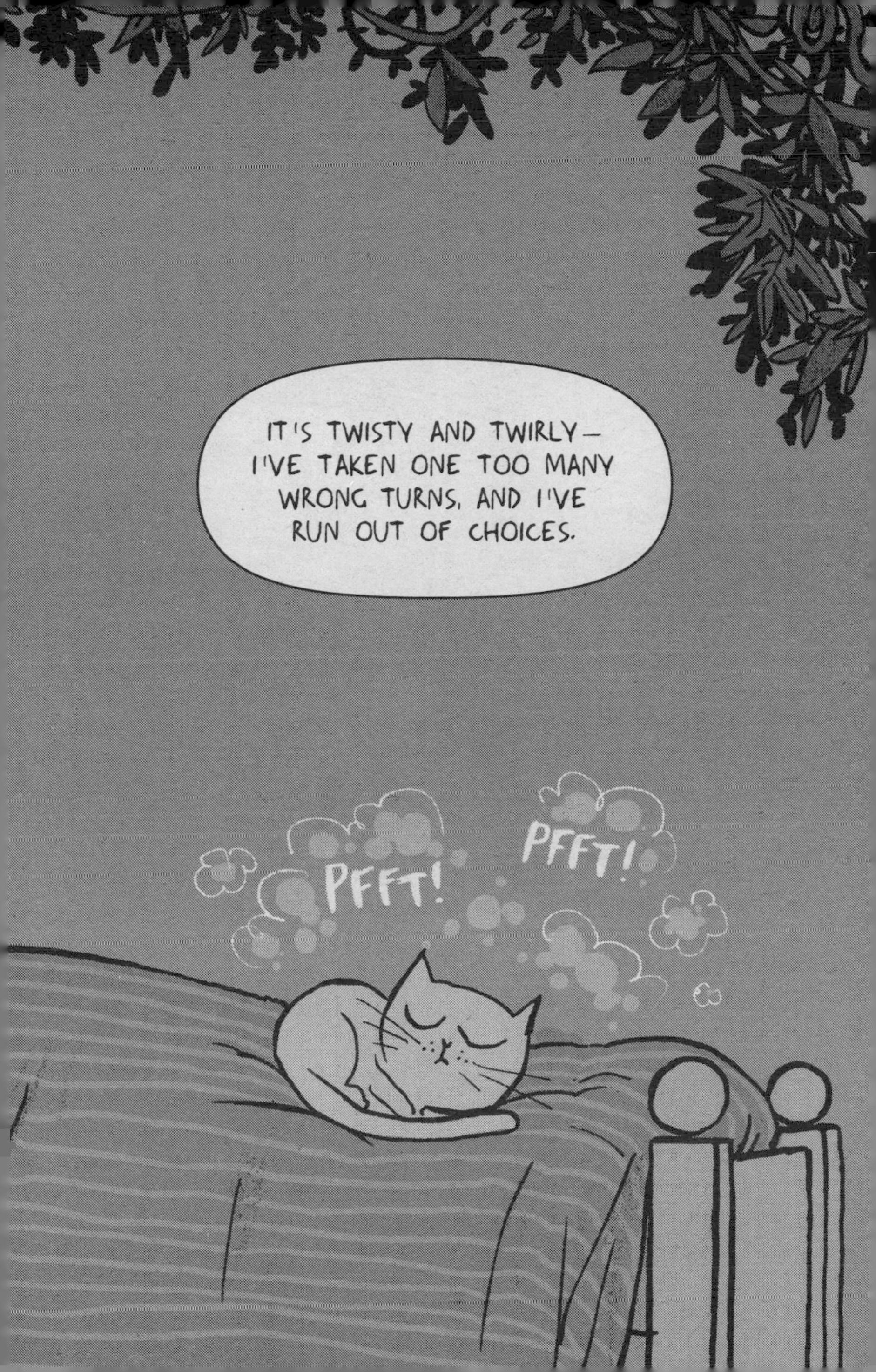
IT'S TWISTY AND TWIRLY— I'VE TAKEN ONE TOO MANY WRONG TURNS, AND I'VE RUN OUT OF CHOICES.
PFFT!
PFFT!

You're probably thinking, "What's the big deal? You've won the challenge. You've even got a shiny new bike." But it's impossible to enjoy this stuff when there's something weighing on your conscience.

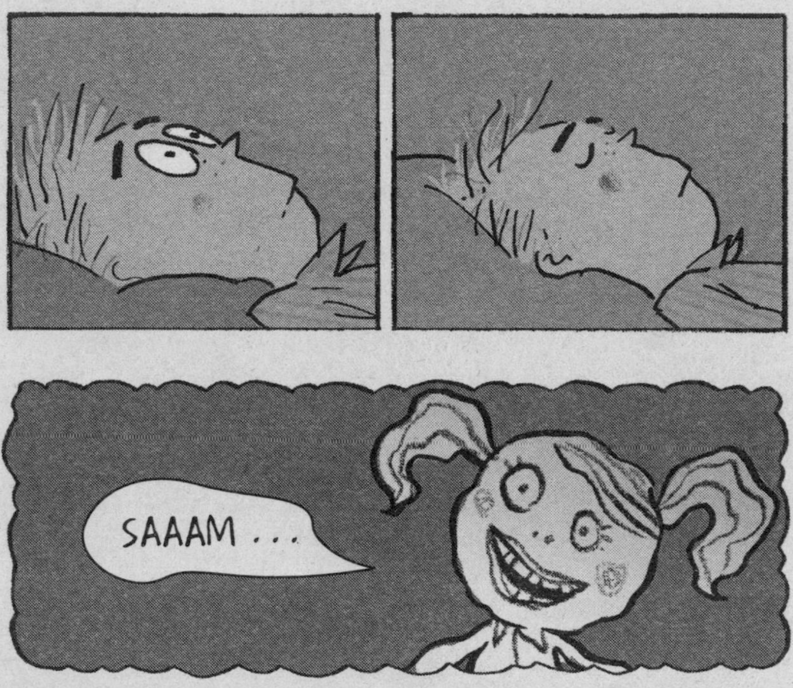
SAAAM . . .

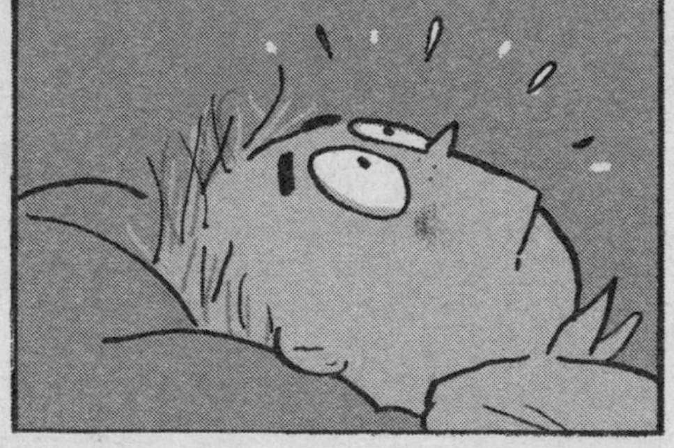

Just impossible.

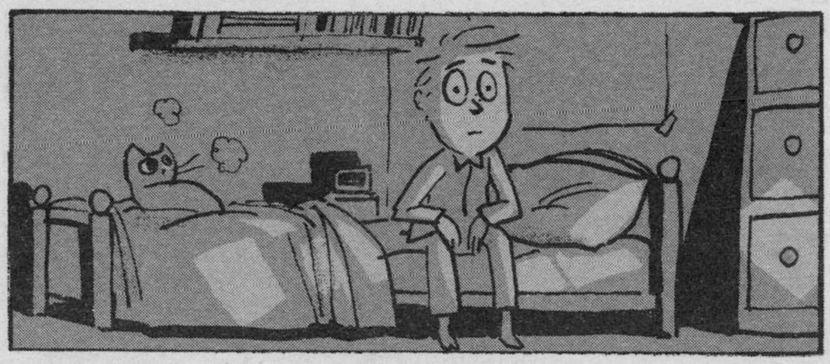

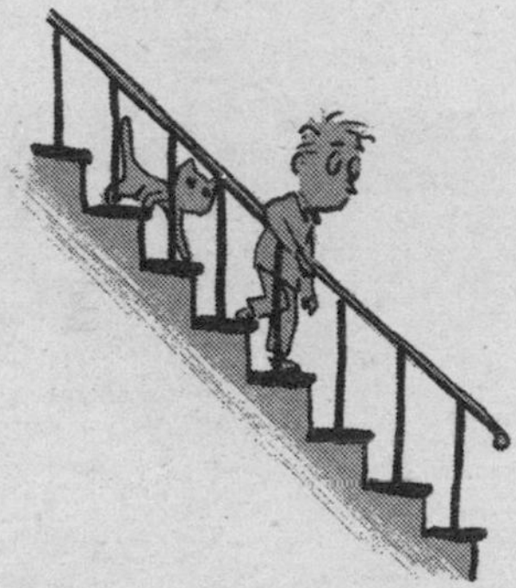

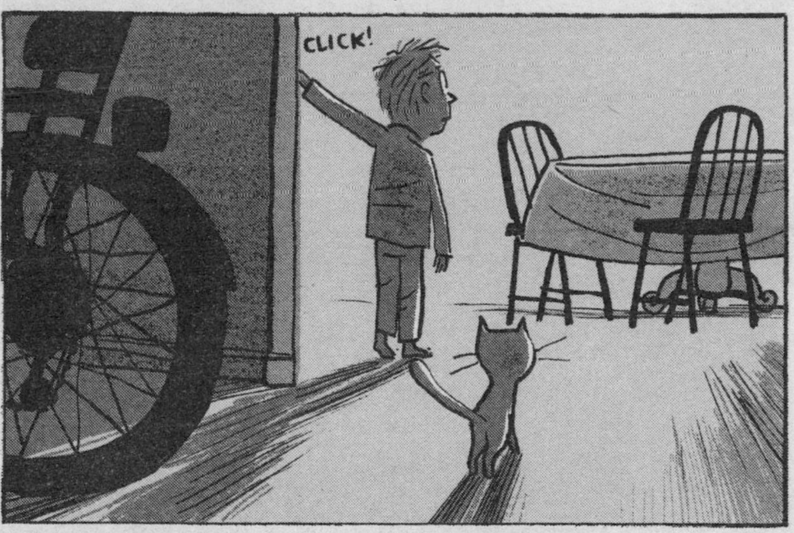
CLICK!

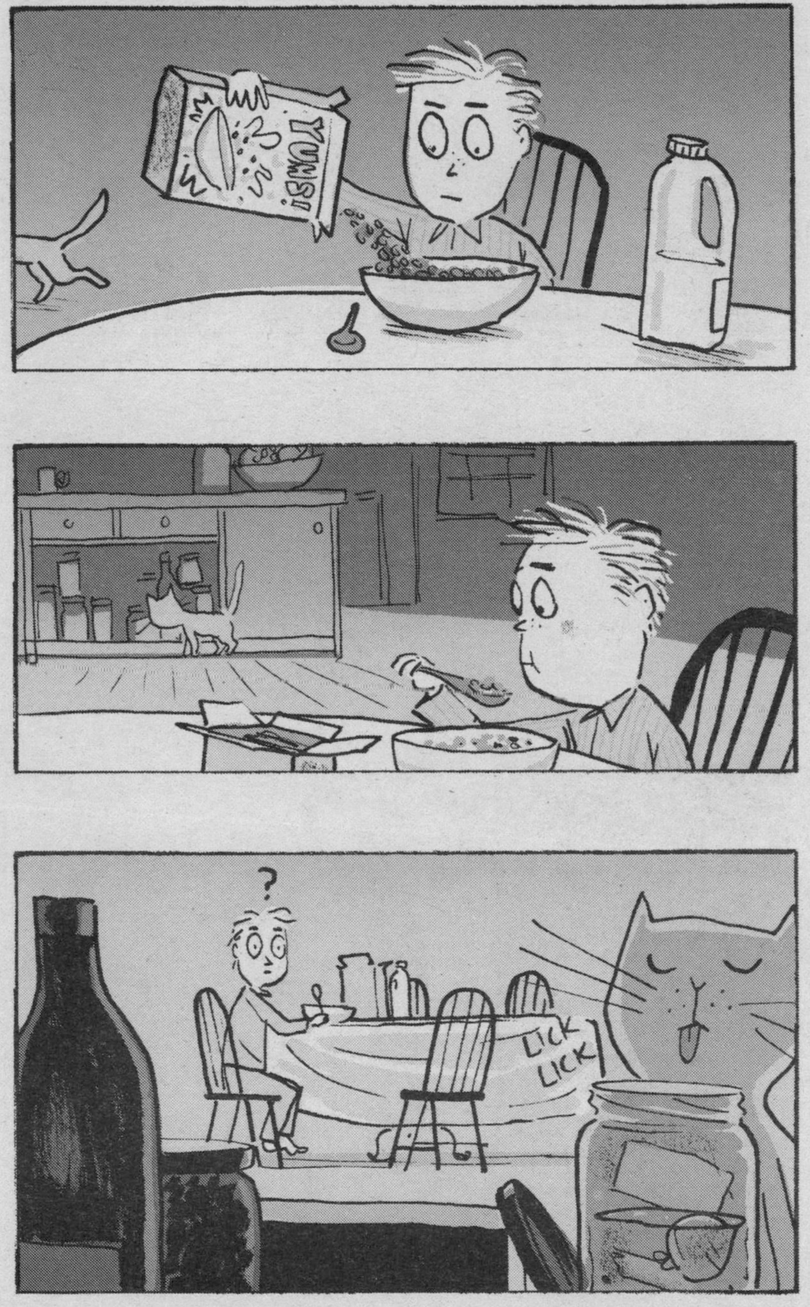
YUMS!
?
LICK
LICK

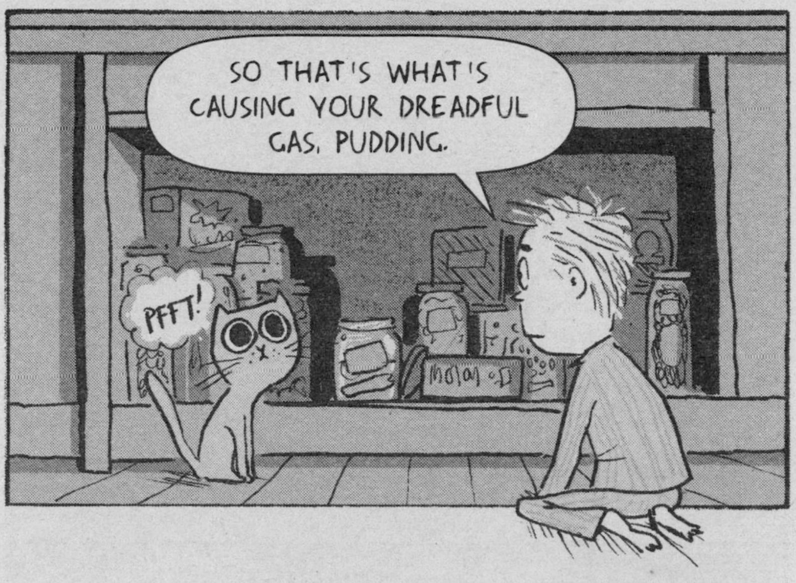
SO THAT'S WHAT'S CAUSING YOUR DREADFUL GAS, PUDDING.
PFFT!

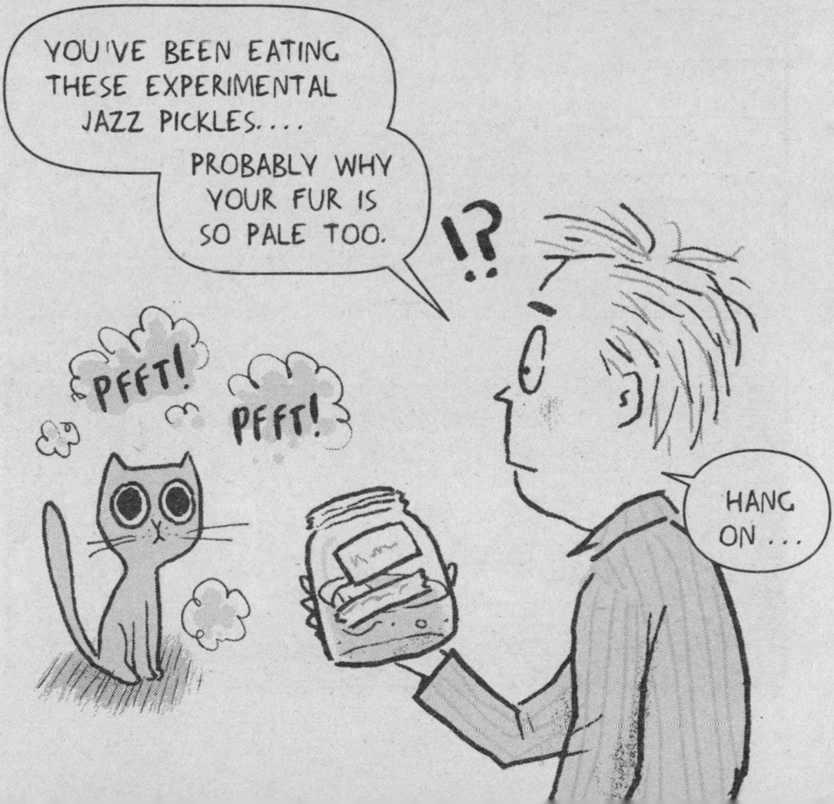
YOU'VE BEEN EATING THESE EXPERIMENTAL JAZZ PICKLES. . . .
PROBABLY WHY YOUR FUR IS SO PALE TOO.
!?
PFFT!
PFFT!
HANG ON . . .

EXPER
7
WIND JAMMER
THIS PICKLE JUICE ...
... DISSOLVES PERMANENT MARKER!

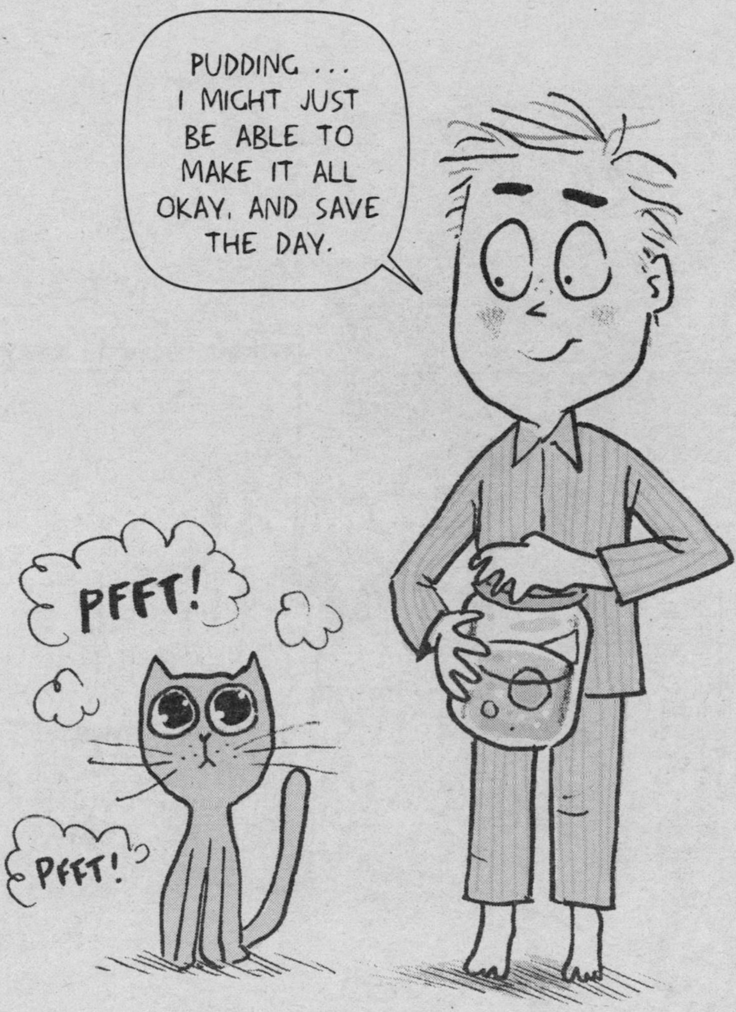
PUDDING . . . I MIGHT JUST BE ABLE TO MAKE IT ALL OKAY, AND SAVE THE DAY.
PFFT!
PFFT!

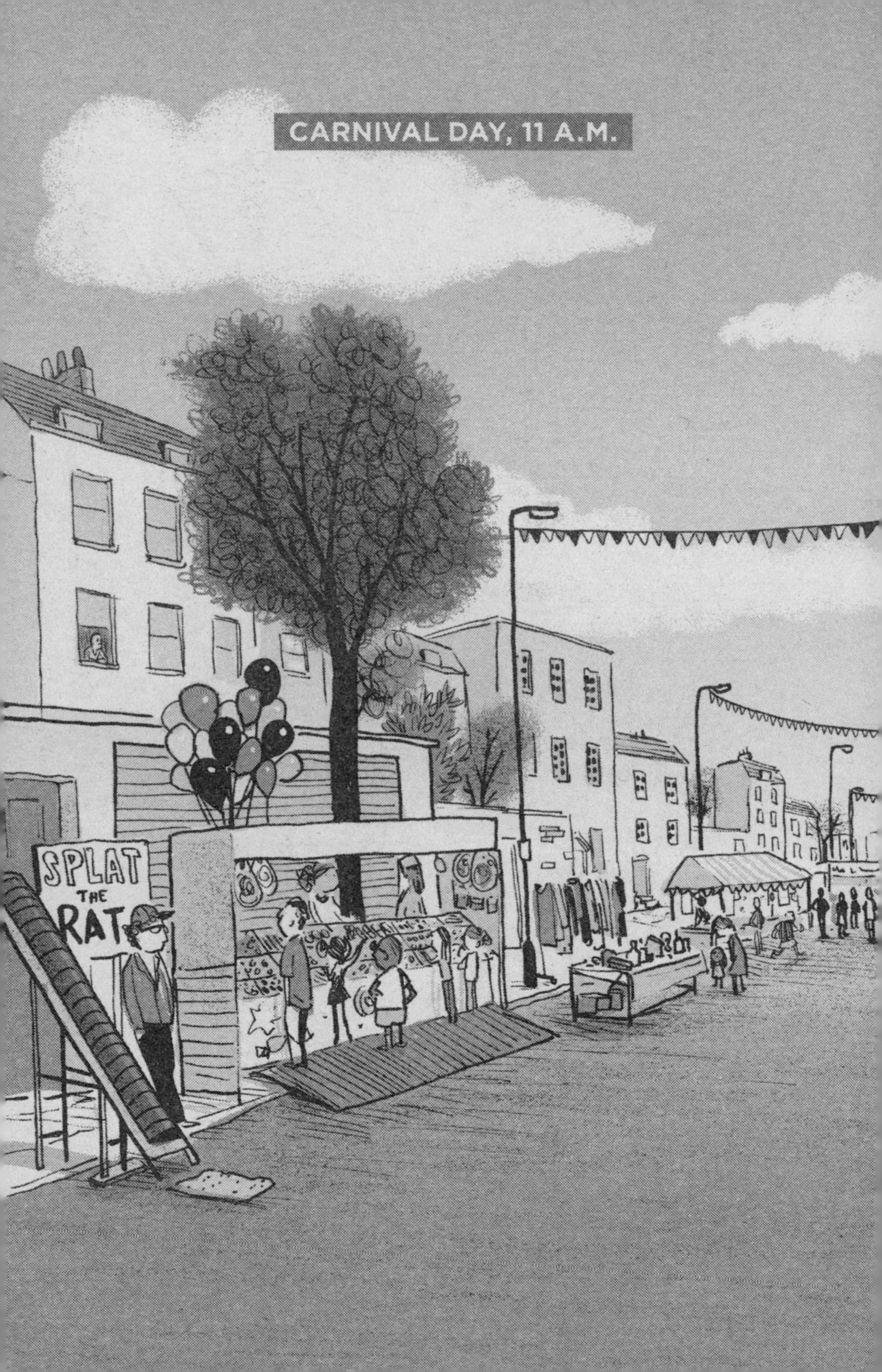
CARNIVAL DAY, 11 A.M.
SPLAT THE RAT

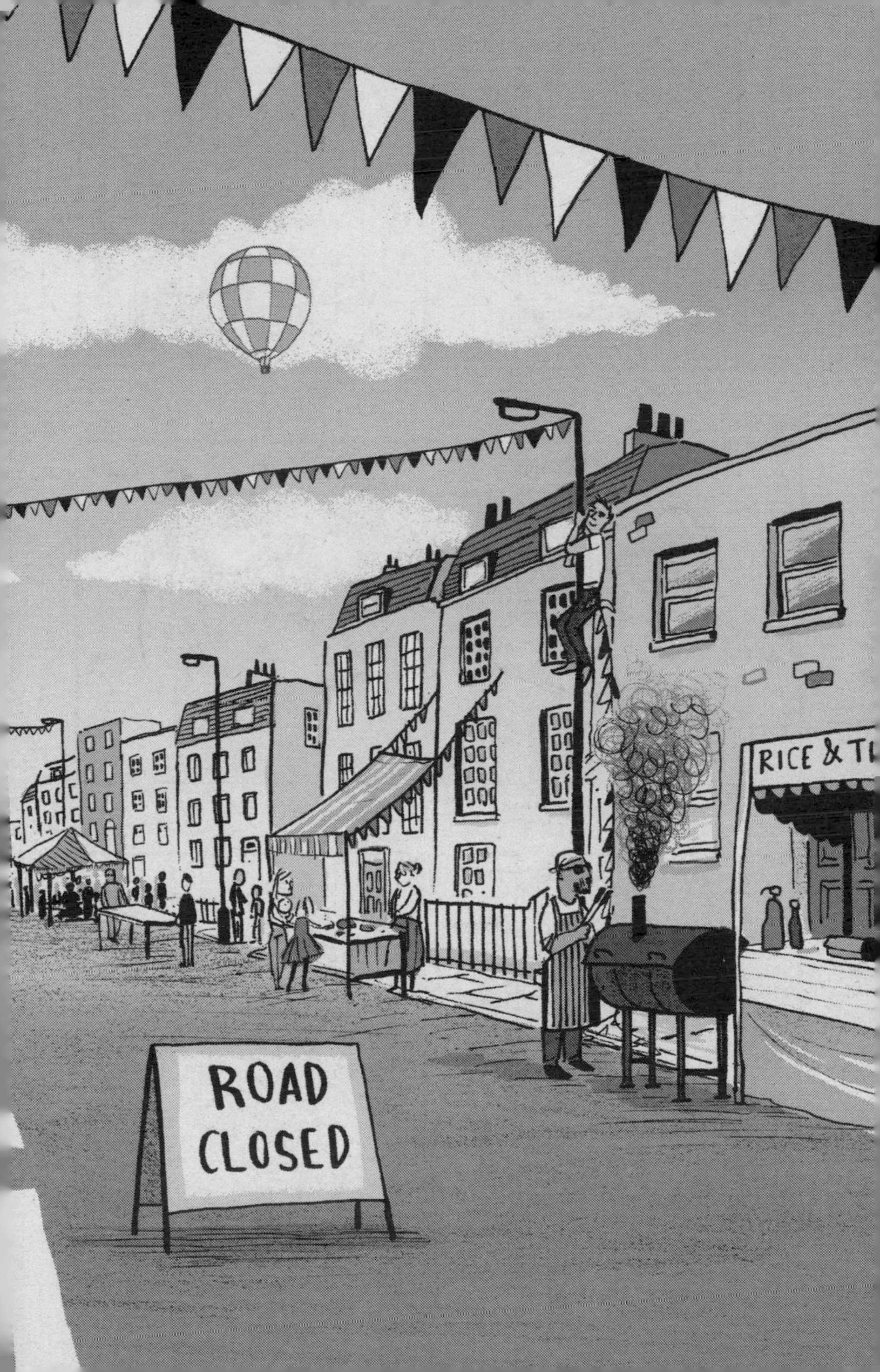

RICE & T
ROAD CLOSED

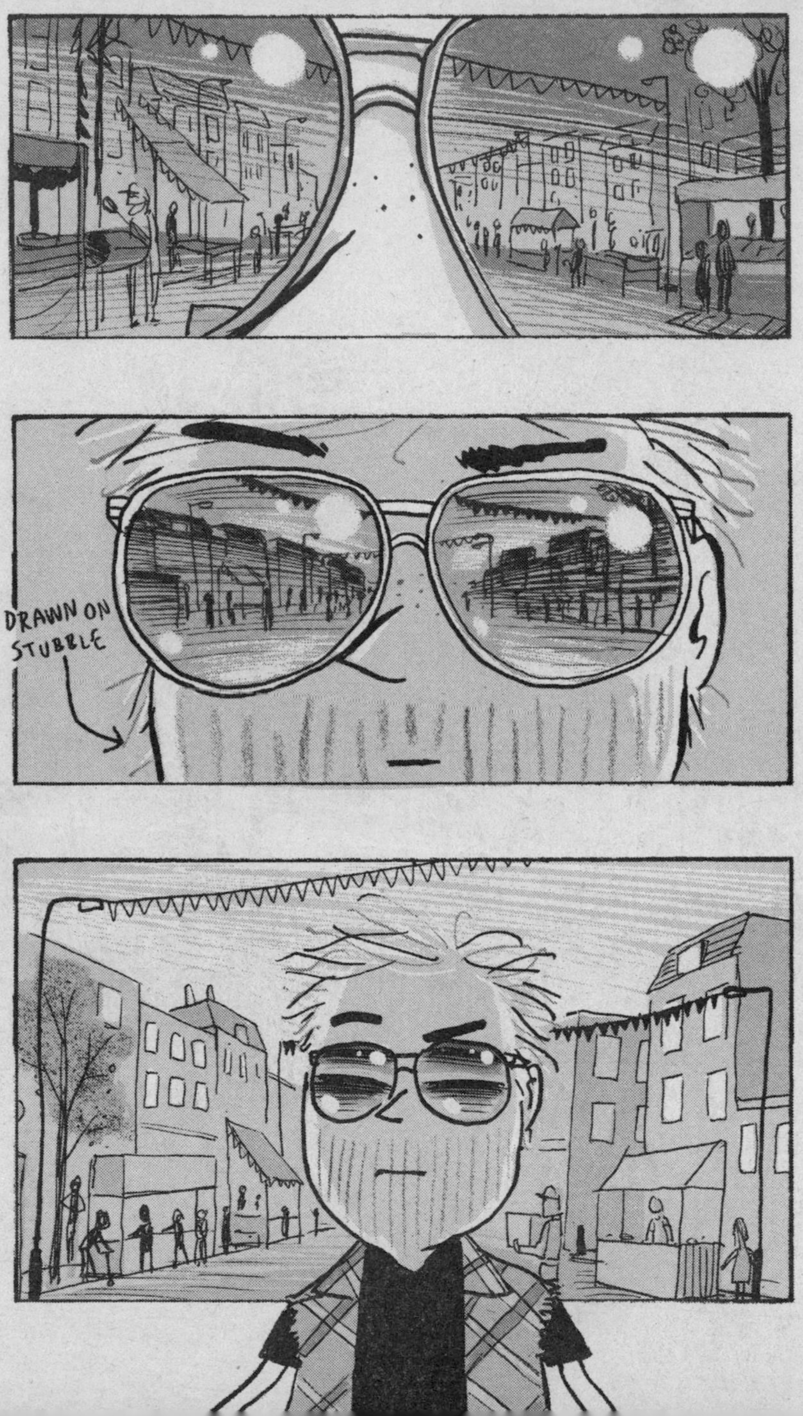
DRAWN ON STUBBLE

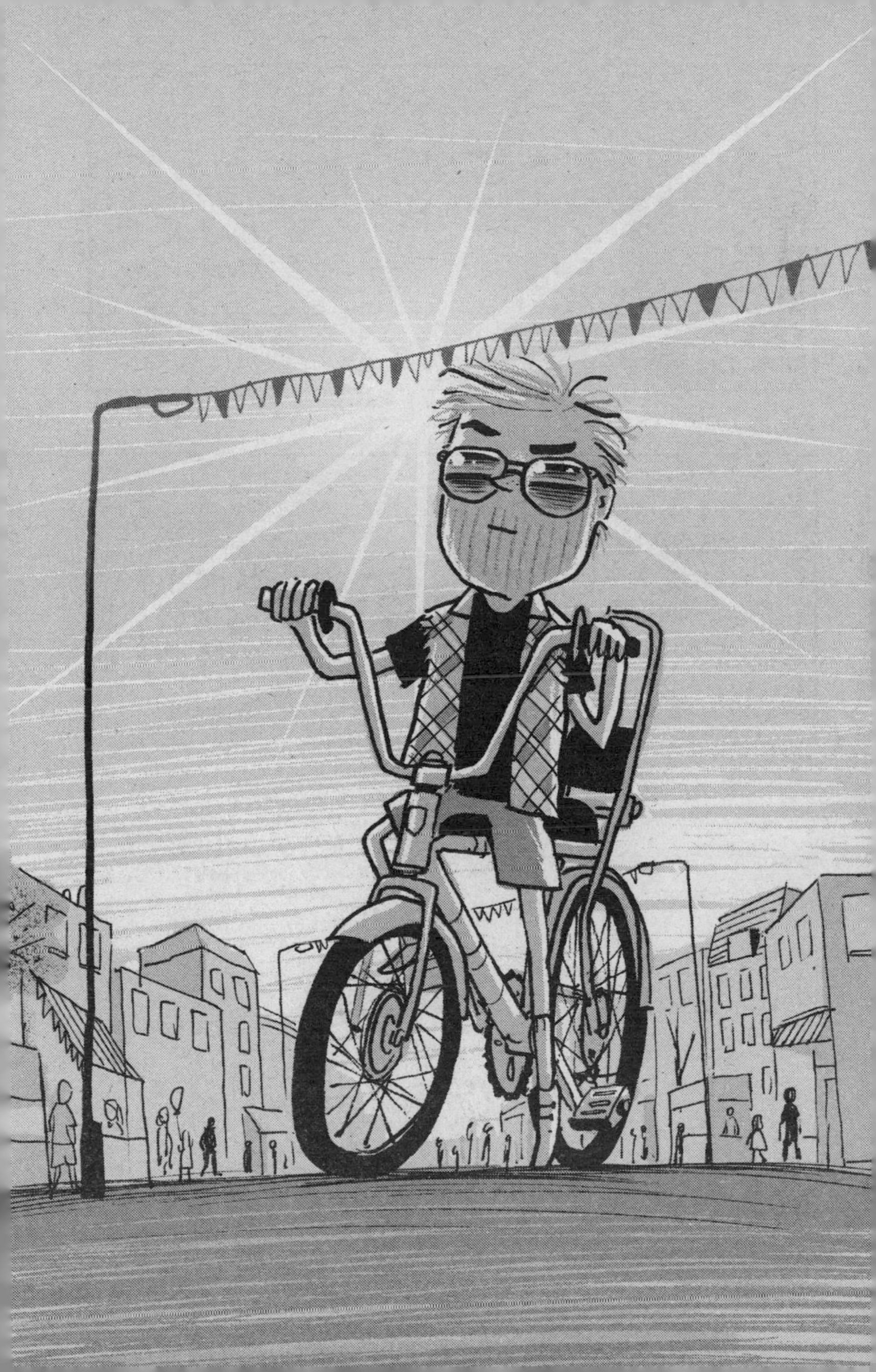

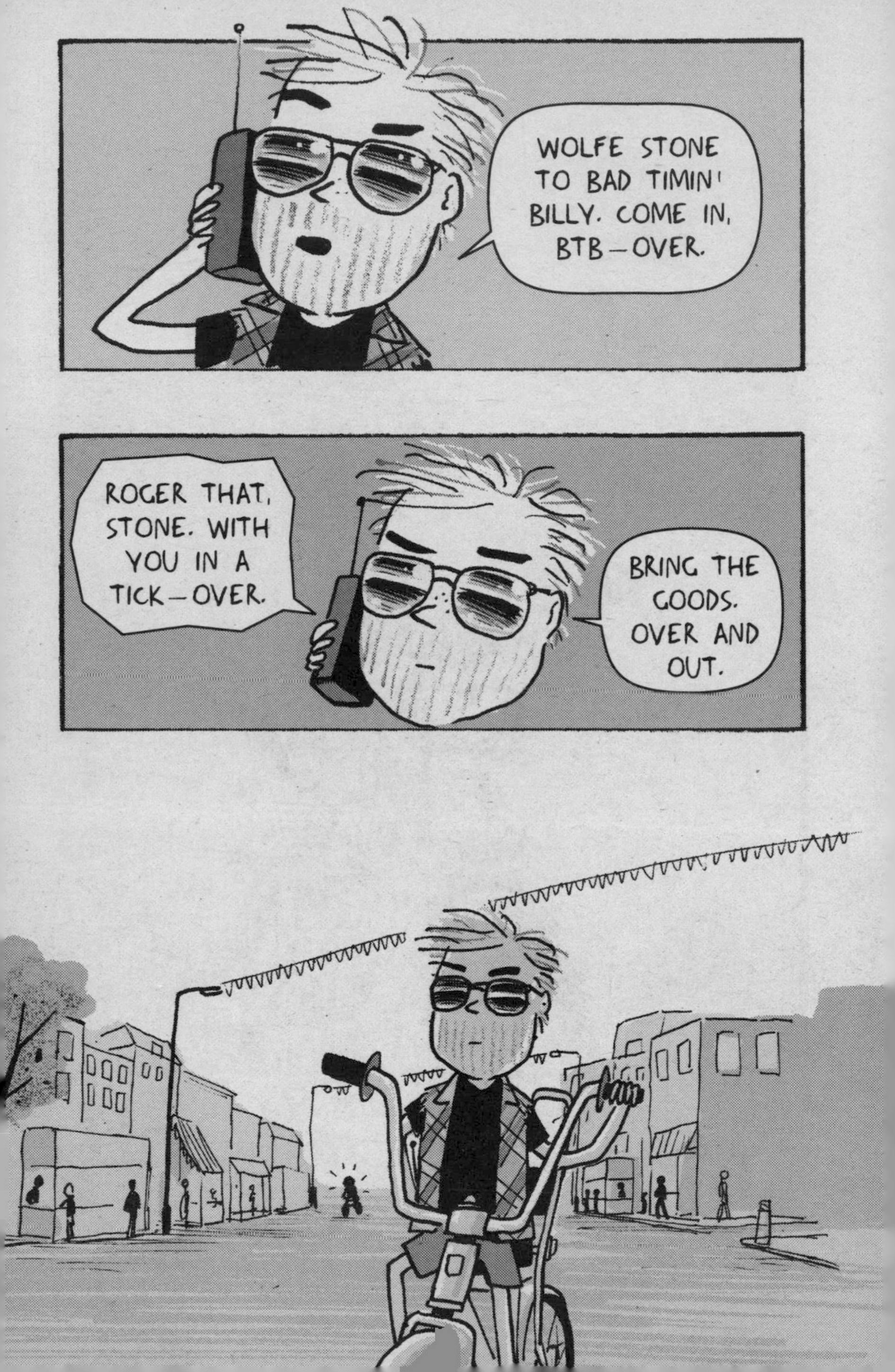
WOLFE STONE TO BAD TIMIN' BILLY. COME IN, BTB—OVER.
ROGER THAT, STONE. WITH YOU IN A TICK—OVER.
BRING THE GOODS. OVER AND OUT.

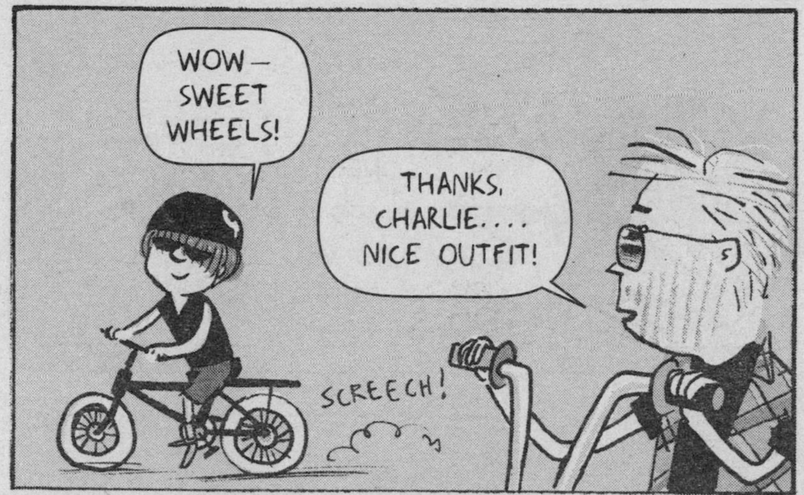
WOW—
SWEET
WHEELS!
THANKS,
CHARLIE. . . .
NICE OUTFIT!
SCREECH!

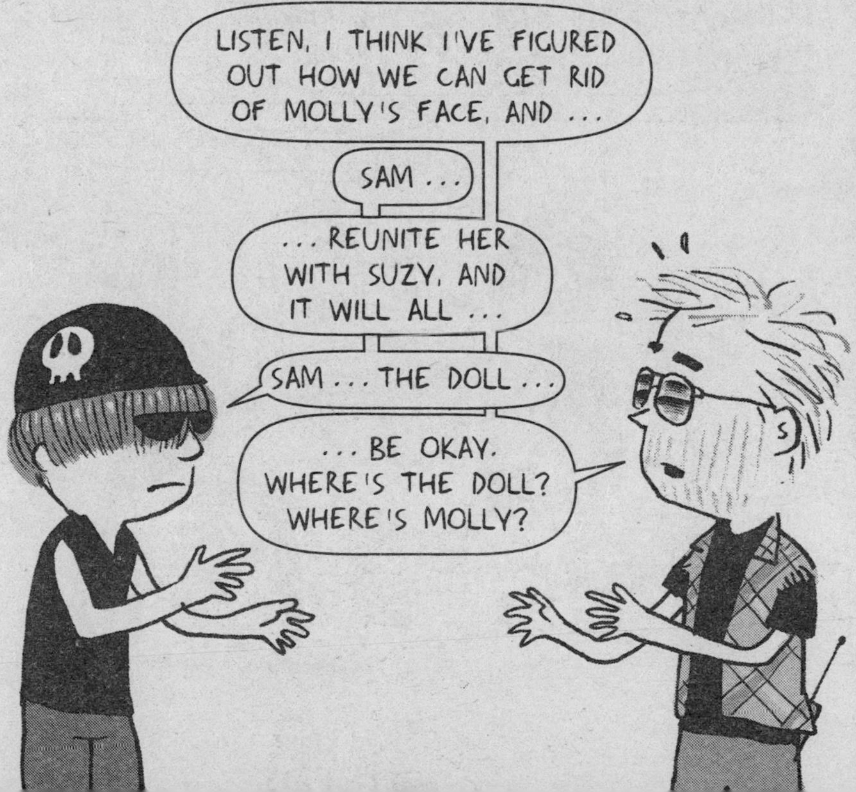
LISTEN, I THINK I'VE FIGURED OUT HOW WE CAN GET RID OF MOLLY'S FACE, AND . . .
SAM . . .
. . . REUNITE HER WITH SUZY, AND IT WILL ALL . . .
SAM . . . THE DOLL . . .
. . . BE OKAY. WHERE'S THE DOLL? WHERE'S MOLLY?

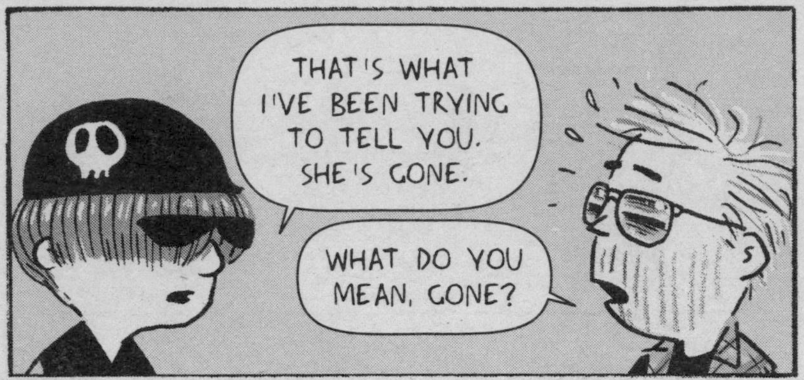
THAT'S WHAT I'VE BEEN TRYING TO TELL YOU. SHE'S GONE.
WHAT DO YOU MEAN, GONE?

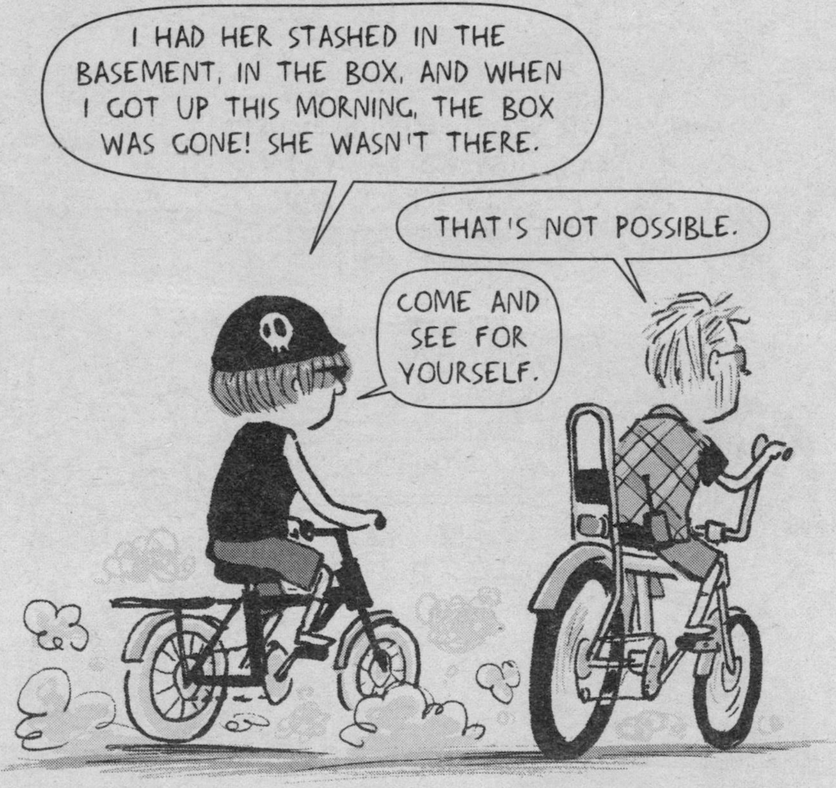
I HAD HER STASHED IN THE BASEMENT, IN THE BOX, AND WHEN I GOT UP THIS MORNING, THE BOX WAS GONE! SHE WASN'T THERE.
THAT'S NOT POSSIBLE.
COME AND SEE FOR YOURSELF.

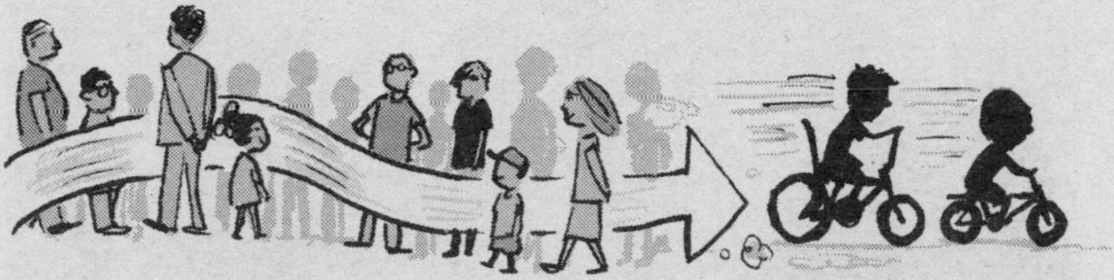

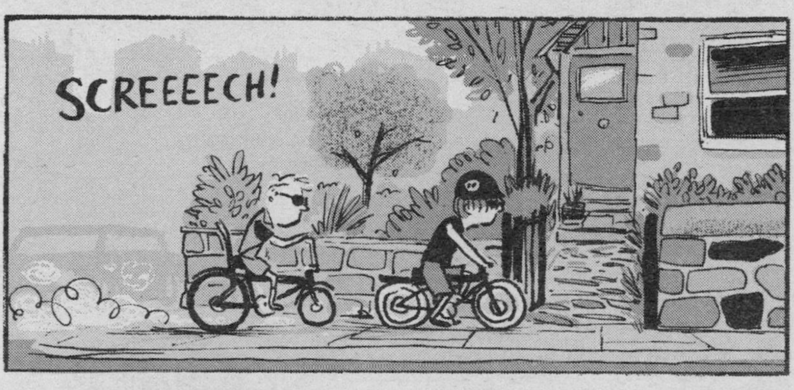
SCREEEECH!

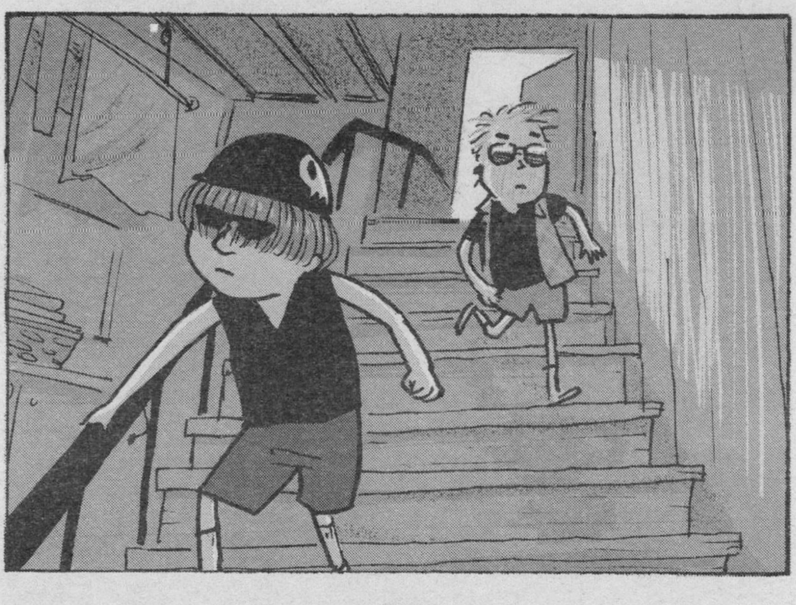

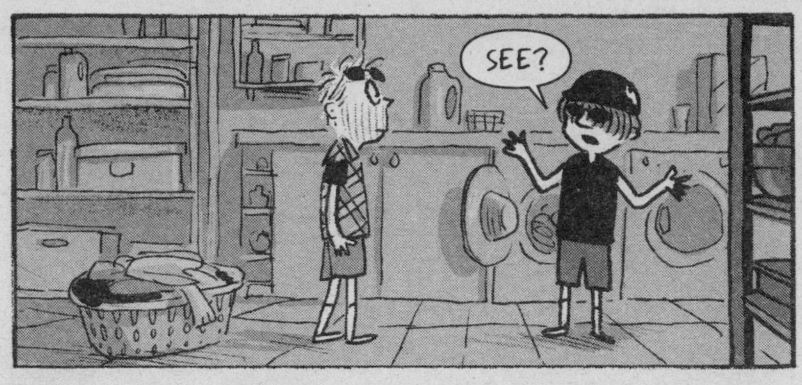
SEE?

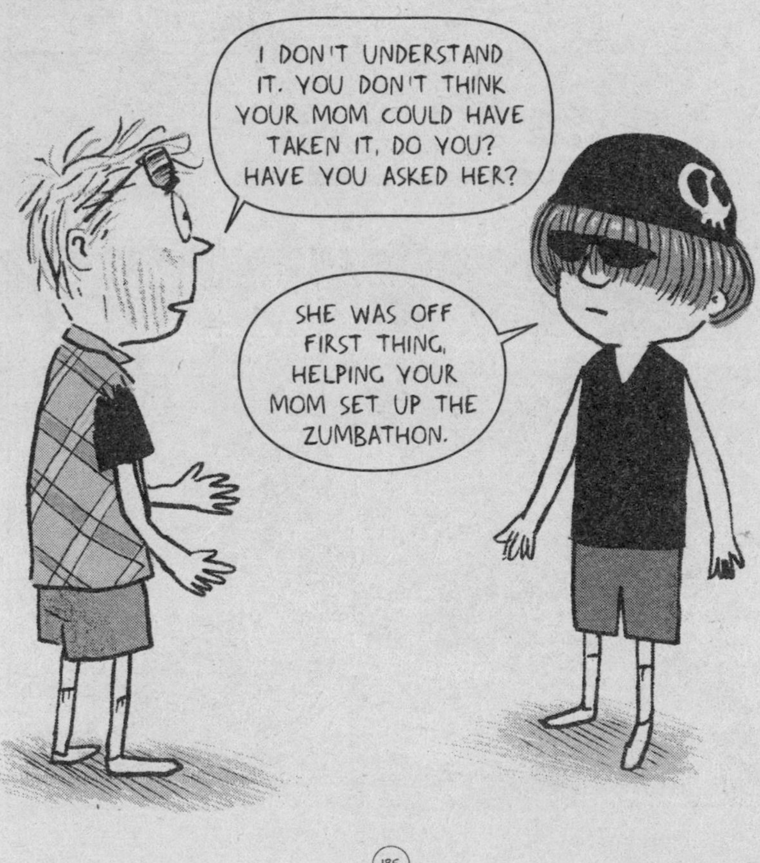
I DON'T UNDERSTAND IT. YOU DON'T THINK YOUR MOM COULD HAVE TAKEN IT, DO YOU? HAVE YOU ASKED HER?
SHE WAS OFF FIRST THING, HELPING YOUR MOM SET UP THE ZUMBATHON.

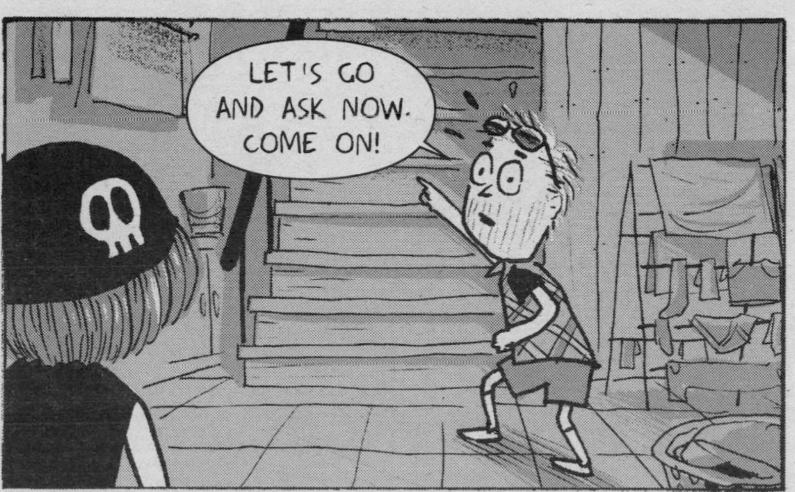
LET'S GO AND ASK NOW. COME ON!

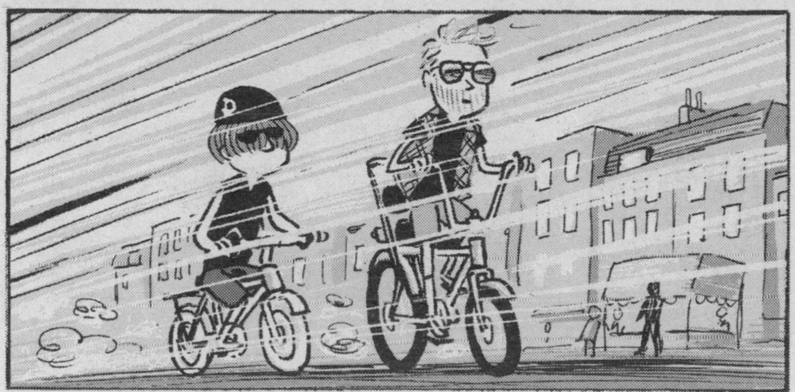

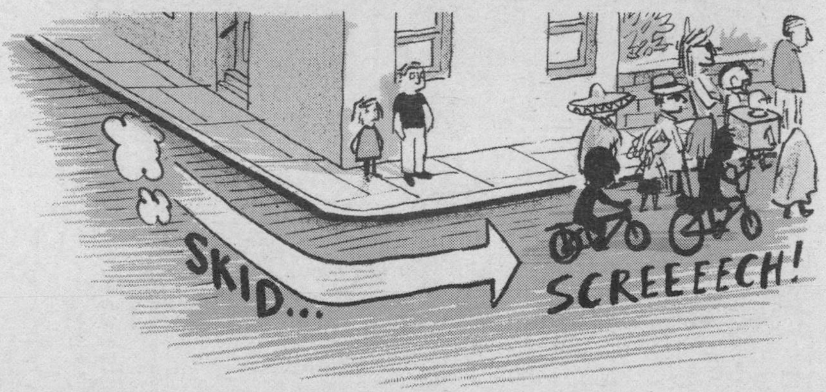
SKID...
SCREEEECH!

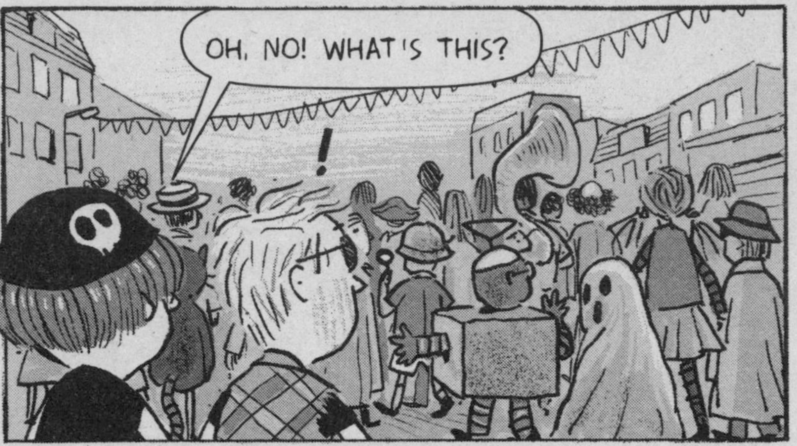
OH, NO! WHAT'S THIS?
!

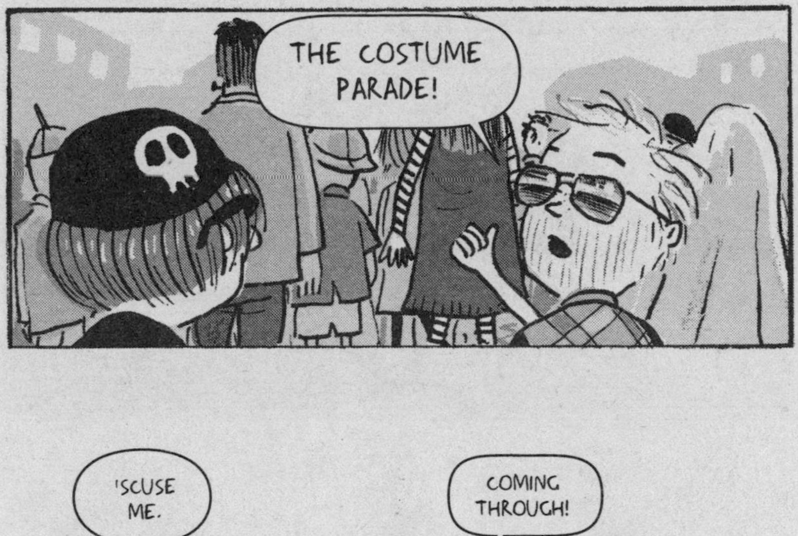
THE COSTUME PARADE!

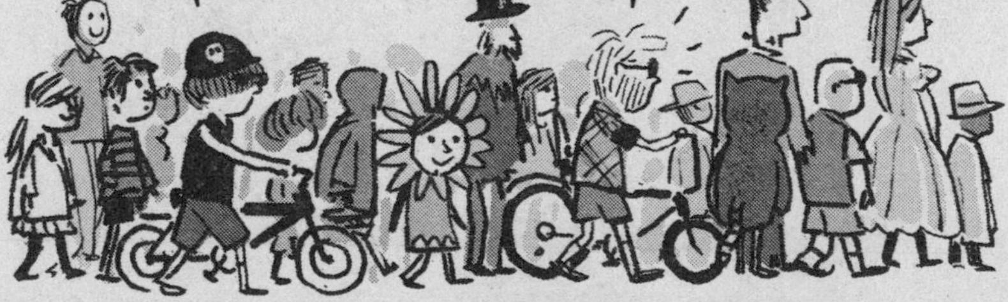
'SCUSE ME.
COMING THROUGH!

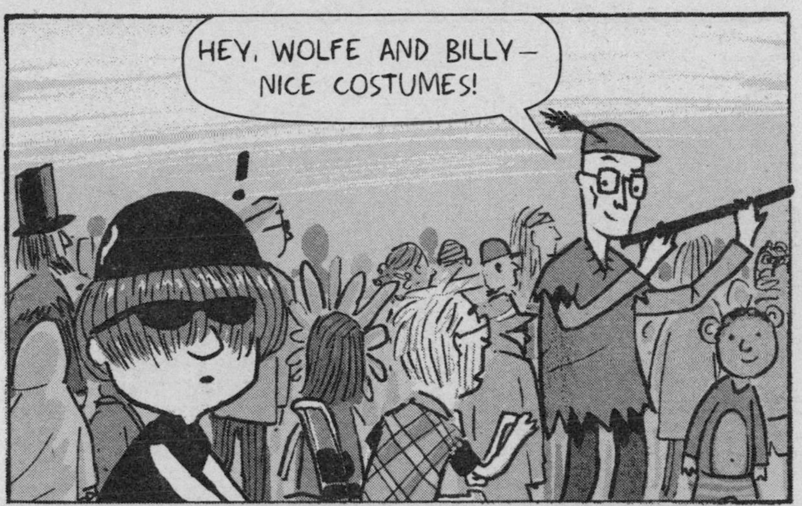
HEY, WOLFE AND BILLY—
NICE COSTUMES!

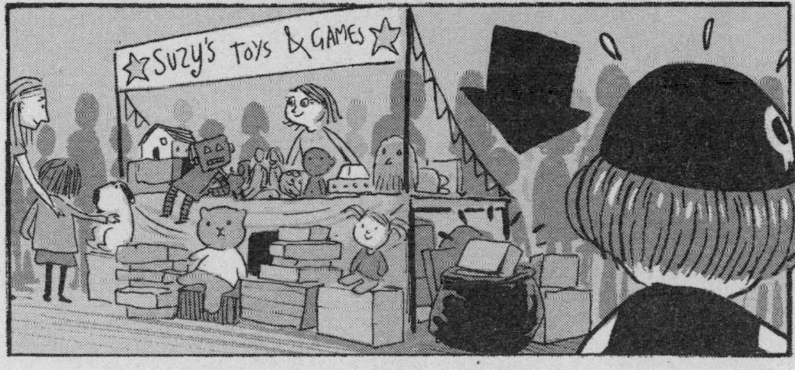
SUZY'S TOYS & GAMES

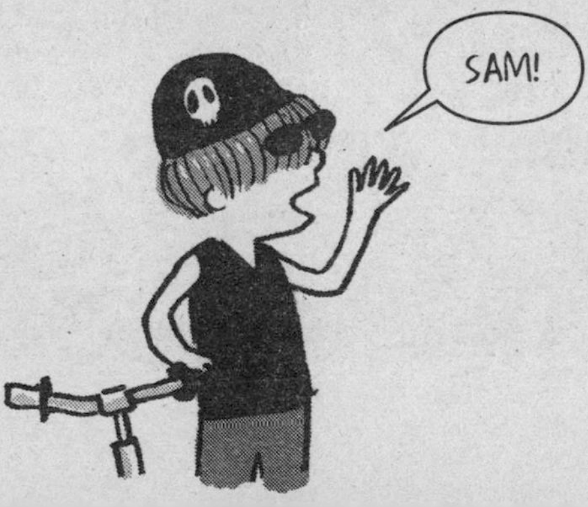
SAM!

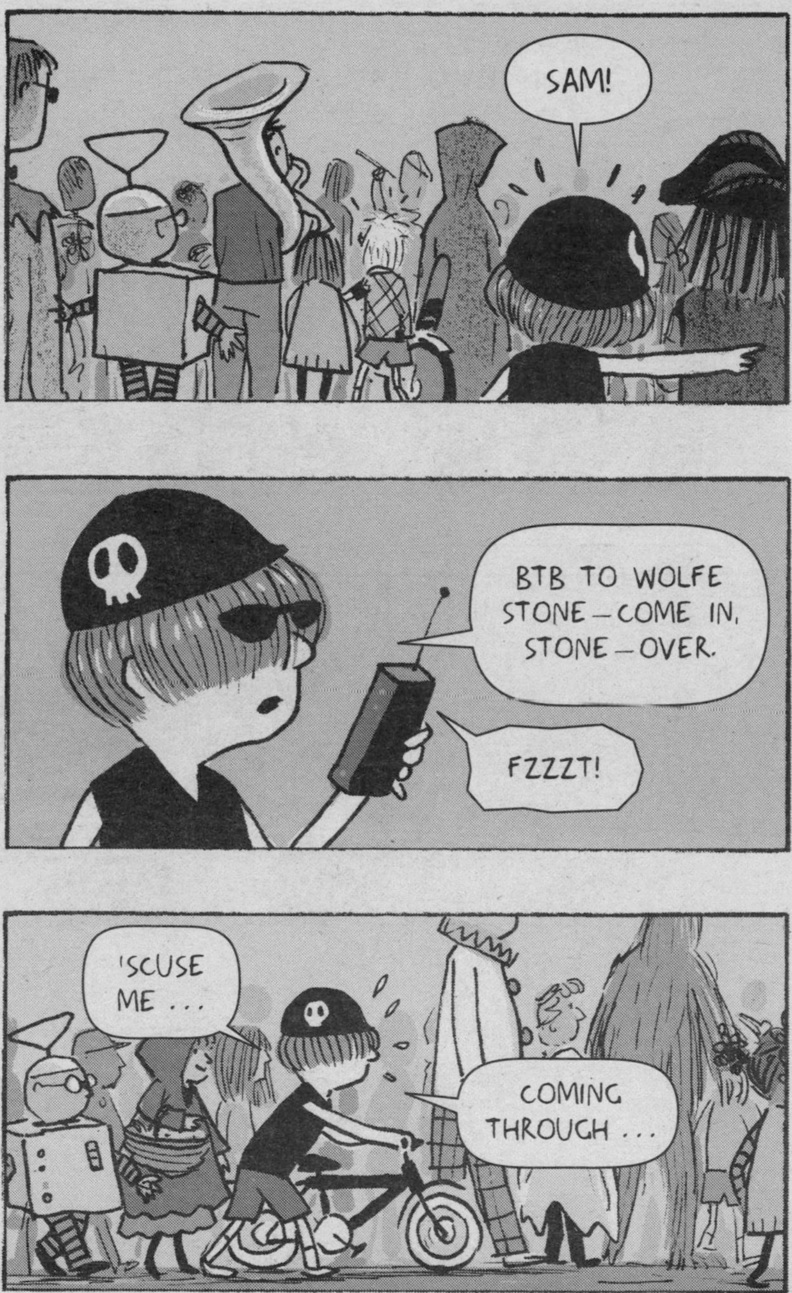
SAM!
BTB TO WOLFE STONE—COME IN, STONE—OVER.
FZZZT!
'SCUSE ME . . .
COMING THROUGH . . .

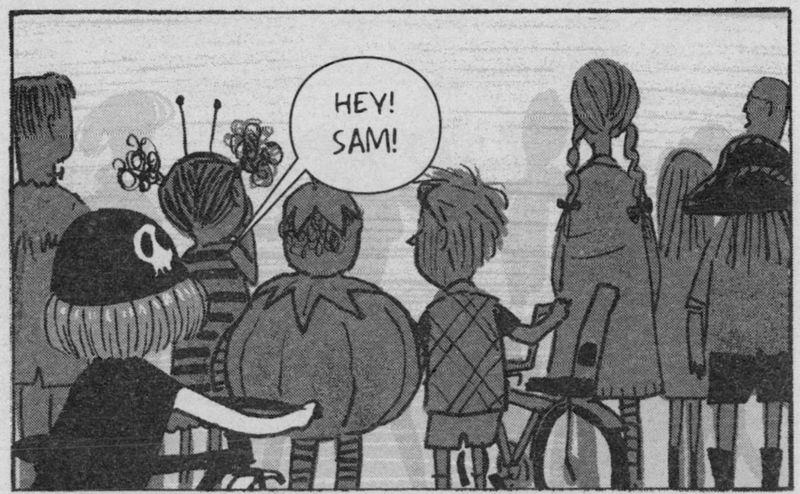
HEY!
SAM!

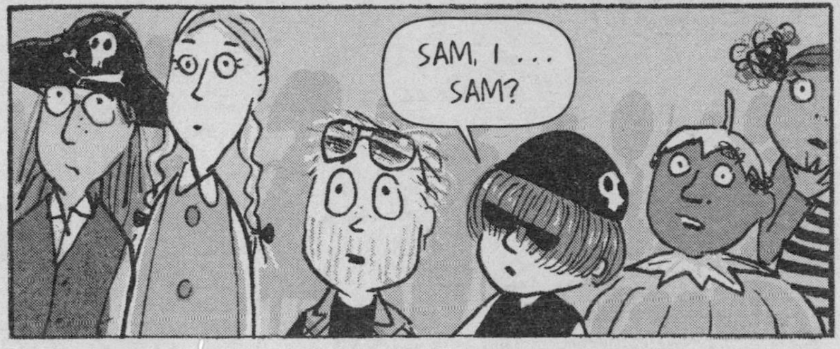
SAM, I . . .
SAM?

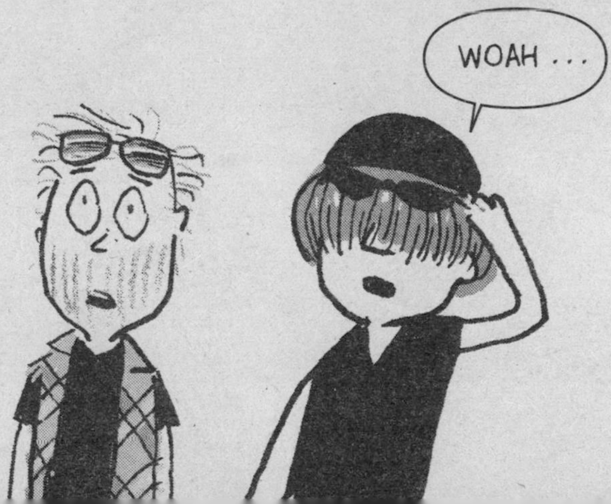
WOAH . . .

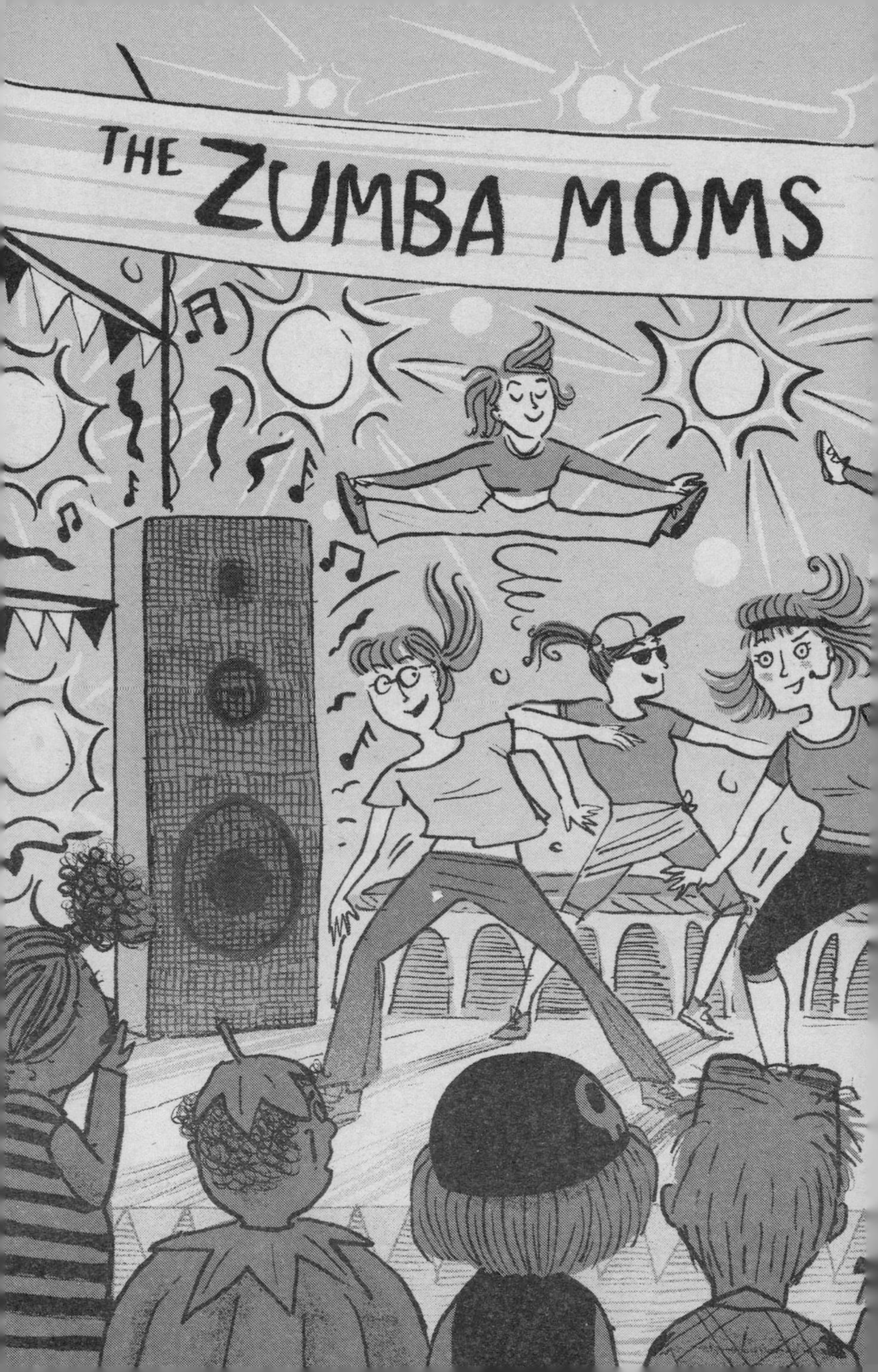
THE ZUMBA MOMS

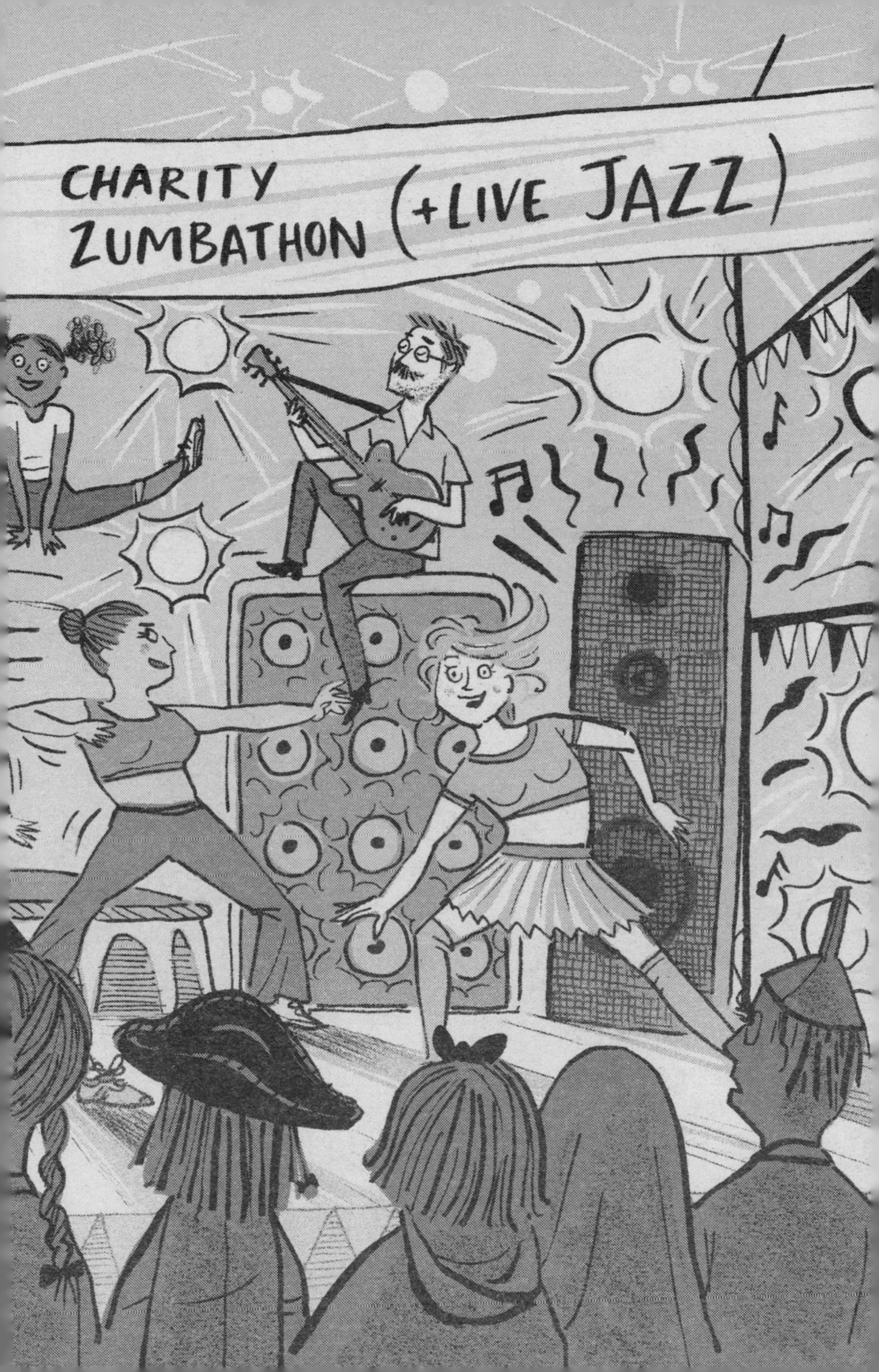
CHARITY ZUMBATHON (+LIVE JAZZ)

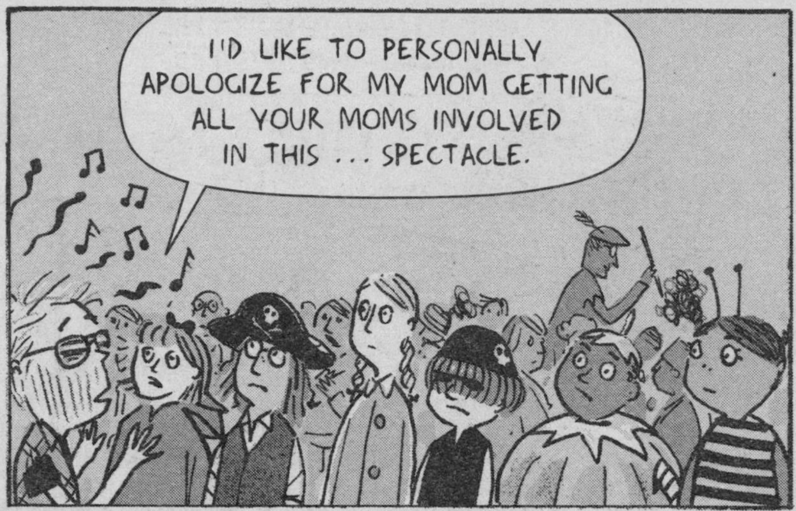
I'D LIKE TO PERSONALLY APOLOGIZE FOR MY MOM GETTING ALL YOUR MOMS INVOLVED IN THIS . . . SPECTACLE.

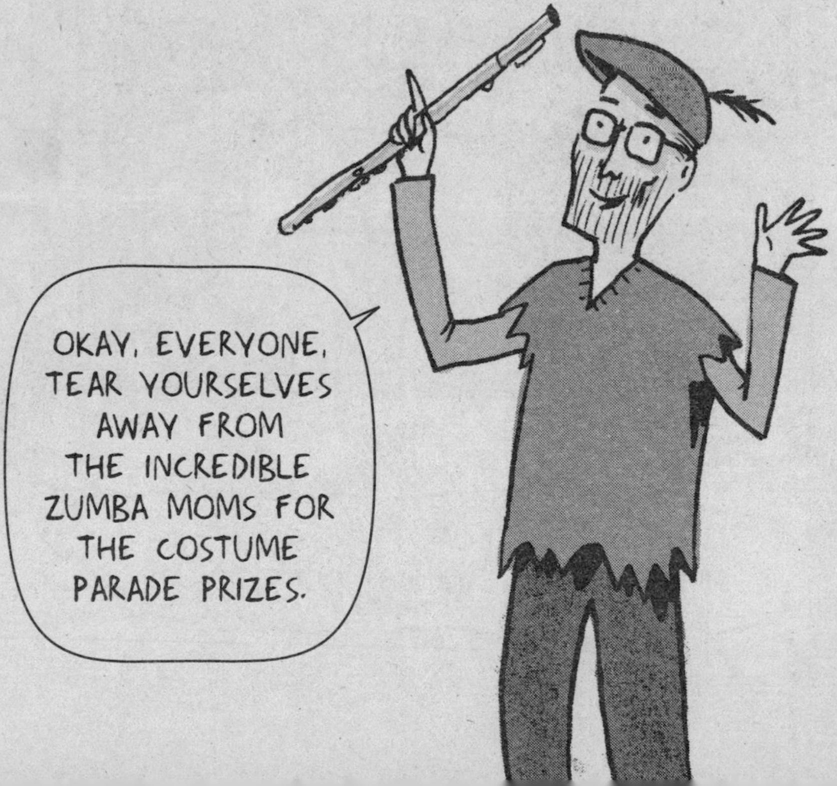
OKAY, EVERYONE, TEAR YOURSELVES AWAY FROM THE INCREDIBLE ZUMBA MOMS FOR THE COSTUME PARADE PRIZES.

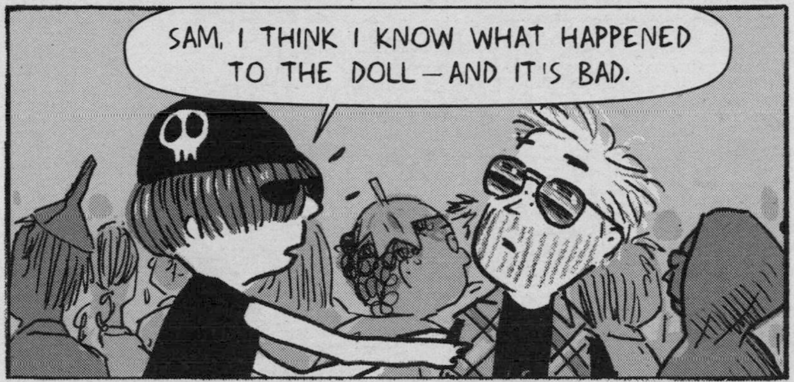
SAM, I THINK I KNOW WHAT HAPPENED TO THE DOLL—AND IT'S BAD.

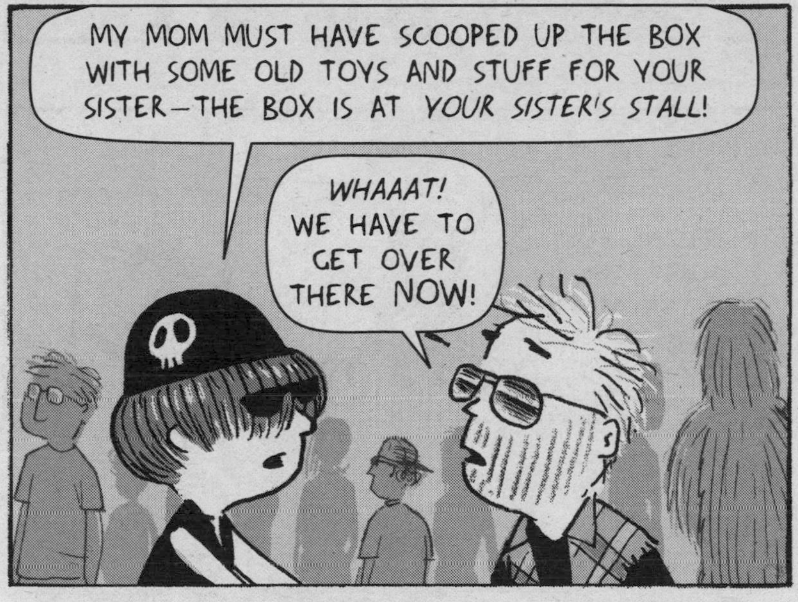
MY MOM MUST HAVE SCOOPED UP THE BOX WITH SOME OLD TOYS AND STUFF FOR YOUR SISTER—THE BOX IS AT *YOUR SISTER'S STALL!*
WHAAAT! WE HAVE TO GET OVER THERE NOW!

AND A SPECAL PRIZE FOR "THEMATIC RELEVANCE" GOES TO ...

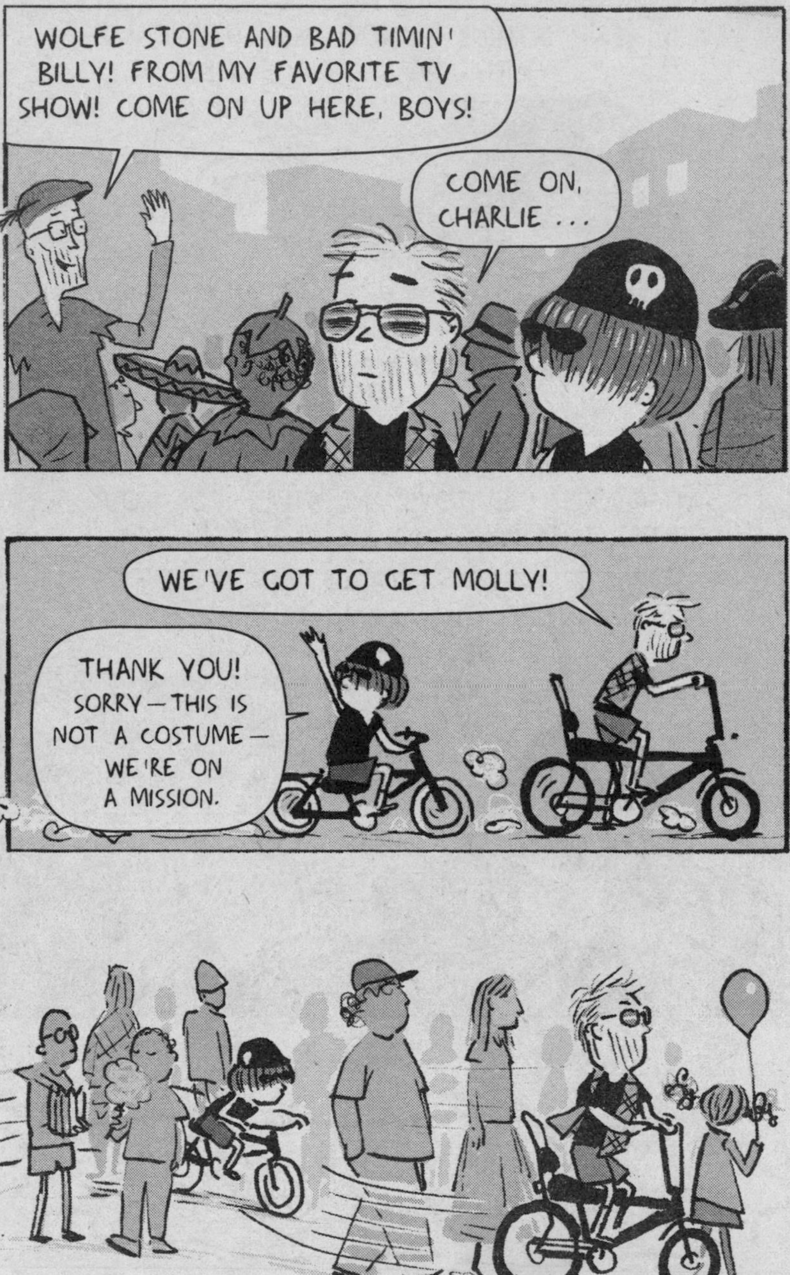
WOLFE STONE AND BAD TIMIN' BILLY! FROM MY FAVORITE TV SHOW! COME ON UP HERE, BOYS!
COME ON, CHARLIE . . .
WE'VE GOT TO GET MOLLY!
THANK YOU! SORRY—THIS IS NOT A COSTUME—WE'RE ON A MISSION.

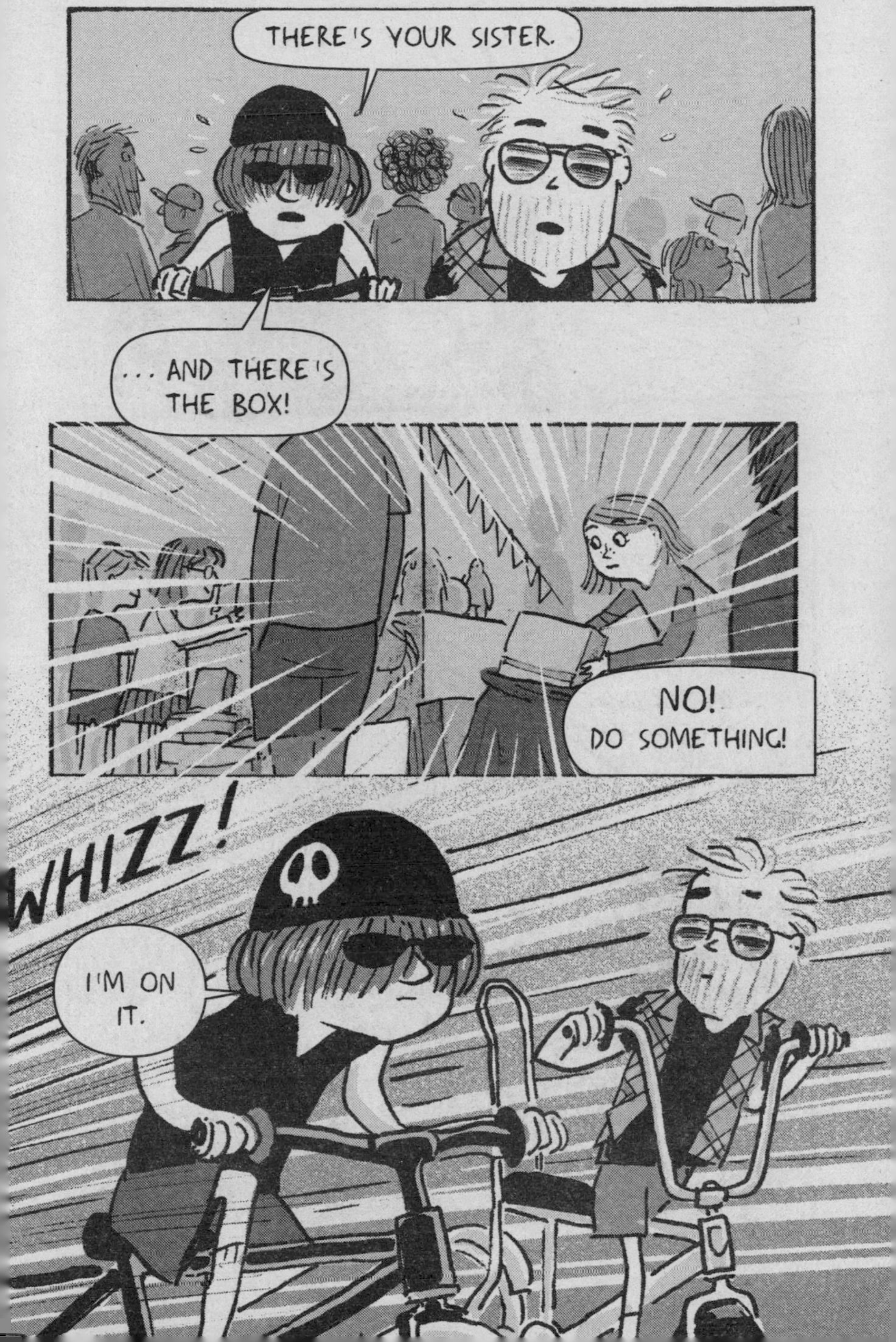
THERE'S YOUR SISTER.
... AND THERE'S THE BOX!
NO! DO SOMETHING!
WHIZZ!
I'M ON IT.

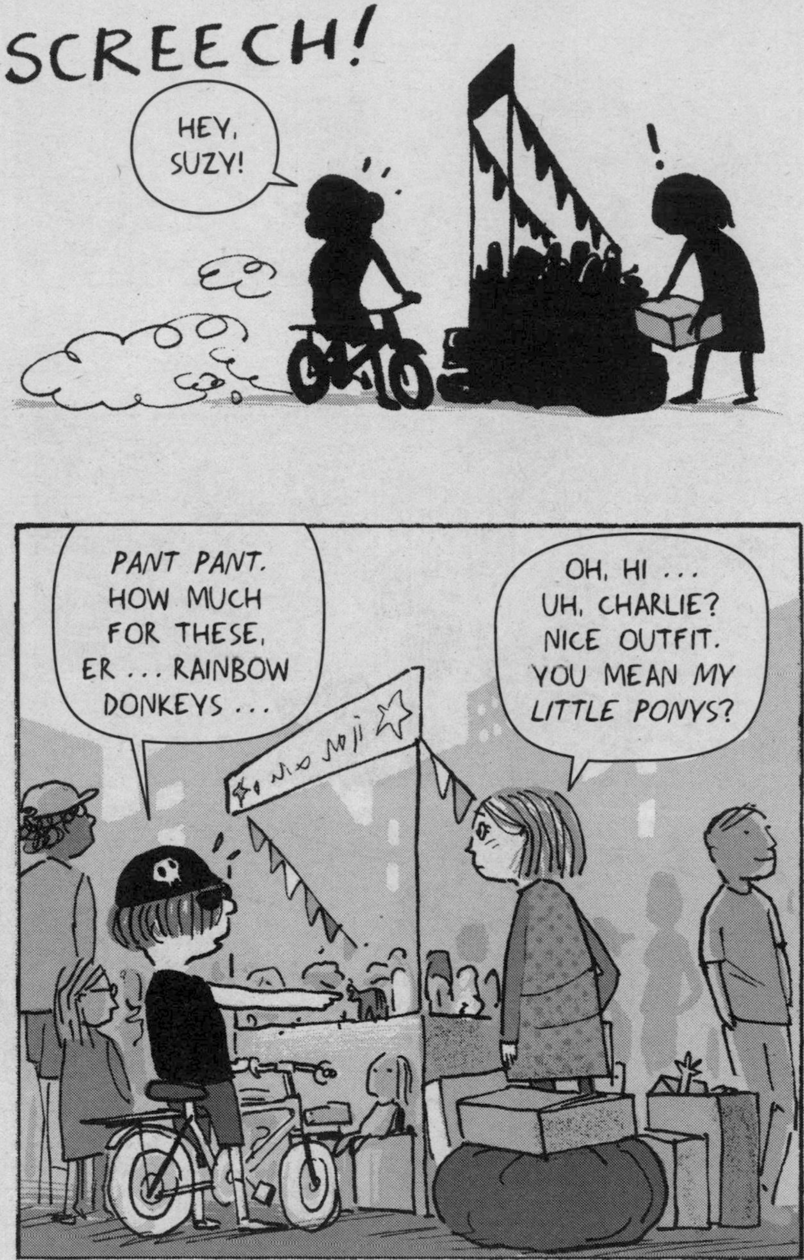
SCREECH!
HEY, SUZY!
!
PANT PANT. HOW MUCH FOR THESE, ER . . . RAINBOW DONKEYS . . .
OH, HI . . . UH, CHARLIE? NICE OUTFIT. YOU MEAN *MY LITTLE PONYS*?

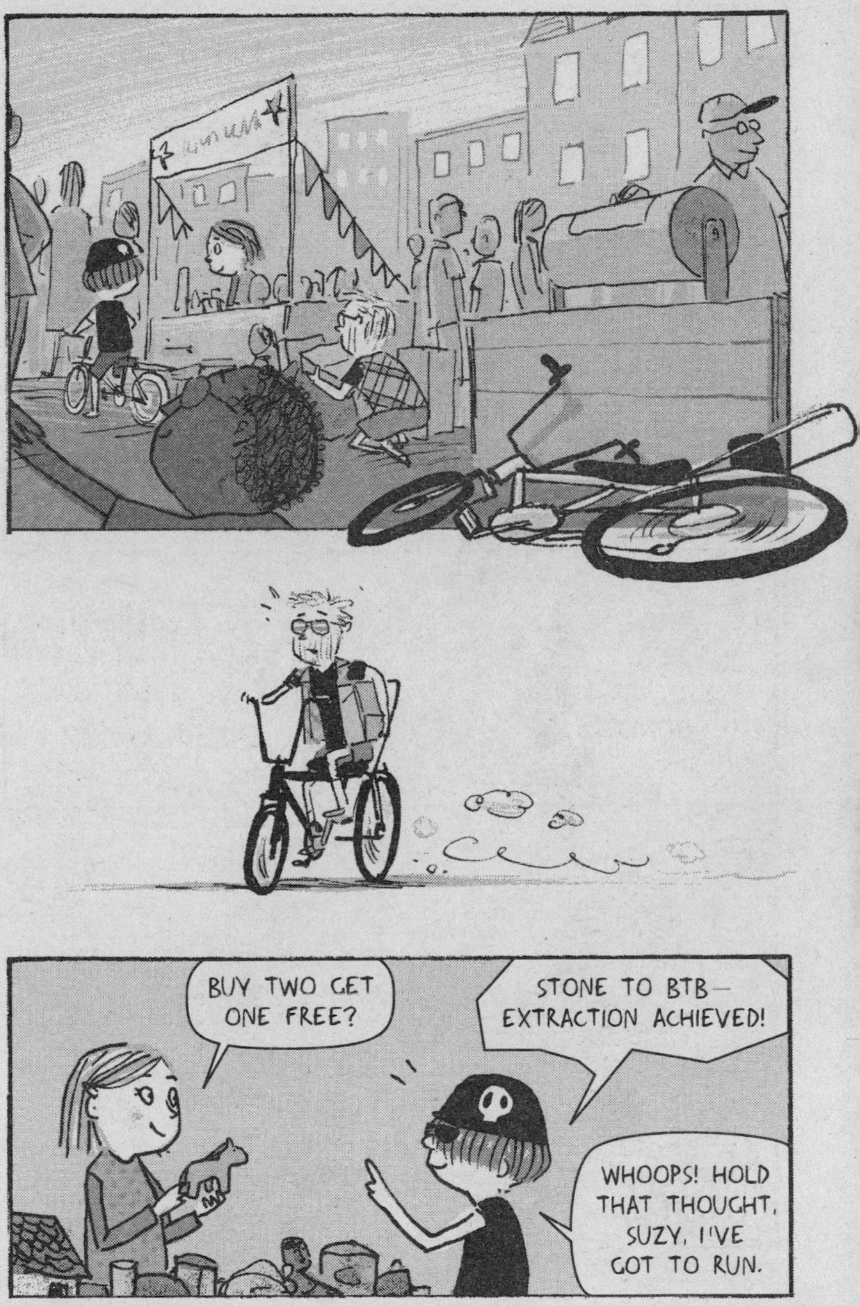
BUY TWO GET ONE FREE?
STONE TO BTB— EXTRACTION ACHIEVED!
WHOOPS! HOLD THAT THOUGHT, SUZY, I'VE GOT TO RUN.

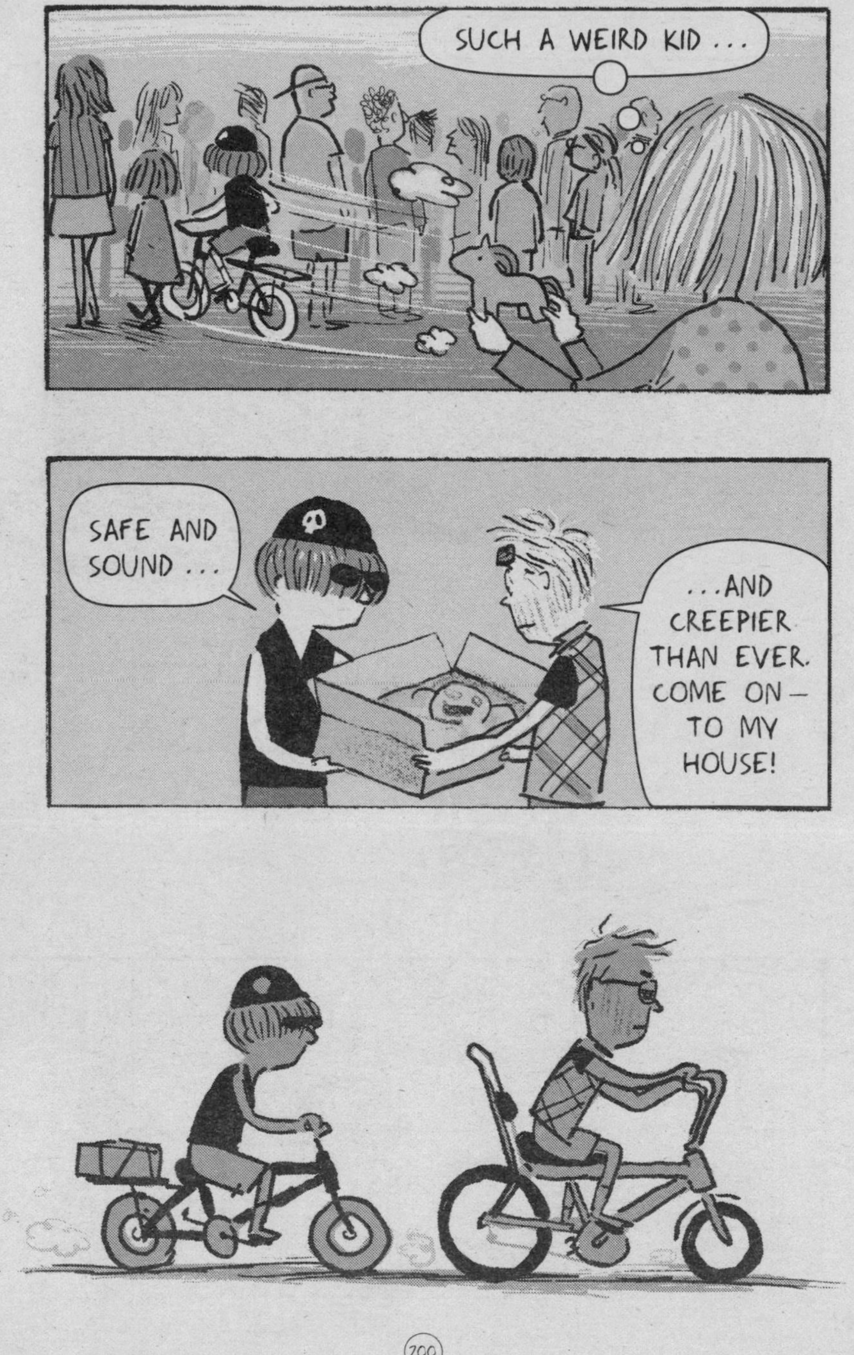
SUCH A WEIRD KID . . .
SAFE AND SOUND . . .
. . .AND CREEPIER THAN EVER. COME ON— TO MY HOUSE!

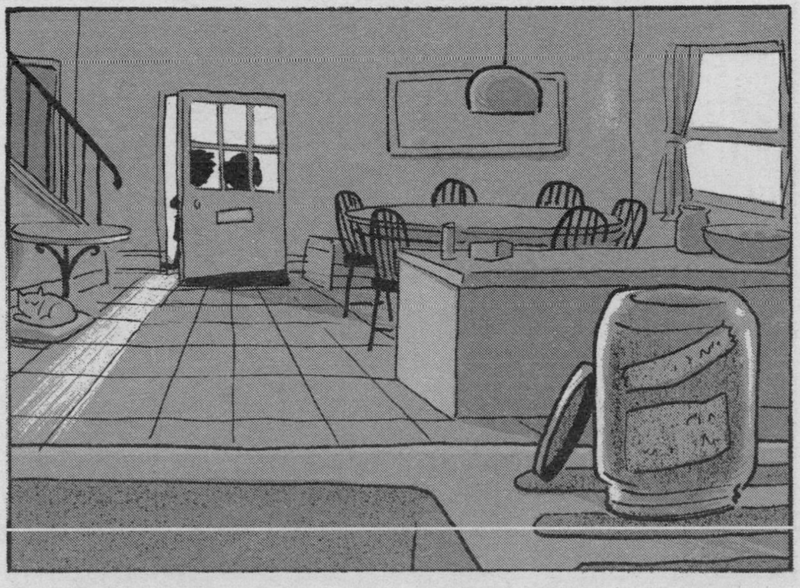

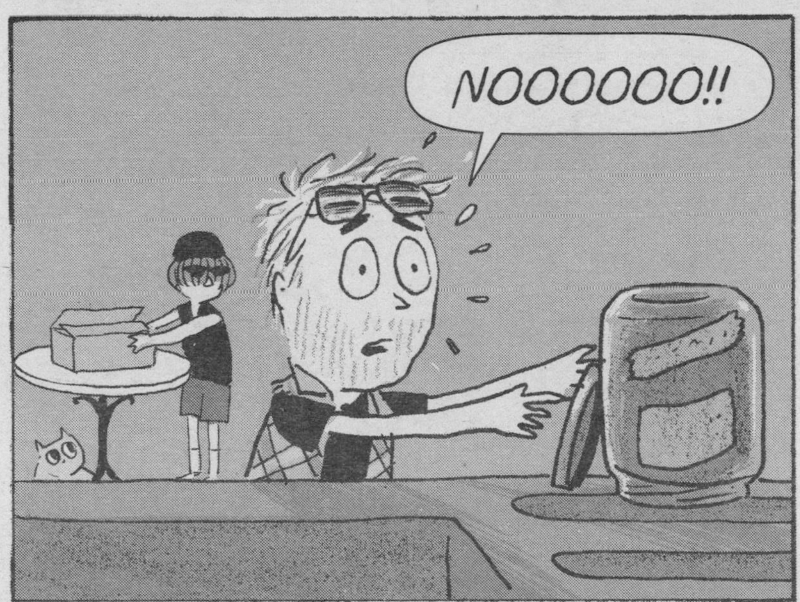
NOOOOOO!!

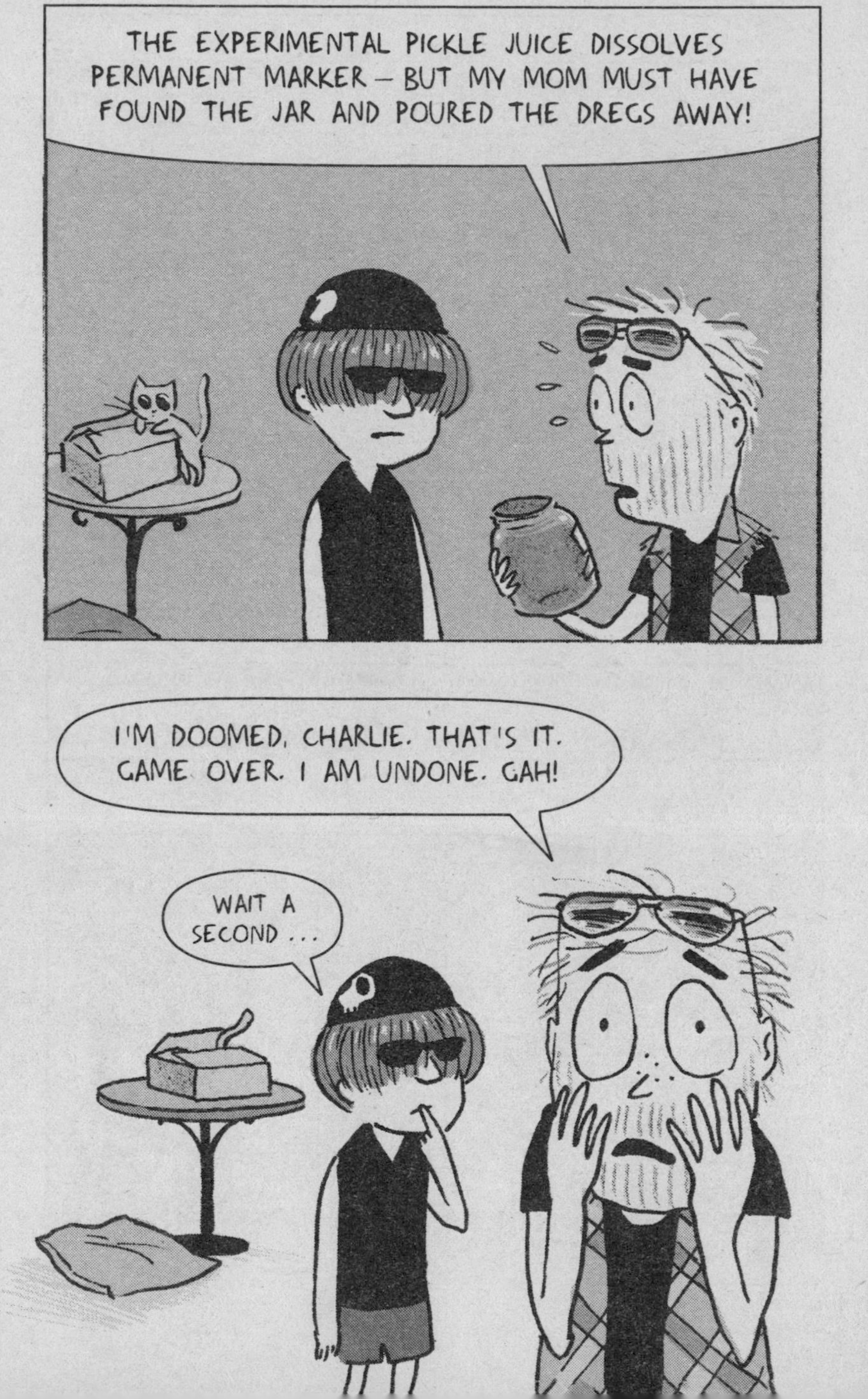
THE EXPERIMENTAL PICKLE JUICE DISSOLVES PERMANENT MARKER—BUT MY MOM MUST HAVE FOUND THE JAR AND POURED THE DREGS AWAY!
I'M DOOMED, CHARLIE. THAT'S IT. GAME OVER. I AM UNDONE. GAH!
WAIT A SECOND . . .

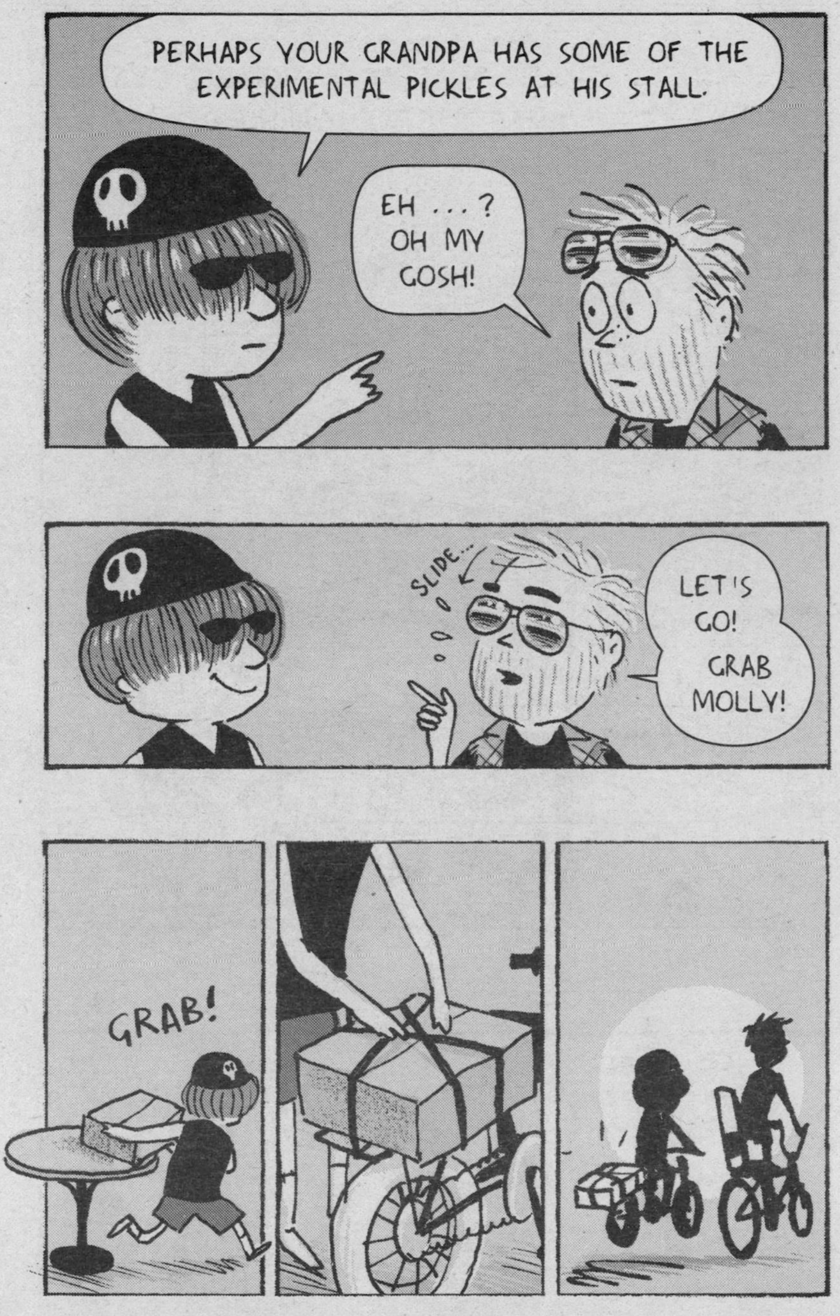
PERHAPS YOUR GRANDPA HAS SOME OF THE EXPERIMENTAL PICKLES AT HIS STALL.
EH ...? OH MY GOSH!
SLIDE...
LET'S GO!
GRAB MOLLY!
GRAB!

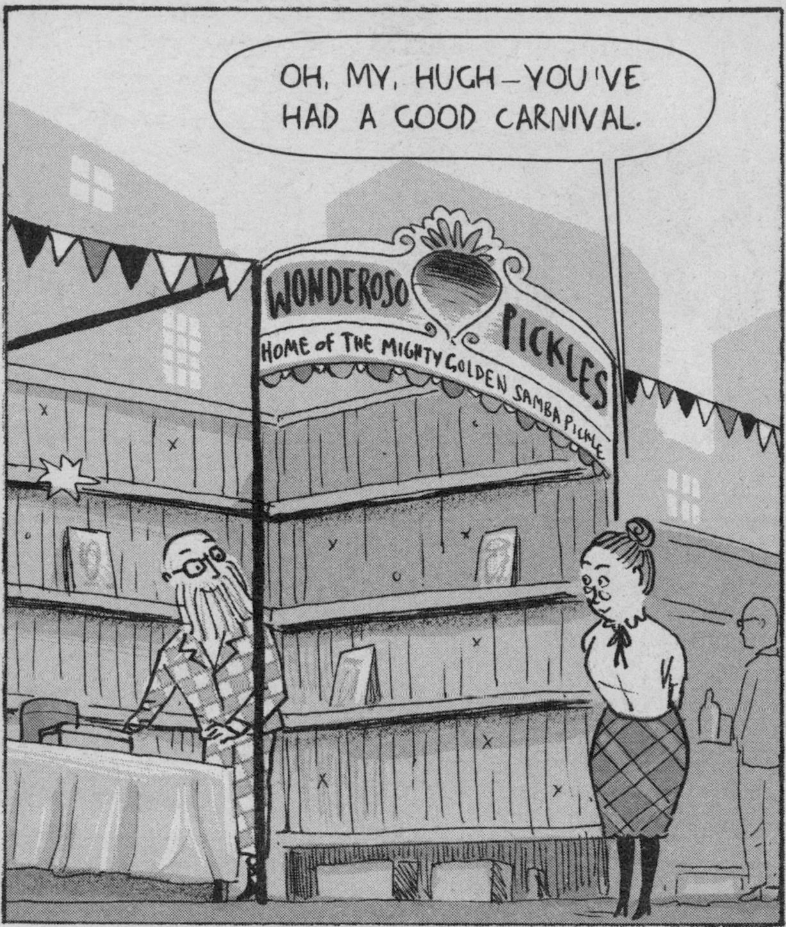
OH, MY, HUGH—YOU'VE HAD A GOOD CARNIVAL.
WONDEROSO PICKLES
HOME of THE MIGHTY GOLDEN SAMBA PICKLE

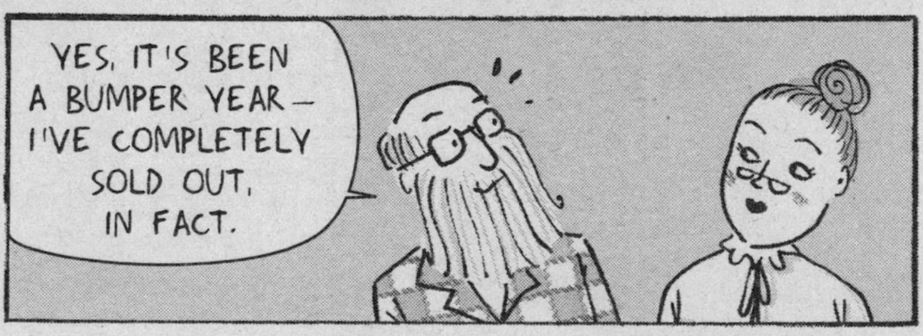
YES, IT'S BEEN A BUMPER YEAR—I'VE COMPLETELY SOLD OUT, IN FACT.

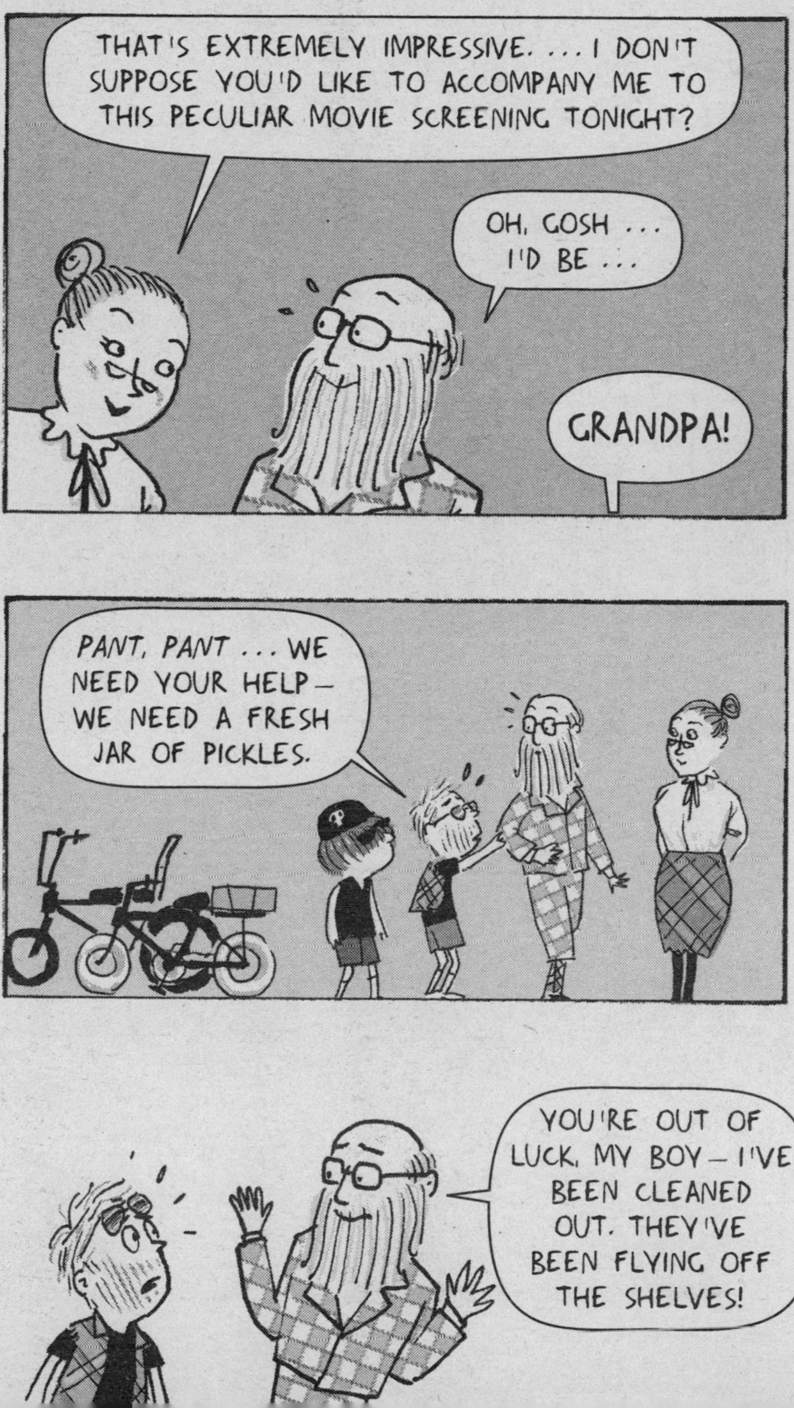
THAT'S EXTREMELY IMPRESSIVE. ... I DON'T SUPPOSE YOU'D LIKE TO ACCOMPANY ME TO THIS PECULIAR MOVIE SCREENING TONIGHT?
OH, GOSH ... I'D BE ...
GRANDPA!
PANT, PANT ... WE NEED YOUR HELP— WE NEED A FRESH JAR OF PICKLES.
YOU'RE OUT OF LUCK, MY BOY—I'VE BEEN CLEANED OUT. THEY'VE BEEN FLYING OFF THE SHELVES!

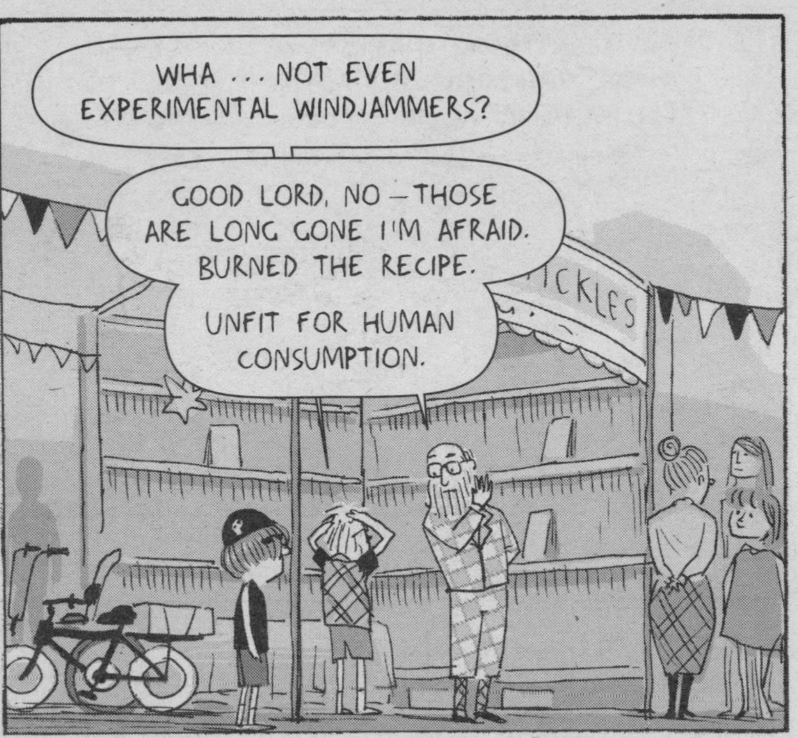
WHA ... NOT EVEN EXPERIMENTAL WINDJAMMERS?
GOOD LORD, NO – THOSE ARE LONG GONE I'M AFRAID. BURNED THE RECIPE.
UNFIT FOR HUMAN CONSUMPTION.
PICKLES

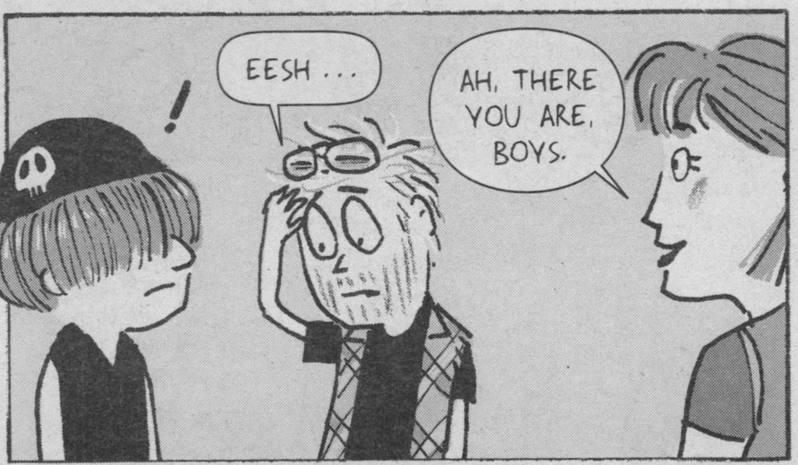
!
EESH ...
AH, THERE YOU ARE, BOYS.

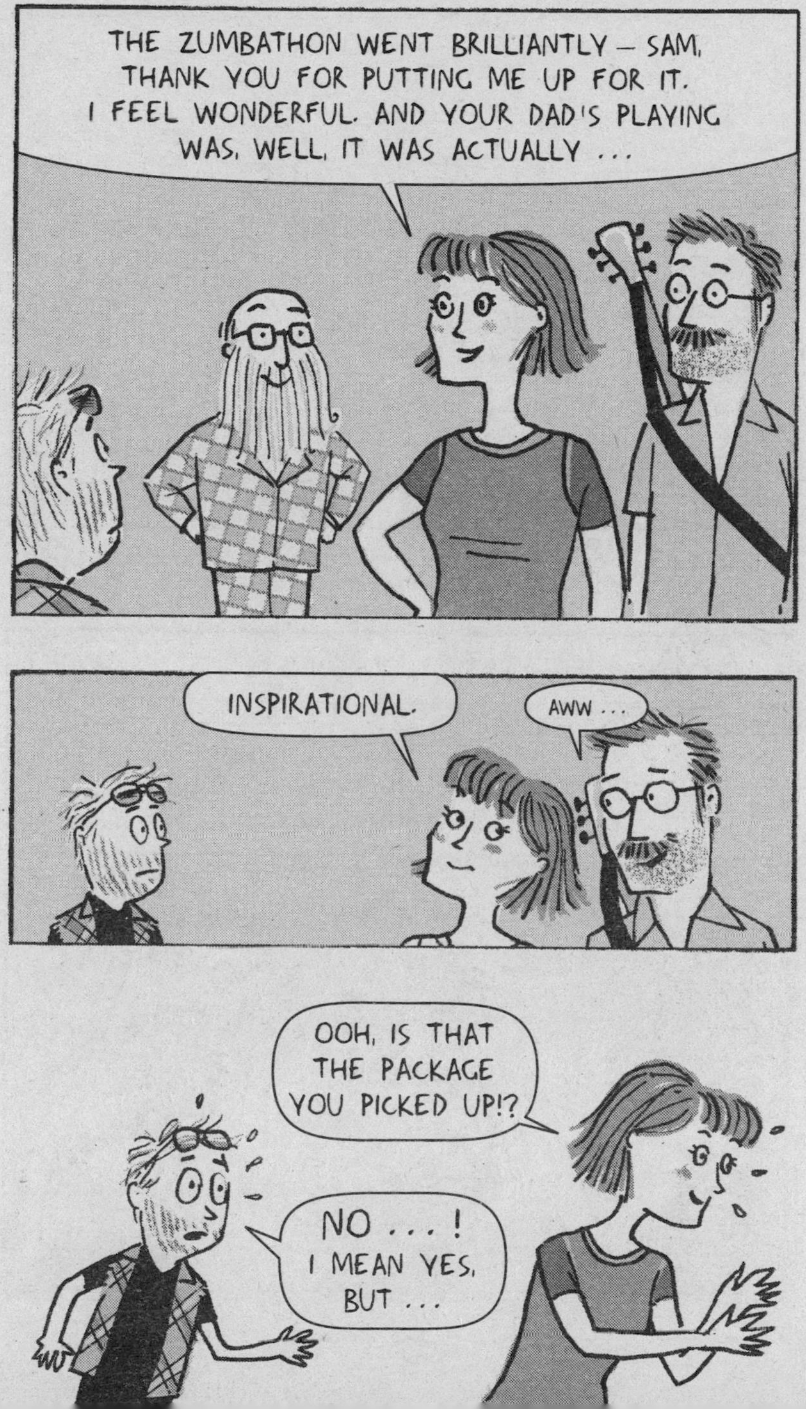
THE ZUMBATHON WENT BRILLIANTLY – SAM, THANK YOU FOR PUTTING ME UP FOR IT. I FEEL WONDERFUL. AND YOUR DAD'S PLAYING WAS, WELL, IT WAS ACTUALLY ...
INSPIRATIONAL.
AWW ...
OOH, IS THAT THE PACKAGE YOU PICKED UP!?
NO ... ! I MEAN YES, BUT ...

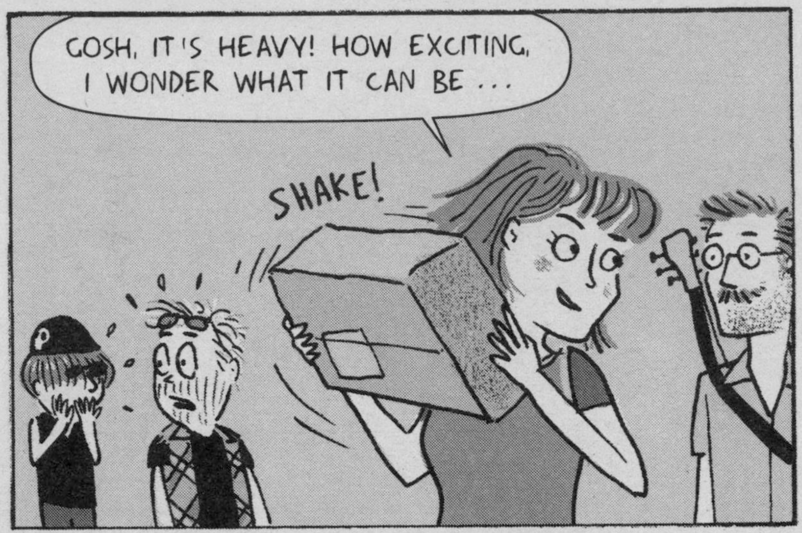
GOSH, IT'S HEAVY! HOW EXCITING. I WONDER WHAT IT CAN BE . . .
SHAKE!

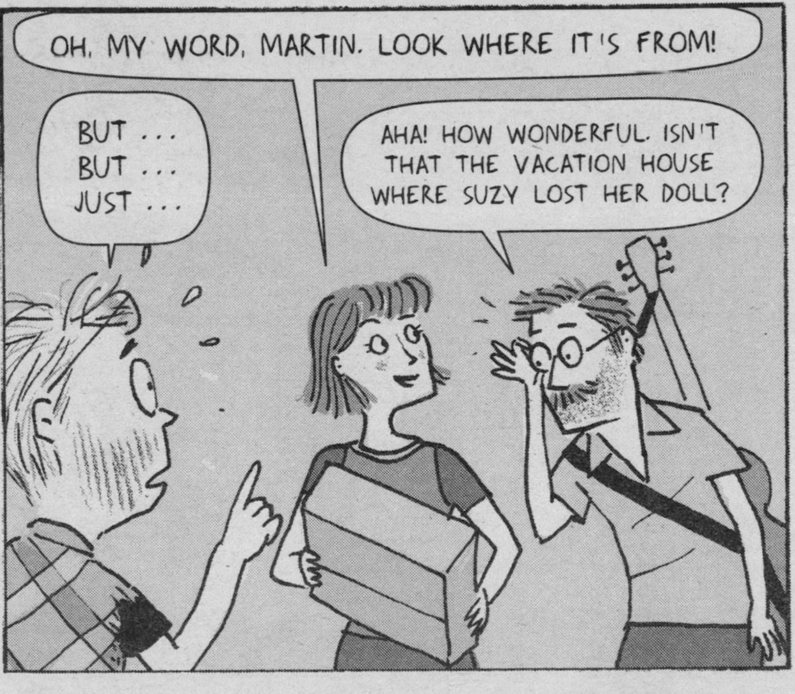
OH, MY WORD, MARTIN. LOOK WHERE IT'S FROM!
BUT . . . BUT . . . JUST . . .
AHA! HOW WONDERFUL. ISN'T THAT THE VACATION HOUSE WHERE SUZY LOST HER DOLL?

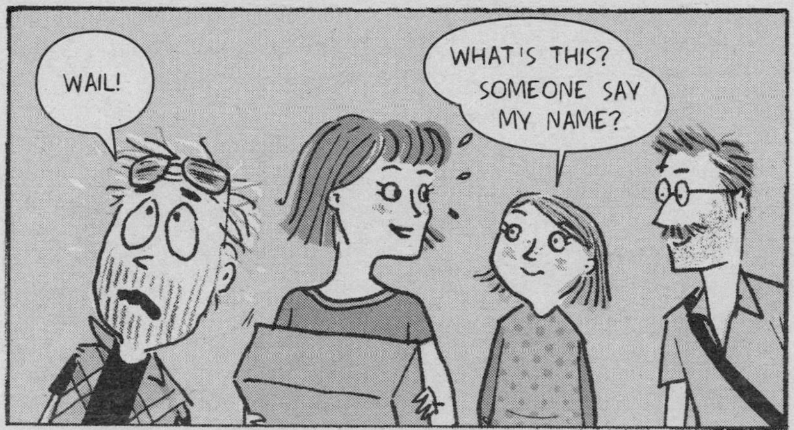
WAIL!
WHAT'S THIS? SOMEONE SAY MY NAME?

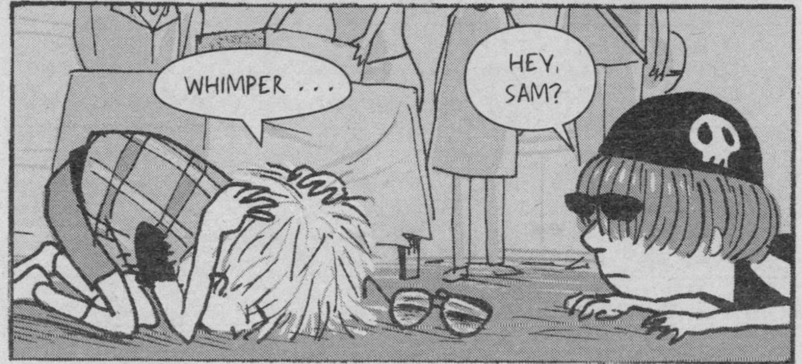
WHIMPER . . .
HEY, SAM?

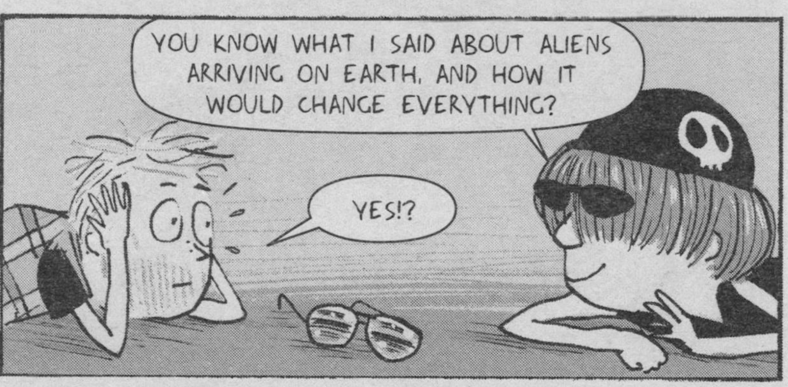
YOU KNOW WHAT I SAID ABOUT ALIENS ARRIVING ON EARTH, AND HOW IT WOULD CHANGE EVERYTHING?
YES!?

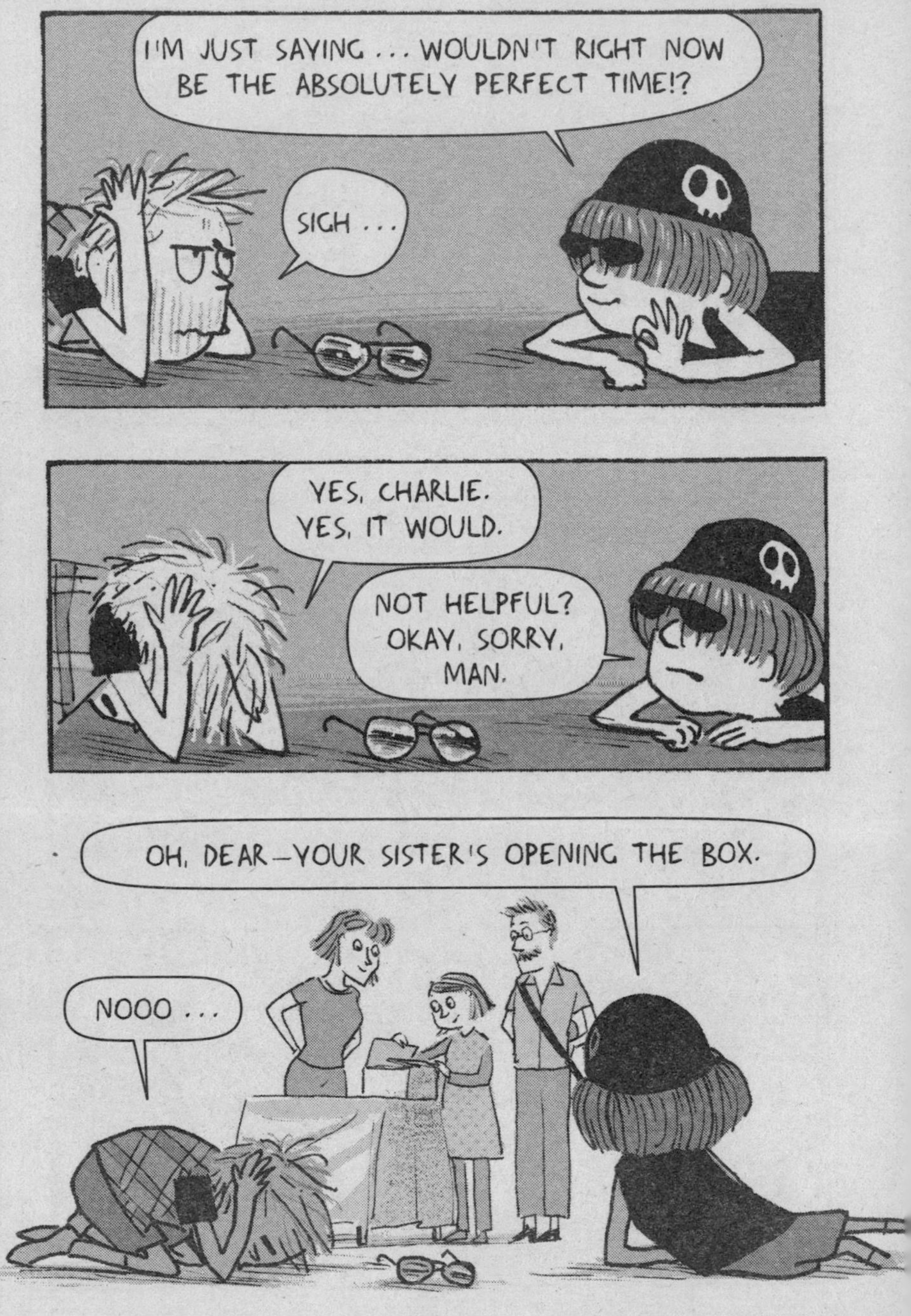
I'M JUST SAYING . . . WOULDN'T RIGHT NOW BE THE ABSOLUTELY PERFECT TIME!?
SIGH . . .
YES, CHARLIE. YES, IT WOULD.
NOT HELPFUL? OKAY, SORRY, MAN.
OH, DEAR—YOUR SISTER'S OPENING THE BOX.
NOOO . . .

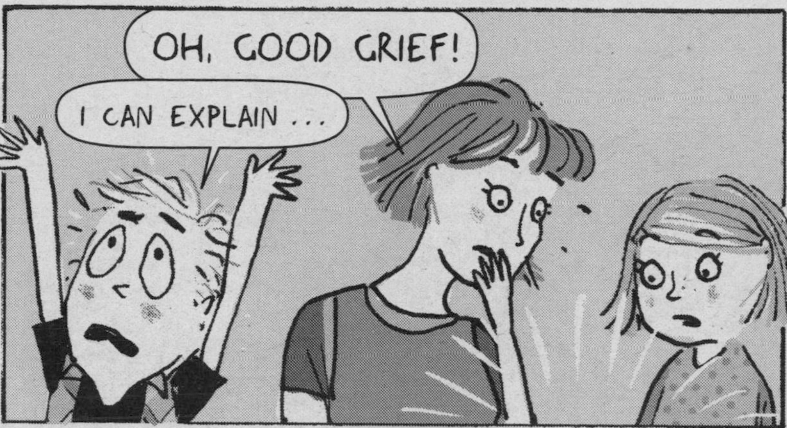
OH, GOOD GRIEF!
I CAN EXPLAIN . . .

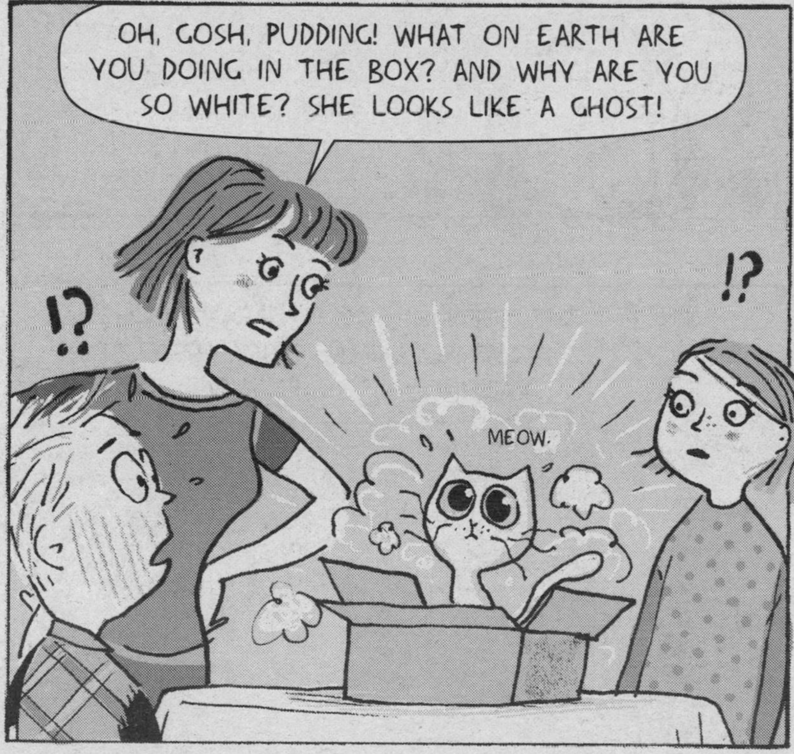
OH, GOSH, PUDDING! WHAT ON EARTH ARE YOU DOING IN THE BOX? AND WHY ARE YOU SO WHITE? SHE LOOKS LIKE A GHOST!
!?
!?
MEOW.

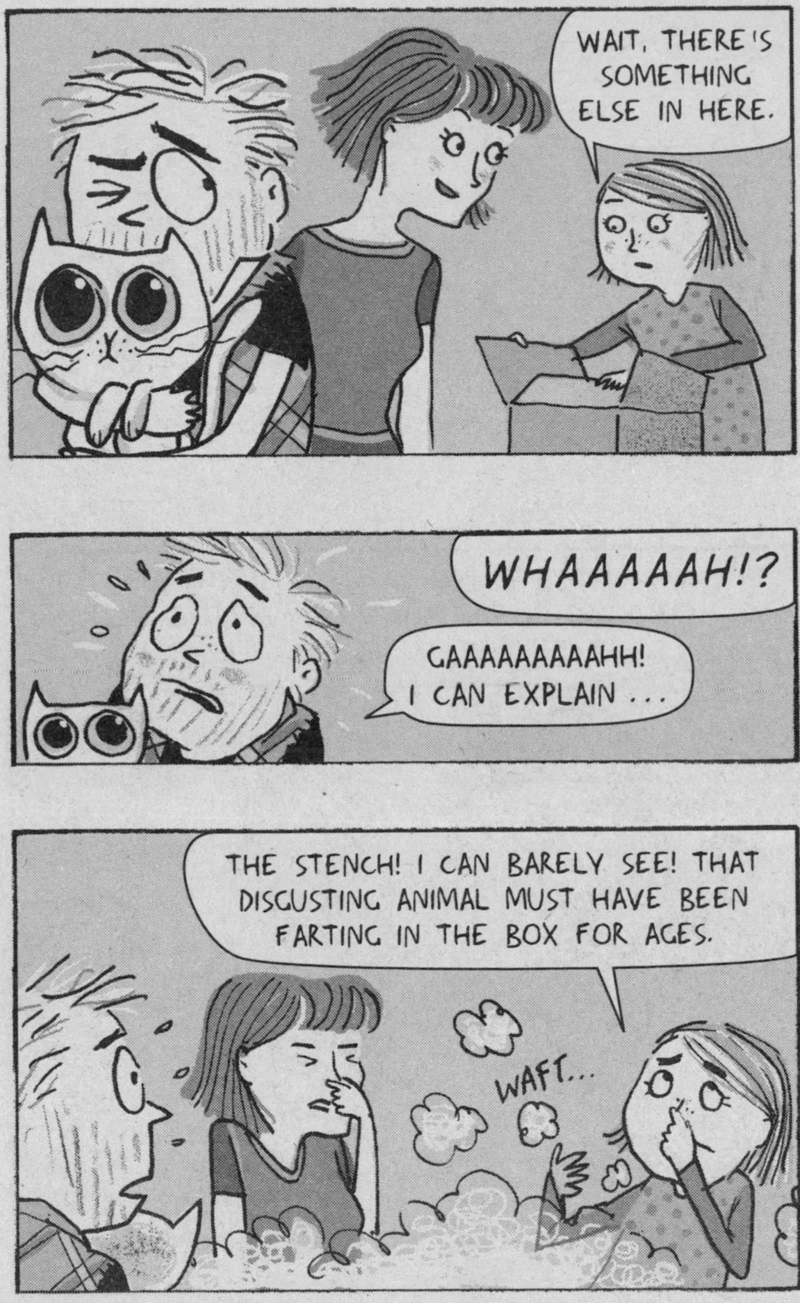
WAIT, THERE'S SOMETHING ELSE IN HERE.
WHAAAAAH!?
GAAAAAAAAAHH! I CAN EXPLAIN . . .
THE STENCH! I CAN BARELY SEE! THAT DISGUSTING ANIMAL MUST HAVE BEEN FARTING IN THE BOX FOR AGES.
WAFT...

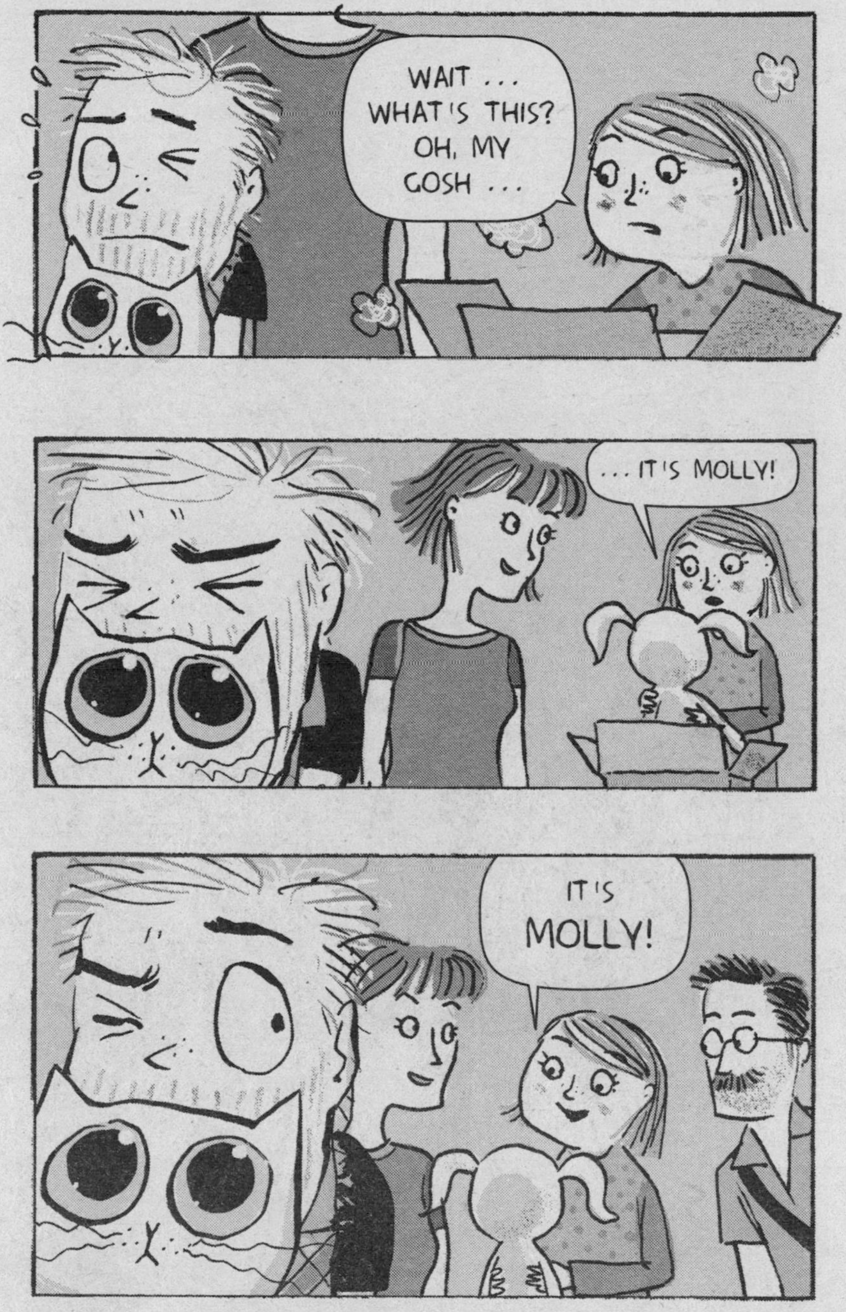
WAIT ...
WHAT'S THIS?
OH, MY
GOSH ...
... IT'S MOLLY!
IT'S
MOLLY!

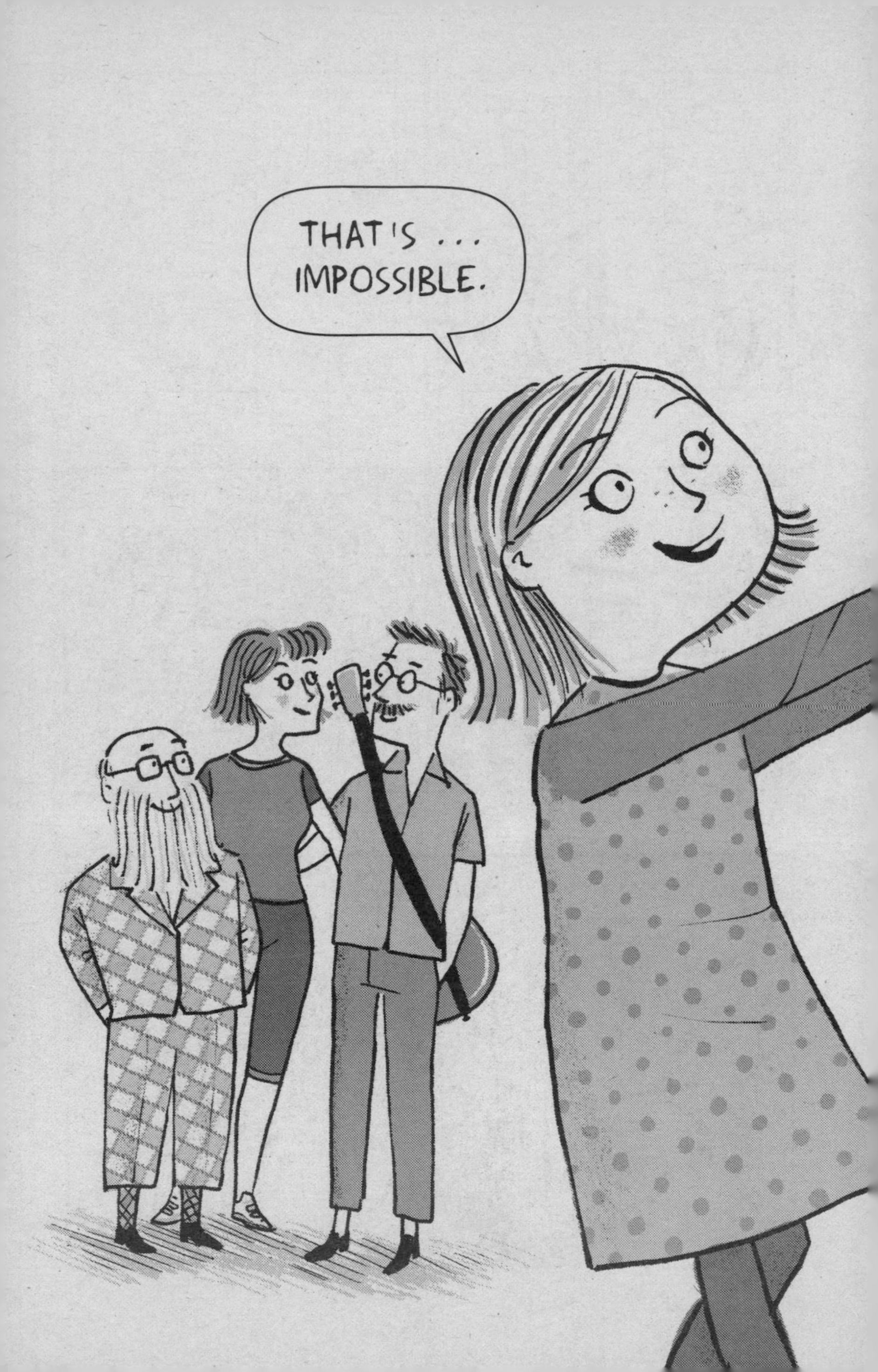
THAT'S ... IMPOSSIBLE.

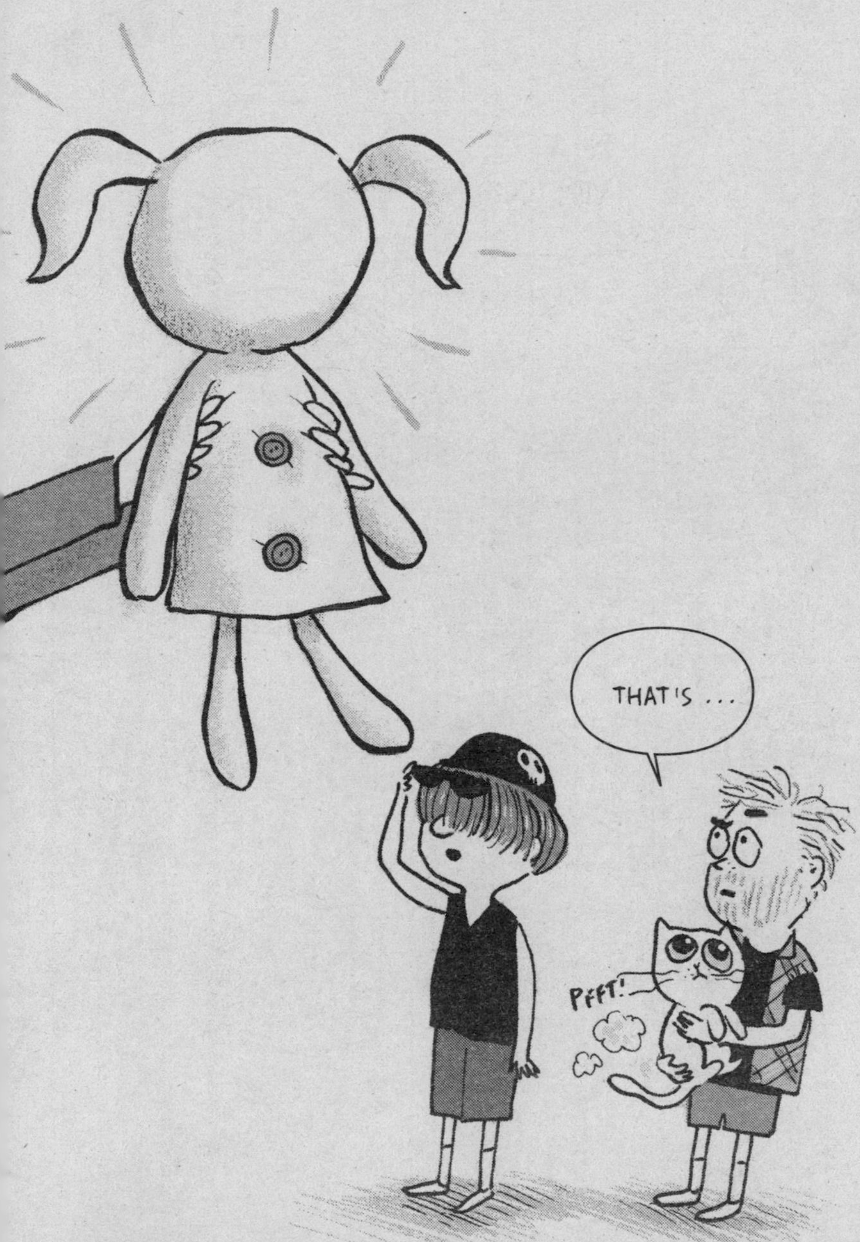
THAT'S . . .
PFFT!

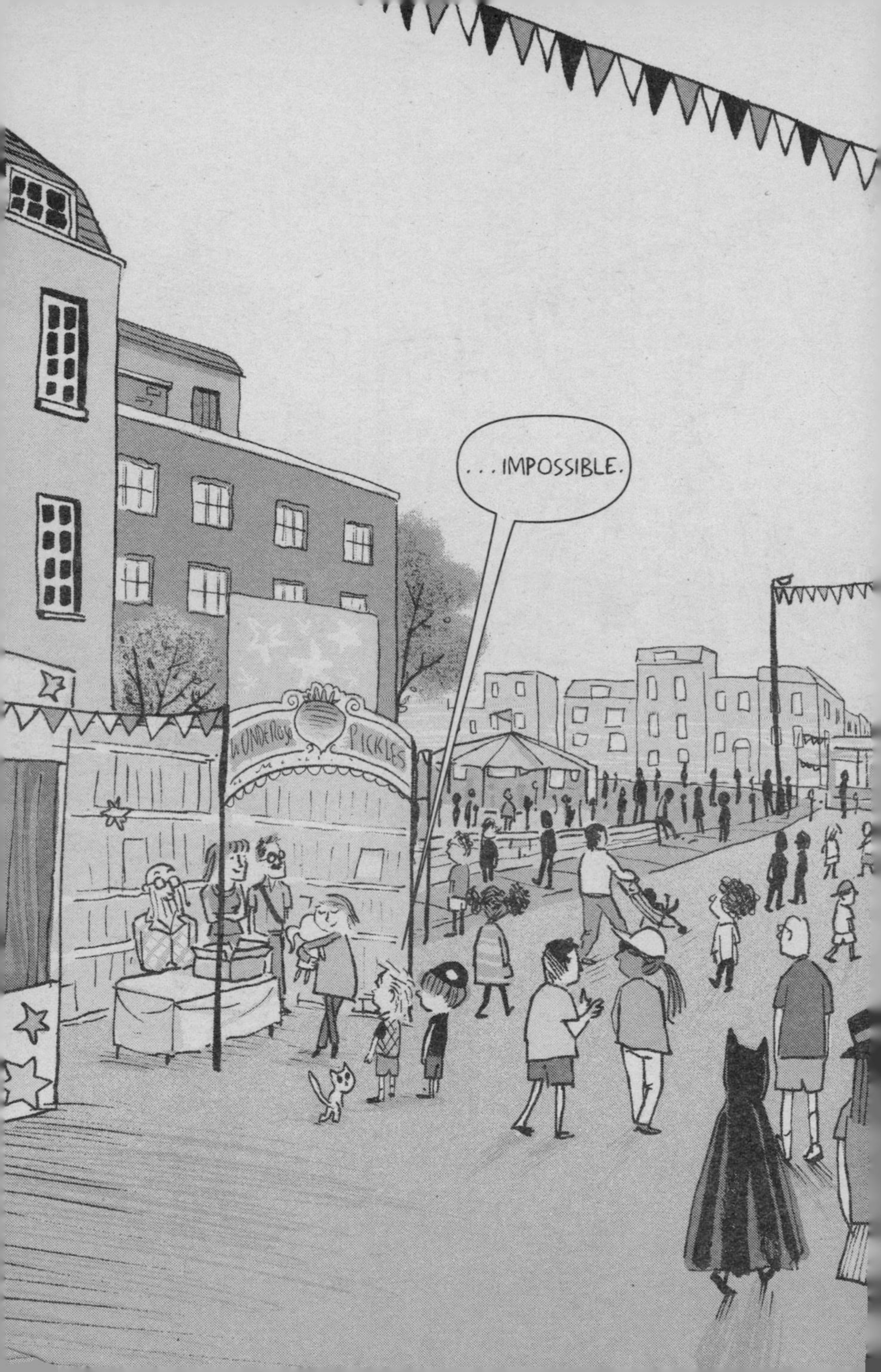

...IMPOSSIBLE.
PICKLES

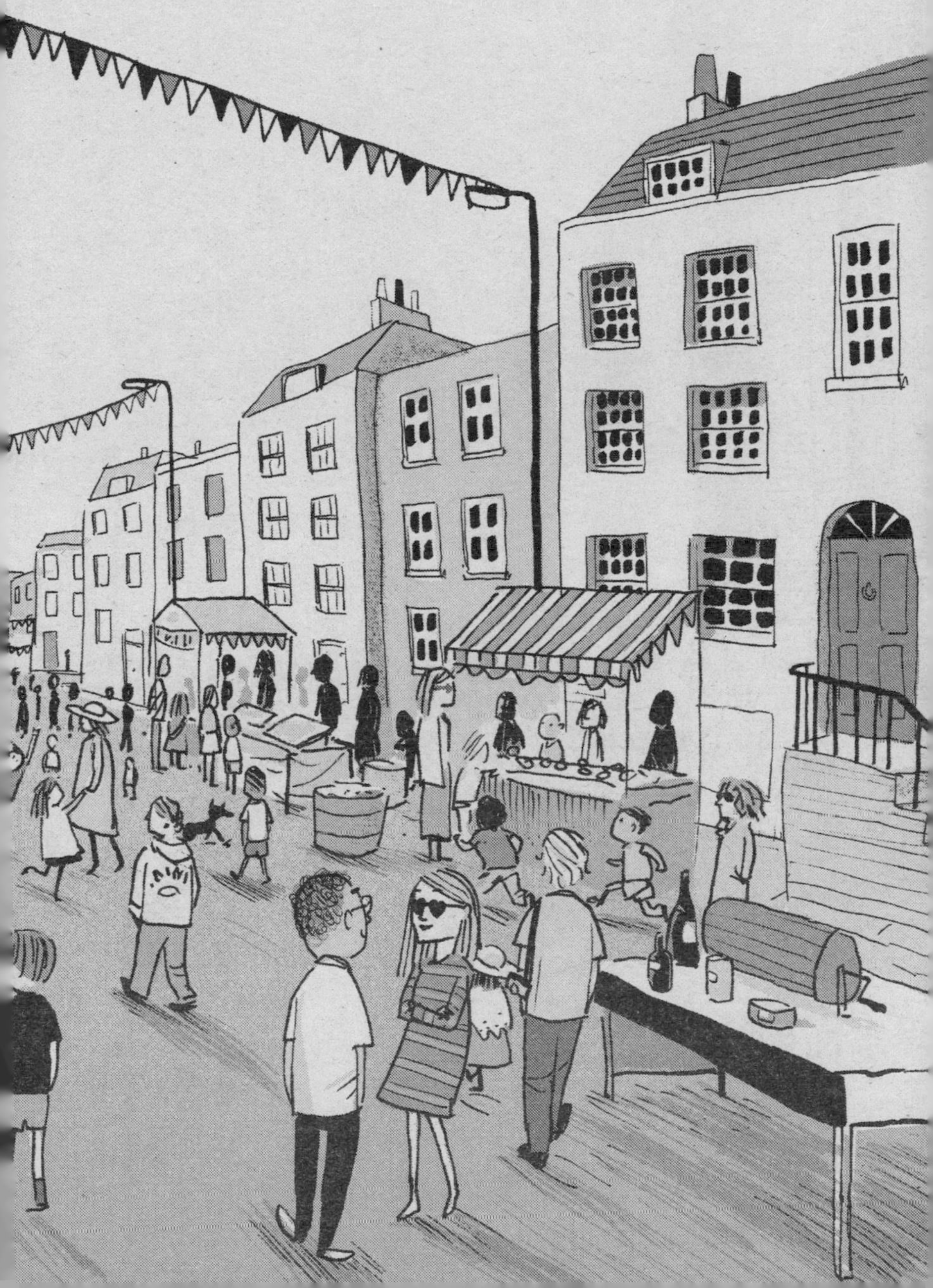

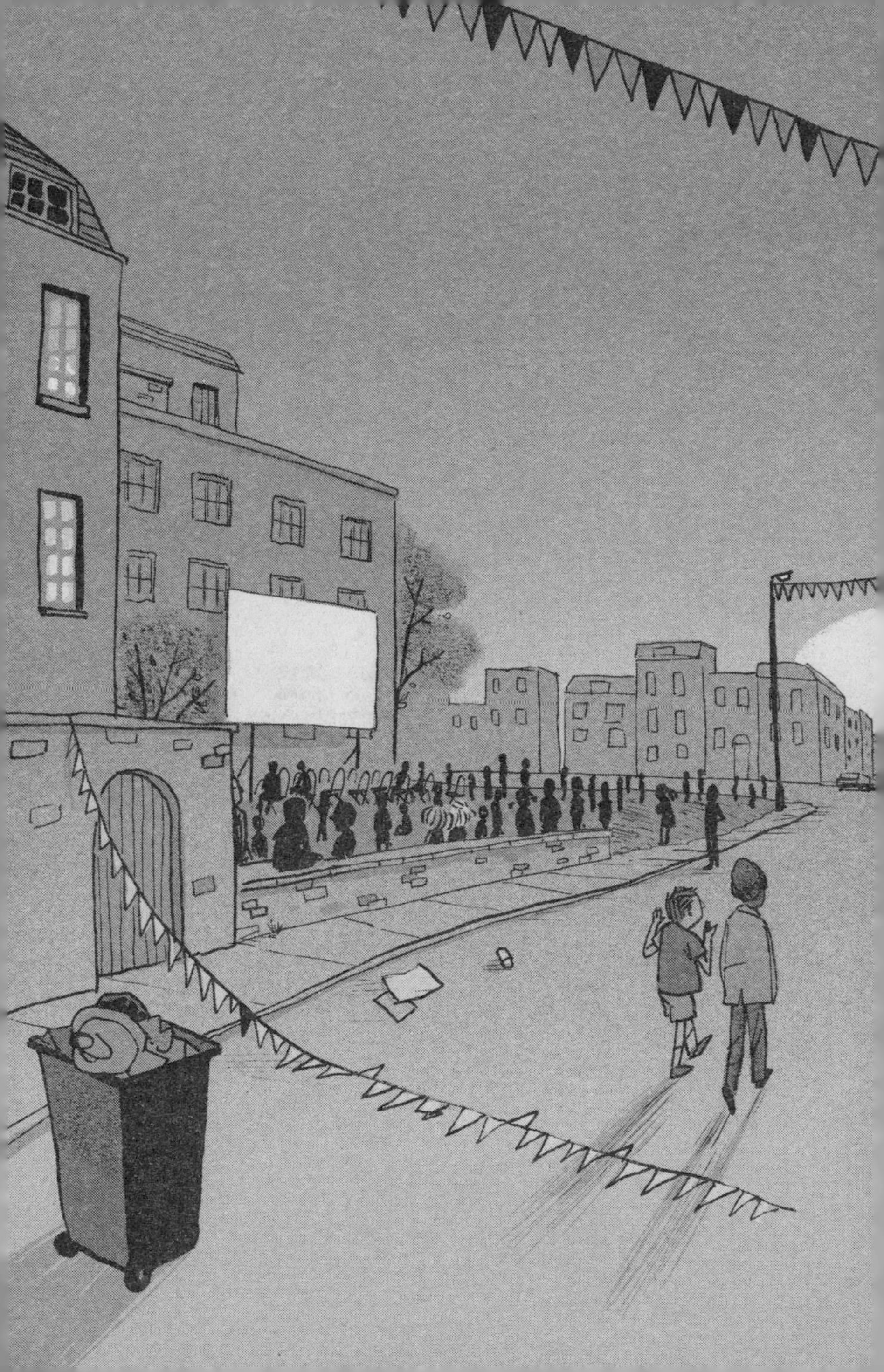

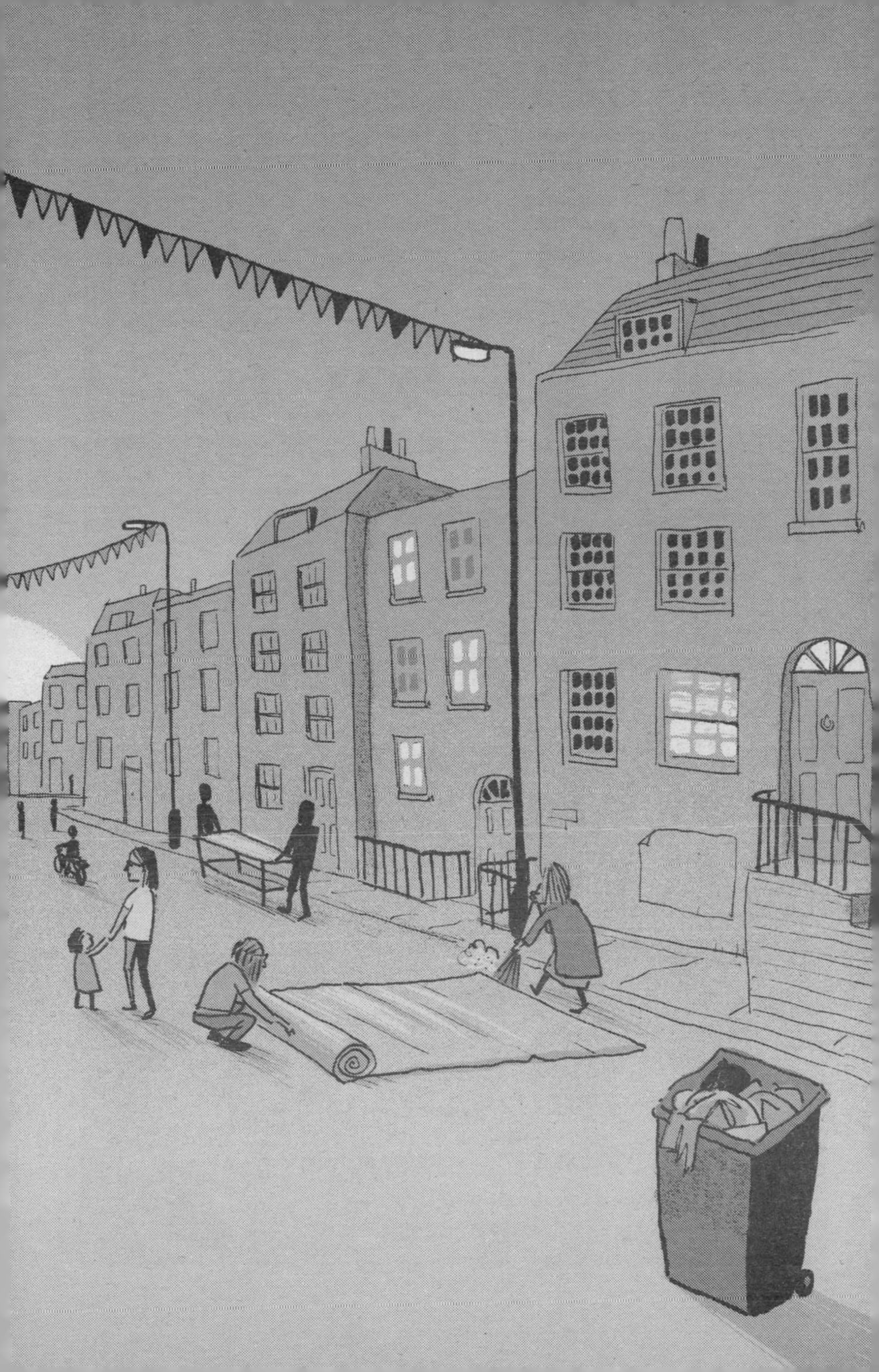

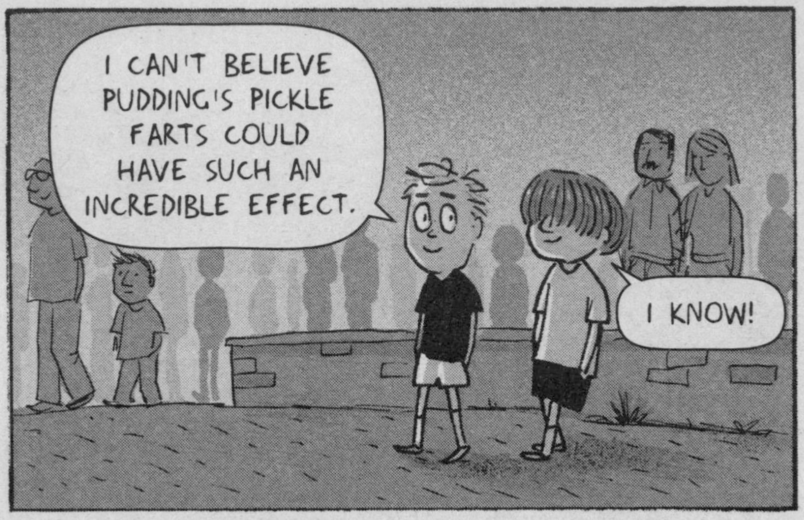
I CAN'T BELIEVE PUDDING'S PICKLE FARTS COULD HAVE SUCH AN INCREDIBLE EFFECT.
I KNOW!

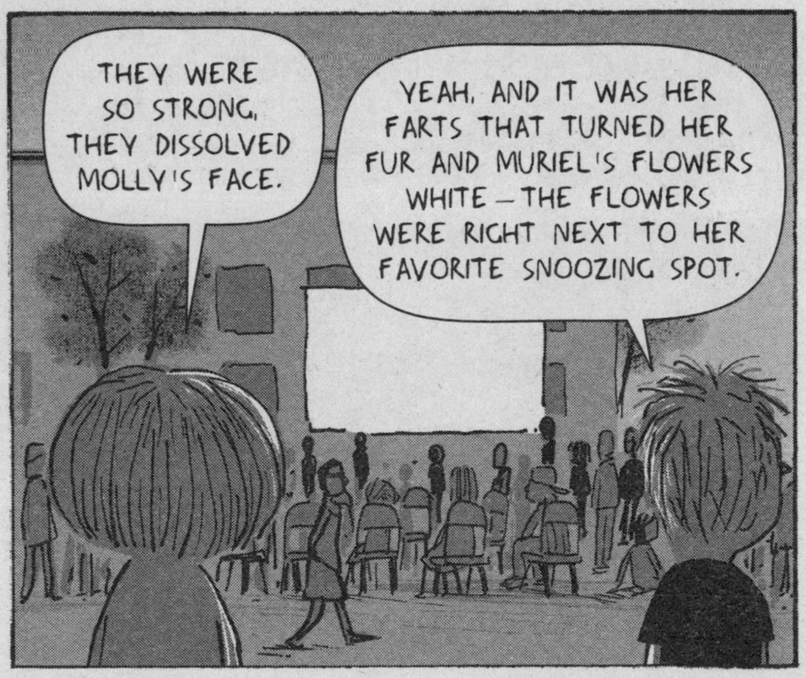
THEY WERE SO STRONG, THEY DISSOLVED MOLLY'S FACE.
YEAH, AND IT WAS HER FARTS THAT TURNED HER FUR AND MURIEL'S FLOWERS WHITE – THE FLOWERS WERE RIGHT NEXT TO HER FAVORITE SNOOZING SPOT.

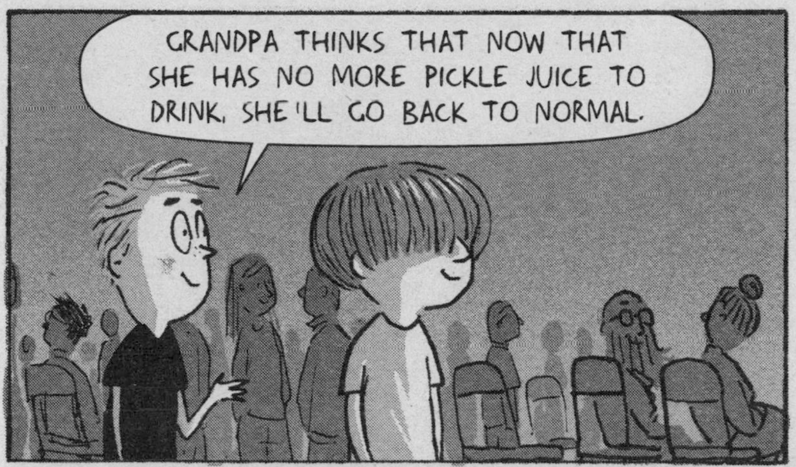
GRANDPA THINKS THAT NOW THAT SHE HAS NO MORE PICKLE JUICE TO DRINK, SHE'LL GO BACK TO NORMAL.

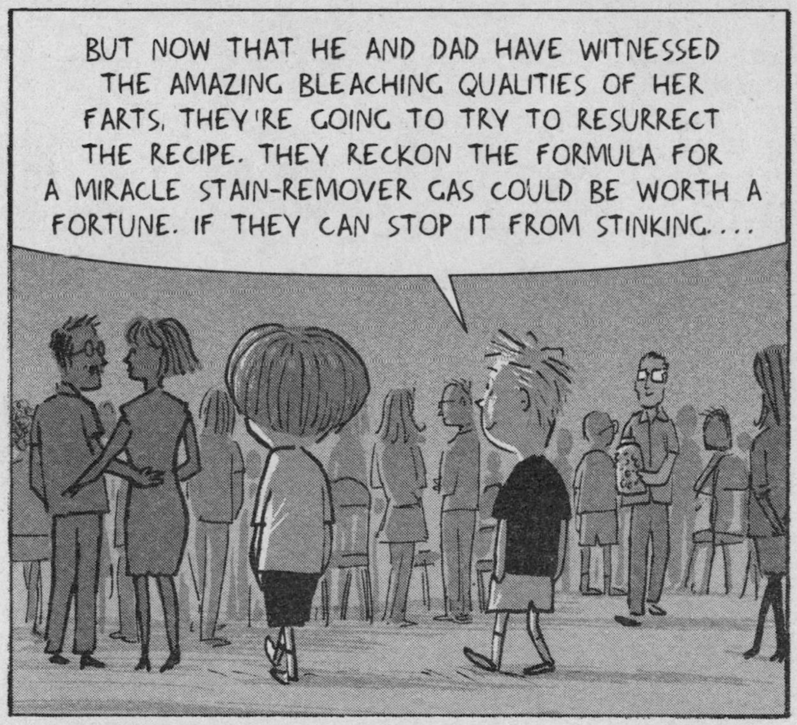
BUT NOW THAT HE AND DAD HAVE WITNESSED THE AMAZING BLEACHING QUALITIES OF HER FARTS, THEY'RE GOING TO TRY TO RESURRECT THE RECIPE. THEY RECKON THE FORMULA FOR A MIRACLE STAIN-REMOVER GAS COULD BE WORTH A FORTUNE. IF THEY CAN STOP IT FROM STINKING. . . .

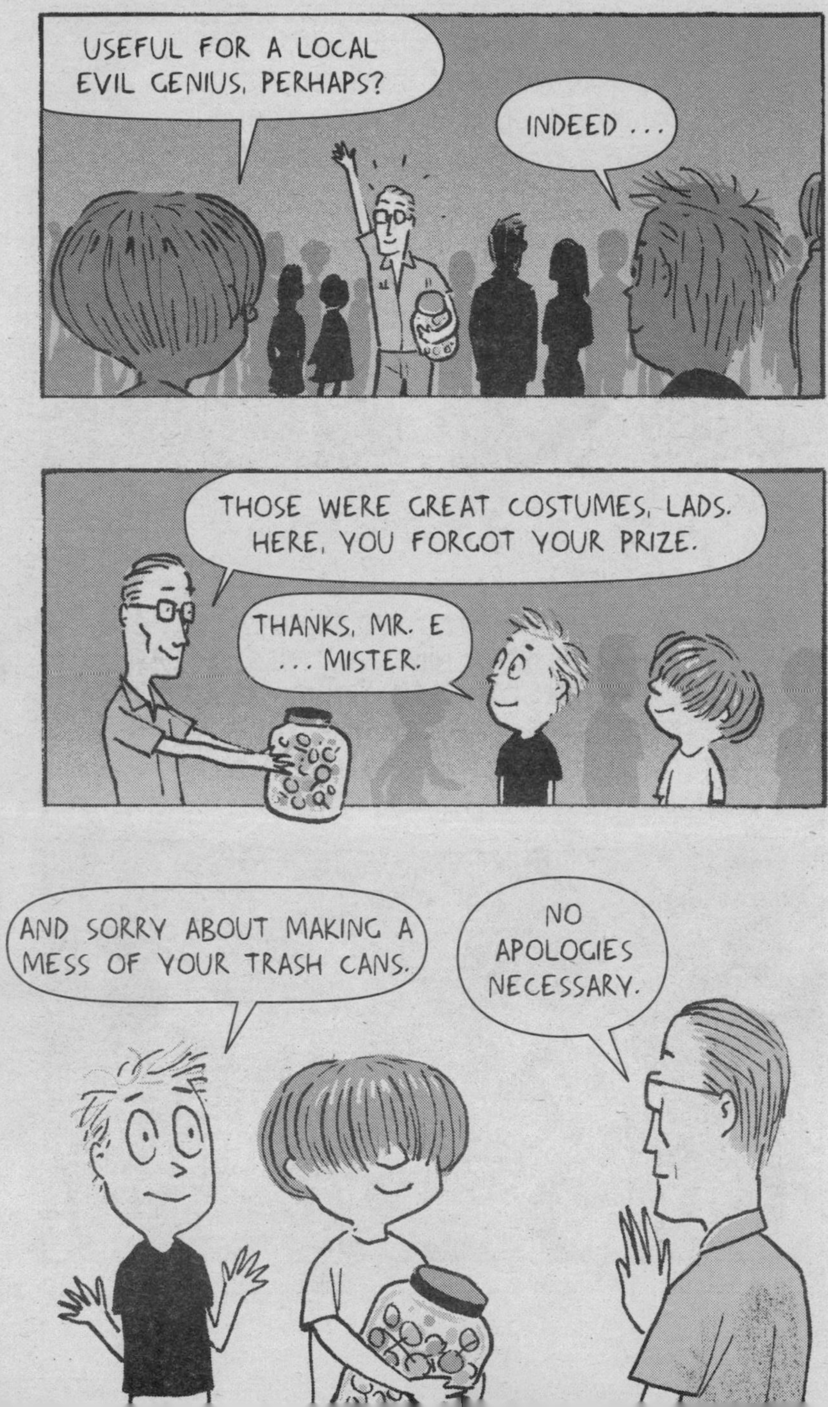
USEFUL FOR A LOCAL EVIL GENIUS, PERHAPS?
INDEED . . .
THOSE WERE GREAT COSTUMES, LADS. HERE, YOU FORGOT YOUR PRIZE.
THANKS, MR. E . . . MISTER.
AND SORRY ABOUT MAKING A MESS OF YOUR TRASH CANS.
NO APOLOGIES NECESSARY.

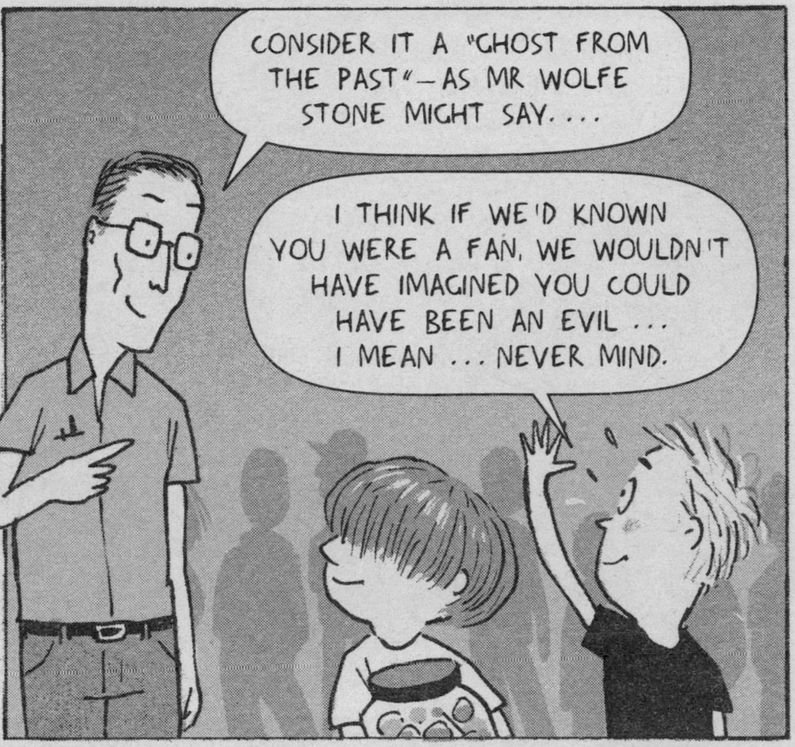
CONSIDER IT A "GHOST FROM THE PAST"—AS MR WOLFE STONE MIGHT SAY. . . .
I THINK IF WE'D KNOWN YOU WERE A FAN, WE WOULDN'T HAVE IMAGINED YOU COULD HAVE BEEN AN EVIL . . . I MEAN . . . NEVER MIND.

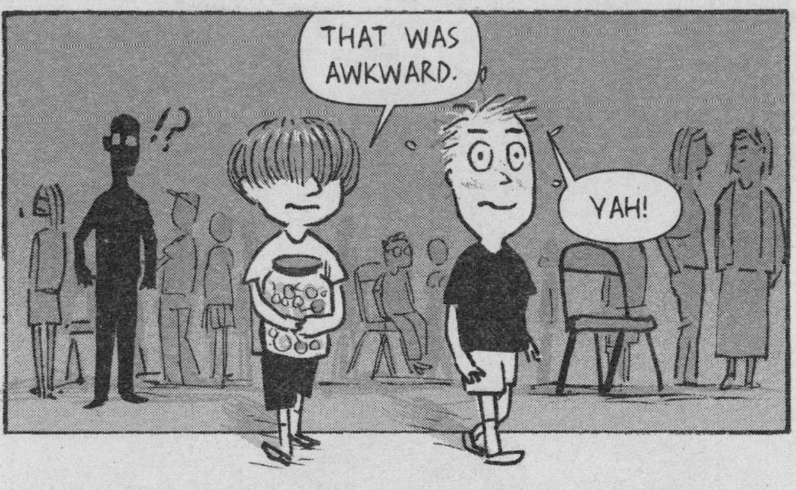
THAT WAS AWKWARD.
YAH!

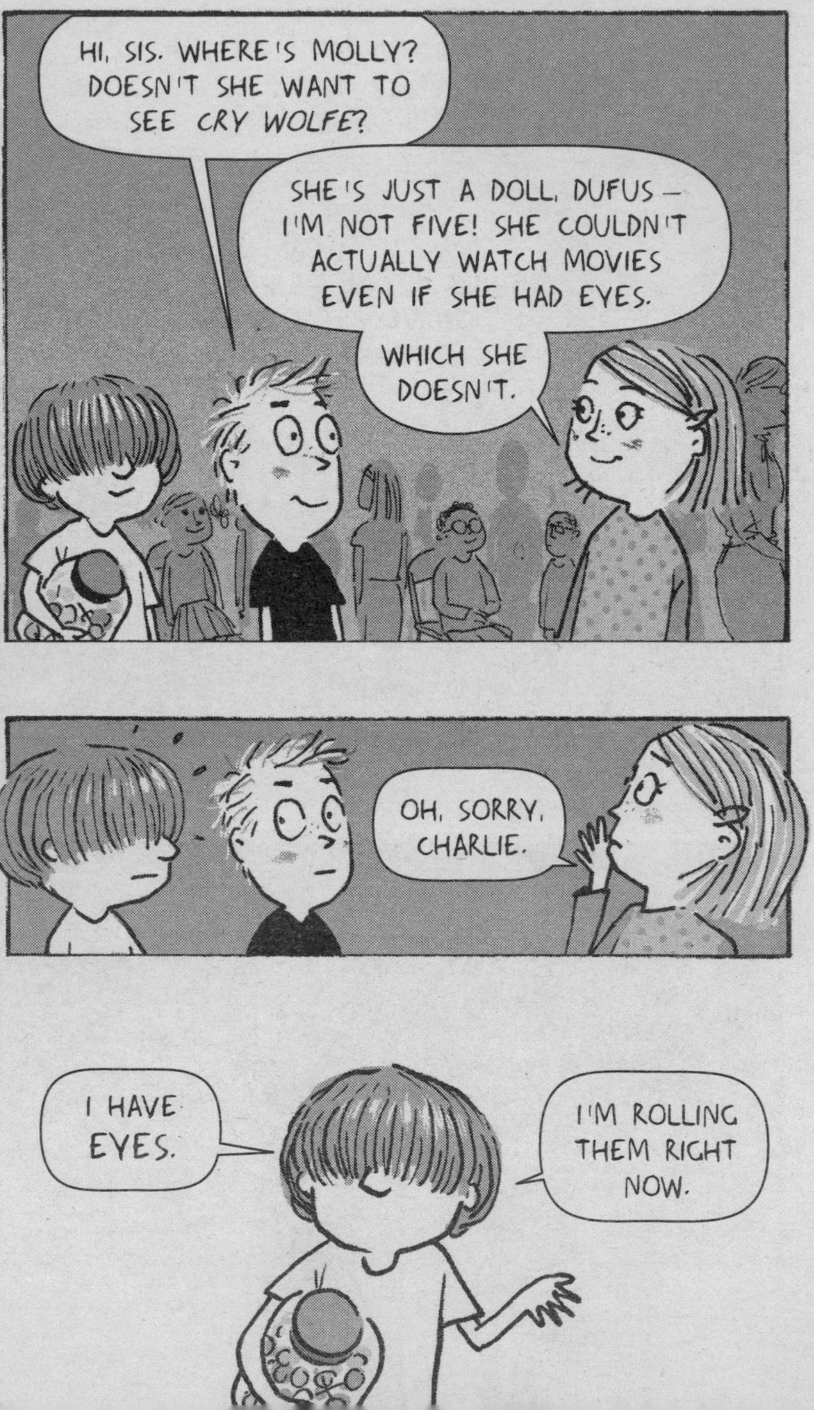
HI, SIS. WHERE'S MOLLY? DOESN'T SHE WANT TO SEE *CRY WOLFE*?
SHE'S JUST A DOLL, DUFUS— I'M NOT FIVE! SHE COULDN'T ACTUALLY WATCH MOVIES EVEN IF SHE HAD EYES.
WHICH SHE DOESN'T.
OH, SORRY, CHARLIE.
I HAVE EYES.
I'M ROLLING THEM RIGHT NOW.

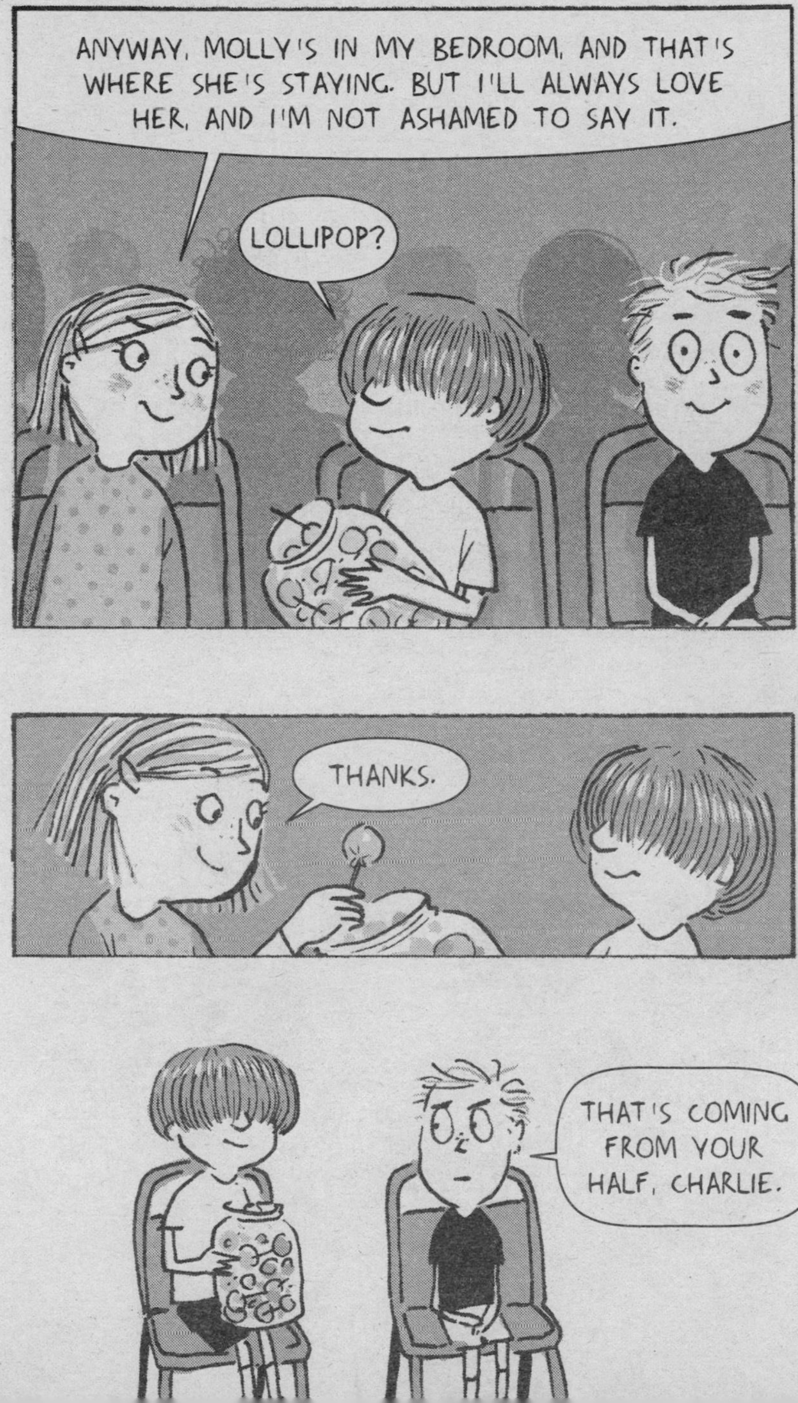
ANYWAY, MOLLY'S IN MY BEDROOM, AND THAT'S WHERE SHE'S STAYING. BUT I'LL ALWAYS LOVE HER, AND I'M NOT ASHAMED TO SAY IT.
LOLLIPOP?
THANKS.
THAT'S COMING FROM YOUR HALF, CHARLIE.

Well, against the odds, I made it through the **STINKY SWAMP OF TRUTH**. I thought I was just looking forward to a movie, but it turns out I was after something a little bit more precious and hard to get hold of. A sense of contentment, the bliss of not being responsible for causing any bad stuff.

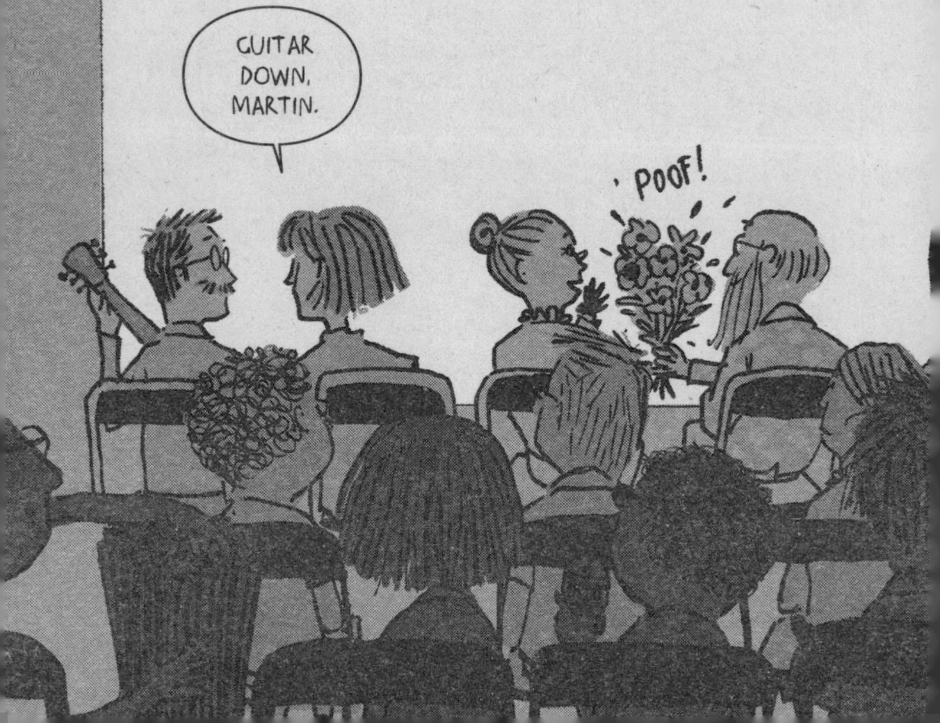
GUITAR DOWN, MARTIN.
POOF!

In my experience, moments like this never last long, but I'm going to savor every last second of it. . . .

Until the next inevitable homegrown calamity.

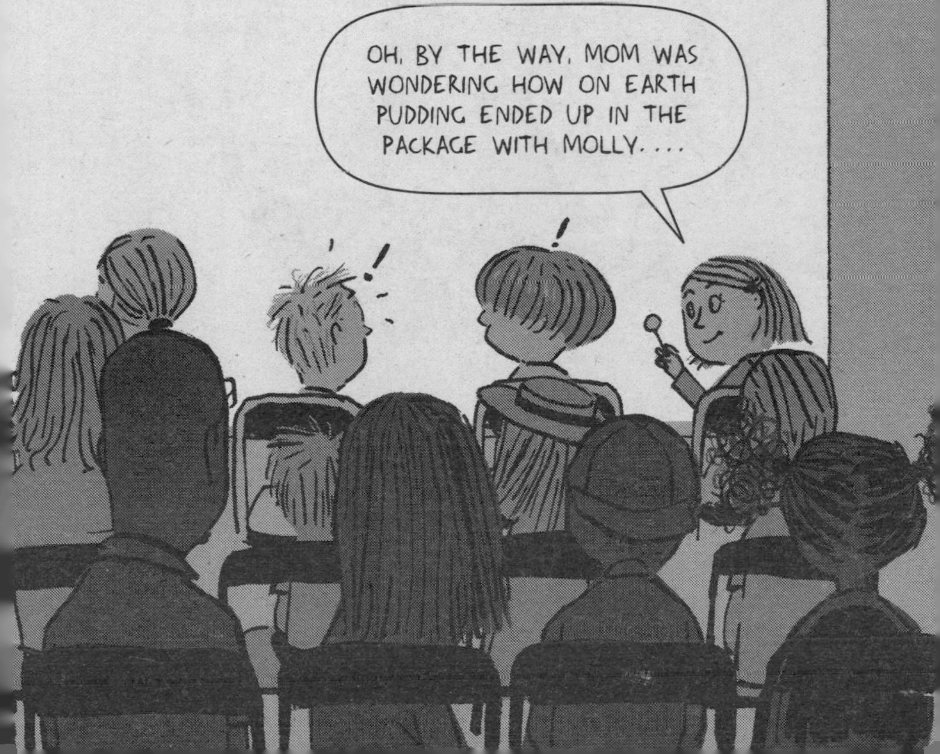
OH, BY THE WAY, MOM WAS WONDERING HOW ON EARTH PUDDING ENDED UP IN THE PACKAGE WITH MOLLY. . . .

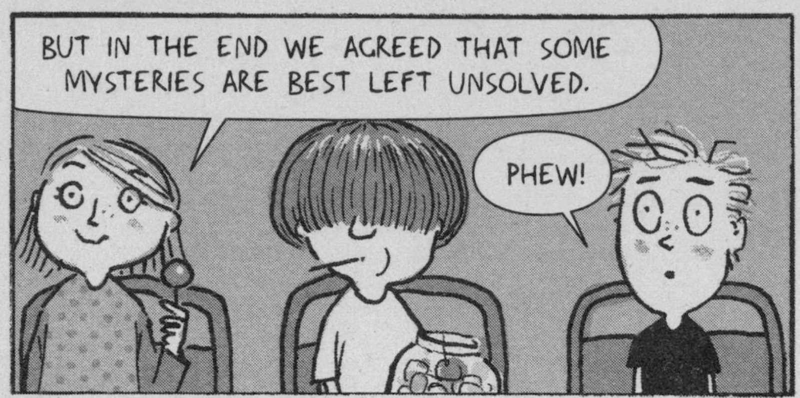
BUT IN THE END WE AGREED THAT SOME MYSTERIES ARE BEST LEFT UNSOLVED.
PHEW!

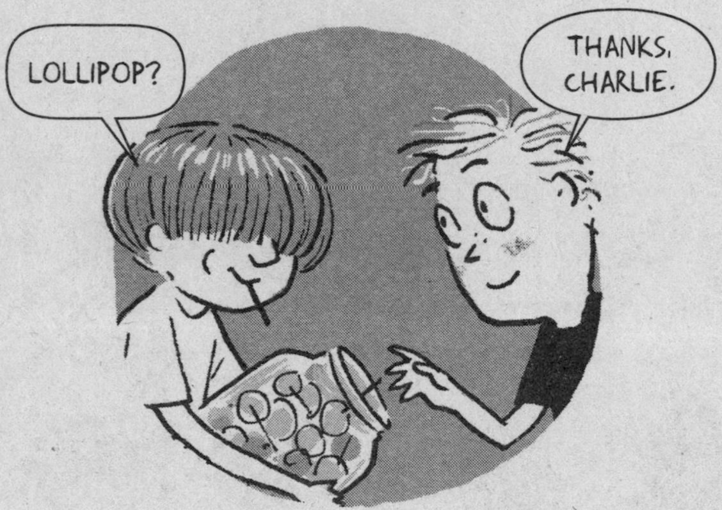
LOLLIPOP?
THANKS, CHARLIE.

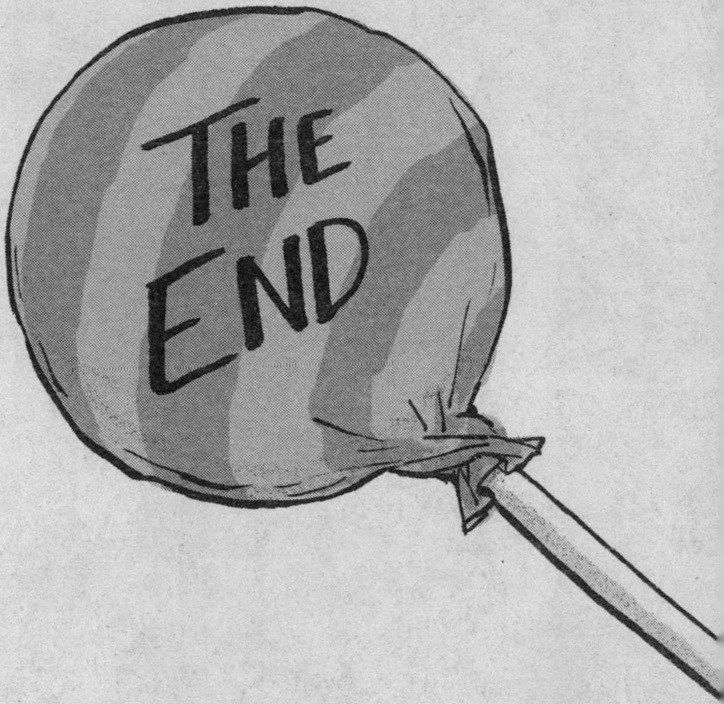
THE END

CRY WOLFE

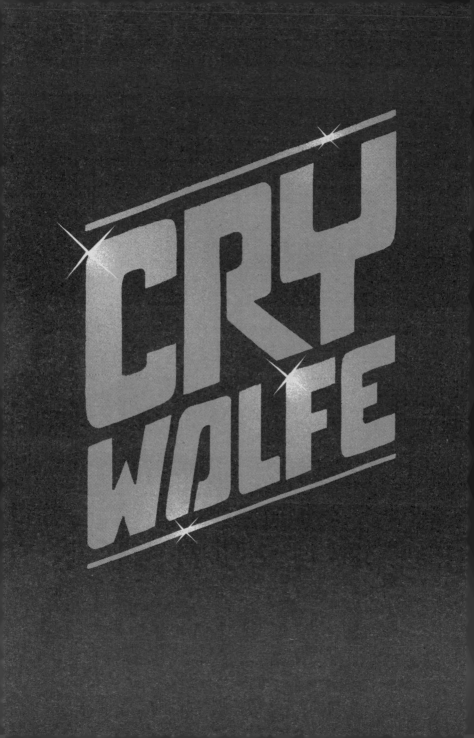

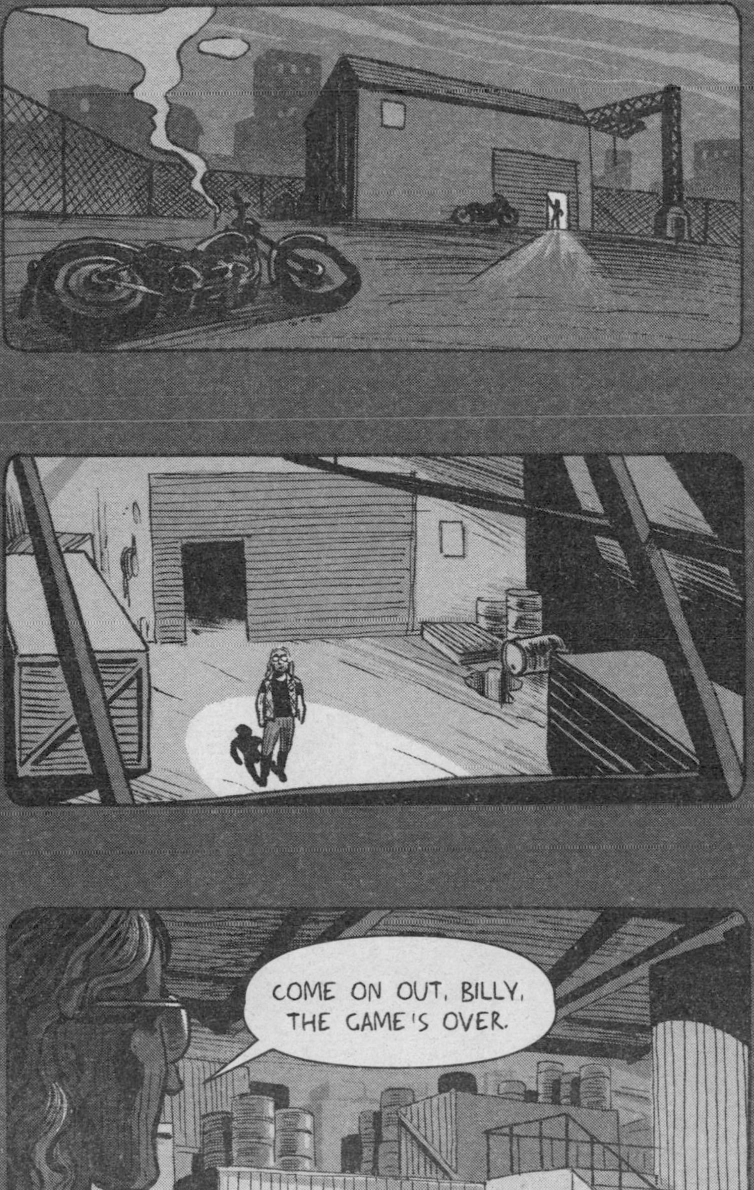
COME ON OUT, BILLY. THE GAME'S OVER.

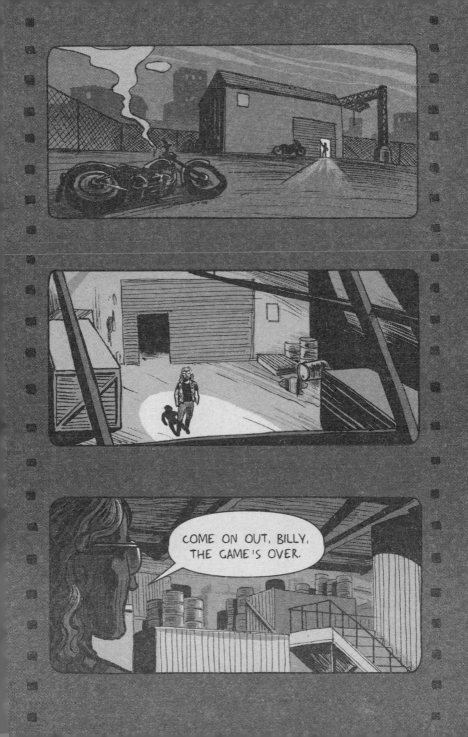

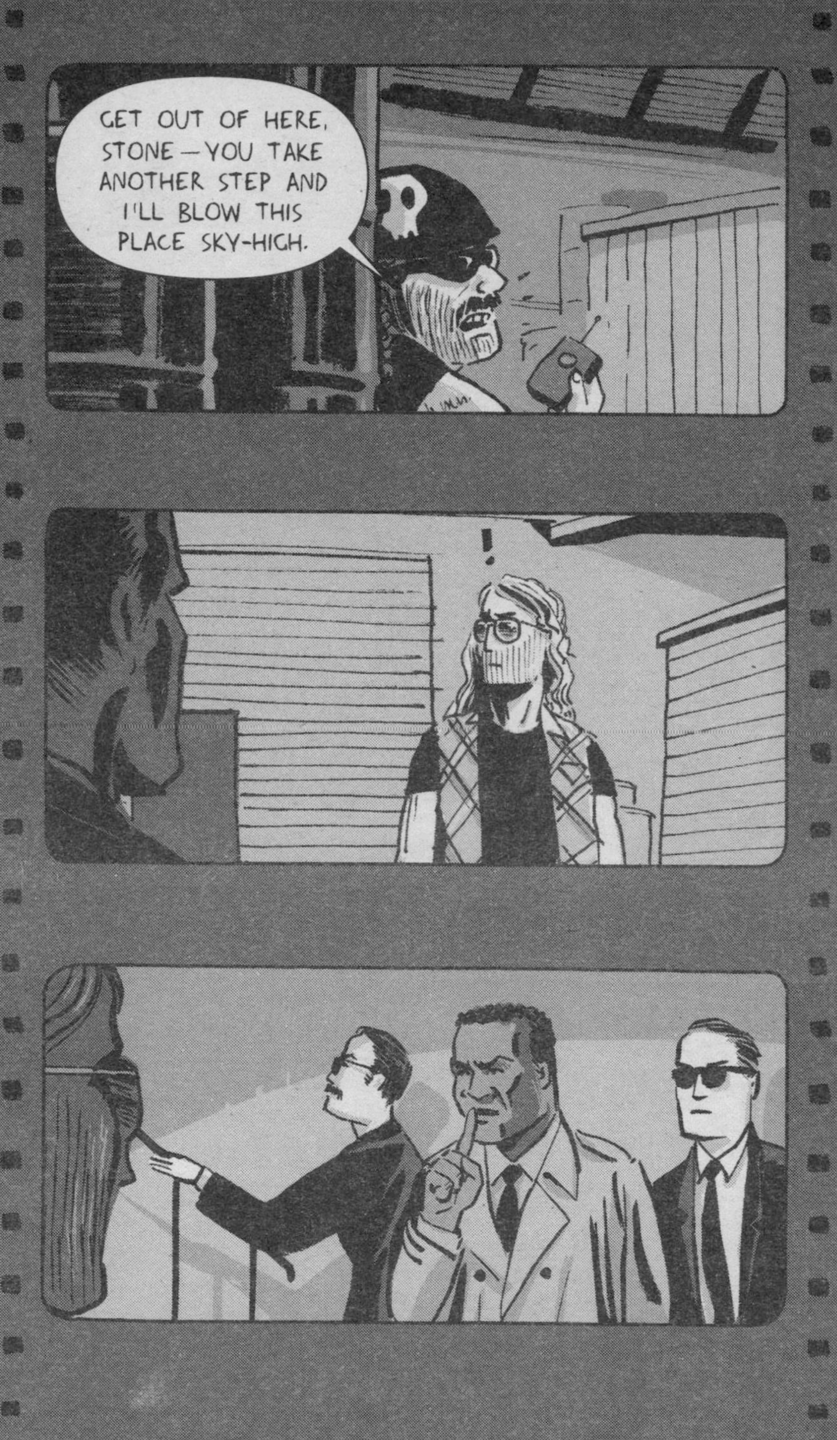
GET OUT OF HERE, STONE—YOU TAKE ANOTHER STEP AND I'LL BLOW THIS PLACE SKY-HIGH.
!

WE'VE ALL GOT THINGS FROM OUR PAST WE'D RATHER FORGET, BILLY. THING'S WE'D DO DIFFERENTLY, GIVEN THE CHANCE...

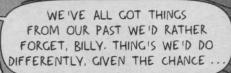

IT'S A LITTLE LATE FOR REGRETS, STONE, DON'T YOU THINK? THE DAMAGE IS DONE. IT'S TIME TO PAY THE PIPER.

YOU EVER HEAR OF "CHICKENS COMING HOME TO ROOST"? WELL LOOK UP, BECAUSE THAT SKY IS FULL OF HENS.

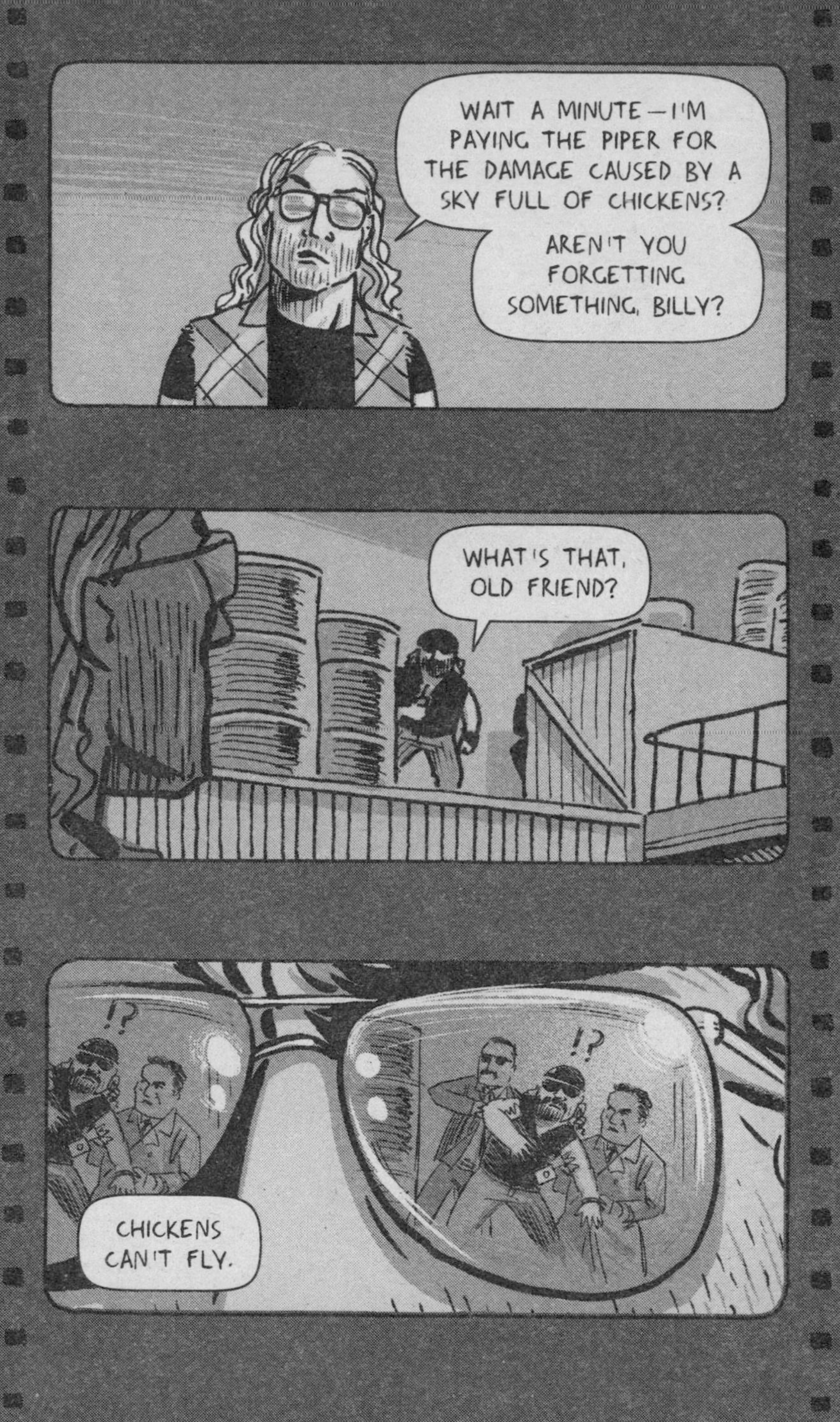
WAIT A MINUTE—I'M PAYING THE PIPER FOR THE DAMAGE CAUSED BY A SKY FULL OF CHICKENS?
AREN'T YOU FORGETTING SOMETHING, BILLY?
WHAT'S THAT, OLD FRIEND?
!?
!?
CHICKENS CAN'T FLY.

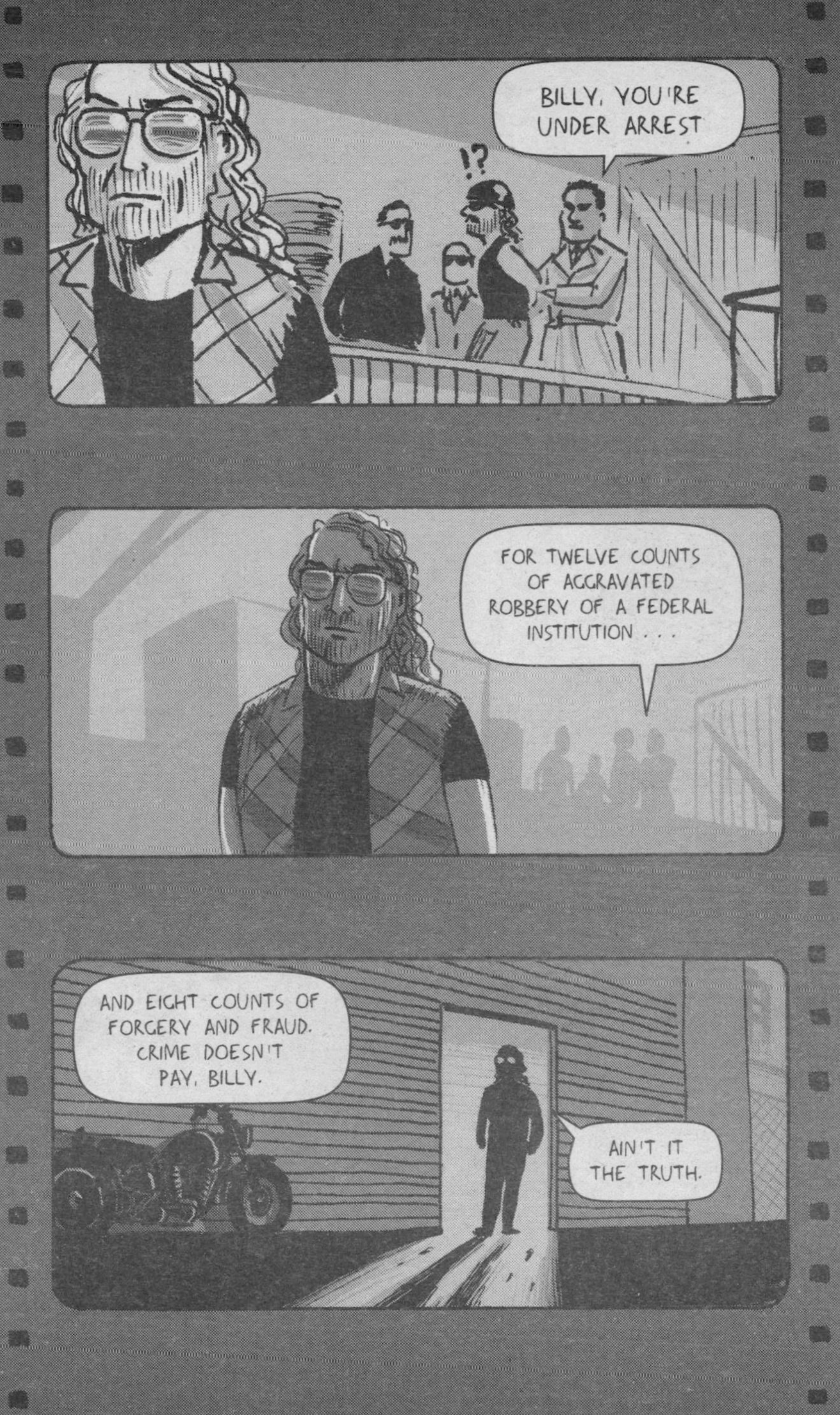
BILLY, YOU'RE UNDER ARREST
!?
FOR TWELVE COUNTS OF AGGRAVATED ROBBERY OF A FEDERAL INSTITUTION . . .
AND EIGHT COUNTS OF FORGERY AND FRAUD. CRIME DOESN'T PAY, BILLY.
AIN'T IT THE TRUTH.